It's Not Your Hair...

Copyright 2013 Pamela Pantea, "Miss Thing," and Brian Wallace

TABLE OF CONTENTS

Chapter 1: Beauty School Savoir-faire……………………………..page 4

Chapter 2: Welcome to The Gayborhood……………………….page 16

Chapter 3: Here He Is: Mr. America…………………………….page 33

Chapter 4: Curbside Queen……………………………………….page 44

Chapter 5: Thunder Pussy………………………………………...page 53

Chapter 6: Handbags, Lipstick and Blow……………………….page 65

Chapter 7: Remedial Groupies…………………………………...page 75

Chapter 8: Lbs. And Biscuits…………………………………….page 82

Chapter 9: Christmas Island……………………………………...page 89

Chapter 10: Trannies, Plantains and Festivas…………………….page 97

Chapter 11: Added Value………………………………………...page 110

Chapter 12: Don't Throw Away a Perfectly Good White Boy…….page 123

Chapter 13: Let's Get Physical…………………………………..page 134

Chapter 14: Hierarchy of Breeds……………………………….page 144

Chapter 15: It's a Spiritual-Love……………………………….page 148

Chapter 16: That Queen Had Balls……………………………..page 156

Chapter 17: Celebrity Hooker Like……………………………..page 167

Chapter 18: Bitchin' Laws……………………………………….page 178

Chapter 19: Dark Side of The Rainbow…………………………page 190

Chapter 20: From Gluttony to Transmology…………………...page 197

Chapter 21: Pity Party For Two..page 210

Chapter 22: Hi Fi Mama..page 217

Chapter 23: Magically Delicious.......................................page 226

Chapter 24: Prehistoric Will Destroy It................................page 234

Chapter 25: Raggedy Ann and Dandy..................................page 238

Chapter 26: Unarmed Forces..page 244

Chapter 27: It's a Comb, Not a Wand..................................page 253

Chapter 28: The Mane Attraction......................................page 262

Chapter 29: Edwina Scissorhands......................................page 270

Chapter 30: Hurts So Good..page 281

Chapter 31: Switch Hitter Highway....................................page 287

Chapter 32: Constantly Craving Surprises............................page 296

Chapter 33: Final Chapter…The New Frontier,
 But Not The Final One.....................................page 307

Intro: This book is dedicated to all hairdressers, hair-burners, and hairstylists worldwide. If you would put us all together in an arena, it would take 20 years for us to tell of our experiences. After hearing them, you would think we all worked together in the same prison!

Chapter 1: Beauty School Savoir-faire

I will not expose my age right now, because I don't want you all to come to the conclusion that I'm just some old bitch complaining about what I coulda, shoulda, woulda done with the deck that was handed to me; but if you studied cosmetology in the 80's, it was a frigging joke! The instructors were from the old school era of the 50's and 60's, but these women did not study under Vidal Sassoon, ohhh nooo. The majority of them couldn't cut it in the real life salon experience; so they were reduced to teaching ugly ass updo's that you wouldn't put on your Baby Chrissy doll.

I started beauty school at the tender age of 16. I was very shy, with horrifically low self-esteem, and was pretty much pissed off most of the time. I hated high school, so I knew I would never attend college. The idea of spending 4 to 5 more years in a stinky classroom — with crazy ass professors — was never appealing to me. So, a friend of mine and I decided: "Huh, why not beauty school; we like to do each other's hair." *What the fuck was I thinking?* Dammit!

We had two female instructors: Miss Anderson and Miss Flowers. They were both pretty cool, and I was pretty quiet, which they loved. Miss Anderson was a very tall black woman who was probably in her middle 50's. She wore her hair so extremely short that it looked like a bull dyke's cut. Hardly wearing any makeup, she was pretty harsh to look at. She wore very tight-fitting stretch pants over a quite large pear-shaped ass. She never wore blouses that would cover that thing. She also had the loudest speaking voice I had ever heard. It was like being in a cave with Alice the Goon from that Popeye cartoon. You would almost cringe after you asked her a question; because the answer would come out so frigging loud, that you were backing up before she finished. One day, the topic was on finger waves, and I know how much all of you loved doing those! When we first started, I freaked, thinking, "I can't do this!" Plus, it's ugly. But Miss Anderson was like a drill sergeant when it came to this particular topic. You would think she invented the finger wave — the way she would go on, and on, and on, about it.

There was a student, named Rose, who Miss Anderson just adored. Rose was the most annoying girl in that class. Miss Anderson just loved her, probably because she was always kissing that gargantuan ass of hers. So, on the day of the finger wave extravaganza, Buck-tooth Rose started giving me advice on what to do. Then Miss Anderson started screaming in my other ear. Finally, I put my rat-tail comb down to avoid having to stab them both in their titties, and said in a very calm, controlled voice: "If you both don't back off of me, I'm going to kick you both in the pussy....." Oh, my, did I actually say that out loud? I always thought it, but usually didn't say it! But guess what, they backed the fuck off! I then picked my comb up again and I aced that finger wave class. After that day, I noticed Miss Anderson started wearing longer blouses, hmmm...

Miss Flowers was the totally opposite of Miss Anderson. She was a short, piggy white woman in her early 60's. Her hair had a slight blue hue to it, and was piled high in the most amazing bee-hive I had ever seen. Actually, this was the first bee-hive I'd ever seen in person, and it was fuckin' blue! She also barely spoke above a whisper. After instructing you on something, she would walk off while muttering to herself. That was fuckin' crazy. And, on top of that, her right eye was always twitching; so you were so busy paying attention to that eye of hers, that you didn't hear a damn thing she said. She had the most horrible outfits I had ever seen. I think you would call them muumuu's, with huge floral patterns that clashed with her pasty skin. Yuck! And she wore these pink rhinestone cat-eye reading glasses. For some strange reason, she took a liking to me. Every morning before class, she would always bring me a Charleston candy bar, weird... But I would accept it, graciously.

    I soon found out that Miss Flowers had a boyfriend, named Mr. George. Since I was one of her favorite students, she always wanted me to practice cutting his hair. Mr. George was a really good-looking guy, very tall and thin. It made you wonder how in the hell she got him! His hair was very thick and wavy, and a beautiful white-grey. He always wore a slick grey suit. There was just one major problem. His breath smelled like old dirty diapers! News flash: before you have an appointment anywhere, especially if there is going to be close contact for about an hour, TRY PUTTING IN A BREATH MINT. WOW! That should have made me consider a whole new career right then. To top it off, he always requested for me to trim his protruding, twisting nose hairs! Ugghhh, sorry, Mama doesn't do personal hygiene on anybody. So, every time I knew Mr. Man was coming in, I would hide in my ceiling-to-floor personal locker secretly hoping that Miss Flowers would get someone else to do it. That, of course, never happened.

The uniforms they issued to us were awful. The jackets had every color you could imagine in stripes, with white pants, and white Herman Munster nurse shoes that felt like weighted blocks. We looked so fuckin' stupid.

And don't let me get started on what my own hair looked like. Oh, my God, I looked like Adam Ant. Of course, we were all so delusional that we thought we could make each other look like super-models. Rather, we ended up looking rather drag queenish. Everyday we would try to fix what we did to someone the day before. To this day, I can still smell that cheap, disgusting hairspray, and that incredibly gross setting lotion we put on each other, as that song "She Blinded Me With Science" was blaring through the room. Whew, I almost passed out just thinking about it.

Throughout the whole ordeal of cosmetology school, they would always try to scare us about the state board exam: how hard it was going to be…some never make it through… blah, blah, blah. We were all so terrified that I actually ended up having nightmares about that day coming; how horrible is that? Then, I would think, referring to the instructors, "You mother-fuckers passed, so it couldn't be like going for a PhD."

Finally, we were told when we got to the date of our exam that there would be two parts to it: a written, then a lab. I prepared for weeks for this thing. I checked and rechecked. I went over, and over, everything. I had this bitch in the bag. Yes Maam, sho' did!

As many of you remember, you had to have a live model at the exam, whether it was your Mom, sister, or your transsexual cousin; they didn't care. Just have one! My mother was very gracious to accept my offer, which actually surprised me a little. Our relationship during my upbringing hadn't been all peaches and cream. I knew from a very early age that I was different from everyone in my family. I know a lot of people who are artists can totally identify with what I'm saying here. As I got older, I had a "passion for fashion" and would pour myself into magazines, trying to copy the look that the models were sporting. My two younger sisters would laugh and make fun of me when they saw the wild make-shift costumes I created for myself. However, when I would arrive home from school a little early sometimes, I would find my clothes on the floor in my closet. Soon, I realized that they were only laughing to my face to get me off track. The little thieving bitches were actually wearing my early couture to school!

Also, I could never go to my Mom with any of my problems. The one time I did try to confide in her, she sharply replied: "What do you want me to do about it? It's your problem!" After that rebuke, if I ever had any type of heartrenching situation arise, I would tackle it on my own. But I have to be fair about it all, too. Mom's upbringing was much worse than mine. So, sometimes, I would try to cut her a little slack. But, after a while, don't you think people should just move on and quit blaming their parents for the fucked up decisions they made? The reason why I asked her to be my model for the state board was for the simple fact that I knew there was no one else I could ask. Also, she had a little pea head. One thing I learned during those fabulous months of school: If you have to roll a perm, or do a wet set, on some monster water head, it will take you forever to get it done!

The sizes of the school classrooms were so big, and spacious, the examiners decided that instead of us going to Austin to take the exam, we could take it within the school. Praise God! I was ecstatic. Yay! No travel ordeals. So, when that blessed day finally came, though I didn't sleep at all the previous night, I was totally prepared. My mother and I arrived, and stood in line with the others, as people were being checked off a list. I realized that everyone had a piece of paper in their hand. I didn't have that paper! In fact, what the fuck is that piece of paper? Oh my God, what was going on? If you didn't have that entry form, you couldn't start your exam. I wanted to scream, strip naked, and go running into traffic. No fuckin' way! Then, I suddenly remembered that the paper was sitting in a binder, in my bedroom closet, back at home. Of course, I was told that I couldn't take the exam without it. Why was this happening? I thought I had done everything right! Shit, shit, shit! Full-blown panic set in.

I looked at my Mom, and said, "You have to go get that thing, NOW!" So she took off down the hall. It seemed like a thousand lifetimes… What was taking her soooo long? All I could hear was white noise. Oh, my God, what the fuck was she doing!?! Then, I heard someone behind me say some precious words of encouragement, "You won't be able to take the exam; and if you do start, you won't finish on time." As I turned around, I noticed it was Rose saying that to me. It must have been an angel that kept me from kicking her in her pussy! Mom finally got back. The instructors started me in lab first. I rolled that damn perm so fast that I couldn't even believe it. Ok, next, bring it! Then, during the manicure, oh wow, the stupid girl next to me suddenly knocked over a whole bottle of nail polish remover! Get the fuck away from me!
OK, done, I passed lab, now on to written. It was all multiple choice. At first, I thought, "Is this a trick? It couldn't be this easy." I looked around at everyone else. Most of them looked shell-shocked, or drugged. I knew I couldn't pay attention to that. I wanted to finish this crap. After about 45 minutes of answering all the questions, I realized that I had finished way before most of the students who started before me. And that buck-

toothed chick who said those oh so sweet words to me was still in lab: Ha Ha! So, Mama finished with flying colors, baby! Wowwww! When we left, and got home, I think I slept for 2 days. Then what?

If I remember correctly, it took about 30 days to receive my State Board test results. I was pretty nervous when it arrived; but I knew, before I opened it, that I had passed. As I read the letter, it was becoming clearer, and clearer, that a whole new world was going to open up for me. I was 18 years old by this time, so you can imagine all the stuff that was going through my head. Then, I suddenly remembered my girlfriend, so I ran to the phone to call her to tell her the news. She hadn't received her letter yet. I could tell she was a little disappointed, but I assured her it was on the way, and that she, too, had certainly passed. You know, talking to your home-girl like you should, not just thinking of yourself. Well, the next week, her letter arrived. Yay! She passed. Boy, we started making huge plans for our future. We were going to work together in the same salon, build huge ass clienteles, and make lots of money, yeah!

We both started looking in the want ads for assistant positions. Back then, when teenagers were applying for jobs, we knew we were blessed for anyone to even talk to us, let alone give us an interview. It wasn't like the present, where kids expect to be running the place in 2 weeks. I didn't have a car at the time, so whatever I found had to be near a bus line. Boy, I hated that. My girlfriend had a car, so she was pretty set. About a week into it, she called me in a super excited state. She had her first interview at a salon in the downtown area. For one quick second, I could feel the jealousy start to rise... she got an interview first, damn! But then I got a hold of myself, and my voice didn't even change. Hey, I was super excited for her; this was great, right? She began to tell me that the guy seemed really nice, and that it was a brand new salon — with only 4 chairs — and that she mentioned me to him. Wow, thank God I didn't go psycho crazy jealous on her, for she had my back! Wow, that was pretty righteous. Her interview was the next day, and she started on a Friday as his personal assistant. That evening, after she arrived home, she told me that it was so much fun, and he was very talented. Since he had just opened the place a few months prior, he wasn't super busy. He was hoping to start receiving a lot of walk-in traffic from the surrounding office buildings. We made arrangements for me to come to visit and check it out the following Tuesday. When I got there, my mouth hit my chest. It was such a beautiful place. I was really impressed. I was there sitting around and talking most of the day, and he only had one client scheduled, humm…how many clients does he have, anyway? I knew then that I wouldn't be able to even consider working there, because no one was showing up, at all. But I was truly happy for my friend, and told her that I would keep in touch, and let her know when I found something.

    Ok…I couldn't even get hired at fuckin' McDonalds; what the hell was going on! It had been like freakin' forever and I was still sitting there at my Mom's house, as we were both getting on each other's nerves. It had been a full month since I spoke to my friend about me getting a kick ass job; well, it hadn't happened, and I was pissed! I had worked in salons before, mainly part-time work, during the summers, while I was attending beauty school. But I wouldn't have even considered putting those places on a resume. Half the time, if not all, I felt like I was working for Aunt Esther and Grady, because those places were so ghetto fabulous. The first salon at which I apprenticed was a little five-chair establishment. Though the stylists were all pretty nice, I could tell that the owner, whose name was Debbie, was a pretty sneaky bitch. There was a guy named

Lenny who wore his hair in corn-rows. She treated him like he was her child. It was sooo creepy to watch as she would practically breastfeed him. He could never make it to work on time and he always slept in his chair at his station. Wow, that looked professional; and Debbie never said a word to him.

One day, he wanted me to give him a perm. I could barely put the rods in, because his head was flying all over the place. The other stylists were all so loud and they ate at their stations; it was gross! About 2 more weeks went by, and Lenny, on some days, wouldn't even show up for work. I knew then that something was very wrong with him. Nobody would ever discuss it, especially in my presence. One day, he came dragging in, could barely speak — let alone see — and he walked straight to the back dispensary area. I had to go to the restroom; and, when I came out, I heard a huge crash coming from the back of the salon. Everyone dropped what they were doing. Hell, even the customers came running back, because there was ole Lenny passed out face down in a pile of boxes with a bottle of Pepsi in his hand. Man...that was high rollin'!

I just turned around, grabbed my bag and got the hell out of there. About three weeks later, I heard about a hair-weaving salon that needed an assistant. I called and a woman named Desiree answered, asking me if I could come by that day. She was very pleasant, but I wasn't sure if that was what I wanted to get into. She showed me around the place. It was very tiny, just a two-chair salon, and she loved Isaac Hayes; because that's all I heard playing on her stereo the whole time I was there. She told me that I could start the next day, great...I think..! So I was there at 10 a.m., and she started showing me how to set up her stations. Then she asked me that question that I now know to never answer again. Where did you work before? So I started telling her all the sordid details of my horrific experience with Debbie, and how working in her salon was like working in a circus. As I continued to shoot myself in the foot, I watched her smile transform into a disapproving scowl. You see, I just fucked up, royally. Debbie and Desiree were best friends. So once again, I picked up my purse and went home, weeee! I told myself that Friday morning, "You will find something today; and I don't care if it's pickin' cotton, shit!" I looked at that want ad section until I could barely see straight, and then all of a sudden, I saw a little itty bitty ad that read **Help Wanted: assistants needed, 555-5555.** What!?! I had been looking at this thing for hours. How did I miss this ad? My hands started to shake, as I dialed the number. A girl answered immediately, asking me if I had my license. When I told her I did, she said, "Could you come tomorrow for an interview?" Honey, I could hear the angels sing. I GOT AN INTERVIEW, OH MY GOD! Is this for real!?! As she told me where the salon was located, I didn't care if it was located on the planet FAT ASS. I didn't know what area she was talking about. I didn't care, because I had gotten an interview.

  I immediately called my girlfriend to express my excitement! As I told her the details, I couldn't really hear any enthusiasm on her end. I then told her where it was located. Hmmm…more silence. Then, all of a sudden, her boyfriend was at the house and she had to go. Well, that was fuckin' weird. But I didn't care. I finally had my interview!

  Thursday night was another sleepless night. My interview was scheduled for the next day, on Friday at 12 noon. As I rehearsed over and over what I was going to say, it all sounded retarded to me. Finally, I drifted off around 2 a.m. When I awoke, I felt really calm, cool and collected. I went to my closet and stood there trying to decide what to wear to this thing. Though it was a salon, and I knew I had to look professional. I loved color, too. Colors make people happy, right? I finally decided on this pink floral dress I had worn to church the previous Easter, with these pink pumps to match (it was the friggin' 80's...okayyyy?). A week after I got the job, I threw that hideous dress away, for I never again wanted to look like the crazy ass Easter bunny! I then went over the bus route to see where the hell I was going. Oh my, I had to take 2 buses to get there. Well, I couldn't back out now, because this was it. The first bus took me downtown. I had a 10-15 minute wait for the next one to take me to the salon. I sat towards the middle of the bus on the left hand side. As the bus took off, I started getting a little nervous again, but I held it together. I couldn't believe that I was actually doing this.

All of a sudden, the bus made a sudden stop near an older neighborhood, and something got on that bus that I had never seen before in my whole life. Terror flooded my soul. I knew I would never make it to my interview, because everyone on the bus would be murdered! Now, you have to understand, I grew up middle class. Nobody was really well off, but everyone was pretty comfortable and normal looking. I'd seen a few punks in my neighborhood, but they were all pretty harmless, as they pranced around with their hair in rollers and short shorts with fuzzy house shoes on…ummmm, sexy. But I'd never seen this before. He was about 5'10, slight in build, but strong and solid. Bald, shaved head, white t-shirt, black jeans rolled up with combat boots, round spectacle glasses. I then looked down at his wrist. He had thick metal bracelets on that looked like he couldn't take them off without experiencing ball-busting pain. Wow, Lord help us all! All I could think of was, "Please don't sit by me, please, please, please!"

As the bus continued on the route, I noticed that there was not really a lot of real estate development out there. Was I going to work in the boonies? We made a sudden stop. I looked out the window and saw this huge shopping center that was gorgeous. I felt someone brush past me and noticed that it was the scary guy. Suddenly, I knew to follow this man. It was like I knew he was going to lead me to my new job. Divine intervention in the form of this whacked out punk!?! I got up from my seat and exited the bus right behind him, making sure I wasn't too close. He went up some escalators and then right into the salon. Wow, what does he do there? As I walked in, and promptly told the receptionist who I was, she whisked me in right away to the manager. In less than 10 minutes, I had the job. This was insane. I couldn't believe that she wanted me to start the next day, on Saturday. Whoo, hoo!

Chapter 2: Welcome to The Gayborhood

I had to be there before 10 a.m., so I was up super early, and made it there by 9:30 a.m. As I walked in, I noticed that the place was packed, with clients and hairdressers everywhere in total chaos. I looked around to see if I could spot the manager. Nada. I knew nobody, except the scary guy. So I walked around a little. It was a huge place, and I saw him, thank God! I was a little nervous. I decided to approach the scary guy. As I went up to him, and introduced myself, he broke out into the nicest smile and started showing me around. He was the massage therapist there. Crazy! And, later, he became one of my dearest friends. He directed me back up to the front desk.

One of the receptionists, and another assistant, kind of showed me what to do. I pretty much shampooed someone's client when needed; but, other than that, I stayed pressed up against the wall in total shock. These were the wildest looking and wildest acting people I had ever seen. I'd never even seen this on TV. Then, all of a sudden, I felt something twirl by me with the aroma of nice cologne. I looked to my left and noticed a man with white hair who was wearing a tutu, and skating by on roller-skates. DAMN! Then, to my right, I heard a man, with a very "Nellie" voice, yell, "Hey everyone, my scars have healed; come and see my new...!" What the fuck did he/she just say? I knew not to go running back there and see what was going to get exposed. Something told me that it would haunt me for the rest of my days! The only thought running through my mind as I stood there in disbelief was, "I can't tell Mom about this. No way! She would make me quit..."

The first week working there was a huge blur. There were around 30 employees with all different personalities and attitudes. What I loved most about these people was that everyone had their own style and their own look. As I mentioned before, I had to take public transportation to get to work; and, I tell you what, experiencing that for a couple of years will definitely keep you humble. Until this day, Mama has never forgotten where she came from, if I ever start to think that I'm "all that." All it takes to knock me back down to earth is to drive by people standing in the extreme heat, cold or just plain windy ass days.

One morning, on my way to work, I noticed a very nice looking, muscular man in his mid twenties, at the bus stop downtown. He had dark brown hair and brown eyes. We struck up a conversation. His name was Kevin. It turned out that he worked at the same place as me; and that he just gotten back in town from having a Hairdresser Breakdown.... Now, I want to explain the meaning of that phrase. A hairdresser breakdown is when you have come to the very end of your end, and you don't give a rat's ass if you ever see a client again. I had never experienced it myself; but I heard that you lose all feeling in your body, and you have about twenty emotions flooding you all at once. Then, you take a deep breath and gently put your scissors down, so you won't use them as a butcher knife on the fat ass client complaining about the work you do. You calmly pack your bag and walk out of the salon. And, when you finally "come to," you are in a dazed out mental state at your Mom's house in Florida, sitting on the screened-in porch, and she's handing you your favorite cocktail. So, that's probably what happened to Kevin. He had the best, most sarcastic "cut to the throat" sense of humor, and the best laugh I had ever encountered. He also told me that he had sold his car to a friend before he left, because he needed the money. I could tell that Kevin had a lot of skeletons in HIS

CLOSET, so to speak. To be totally honest, when I first met him, I kind of developed a little crush. Then, one day I saw him queen out; wow, I had no idea that he was gay! One Wednesday afternoon, we were in the back dispensary having lunch. Kevin asked me if I would like to go out that night for Wednesday night ten cent drink night. Okay, I was 18 years old, and the only alcohol I'd ever tasted was some Blue Nun white wine I had seen on a television commercial. It looked so good that I begged my dad to buy it. I took one sip and couldn't believe that something that looked so good tasted so vile. So when Kevin invited me out, I played along like I knew what I was getting into. Boy, was I in for a shocker! I was never, ever the same after that night.

After work that day, we went to Kevin's apartment, a very spacious two-bedroom that was decorated amazingly well. Kevin had a roommate name Bill, who also worked at the salon, but was out of town that week at a hair-show. Kevin got all dolled up for the night. Damn, he looked good and smelled even better; his cologne was right on! After he called a cab for us, and we headed out, he told me we were going to a gay bar that held live drag shows, and then dance till the break of dawn. My heart started beating fast; I'd never been to anything like this. The only gay men I had seen growing up wore flip-flops, with rollers in their hair, not exactly posh. As we finally arrived, we could hear the electro music pouring out into the street. We noticed a line wrapped around the building. Kevin just grabbed my hand as we walked right up to the front of the line, passing all those people. Wow, this was Hollywood, baby! Kevin knew the front door guys, and they just let us right in. This place was huge, with wall-to-wall gorgeous men! To my left was a stage, upon which stood a 7-foot tall thing dressed in an evening gown, telling jokes and smoking a cigarette. Wooo Weee! In front of the stage was a huge dance floor with seating around it, but everyone was standing up laughing, and yelling, out to the "thing" on stage. Kevin must have seen my mouth drop to the carpeted floor, because he leaned over and said, "We won't stay and watch her. Her jokes are sooo tired!" I laughed my ass off as we walked briskly to the other side of the building to a more loungy area, where he ordered us both a gin and tonic. By that time, the dragon had exited the stage and the music started pumping. Oh my God, this was the best dance music ever. Kevin knew a lot of people. Throughout the night, if we were either dancing, or having yet another drink at the bar, people would come up and talk to him. He would introduce me, everyone was sooo nice, and I was getting sooo drunk. The last thing I remember was someone holding my arms, and my legs, as I was carried out of the bar. Then it was night, night, nurse!

Uh oh, what the hell happened last night? Oh shit, where was I, and what day was it? I was sooo fuckin' nauseous that my head felt like someone kicked it with steel-plated boots. Uggggh, I'm sooo sick. All of a sudden, I heard talking in the other room. I got up, off of a leather couch, and realized that I still had my clothes on from yesterday and last night. Wow, this was not good. Kevin came in the room with a big shit ass grin on his face. "Boy, you really tied one on last night. We had to carry your happy ass out of the club, ha ha." I was like: what's so fuckin' funny! After that night, I started learning how to laugh at myself when gays made fun of me. If you didn't, you would be a bitter ole hag later in life. But what little I did remember about that night, I knew we had a lot of fun. I had to be at the salon at 1:00 p.m. that afternoon. Thank God, because I felt like hell. You see, this was my first of many hangovers to come.

Kevin's roommate Bill was back in town, so he offered to drive us both to my house to shower, change, and then take us to work. I knew one thing: Mom was not going to be happy, because she didn't know where I was, and what I was up to the previous night. I knew that not only would I be getting ready for work, I also would be packing my belongings. It took about 20 minutes to get to my house. I opened the door, and Mom was standing there pissed. I said to her, "I know, I know, I will pack my clothes." She then yelled, "Wherever you were last night, you can go back!" She wouldn't even let Kevin and Bill in the house. Wow, she was truly outraged! I took a quick ho bath, grabbed a duffel bag, and threw all the clothes and shoes I could fit in it. I quickly changed into some jeans and a cute top. Hey, if you're going to leave home, at least do it in style, right?

Working was pretty painful. Thank God all I had to do was shampoo clients and sweep the floors, and all the other little shitty tasks you perform as an assistant. I had to work from 1 p.m. till 9 p.m., ouch! I couldn't wait to lay my nappy head on something and go to sleep. By 5 p.m., I could barely hold my eyes open. I swore to never drink like that again, RIGHT!!! About an hour earlier, I heard yelling from the back room. I saw Bill go running towards the front of the salon, with Kevin close behind, telling him that he was going to kick his fat ass!!! Oh no, what now!?! Kevin came over to me and said, "Honey, I'm packing my bags tonight. I'm not staying in that apartment with that bitch another night! We're going to spend the night at one of my friend's places tonight. And then we will get our own place together."

Whoa, everything was happening so damn fast, but what was I supposed to do? All I could do was nod my head in agreement. Man, Kevin sure was a Butch Daddy when he was upset. I didn't even ask him what Bill did. I knew to stay out of it, and he would tell me when he was ready. Awww, work was over! Kevin called a cab for us, and when we arrived at the apartment, Bill wasn't there. That was really good, for his sake, for sure.

I made it a point that night: to never piss Kevin off. He packed all his things and then made a brief phone call in his bedroom. That was crazy. I was in total shock. I had never lived with anyone before, except my family. Where were we going?

We finally arrived at a two-story apartment building. As the cab came to a stop, Kevin turned to me and said: "Ok, here is the thing; his name is glass-eyed Phil, and he's a weird mother-fucker. But we will only be here for maybe 2 weeks, or less. So, don't fuckin' laugh when you see him." Then he started laughing. Of course, I started laughing hysterically, too, until we got it out of our systems. Then, as he knocked on the door, I realized that this was it. Welcome to the gayborhood.

So we had arrived at our temporary poon palace, and it was disgusting. Newspapers and magazines were everywhere. The kitchen was even more vile; and, oh joy, he had a cat, too. *Oh my God,* I thought, *I think the cat has a glass eye, too.* Kevin introduced me to Phil, and I noticed he was giving me the once over with that eye. I turned around to look at a picture on the wall, because I was getting ready to burst out laughing, and I didn't want to ruin everything. I didn't want Kevin on my case, either! To make matters worse, Phil had a very high-pitched nellie voice. Shit, I didn't think I could contain myself any longer! He showed us where we would sleep. Hummmm, who gets the box spring? Oh wait, how about that mattress on the floor over there? I just kept my pie hole shut and we both thanked him. After Phil walked out, Kevin said to me: "I knew it was going to be bad, are you ok?" I told him, "Hey, I know this is only temporary, until we find something." Kevin agreed and then said, "Tomorrow, when numb-nuts leaves for work, we will clean this shit-hole, so we can tolerate it."

Kevin, having the day off, had explained our situation to our manager, whose name was Kathy. She was really cool about letting me have the day off, too. So the next morning, after Phil left, we went to the store to get cleaning supplies; because, guess what, he didn't own any! We started in the kitchen, and when we walked in and saw the front of the refrigerator, we both screamed like bitches. There was something on the door that looked human! This was going to be really scary. I think he grabbed a hammer and started chiseling away, while we both tried not to blow chow. Then we tackled that mother-fucker for 5 hours. Actually, it was so much fun, because Kevin had a way of making the most horrible situations smell like roses. Phil had a real dated stereo (dated even for the 80's) and the whole time we cleaned, we danced, and sang, to all of Kevin's favorite love ballads. We performed to Patti Labelle, Chaka Khan, Donna Summer — and oh so many other diva's — while we worked our asses off, like two Georgian slaves. The place looked magnificent!

We went to the grocery store, which was right down the street, and got food and toiletries that we needed. When Phil finally came home from work, I thought he would be overjoyed about how his apartment looked. He just mumbled hello, walked into the kitchen, opened the frig and grabbed one of MY COKES!!! And he didn't even say: "Wow, the place looks great, thank you for cleaning my disgusting rat hole!" Kevin just looked at him and said, "Hey girl, why don't you take me, and Miss Thing, out on the town, for cleaning your fuck-upped mess?" Surprisingly, Phil agreed! It was Friday night, so here we went again, but this time, Mama drank vodka and cranberry. The next day was Saturday, and I knew I did not want to re-live the other night of being carried out of a club. Step 1 of becoming a Diva: always make it a point to walk out of a bar, not be carried out.

The next week, Kevin and I started thinking about where we wanted to move. The box spring, and the pee-stained couch with the K-mart sheets thrown over them, was not going to cut it much longer. We decided on a place not far from where we worked. Actually, we could walk to work, which was awesome. I knew that Kevin was also going to start looking for a new vehicle soon; and I could at least start saving for my own. I wasn't making much as an assistant, but I knew it would not be long before I became a full time hairstylist. It was a two-bedroom, two-bath apartment, with tons of windows and a huge patio. Man, my first place, ever! It was sooo exciting! After we signed the lease, the agent told us we could move in right away, because the apartment had been unoccupied for months. They also had a great summer rate special. All we had were our clothes and shoes; so moving in was a breeze. We took a cab back to Phil's place, grabbed our shit, and were happily whisked away to our new party shack.

Home sweet home, bitches! Yeah, our very own place, with not one stick of furniture in sight. But we didn't give a shit; because it was our place, with no mother, and no nellie-queen, backstabbing fag around. Kevin explained to me what had happened between him and Bill. It was funny how I knew to keep quiet and let him tell me in his own time. It was like we had somehow gotten this closeness, and we knew how to feel each other out in such a short amount of time. It turned out that Kevin had told Bill a secret about one of their friends who was messin' around; and Bill shot his big mouth off by telling several friends in their circle. Wow, I knew then to never trust that one. Kevin said that she could never keep her pie-hole shut; she would still be talking in her casket at the gravesite. Hmmm, step 2 in becoming a diva: keep your pie-hole shut!

We set out that day to go shopping. Kevin was going to buy all of the furniture, because he knew my salary was only $150.00 a week, before taxes. Yeah, it was the 80's. So he bought all of the furniture for the living room and the bedrooms! Such magnificent taste! Even though my salary was meager, I had saved my tips, so I offered to at least buy the groceries. Hey, I'm no bum!! It took two days to get the place together; and boy, did it look good. The next day was a workday, and Kevin was booked solid that week. He said we would behave ourselves by not going out all week. Then we would party on the weekend only. That Tuesday, at work, our Manager Kathy called me into her office. She said that she had a little discussion with two of her top hairstylists. They both needed an assistant. They were willing to share one person and split paying that person's salary. Kathy asked me if I would be interested. I was actually so stunned that I didn't know what to say. Someone actually wanted me to be her personal assistant, wow! She told me I would be assisting two of the male stylists, Fredrick and Lance. Uh oh, this was going to be fun, because these guys were polar opposites of each other. Fredrick was really quiet, and reserved, and gay; while Lance was loud, wild and straight. And they were both very, very busy, which meant lots and lots of tips. When Kathy called them both into her office, and gave them the low-down, they both seemed cool about it. Lance kept sizing me up with his baby-blues. While Fredrick seemed a little indifferent about it, I found out later that this was just his way. Everything was always high-drama with him, and he was always OVER IT!! Do you know what I mean!?!

They both went over their requirements and the things they needed throughout the day. They explained how they wanted their stations set up, etc., etc. It was pretty easy enough. I started working for them that day. On one of my breaks, I went over to see what Kevin was doing, so I could tell him what had just happened. I quickly discovered that he had Bill by the neck in the break-room! So, I decided to tell him later that night...

Awww, the weekend was finally there, and Mama needed some new couture. The high school shit wasn't cutting it anymore. Once again, Kevin and I went shopping; and he picked out a skintight little number. I was so used to wearing loose-fitting things. After I fought him for a few minutes, I tried it on, and guess what! I looked fuckin' hot! Then he promptly had to buy himself a new blouse.

That night, he wanted to go to a piano bar. Wow, Kevin was so sophisticated, too! When we walked in, it was not very crowded. Most of the people there were in their 40's or 50's, which, Kevin told me later, meant 80-plus in gay years. Wow, that sucks! The host came over and directed us to a nice table in a corner of the room; it had a very good view of the place. The waiter practically skipped over to the table. He seemed really happy to see Kevin. Wait! Do they know each other? The guy was almost gushing with joy. Kevin introduced us. His name was Michael; and, boy, was he a cutie pie. Michael took our drink orders and pranced away...wait a minute, was he walking like that on purpose!?! All of a sudden, there was a drum roll. I looked towards the stage and a HUGE dragon slayer was at the piano. He started singing, and telling jokes, in between his numbers. Actually, he was really good.

Michael was at our table so much that it was almost like he wasn't working. We were there for probably two hours. Afterwards, I thought that we were going to tear it up on the dance floor somewhere. To my surprise, Kevin said he was tired and wanted to go home to bed. What! It's not even a school night, and you want to go to sleep! But I didn't argue much. We headed home, and when we got there, Kevin said goodnight. I went to my room, washed my face, watched some TV, and then drifted off to sleep.

What's that smell? Was it morning already? I felt like I had just lain down. I could smell bacon and toast being made as Diana Ross was blaring. I got up, brushed my teeth and ran into the kitchen. Whoaaaa Nellie, what the fuck was going on!?! Guess who was in the kitchen with nothing but shorts on! Well lookie, lookie here, it was Mr. Michael. Tired…my ass. That's why Kevin wanted to go home so early: they had a fuckin' date, or whatever, and I was not even invited. As I got really pissed off, Michael looked really scared. Then Kevin came into the kitchen all happy and shit. "Hey girl, morning, did you sleep well?" Then I knew not to act like a crazy bitch, because I was hungry and I wanted what Michael was cooking up. And if he was using our kitchen like it was no big deal, I knew his ass was here to stay. Man, that changed everything!

Oh joy, another workweek. I'd pretty much gotten the hang of this assistant thing. I knew what Fredrick, or Lance's, next move would be before they even knew it. We got to a place where all they had to do was look my way and I knew what needed to be done with the next client, etc. All the other stylists were acting jealous, because they were stuck with the lame-o assistants who were pretty much stoned most of the time, or talking perpetually in the break-room. So, if my guys didn't need me, the other stylists would ask them if I could help them out, which meant more money for me. All of the regular clients knew me, and they all liked me, so that was a real plus. That was my second month at the salon, and I'd noticed there was a station towards the end of the salon that was unoccupied. I walked in one Wednesday morning and saw a man standing there with a client in his chair. The hairstylist was in maybe his late 40's to early 50's. He was about

6'2 and with a pretty nice physique. I asked Debra, one of the assistants, who he was. She told me that he was the owner of the place, and his name was Danny. He had been out of town on personal family business and had just returned. Then she dropped this bombshell: he's straight! From afar, I watched him with his client, and was amazed how he could do a haircut, and blow-dry, in 15 minutes; and it was perfection. I'd never observed anyone there finish out a client so fast! And he did it while carrying on a conversation with them, too. Would I ever be able to do that!?!

When his client got up to leave, I then made a mad dash to the break-room to fold towels. All of a sudden, I heard a man's voice say, "When did you arrive here, cutie?" I looked around to see who was speaking. Then I looked behind me to see whom he was addressing. There was no one cute in there but me, so I caught on. After I nervously told him which day I started, he asked, "Has anyone talked to you about the classes we have here?" "No," I said. "Well, they are every Tuesday night, so make sure you have a model for each one, or you will not make it on the floor working in this salon." Then, with a wink and a smile, he grabbed a cigarette from his shirt pocket and walked out. Awww, man, where the fuck was I going to find people to let me practice on them!?! This was going to suck balls! Remember, I was still pretty shy, so the idea of going up to a stranger and asking him if I could hack on his hair for 2 to 3 hours was scary as hell.

Later that night, I spoke to Kevin about it; and his reply was, "Girl, you will be fine. You're going to have to start sometime, and now you're ready for the next step. You have to start building your confidence." So, I knew then that I had the rest of the week, and weekend, to find a model for next Tuesday night. The next day, on my break, I decided to suck it up and comb the area for a desperate individual. I put my radar on, looked in shop windows, and glanced over to a food court. Then I saw IT! Big, wild frizzy hair and standing hauntingly near a watch shop. I didn't know if it was male, or female, because its back was to me; and "IT" was wearing jeans. So, I slowly and quietly approached this person. All of a sudden, as I opened my mouth, all of these professional words came flying out! The "IT" was a woman, by the way. I introduced myself and explained to her the situation. She was overjoyed. I gave her one of the salon business cards and took her number, so I could confirm the day before the appointment. Wow, that was sooo easy. Man, I did it! I actually approached a stranger and wasn't cursed out!

I had been told that this particular class was for whatever you wanted to work on. I had no clue about what I was going to do to this woman, but I had confidence that it would come out ok. Thank God Lance was teaching the class, because he was so light-hearted and funny, I knew that it couldn't be painful. There were five assistants that brought models, and mine seemed to be the scariest of them all. When Lance came over, I could see he was trying to conceal a chuckle, so I looked down at my scissors in order to avoid laughing myself. He asked her a few questions about the products she used. Then he told me that he wanted me to shampoo her first and he would teach me how to blow dry her out. Then we would do the cut together. Incredible, it all made so much sense, because her hair was so fuckin' wild. How would you even begin to know what to cut, and how to cut, if this shit wasn't tamed down? Despite the class taking five hours, Lance was so patient with us all and somehow made the time fly. But when I was done, my model looked sooo beautiful. I did it! I did it! My first real professional cut and style. Lance was very pleased, too. Afterwards, he told me that he wanted me to start finishing out his clients now, because I had a knack for blow-drying. Yeaahhh, this was the best day ever!

Debra asked me if I would like to come by her house and have a drink to celebrate. Sure, why not? We both needed to wind down after that class; we were both so keyed up. Debra had a very cool apartment. She seemed to love feather boas, as they were hanging everywhere. She turned her stereo on and this magical music came on that I'd never heard before. I asked who it was. She said it was The Cure. Wow, pretty cool! As we hung out for a while, and she shared with me all of the salon gossip, I realized that I never told Kevin what I was up to. It's not like we had to check in on each other all the time, but at least be courteous. I asked Debra if I could use her phone.

When Kevin answered the phone, I heard music and people in the background. Ooohhh, this is a Tuesday night, what's going on over there? He said that a good friend popped in town out of the blue, so he invited some people over for cocktails. Well, that sounded harmless. I told him I was at Debra's. He said, "Bring her, too."

When we got to the front door, it sounded more like a nightclub than a small gathering among friends. I opened the door, and just when you think you've seen it all.... There were about 40 people milling around, dancing and talking. In the middle of the living room sat a huge drag queen, in a chair, with a small brown bottle in her hand. The boys took sniffs out of the bottle and then started dancing around like pogo sticks. Oh my God, Kevin, where are you??!! Fuck!

I heard laughter in the den. There was Kevin, with five other guys, sitting around the tv and joking. Of all things, they were watching cheerleading competitions. Oh My God, how weird is that: grown ass men critiquing teenage girls' cheerleading moves!

Kevin shouted, "Hey girl, it's about time you two got here. Here, do a bump and shut up!" Oh man, I forgot that Debra was here…what is she thinking about all this? Next thing I knew, he shoved a key, with a powdery substance on it, into one of my nostrils. In just a few seconds, I felt an amazing rush go from the top of my brain all the way to my toes. "Wow, what the fuck is this!?!" "It's cocaine, girl. It'll put you in the party mood, so you won't get pissy like you normally do." Then he started laughing, with the others, after his quirky little comment. All of a sudden, I replied to him: "Whatever Mary, somebody has to keep your dumb ass straight!" The whole room cracked up. Wow, this cocaine stuff made me turn into a quick-witted comedian! Then Debra joined in on the festivities. Ugghhh, I thought that she must have done this before, because she lined out that powder like a world-class pro, then snorted it up like a hoover vacuum…damn!

Well, our little gathering didn't end til almost 4 a.m., and we both had to be at the salon later in the day. How in the world was I going to be able to dress myself, let alone do a shampoo on someone, without shampooing them to death? Oh, wait. How about carrying on a conversation with them, and actually giving a shit? Kevin and I both dragged ass the first two hours. Usually, I could hear him laughing all through the salon, but not that day. And I could actually see little beads of sweat on his forehead. Wow, he don't look so good. On my break, I knew I needed to eat something, so I went to the break-room to find him to see if he wanted something, too. "No girl," he said, "I just did another toot to get me through the day." "What, you did more?" Oh man, I would have been vomiting, with my arms flailing behind me, if I had done anymore of that stuff at that point! But he was a big boy, so I left and went and grabbed a sub sandwich. After I ate, I actually felt almost normal. Hey, that coke stuff wasn't so bad to recover from. It was wayyy better than recovering from alcohol. Ok…step 3 in becoming a Diva: PACE YOURSELF!!

That afternoon, I realized that Debra didn't come in to work. I asked around if anyone had heard from her. I was told that she had called in sick. Oh nooo, I hoped she was ok, because she had done way more than I had. I started getting a little nervous, so I went to the back of the salon and called her. She answered before the second ring, and I could hear The Cure playing in the background. "Hey Girl, are you ok," I asked. "Oh yeah," she said. "After I left your place, I didn't want to go to bed, so I called a friend of mine who can get stuff. Sooo… I haven't even been to bed yet!" "Holy Crap!! How can you mother-fuckers do that?" "Mama has to go to bed!" "Okay, Girl, I will let you go." Wow, I was never gonna worry about anyone like that again. These people were professionals.

Kevin and I finally made it through the day. We could not wait to lie on our couches, have a cocktail, and go to bed. Michael didn't go in to work, either. His happy ass was in bed, all day…that bitch! We were both sooo jealous; and we were sooo broken down. We looked like 2 sway-backed nags ready to be put out to pasture. As the weekend was approaching, I was wondering, *uh oh, what are we going to be involved in this time?* I heard Kevin and Michael talking in the kitchen. When I came in, Kevin was really excited. They had just joined a gay volleyball league. They were going to start working out, get in better shape, and party less. Wow, what a turnaround from 48 hours ago. I was actually happy for them, because they were so excited. Practices started on Saturday night, so I told them I would go and support them. I also promised to do some of those cheerleading moves they taught me! Kevin said: "That's ok, girl, don't embarrass yourself with those fucked-up moves of yours!" Calmly, I replied: "Suck my dodie, like an ice cream sodie." Ahhhhh, such good times.

Chapter 3: Here He Is: Mr. America

Well, I was then in my 6th month of working as an assistant at the salon, and I knew that I could totally do the job with my eyes closed. Christmas was approaching rapidly, and I hadn't spoken to my mom since I left. Ok, I know what you're thinking... how I'm such an ungrateful child. And that I should let by-gone's be by-gone's. Fuck you! There was absolutely nothing to discuss with her. She threw me out of the house; and, actually, I was ready to go. She just gave me the boot I needed. Anyway, I was excited about the salon Christmas party that was coming up, because I heard it was the shit! It was going to be held at this really cool rockin' nightclub that I'd only been to once. The first time I went was with a girl from the salon named Patricia, who supposedly had clout at the front door; but when we arrived, the clown working the front gave me a hard time about my fake ID.

So the next weekend, Debra took me. Damn, that bitch knew everybody, probably because of her party favor connections. We partied til the break of dawn, boy! The salon was crazy busy because of the holidays, but everyone — clients and hairdressers — were in the Christmas cheer. And remember, in the 80's, money was flowing like champagne, so mama was raking it in, yippee! The party was coming up the following Saturday night; and I really, really wanted to look good for it, because I knew there would be pictures. So Kevin and I set out on Thursday to find the Diva outfit of the century. We went near downtown to an area that had eclectic boutiques and little hole-in-the-wall bars, with rock-a-billy, and underground dance music, blaring from the store fronts. It didn't take long before Kevin found a little black number with metal studs and rhinestones attached to it. Oh yeah, baby, that was the one! He offered to pay for the whole thing, but I told him to at least let me pay my half, because that thing wasn't cheap.

      The big night finally came! The party was supposed to start at 9 p.m. Kevin said that nobody would show up that early, except the ones that wanted to eat up the buffet. So we arrived at 10:45 to make our grand entrance. Danny had rented out the whole club til 12 midnight. Then, after that, the main public could arrive. Everyone looked sooo cool. The one thing I truly loved about my co-workers was that everyone had their own look, their own style. No one ever copied each other. The DJ was so incredible that every song he played made you never want to leave the dance floor. Debra arrived with a date that looked like the lead singer of the Flock of Seagulls, but with thicker bangs falling across his face: wow! Then I saw Lance come in right behind them. He was decked out in a very nice suit and looked amazing! I ran over and gave him a hug, and asked him where his date was. He told me that he went to her house to pick her up and she was already drunk; so he left her standing there at her front door, looking stupid as hell. He was so pissed. I then told him: "Hey, I will be your date, let's get this party started!" All of a sudden, the DJ started playing that Grace Jones song, "Slave to The Rhythm," and we all stampeded down to the dance floor like a herd of buffalo. Even the owner Danny was shakin' his groove thang, cause it was such a fuckin' blast. Suddenly, I saw people I didn't recognize start to attack the buffet table, so I realized it was already midnight. Lance and I struck up a conversation with one of the bartenders, whom we were also tipping pretty well. His name was J.J. and he asked us if we were on the guest list: Lance was on it, but I wasn't. J.J. then replied, "Well, I'll take care of that." He then called one of the door people over and whispered to him while pointing at me. The guy wrote something down on his clipboard and ran off. He then came back over to his post and said to me, "You're now in, Miss Thing!" Oh My God, I was on the guest-list of the hippest, baddest club on the planet!!! Lance looked at me and said: "Wow, you didn't even have to sleep with someone to make the list!!!"

I was sooo excited that I ran to tell Kevin and, boy, he was already wasted. I'd never seen him drunk before. He could barely understand what I was telling him. Oh well. So Lance and I pretty much hung out together with the rest of the crew, dancing, talking, and laughing at each other. Finally, the party was coming to an end; and, I was actually hungry because I had barely eaten anything at the party. I didn't see Kevin anywhere, so I asked Lance if he could take me home. He then replied: "Hey, let's go get something to eat, I'm starving!" Thank God, my prayer was answered! I could have eaten one of those divider ropes in front of the club. Lance told me there was a little eatery that stayed opened all night and served amazing food. He drove a cute little silver BMW that totally suited his personality, and it was spotless inside and out. This was actually pretty cool; because other than work, Lance and I had never talked or hung out. And boy, he drove like such a mother-fucker that I had to hang on to my seat! When we arrived at the place, there were people sitting outside, smoking, drinking coffee, and just milling around. It was very laid back, exactly what we both needed. I followed Lance through the restaurant, to a small enclosed patio area in the back. It was like freakin' Alice in Wonderland out there. Every freak that you could possibly conjure up in your mind was on this back patio: werewolves, vampires, etc. A young guy — with dread-locks hanging down his back — walked over to the table, mumbled something while he laid down two menus, and then floated off. As Lance saw me staring at all of the droids, he started laughing his ass off. I then proceeded to close my mouth.

Lance was in a very talkative mood, and he started telling me about his family background. He said the waiter reminded him of his stoner older brother, who still lived with his parents. I asked him where he was from, and he told me that most of his family lived in California. His dad was a big time lawyer out in L.A, and always wanted Lance to follow in Big Daddy's shoes. But Lance didn't want that type of life, involving yelling, arguing, and stealing from clients. He went on to say that's why he decided to become a hair-dresser. He wanted to do something totally opposite of what Dear ole Daddy would approve. Years before, he had thought about becoming a preacher, but he knew he would end up in the tabloids for doing the female parishioners. He said that his mom's sole occupation was traveling and having plastic surgeries.

I knew I could then open up a little about my own up-bringing, how my parents were divorced, and the details that led to my moving in with Kevin. Lance said that he had heard a little about the crap between Kevin and Bill, but he didn't get involved with the drama-queens at the salon. He had enough on his plate trying to keep his older female clients from grabbing his crotch during a haircut! All of a sudden, our waiter magically appeared at our table. Damn, how did he do that? You never saw him coming your way. We ordered our food, and then he floated away like some ghoul in a horror flick. I turned to Lance and said: "Do you notice how he kinda just floats away like that, like he's not even walking? Yeah, that's fuckin' creepy man..."

The food was totally awesome, and I think we both finished our meals in 15 minutes. Lance suggested that I stay at his place, since it was so late. Oh my God, it was 4 a.m.! His place, he said, was only 5 minutes from the restaurant, so it made better sense to just sleep there and then get a fresh start, since it was Sunday. He owned a condo that had beautiful flowers and trees out front. His place was decorated Liberace style, glamour to the hilt. I would have never guessed that Lance's place was decorated better than a gay man's. Chandeliers, fur throws, and fleur de lis symbols were everywhere. I heard a soft meow behind me, and saw a huge fluffy cat, that was also gorgeous, and blended in with the decor. Lance introduced the cat as Mr. French; how cute was that? He showed me to the guest bedroom, which had an adjoining bathroom, wow... I wanted to move there!!! There were all kinds of facial products for women on the bathroom vanity. I was amazed that his house was so perfect. It then came to me that Lance had to have been born with a girlfriend. Everything he had in his condo was what a woman would want. I washed my greasy face before drifting off into a dreamless sleep.

Wow, I slept like a baby monkey in the bushes and I didn't have a hangover! I could smell coffee brewing, so I got up and looked through one of the dresser drawers for something to change into. And just like I thought: there were shorts and t-shirts, and sweat pants of all colors and sizes. Shit, this guy was a Mack Daddy. No wonder women were clinging to his crotch! I chose some blue and white paisley pants with a blue hoodie to match: cuteness. Then I took a shower and changed. I tip-toed to the kitchen and Lance was there seated at his kitchen table drinking a cup of coffee and smoking a cigarette. He looked up and said, "Morning, Miss Thing, did you sleep well?" I replied: "Yes, that bed in there is sooo posh!" I was pretty sure he had plans with some chippie that day, so I asked if he could he take me home as soon as possible. After he rapidly agreed, he hauled ass to my place within minutes. See ya Tuesday! And he was out of sight.

Outside the front door, I heard Chaka Khan's "I'm Every Woman" turned up as loud as it would go with Kevin and Michael piping in with their manly voices. I walked in and discovered that Kevin and Michael were dancing around the living-room in wigs! "Hey Girl, guess what? We're going on a trip. The Miss Gay America Pageant is in 2 weeks, and I've already told Kathy we're going, so it's all arranged." The Miss What Pageant? I had never heard of anything like that before in my life. This was going to be crazy. We were to leave on a Thursday, early in the morning, because this was supposedly going to be a huge extravaganza: just like the real deal, only with men performing in dresses and high heels. The pageant was going to be held in San Francisco, at a huge stadium-like auditorium. Kevin already had his plane ticket months before, so he hurriedly booked mine, and Michael's, and told us we could pay him back later. Boy, he was really excited, because he was going to be helping out one of the performers with their hair, makeup, padding, etc.

Thursday morning finally arrived, and Debra took us to the airport. The flight was packed with every type of personality you could imagine: fun, fun, fun. We had arrangements to stay at Larry and Jake's, who were two friends of Kevin's. They had been together for almost 20 years. The flight was nice and smooth, and Kevin told us that they would not meet us at the airport. We would need to take a cab to their home, instead, because he knew that Larry would freak out if we arrived and the house wasn't perfect for us. Wow, how nice was that? Their house was a 30-minute drive from the airport. We arrived at huge gates covered with ivy; they opened automatically as we approached. I found out later that they had seen us on camera. Shit, this was going to be insane! The front door blew open and two men came running out. "Oh My God, we haven't seen you forever, you look sooo butch, girl!!!" Kevin laughed, hysterically, and gave them both a huge hug; then he turned to introduce Michael and me. These were the nicest people I had ever met. They were so sweet and funny. They helped us with our luggage and showed us to our rooms. The house was gynormous! We were all arranged on the second floor, for more privacy, we were told. Larry was obviously the woman of the house. He was flying around making sure that every little thing was in its place, and that we had everything we needed. Jake just sort of stood back with his arms crossed, ignoring Larry, and talking and cracking jokes. As I was unpacking, I heard more people arrive downstairs. I threw some things in the dresser drawers, and hung up some outfits that would have wrinkled. Then I put my suitcase in the closet and ran downstairs. As I descended the stairs, I saw four very attractive men looking up at me and smiling. Kevin was there smiling big, too, before introducing me to them all: Paul, Dutch, Eric and Mike.

Larry had made a feast for us all. As we went to the dining room, commotion erupted behind me as Paul frantically ran past Eric to sit in a chair next to me. What the fuck was he doing? The meal was incredible, and Jake made the best cape cods ever. Kevin had known Larry and Jake for many years, so they were pretty much talking about the old days, when they were fresh little chickens. But the weirdest thing that kept happening all night was I would catch the other men staring at me. Larry and Jake never did, but the others kept doing it. What the hell were they looking at!?! It's like they were watching my every move. The pageant was starting on Friday, and ending Saturday, so there was a lot of work to do. As we arrived there at 8 a.m., Michael and I were going to act as Kevin's assistants. We went backstage and a young man directed us to the dressing rooms and makeup stations. Wow! It was a huge room with female impersonators in every size, shape and attitude! Black, White, Hispanic, Asian, "Blackanese," Chinese, Indian — you name it, it was there. I could feel my mouth dropping again, so I closed it quickly. Kevin was going to help out one of the contestants named Priscilla; so we looked around to see if he had shown up yet. All of a sudden, I heard behind me, "Ohhhh, quick, give me a cocktail before we start. I'm sooo thirsty!" Kevin then replied, "You are not getting a cocktail. You are going to drink water for the rest of this pageant so your face won't crack during your performances!" Hilarious! We all started laughing, even Priscilla, as Kevin got to work. He started on the wigs, while a dwarf-like queen ran in with a huge black bag and started putting out the putty he was going to use to glam this man up. Priscilla's real name was Sean. I don't know why he didn't use his real name, but oh well. He was hilarious! He also was very good looking as a man, so I couldn't wait to see the transformation take place. I started scoping out the place, looking around at the other contestants. I was wondering if this pageant was going to be fixed liked the real ones; because at least half of what I saw getting ready in this dressing room couldn't imaginably win any kind of contest!

I saw a woman across the room helping a man with his panty-hose, then zipping him up in an amazing red dress. I went over and complimented him on his outfit. We then started talking and, come to find out, he was straight. The woman was his wife. Damn, that's crazy! He said that one night they had a party at their house; and he got drunk and put on his wife's shoes, and started dancing around singing Judy Garland show tunes. His gay neighbor screamed out, "Bitch, you can make so much money doing that!" So, he quit his day job, started performing in clubs, and began grossing over 70,000 a year dressing up and performing in ladies evening wear.

I went back over to where Kevin and Michael were working. Kevin directed me over to a steamer, to steam out one of Priscilla's costumes. I felt like I was behind the scenes of a theater. It was so incredible. All of a sudden, someone yelled, "Ok, girls. Twenty minutes to go. Get those mugs ready!" Priscilla was the 4th contestant to go out, so I finished steaming the gown, whisked it over to them, and he had it on in ten seconds. Wow, he looked so real that I was in shock, until he started talking; and then it was like a needle scratching across a record and I quickly came back to reality. When his time finally came, we all could tell he was nervous, but Kevin kept talking to him before he went out on that stage like a diva. Priscilla sat down on a white baby grand piano and started singing that Karen Carpenter song, "We've Only Just Begun." Oh my, his voice sounded just like the original, it was so smooth and clear. I turned to look at Kevin and Michael. Their eyes were filling up with tears. "Shit, don't make me cry, too!" It was a great performance. I was totally taken aback. Priscilla did well, really well. He came back to the dressing room flushed; so Kevin broke down and handed Priscilla a cocktail. After all, he definitely needed it. Contestant #5 ran by in a Statue of Liberty/ Uncle Sam combination costume, and started singing God Bless America in a full man's voice. Priscilla then barked out, "If that thing wins this pageant, I will change my name to Yankee Doodle Dandy!!!

On Saturday, the final day of the pageant, we were all really nervous. I even noticed that the boys were so nervous that they kept forgetting to stare at me. It's like they were confused on where to direct their attention. I still didn't get it. That morning, two more friends of Kevin's arrived at the house: Frank and Patrick. They both worked as bartenders in a bar that Kevin frequented back in the day. Patrick was tall, fat, and profusely hairy. Frank was about 5'10 with a slight build, and not hairy. They all ran to each other screaming like schoolgirls. Wow, I don't even act like that. It had been a few years since they had seen each other, so they were all talking at once. I looked over at Michael, who looked pretty bored with it all. We were all introduced, and then Larry called everyone into the dining room for breakfast before heading out to the venue.

When we got there, it was even more insane. You could feel the intensity in the air. Priscilla was already there, screaming at someone on the phone. Uh ohhh, this didn't look good. You don't ever want to see a drag queen upset; it's pretty scary, because they tend to throw things. Kevin went over to calm him down, because it seemed that one of Priscilla's gowns had been stolen. Oh shit, somebody was going to die. You never touch a queen's evening wear! We looked everywhere, but nothing; and, of course, no one around knew anything. So Kevin went through all of the gowns until Priscilla decided on a beautiful sparkly white one. Instead of his wearing a long blonde wig, Kevin suggested that he wear a dark one with the white gown, and pull the wig back in a sleek ponytail for more dramatic effect. Wow, that sounded fantastic! The little makeup guy came out of nowhere and started beating Priscilla's mug, while Kevin handed him a shot of vodka.

Finally, the big moment: I asked Kevin what number he was going to do. Kevin replied cryptically, "It's a surprise, but you will love it." As the music started, two male dancers showed up on stage. Priscilla sashayed out, and started singing that Chaka Khan song I loved so much, "I'm Every Woman!" The audience went wild as he was dancing and singing his ass off. It was incredible. Where the hell did they find those back-up dancers? At the end of the performance, they picked up Priscilla and carried him off stage. I was dumb-founded. He was going to win for sure, totally in the bag.

Miss Statue of Liberty/Uncle Sam contestant went out; he was the last one, and started singing God Bless America in that man's voice again. Ok, I love my country and I love that song, but for a pageant? That kind of pageant? What was he trying to do, anyway? I looked around at the boys and you could tell everyone hated it, except for his fans in the audience.

There were four contestants left. The moment had finally arrived. Blood, sweat, tears! "The winner is...UNCLE SAM!!!" I almost fainted. Priscilla actually did. Kevin then turned to me and said, "I guess she'll have to make an appointment on Monday now to get her name changed to Yankee Doodle Dandy!"

On the way back to the house, everyone was silent. "That thing was totally fixed," we thought. Priscilla placed second. He was so pissed that he threw his wig out the window of the cab. All I wanted to do was take a shower, have a drink, and relax. The boys all went into the living room to have cocktails. I told them I would be down later after I freshened up. As I was taking my shower, I realized that I had forgotten a pair of jeans in the laundry room downstairs. So I wrapped a towel around me, and went downstairs to ask Kevin, or Michael, to grab them for me. When I did, the boys that were staring at me the whole time all screamed in unison, SHE'S A REAL FISH!!! Kevin immediately fell on the floor laughing hysterically; so did Larry and Jake. You see, Kevin had told all of his friends that I was a trans-sexual, and that I had my final surgery earlier in the year. Also, that I was then going through therapy. He told them to be very careful about how they treated me, because I was still very emotional and fragile. OH MY GOD, no wonder they kept staring! Fuck!!

Chapter 4: Curbside Queen

Another workweek had started. It was really hard getting back into the swing of things after that pageant weekend; we were all so drained. But I sucked it up and continued to find models for the haircutting classes and being diligent with taking care of Lance and Fredrick's clients. I have to be honest though. I was really getting pretty bored with the assistant gig. I knew it was getting closer for me to start at least part-time on the floor. I made a mental note to run it by Kevin as soon as possible. One morning, a few weeks later, I went out to check the mail and got sidetracked talking to one of our nosey neighbors. I really wanted to talk to Kevin about me cutting back on the assisting.

I finally got away from that nosey bitch, and ran into the apartment. I could see that the back patio door was slightly opened and Michael was out smoking. He didn't look too happy. So I went into the kitchen and dropped the mail on the counter. When I came out, I heard Kevin talking on the phone, and laughing hysterically. I looked at Michael, who appeared as if he wanted to strangle someone. I asked him what was the deal, and he replied, "Girl, that mother-fucker is going to have those annoying little friends from his hometown, Frank and Patrick — the ones that we met the weekend of the pageant — come and move here! WTF!!! More here, in this apartment!!! No fuckin' way is that going to happen." Well, yes, fuckin' *way* it did. Supposedly these two "friends of his" wanted to get out of their dead-beat town. Since Kevin was Mr. Hollywood now, why not come to the big-city and give it a shot? Wow, this was all happening so suddenly. It was like every time I turned around, something new was happening. Well, I thought, "Get used to it honey, because when you live with people, there will always be SOMETHING going on." So the big question was, when are they coming? The answer: Next Friday! So we had a lot of work to do getting the place ready. Michael was still pissed, but I knew he would be okay; he never remained mad for long, especially after a few Crown and cokes.

I didn't know what to expect, but I wasn't expecting much. Their bus was supposed to arrive at around 7 p.m. that night, and it was right on time. When the passengers were stepping off, I asked Kevin, "Do you see them?" Yeah, there they were, the last ones off, of course. They all ran over to each other again, screaming like bitches. Michael looked like he was going to vomit. By this time, Kevin had already invested in a nice car, so the country girls were going to be riding in style. We headed back home so that they could unpack and freshen up. Of course, they wanted to hit the bars running.

Kevin decided to take them to a bar so they could check out the big city meat. Michael had to work that evening. So, it was only going to be the 3 of us. We ended up at a place that was swimming with guys and fag-hags. Frank went to the left and Patrick scurried to the right. Wow, they hadn't even ordered a drink before they were already cruising. Kevin said: "They're too fuckin' cheap to buy the first round. That's why they ran off. Some dumb ass desperado will buy one for them."

Finally, this was my chance to speak to Kevin about my assistant situation. I knew it was time for me to step forward into the hairdressing realm, because it had then been almost over a year. He agreed with me whole-heartedly, saying that I needed to work on a few more clipper cuts. Actually, Danny had approached him the previous week, saying that he wanted to show me a few blow-drying techniques. Thank God, my prayers have been answered: Looks like we're all definitely on the same page! We had a couple of drinks, and frankly I was bored, as I noticed that Kevin looked tired. So, I suggested that we grab a burger at a place on the strip and then go home. He said, "Girl, you just read my mind! Let me go find those whores and tell them our plan. They can get their tricks to take them back or take a damn cab. Let's get out of this hole!"

The next day was Saturday, and Kevin and I both had to be at work before 10 a.m. Frank and Patrick had not made it home yet. I was not going to worry about two grown ass men; I was not falling into that drama again. On the way there, Kevin promised me that he would set up a little pow wow with Danny, Kathy, Lance and Fredrick: about me moving on to the floor on a part-time basis. This meant that if I was assisting someone and a walk-in came in, I could finish the shampoo — or whatever I was doing — and then tend to my client. All of a sudden, my heart started beating really fast. I was thinking, "Uh oh, am I ready for this? Hmmm, maybe I should wait a month, or two, longer." Kevin, sensing my hesitation, became really stern for just a moment. "You will not wait a month, or two. You will start as soon as possible! We will talk to them next Tuesday." "All right, all right, you don't have to scream, Mary," I exclaimed. He replied, "I'm creating a monster, your come backs now are becoming quicker and sharper." He then acted like he was wiping away tears and said: "You are making your Mama proud!"

Saturday was a blur. All I could dwell on was the meeting on Tuesday; but I knew in my heart that I was ready. That weekend I stayed at home while the boys went out, because I wanted to be totally fresh and clear-headed for the week. This was certainly going to be a turning point in my life: starting a career at 19 years of age. I don't think I really had a full understanding of that, until I was much older. Tuesday came around pretty damn fast. The meeting was very brief and to the point. I would start out part-time, just like Kevin said, assist Lance and Fredrick until a client walked in (at the time, I was the only assistant ready to go on), finish helping them, and then attend to the client. Also, Danny told me, "I want you to practice keeping all the implements in your hand: blow-dryer, brush, and clips, at all times. I don't want to see you ever, ever stop that blow-dryer, or put it down, while styling out a client!" Then Kevin told me, "I want you to bring in a couple of models for flat-tops, too, because that Top Gun movie with Tom Cruise is all the rage right now; and every Tom, Dick and Susie are going to want to look like that mother-fucker!" I could hardly take this all in. It was so much information overload, that I felt like the robot on Lost In Space: does not compute, does not compute…Then everyone got up and walked out of the office. Kathy looked straight at me and said, "Well... you might as well start today!" All of a sudden, my hands got clammy, my throat became very dry, and I couldn't answer her. I had become a deaf mute.

"Yep, let me go and tell the desk girls now, and put you on the main appointment book." I wanted to reach out, grab her by her hair, and tie her up to her office chair. NOOOOOOO, let's start next week. But all I could do was nod my head like a puppet. I walked like a zombie towards Fredrick's station in total shock, waiting for that intercom to go off saying that I had a client up front. About 2 hours had gone by: no walk-in, whew. It was also Tuesday; walk-ins usually came in the later part of the week, and weekend. Then I heard it, that sound I'd heard for a year and a half: "Your client is in!" I floated up to the reception area, and thought: "Hey, maybe that waiter was scared to work at that restaurant, and that's how he floated around like he did." Anyway, I was praying it wasn't some bald fucker who was picky about his 3 long hairs he had left. One of the receptionists said, "Here is your client, and her name is Cindy." It was a little girl about 3 years old, with white blonde hair and blue eyes. She looked like a little doll and she actually had a doll in her arms that looked like her, too. Her parents were a nice-looking couple, and seemed pleasant; so I could feel the fear and tension leaving. Thank God, my first client was going to be sooo easy.

I placed her on top of a booster seat at my station. She was so cute as she talked about what she was going to do that weekend. Her mom told me: "She really doesn't need much, just trim the ends, and that's it." Wow, I couldn't believe how fun this was. I finished her in about twenty minutes. I could feel every co-worker's eyeballs watching my every move. She even gave me a hug. Back then, we didn't charge much for children, but I didn't care. I did my first client and she was pleased! I walked them all up to the front desk, gave them a business card and then went back to my station to clean up. I heard that little girl behind me a few minutes later. She was holding some money in her hand to give to me. Insane, I was so busy thinking about the first client, I totally forgot about my first tip! Rock n' Roll!!!

    For the rest of the week, I was pretty busy with clients. So Kathy decided to put an ad in the paper to hire more assistants. Debra was also pretty much on her way to graduate to the next level. I noticed Debra and Danny talking a lot and walking out of the salon together during her break. "Hmmmm, do I smell love a brewing?" Two weeks later, a couple of girls came in to apply for the assistant job; man, that was fast! They started working the next day, just like I did. Their names were Tammy and Louise. They were both tall and had pretty blonde hair. They had incredibly thick New York accents and talked really loud. I could tell that both of them were pretty wild, and liked to party. After a few conversations with Louise, I knew I didn't want to hang with her; because her whole purpose in life was to get laid. That's all she talked about: getting laid, laid, laid. I guess I couldn't really relate to that subject, since my first experience was downright awful. I didn't think it was such a big deal. I loved the fact that I could hang out with the gays and never have to worry about being hit on. Except on those rare occasions when you would meet a guy out who was "sugar tank," meaning you spent the whole evening trying to guess: Is he straight is he gay? And, after a while, you wear yourself out trying to guess what he is. Tammy was just the opposite of Louise. Tammy was real laid back, and aloof, almost like she had a little poker chip on her shoulder. Both were pretty suspect, so I was definitely going to keep it on the down low with those two.

It had been about 3 weeks since Patrick and Frank had moved in. I arrived home one Wednesday evening and they were all sitting in the living-room. Patrick was smoking a cigarette and looking really nervous. Kevin was playing his stern butch daddy role again. Michael was over in the corner of the room with a smirk on his face. Uh oh, something was going down! As Kevin laid down some ground rules to the boys, Frank seemed to be fine with the fact that they had to find employment. Patrick, on the other hand, wasn't too keen on the idea. As I watched him more closely, I could tell he was afraid. "Girl, you're going to have to either be a bartender on the strip, or sack groceries. I don't give a shit what you do, but I'm not taking care of your happy ass forever. My titties are not full of milk anymore!" At that moment, Michael and I lost it and started laughing ours asses off, picturing Kevin with two huge cow udders! Finally, Frank spoke up and said that he found a position open at a French restaurant that he was going to check out. "Would Kevin or Michael take him if he got an interview?" Kevin instantly replied, "Hell yeah, girl, of course I will take you, just let me know when." Frank also said that he was thinking about maybe going to beauty school, because he didn't want to be in the restaurant/bar business forever. That was pretty cool. Frank was really trying to figure out what to do with his life. Patrick still looked pretty upset, so Kevin said, "Girl, I'm giving you two more weeks to find a job. After that, I'm sending your broke ass back home. Ok, meeting adjourned; let's have a cocktail."

Frank aced his interview and started training that week. All of us would come home broken down tired every day, and Patrick would be on the couch sprawled out watching sit-coms. The TV would be turned up so loud that you could hear it from the front door. I was starting to get pissed now, because he was totally taking advantage of Kevin's kindness. Finally, one evening we came home and all of us witnessed the same scenario: Patrick on the couch smoking, and missing the ashtray, of course. I thought Michael was going to smother him with one of the couch pillows. "Girlllll, I'm hungry; where are we going to eat tonight!" I just knew that this was the question that would end his life that night. But Kevin simply smiled and said, "Why don't we all go see Frank at his restaurant. Let's all show him our support." Whoa Nellie, I was shocked! He wasn't going to kick his lazy ass!?!

We all got dressed up and headed out to see Frank. I would have been so embarrassed if my friend was working, and I wasn't, and I showed up to his job to have my dinner paid for. Wow, free-loaders have no boundaries. When he was out of site, I turned to Kevin and said, "Did you notice how Patrick seems afraid to go out and get a job?" "Yes girl, I know he's afraid. I'm going to tell you something and don't you dare tell Michael!" "Ok, ok, what is it?" "You see…Patrick can't read or write. And I know he can't; and all he has to do is admit it and quit being a prideful prick. I would help him get enrolled in some classes. However, he's being such a dick about it; but don't worry, tonight it will all end." Oh shit, what was Kevin up to?

The restaurant was absolutely fabulous! There were wonderfully ornate chandeliers and gorgeous paintings everywhere. Frank saw us walk in and was beaming as he immediately ran over to greet us. I was so happy for him; what a great gig! Frank looked at Patrick and said, "Girl, couldn't you have saved wearing your cover-alls for another night?" "Shut up, bitch!" Patrick replied.

Frank took our drink orders as we all started to look over our menus. I glanced over at Patrick, who was pretending like he was giving the place a good once over, even looking under the tablecloth. Awww man, I felt so bad for him, "Why don't you say something, you dumb ass?" I thought. Kevin leaned over to Patrick and said, "Why don't you have the filet mignon? That's what I'm having, you'll love it." "Oh yeah, girl, that's exactly what I was thinking about having!" Our drinks finally came. Boy, I needed mine really bad tonight (I thought) — as Frank took our orders. Dinner was great. I thought that Patrick was going to tongue his plate, he was so ravenous.

Frank came over after we were done and asked how everything was; of course, we were thrilled with the whole experience. Suddenly Kevin looked over at Patrick and dropped the bomb: "Well, Girl, say goodbye to everyone; say goodbye to Frank. Your bus leaves in an hour and a half!" All of our mouths dropped open, even the waiter who was eavesdropping at our table. What, what…what are you talking about!?! "This is your goodbye dinner; say goodbye to Frank, so you can go home and pack. Your ticket is sitting on top of your suitcase." Damn, that was fuckin' harsh but smooth. Patrick got up like a toy soldier and woodenly marched over to Frank. They hugged each other while Kevin paid the bill. I've never ridden in the family car at a funeral before, but I figured this was what it probably felt like: dead silence, all the way home. Patrick packed his few belongings, as Michael and I said our goodbyes. Kevin escorted him to the car and that was that. Michael then ran over to the stereo and turned up his favorite song: "It's Raining Men," by the Weather Girls. We promptly danced and lip-synced our hearts out!

Chapter 5: Thunder Pussy

Everyone's life seemed to be moving at warp speed. Patrick was back home, nursing a beer bottle. Frank had made enough money to purchase a car, and he enrolled in a beauty school very close to the restaurant. I finally purchased one, too. I bought it from a client's husband and paid 2,000 cash for it. It was an Oldsmobile, big 4 door, light baby blue in color, with white leather seats. Yes, it was a pimp car, but I didn't care. At least I had my on transportation. Danny decided that week to put me on the floor full-time, and he told me he wanted my station to be four chairs down from his. I thought, "Awww, man, what the fuck for?" But I did what I was told, and transferred all of my things to the new station. I knew he wanted to make sure I was doing everything right. It was his salon, after all. What came out of there would affect his reputation.

Tammy took my place assisting for Lance and Fredrick, which I thought would be a perfect fit for them. At least Tammy wouldn't talk to their clients about getting laid! That afternoon I was blow-drying a female client. Everything was going smooth, but I must have blacked out for a second and placed the blow-dryer down and then began to section the hair. All of a sudden, I felt something flying past my left ear! Oh my God, Danny had just thrown a Denman brush at my head!! Pick up that dryer, Sweetie...he said. My client looked at me, glanced at Danny, then went back to reading her magazine. I was starting to really get busy; my clientele were skyrocketing. The party scene was where I got a small percentage of clients. I would hand out my cards to every cutie pie I met. The club where I was on the guest list was one that my co-workers and I frequented pretty much every weekend. In about 6 months, I had built a pretty steady clientele base upon which I could easily support myself. I was working five days a week, sometimes 11 hours a day. At that point I was 20 years old. I worked hard; and I partied hard, too. I never had close friends in high school, so the party scene was where I met my closest, dearest friends for life.

I could tell that Kevin was starting to get a little anxious. You see, I'd learned some things about his personality. He could accomplish anything he set out to do. But once he did, he got really bored with it all. And I could tell that he was on the verge of another hairdresser breakdown. One Friday night, when I came home from work, I could hear Kevin and Michael laughing in the bedroom. All of a sudden, they both ran out into the living room dressed in full drag! Ok, one thing you have to understand, those two were not built for drag; well, at least, be pretty in drag. They were way too fuckin' muscular! What the hell are you two up to? I could tell that Kevin was higher than Cooter Brown, because his grin was all crazy. "Girl, we're going to enter an amateur night contest." "For what," I asked: "The biggest beast in a dress contest?"

Kevin then replied, "Bitch; that was not even funny!" But he couldn't help but laugh. I also knew that this was strange. "Why the hell would he want to do drag?" He was too fuckin' big: another sign that he was getting really bored.

Two weeks later, on a Sunday morning, the inevitable happened. Kevin said that he and Michael were going to move to California. Frank and I started sobbing like three year olds. Why are you leaving us!?! God, we were so fuckin' selfish then, when I look back at it. Kevin replied, "It's time for you two to make it on your own. You don't need me anymore." I felt like I had been shot in the heart, but what was I to do? Considering their plans to move in two months, I told Frank I would talk to the apartment complex about us moving into a smaller two bedroom together. Frank was still crying when I walked out of the apartment on that very sad, sad day.

Frank and I pulled it together pretty fast, as we knew it was time to put on our big girl panties, and grow up. We were scheduled to move into our new place a week before Kevin and Michael would leave for Cali. When that day came, Frank and I were actually okay with it. We both decided to avoid thinking of ourselves, and just be happy for Kevin and Michael. Hell, it was like we were their kids, and the kids had to let the old folks go live it up. Frank drove us all to the airport, proving another damn silent car ride. I was really going to miss Michael; he was my dance partner. We all went to a bar at the airport to have a goodbye drink together; we were all chain smoking. Finally, their flight was called for boarding. Man, this was so hard. I was going to miss them something awful. But I made sure that I didn't look at Frank; so I wouldn't lose it. Kevin said, "You know we will keep in touch. I will give you all of my info when we get settled." I was trying not to stick my lip out. We all hugged goodbye before they disappeared in a cloud of pixie dust.

I threw myself into work with a vengeance, quickly becoming a hairdressing machine. I took everything that walked through those salon doors. I took shit that nobody wanted to deal with, including all of the picky problem clients. Before Kevin left, he had me bring in several guys to practice the flat-top, and I mastered it pretty well. So I then became the flat-top queen, because no one else would touch that haircut. The men who wore that kind of hairstyle were definitely a different breed. After a while I was so booked during the week, I could only take in maybe one walk-in a week, because I already had regulars coming in. Plus I was getting tons of referrals. I think Frank and I were still trying to get used to the boys being gone. Frank said that for as long as he had known Kevin, he was always that way: here today, gone tomorrow.

Oh fuck, I had just remembered, who the hell was going to do my hair!?! Kevin was the only one I trusted, shit, shit, shit! I also started partying even more, as there was something to do almost every night of the week. When Kevin was here, we did a lot of coke, but now the party favor of choice was crystal meth. You only had to do a tiny bit, and it would last you all night. All we wanted to do was buy new outfits and dance all night. As you very well may remember, through the 80's — and into the late 90's — we didn't go out to get wasted and fistfight each other. It was all about the music and the fashion. To come up with the most badass costume to go out in was the highlight of the week. I had accumulated the most amazing club wardrobe; all the queens and chic's wanted the shit I wore. I was also pretty thin, (and still am, I might add; Mama didn't become morbidly obese in a twenty year period, like some did). So I was having the time of my life. I even had a personal shopper too. His name was Bobby, and he would call me at the salon every Saturday afternoon about an awesome outfit that had just come in, and that I needed to come take a look. I have to tell you that those clothes weren't cheap either; I wasn't shopping at Kmart! I would receive a call from Bobby around 4:30 p.m. and he was always so dramatic. "Girl, I have the outfit for you, it just came in and it has your name written all over it girl!!!" I would then reply, "Bobby, you say that every weekend!" "NO, Girl, this is the one." That was our conversation every week. Well, on one particular Saturday, he really did have THE ONE! Debra and I went to his boutique after work and he brought it out to me. "Oh MY God!" was my immediate reaction. I knew it was the one. He then said, "Look at the name of the tag, girl; this is so you!" Ok hold on to your jock straps. In bold black letters the tag read, THUNDER PUSSY!!! YEAAA! That was it, my signature piece. I grabbed Bobby around the neck and hugged and kissed him.

He finally ordered me something that no one else would ever dare to wear. It was a black romper that went around the neck like a halter outlined in silver studs. Then it went down into a jumpsuit that was actually short, shorts with 6 inch silver chains hanging around the legs! This wasn't some fuzzy pink and blue club kid animal costume. I wore the fuck out of that outfit! When we were getting ready to go out, my friends would ask, "Are you going to wear TP out again?" You see, we did have some class; we didn't just scream out Thunder Pussy in public.

Like I said before, I met a lot of my close friends in the club scene. There were two guys I would see out all the time. They stood out because they were both pretty hip dressers and they were both over 6'0 in height. At first I thought they were together because they always were together. Every once in a while, I would see a girl with them, so I wasn't quite sure about the situation. There was something about one of them I didn't really care for; he never really did anything to me. He just acted like his shit didn't stink. Then one fine day, I walked to the front desk of the salon to grab a product, and those guys were sitting there in the lobby. What the fuck? Are they hairdressers? One had very blonde highlighted hair, and the other one was just the opposite: his hair was black as coal. I quickly went to the office and asked Kathy about them. She told me that only one was interviewing and he would most likely start out as an assistant for a short period of time, then go on from there. I said, "Which one was interviewing?" She peeked around the corner and answered, "the blonde one, I think." I thought, "Dammit, that's the one I don't like! Oh well, I might as well get over it. I don't make the decisions around here. I saw the one with the jet black hair, whose name was Jackson, lean over and whisper to the blonde one Robert. Later I found out that he had said, "Hey, that Thing works here (referring to me). Are you sure you want to apply here; doesn't she get on your nerves!?!"

Robert started assisting at the salon the following week; they had him floating around helping out any stylist that needed it. I watched his ass from a distance and he seemed pretty pleasant. Hmmm...maybe I had the wrong impression about him; he could be ok. Kevin called Frank and me to give us their address and phone numbers. We had each other on speaker so we could all talk at once. I could tell that I'd moved on to a degree because I didn't have that ache in my heart anymore while we were chatting. It was good to hear that they were doing great, but I could tell that I wasn't attached to his apron anymore.

My clientele were developing very nicely and I was starting to build some good relationships. I will tell you one thing, though. There is one thing I wish I knew then that I do now: that a hairdresser really shouldn't ever have to take shit off of any client, ever! I kissed ass and let them slap me around with their bad attitudes and their rudeness for years, before I finally turned into the hair nazi! But I will go into that a bit later. There was a lot of diversity also. I had all of the following: the gay and lesbian clients; the straight couple clients right out of college; the young singles; old singles; business men; and housewives. My days were never boring, for sure. I still really wasn't interested in dating, but I had clients that thought I should date. You're such a cute, nice girl; you need to meet a nice man, yada, yada, yada. Rick was a client of mine who was married and he was always trying to set me up. So, finally, after four months of him bugging me about it, I gave in. I was then twenty-one-years old and Rick wanted to set me up with his thirty three year old mailman. Wow, I don't really think this is going to be good at all, but ok. The mailman's name was Leonard. Uhhh, I didn't like the name much.

Leonard called me and we set up a date for the following Saturday night. His voice was nice so maybe it wouldn't be so gross after all. Right? My friends couldn't believe it: "You're going on a date!" "Yeah," I replied, "but if it's shitty, I will be calling you guys to meet up for sure!" Mr. Man arrived right on time: 7 p.m. I decided to wear a simple little black dress; and not look so funky as to scare him. Sorry TP, you can't come out to play tonight! He was a nice looking black guy, very well dressed and with a great haircut. He asked me what type of food I was in the mood for and I suggested Italian; so he took me to this little quaint spot in a neighboring sub-division near my apartment. I didn't know this place existed, how cool! Leonard was so talkative that he would barely take a breath before he was on to the next topic. I noticed that when he asked me a question, he would cut me off and keep yammering away. I guess it was ok to a point since I talk all day at work; but, shit, when was he going to shut the fuck up? He ordered a bottle of white Zinfandel. Ugghhh, what the fuck is white Zinfandel? I'd never had that before. Kevin told me it's cheap Kool Aid tasting wine. Ohhh boy, here we went starting off with cheap ass wine! We ordered our meal, and I started gulping down the Koolaid as Leonard went on and on. After a while, I didn't even hear what he was saying and I think we finished eating in 15 minutes. So I asked, "What other plans do you have for the evening?" Well, he replied: "I thought we would just go back to your place and talk."

Dammit! I wanted to pick up that wine bottle and smash his fuckin' teeth in! What a cheap ass son of a bitch. I hated this; the gays didn't ever treat me this way! Well, I thought, when Buster Brown takes me back home, I'll give his trifling ass 20 minutes so HE CAN TALK, then he's out the fuckin' door. When we arrived, I told him to have a seat, then I ran to my kitchen to do a shot of vodka. I wasn't going to offer him any for sure — cause it might make him talk even more. I then excused myself so I could change into something more comfortable. All of a sudden his face lit up. Oh, hell no, cowboy! I'm going to put on my pajamas with the feet attached and grab my stuffed tropical penguin named Val, named after Val Kilmer, of course, who is just about the finest motherfucker on the planet.. And Val is going to sit in my lap while you TALK! As Leonard went on and on, I thought, "How could anyone talk so fuckin' much?" If you closed your eyes, it sounded like the radio had been left on. Even Val was starting to look at the clock. Finally, I heard the question that prompted me to shut er' down! "What are your ice cubes shaped like? Mine are sort of oblong shaped." What the fuck was he talking about!?! Ok, time to go night, night nurse. "Uhhh, Leonard, it's been a long week…" as I'm shoving him out the door, and "I'm very tired now and thanks for dinner; bye, bye now!" God, that sucked balls!

On the following Tuesday afternoon, I went into the break room to eat my lunch, and Mr. Robert was back there folding towels. When I walked in, I could tell he hesitated on whether he wanted to speak to me or not. So I went ahead and beat him to the punch. "Hiii Robert, what's up?" "Oh, same ole same ole, just back here doing my slave duties." "Oh, I hear ya, my aunt Jemima scarf still has sweat stains on it!" Robert started cracking up. Well, well, I think we broke the ice a little. "Can I tell you something?" Robert asked.

"Sure," I said. "When I would see you at the club, for some reason I never liked you." I started laughing and said, "I felt the same way about you!" After that, Robert and I became friends. And, after a while, we were inseparable, we did everything together. He even replaced Michael as my new dance partner, I was tickled pink!

It didn't take long for Robert to finish his apprenticeship, as he was a very quick study. He knew a lot of people, so he would sometimes bring in 2 models a week. So any stylist that was available could check his work. Robert even started styling my hair, especially for our big Saturday night extravaganzas. We did everything together: shopping, dining, dancing. It was a dream come true, someone who was around my age who had a sense of style and was funny. Even Jackson eventually warmed up to me, and sometimes all three of us would go out on the town, usually to our favorite spot because we were all on the guest list. It was so rocking to walk up that huge red velvet staircase passing all of the losers waiting in line to get in. And our drinks would be practically almost made before we even stepped up to the bar. So fuckin' cool, right? One thing that kind of ticked me off would be if we wanted party favors, Robert always wanted me to approach the guy from whom we usually we got them. I hated doing it, "Why don't you do it sometimes?" I would ask him. "Noooo, it's best if you do it; they never turn girls down." True, but they always bust them, too. I always got the feeling that if I was busted, he would just vanish. I would be standing there handcuffed looking stupid as hell. But that thought never stopped me, and we always got what we wanted and then some. We never really discussed it much, but I knew that Robert was on the fence about coming out of the closet. He wasn't a Nellie queen, but he wasn't a butch daddy either. He never wanted to date and he was very picky. Jackson would date anybody who would pay his way, but he could get away with being a freeloader because he was cute. A friend once told me that if you are gay, young, and cute, you can get away with anything. But once you hit your mid-forties, in gay years that is 80 years +! And you better have some money, because you will never get anything for free, ever again.

There was a guy at the club who liked Robert. His name was Ben, and he had fire engine red hair that he wore in a shoulder length bob. The restrooms were unisex, with huge mirrors, through which you could check yourself out, and long plushy lounge couches. One night, Robert and I just finished dancing and needed to take a break, so we were sitting on one of the couches with our heads tilted back. And guess who showed up? Old Ben. He started talking to us though it was pretty loud in there with all the people. So I was half ass listening to him but all I could see were his amazingly long red nose hairs. Whoa, he really needed to attack those nasty things. When he finally stopped talking and just walked off, I asked Robert, "Did you hear what he was saying?" Robert then looked at me with a smirk and said, "I couldn't get past the long red nose hairs!" Priceless!

Many of you comrades know, and have experienced, the delight of building your clientele. Everyone starts out so nice; and they are so appreciative of you and your expertise. You are sooo talented that they croon: "I don't know what I would do without you," so on and so forth. Then SHAZAM! They turn on you like white on rice; it's almost like you are married to them; and, after a few years, they are talking to you like you're their husband or wife. As if you are there for their bidding, that red-headed stepchild treatment. How many years did it take for one of yours to go ballistic; what, two to four years maybe? Yep, that sounds about right.

One Wednesday afternoon, a family walked in: Dad, Mom and two kids, a boy and a girl. They had just moved to town a few weeks ago, and were looking for someone who could take on the whole family. The receptionist booked them with me for two weeks out on a Saturday around 11 a.m. Back in the day, I would allow new clients to be booked on a Saturday, but now Hell to the No. The mother-fuckers are always late, then they want to, of course, talk about their last experience — which was a catastrophe, because they wouldn't keep their trap shut and let the hairstylist do their job.

So now the new ones either come on a weekday, or not at all. Damn, I'm mean, huh? When this family came in, I noticed they were all a little off. The dad talked constantly and the daughter, who was about twelve years old, acted just like him. They never shut up! What is it about these people? We have to work all day in this environment. We don't want to hear all about your generational background, how many bunions you had removed from your Flintstone feet, etc. We just want to do your hair! The mom was a nut job, too. She talked a lot, but would get lost in her thoughts and would kind of just sit there and ponder. Shit, at least I got a break in between her outbursts. But the most disturbing was the son, who was about nine. He would crawl up in a ball underneath one of the lobby waiting chairs. While he was sucking his thumb, his family would have to baby talk him out from under the chair. Now that was fuckin' crazy! I put up with that family for two years; now, I wouldn't deal with it for two minutes. I finally got my chance to reprimand the psycho mom one day. She had called for an appointment, just for herself, and she got the days all mixed up. I heard a voice screaming like a banshee from the front desk area. Recognizing the voice, I excused myself from my client. Of course, the screeching was coming from Miss Wack-a-do; so I grabbed her by her elbow and led her out down the hall and away from the salon. "What the hell are you doing?" I asked her. "They got my appointment wrong!" she squealed. "No, they didn't," I replied. "I was standing up there when she took it; you're wrong!" I said. She started stammering, and then I said to her, "One more act like that and don't even think about coming back to me to do your nappy head, got it?" A month later she "no showed" her appointment. Don't you just love when they start doing that? Like we just come to work to sit around and play with ourselves. After that, I never saw the Adams Family again, thank God.

Chapter 6: Handbags, Lipstick and Blow

Ok, I have to finally bring up a subject that may hurt some feelings, but I don't give a damn. Some peops shouldn't be so stupid. Hairstyles don't make a person look fat. Hairstyles don't make a person look thinner. You're either fat, or you're skinny, and you know what the fuck you're doing! Some peops try to put all the blame on the hairdresser. Everything is all our fault. It's our fault that you raid the fridg from the time you get home from work till 12 midnight, I know. It's our fault that your husband left you for a transsexual store clerk. Yep. It's our fault that because you are such a nosy ass busy body, you had to go see a therapist because you were so gung ho on fixing everybody's problems, except your own. I remember when people were ashamed to say they saw a shrink; now, it's as popular as bragging about how many depressants you're on. Why don't you all grow a pair? Whew, I feel better now!

Many hairstylists will remember the client, or clients, that thought it was their duty to try to lip-lock you? Or somehow that captain hook hand just happened to connect with your boobs, crotch or ass. Know what, guys and dolls: you fuckers don't pay us enough to cop a feel; and we're not all that hard up. Not to mention that nine out of ten of you are not even remotely cute to begin with. And believe me: if we want you, you will definitely catch on, because you would need a rodeo clown to interfere!

Reminds me of my old client Jesse who had breath that smelled like decayed flesh. Every time he would start to leave, after his appointment, he would lean forward to try to kiss me on the lips. I put up with that nasty ole goat forever! But there was one client for whom I would have gladly cut his hair, while naked, if he asked me to. Hell, he wouldn't have had to ask. His name was Scott and he used to go to Lance when I was an assistant. Scott was the sexiest mother-fucker I have ever met till this day. After a while, Lance's schedule became so hectic that he couldn't accommodate Scott any longer. So guess who got the honors? Why, little ole me! He would call at the last minute, on a Saturday afternoon, but I didn't give a shit, cause he was fine. So don't try to play all coy and innocent, you hairstylists. I know this pertains to every one of you who have had a client that was hot: you would have canceled a wedding party "the day of" for them. So, one Saturday afternoon, Scott called — needing to get in pronto — so I stayed till 5:30. He came in and…fuck, he was so hot, my heart would start beating so fast. What was funny about it all was the fact that I wasn't in love with him; he just had that something that you only maybe experience once in a lifetime. His voice could melt butter on a vagina, whew! I'm getting all hot and bothered just talking about it now! He asked me what my plans were for that evening. "I have no plans," I hurriedly said. Robert was three stations down, firing off a "go to hell" look. "Uhhh, I meant I have plans with Robert to go to the club, what are you doing?" "Well, baby, I'm meeting some friends out, but we can meet up with you two later." "That will be perfect," I said. He gave me his number; and, while I was cutting his hair, he reached back and grabbed my legs! I almost passed out!

Back then the rage was the drug Ecstasy. I didn't like taking pills, because you never knew how it was going to hit you. And usually it would hit you while you were talking to someone cute; and, all of a sudden, a huge volcano of vomit would erupt to your lips. But one of Kevin's clients, a psychiatrist that still came to the salon after Kevin left, gave me 2 capsules of X. It was the original shit he gave to his whack-job clients. Not the shit made in the bathtub of some strung out weasel.

    Robert and I broke one open and each of us took a half. I'm not quite sure if that was a smart thing to do, but oh well. I knew I didn't need to take the whole thing by myself, or I might have been looking, and acting, like a monkey when I finally hooked up with Scott. Robert and I started dancing and had our usual cocktails. As I felt that shit starting to kick in, it was so nice. I felt so loving and kind, I couldn't stop smiling. I was even talking to people I couldn't stand. Finally, Scott arrived; I had almost forgotten he was coming. I turned to Robert and said, "Here is all of your shit, I'm leaving!" Scott and I jumped into his car and went to another club to meet some of his friends. He had taken something, too, because he was real touchy, feelie…and I likie! He was a wild SOB. We ended up dancing on tables; and, of course, I had on TP, so we definitely got a lot of attention. Afterwards, we ended up going back to his place and it was like that movie War of the Roses, only we didn't hate each other. I won't go into the sordid details. I know you want me to, you nasty thing, you. But I won't. All I will tell you is that lamps were on the floor, we couldn't find our underwear, and why was there dishwashing liquid everywhere?

    Ugghh, I smoked way too many cigarettes last night. I tasted foot and booze and I smelled like ass. Oh shit, where is my purse? I knew I looked like King Kong, so I had to get some makeup on before Scott woke up. I didn't want him thinking that he woke up beside a teenage boy. I tip-toed out of the bedroom; and I started crawling around the apartment, like a combat marine. What the hell was my purse doing on his balcony? I got myself together and Scott came into the living room. "Whatcha' doing, baby?" he asked? "Oh not much," I replied, just trying to put my face back on. "You look good," he said! Wow, that was totally shocking and I could tell he meant it, too. It was Sunday and I had a lot of laundry that was piled up. Plus, my apartment was a wreck. So I asked him to take me home. The ride home was actually pleasant. Scott and I both knew that this was just a one-time deal, and that it would go no further. I think we both just wanted to test out the waters, so to speak. But we would never consider a future together. Actually, it was pretty cool, because there was no weirdness between us later on. He would still call on Saturday, at the last minute, and I would jump through hoops to fit him in. And we would joke and laugh about that evening, but we never met out again.

  Earlier in my career I accumulated a quite large gay clientele of men and women. Since I had frequented the gay bars with Kevin, I had the tendency to stay down on the strip, even after he had gone home, continuing to hang out and party with our friends. And those friends always knew someone who needed a hairdresser. One Saturday night Robert and I were out and a queen came up to us and started yammering away. Boy, he was on something for sure; his underarms were soaked through his shirt. Yucko! I looked down and noticed that he had a huge Gucci purse in his hand. I'd never seen a grown man with a big ass purse in his hand in a club or anywhere else for that matter. Then he leaned in closer and asked us, "Do you guys want a bump? Let's go to my car, because these bitches notice every little thing in here." The queen opened up that purse and there were several bags of coke stuffed in it. Shit, he was carrying a purse in plain view with drugs!

Was he fuckin' nuts, or what? He had the whole set up in his car tray — even a gold straw. You name it: he had it. He gave us both 2 huge hairy lines. Wow, his shit was good.

He finally introduced himself and said, "My name is Kent and what do you two cutie pies do?" We went into the hairstylist song and dance. I didn't want to talk about work and I know Robert didn't, either. Then the queen asked for a business card. Robert didn't have any on him but I did. Kent then proclaimed, "I will be calling you later, girl, for a haircut." Of course I didn't believe he would. People said that all the time and rarely called. Well, two weeks later I went to look at my schedule for the week and there it was in black letters for one of the days: 3:00 p.m. KENT. I thought, "Is that the same Kent that we met at the bar? Couldn't be!!!" Well, Saturday rolled around, and, guess who was coming to dinner? Kent! And guess what he had in his hand as he walked into the salon? He walked down the sidewalk with that fuckin' purse. That queen had some balls! You see, Kent was a well-known dealer who happened to be crazier than a shit house rat! He didn't give a damn what anyone thought of him, and he really had a weird way of showing it, though. So when he came in, he asked me, "Hey girl, do you want to go have a drink after my haircut?" "Sure, that would be great," I said, wondering, when I said it, where was he going to put that purse when we were seated. I started smiling to myself when I thought about the looks we were going to get.

I finished his hair; then we went to the bathroom. We each did a line and then headed off to a restaurant bar that was close. Oh, looky, it has an outside patio! Now everyone could see the man with the purse. I actually knew one of the waiters there, so I asked for his section. When he came over, he started laughing. Kent put that big Gucci purse right on the table next to him, and people's eyes were bugging out of their skulls. We just sat out enjoying the sunshine and the people passing by with either a shocked look or just down right appalled!

It had almost been six months since Tammy and Louise started assisting at the salon. They were more than chomping at the bit to start burning some hair. Kathy started them right away working on Sundays, and Mondays, because most of the senior hairstylists took those days off and the walk-in traffic was tremendous. I had been working Sundays for about one year; so I was more than ready to take a break and I would occasionally work someone in on those days if they had an emergency come up, like a meeting, or a funeral. You know, I still don't get why a person wants their hair done so badly before a funeral? Nobody is paying attention to your ass; how self-centered is that?

On one particular Sunday that I had off, I got a phone call from Louise. She was so damn excited that she could hardly talk and explain the reason for which she had called. As she hyperventilated, she told me that a few guys from an Australian basketball team had come in to get their haircut. They had invited her, Tammy, and whoever else wanted to come out, to join them for drinks! Yeah, I was game, even though it was the end of the weekend. Who cares? Free drinks! Woo hoo! And I'm sure they were cute, cute, cute — with those sexy ass accents of theirs. She gave me the details and told me she and Tammy would go grab some Ho Wear, then come to my apartment to get ready so we could all ride together. Sounded like a perfect plan to me. This, of course, was not a Thunder Pussy night. I knew that we would end up at a top 40's club because that's what the girls liked; so I chose a tight pink dress with high heel pumps to match. The girls arrived around 8:30 p.m. They got ready and, as we admired ourselves in the mirror, we all agreed we would be the hottest ones there. Louise then announced that we were first going to meet some of the guys at a bar near the salon, then go from there. It actually turned out to be the same bar at which I hung out with Kent; so that was cool, because we all knew the layout. When we saw them at their table, I couldn't believe what I saw: the whole table was filled with beer bottles. I'm not talking about 5 or 6; I mean like 30 or 40 bottles! These mother-fuckers were putting it away. My first thought was, "Awww, man, they are going to be so wasted that all we are going to end up doing is baby-sitting the whole night." We all looked at each other and took the plunge, walking straight up to their table anyway. We were greeted with whistles and comments, exactly what we expected, of course! We sat down and had a drink with them. As I observed them, I noticed that they didn't act intoxicated at all. They weren't even slurring their words. Hmmm, that's odd; how is that possible?

The boys then told us that there were more guys from the team they were going to meet. Could we meet them at their hotel lobby? So we drove downtown to this huge hotel on Main Street. When we walked through the carousel doors, all three of us said in unison: Shit!!! There were young girls everywhere in the lobby, hundreds of them! So the boys had been busy. You see, they went out and rounded up every chick they could and invited them to meet them out. Displaying all shapes, sizes, and colors, too, it looked just like an ad from the United Colors of Benetton. Tammy leaned over to us and said, "I feel like a roped steer," as we burst out laughing.

We milled around a bit. When spotting the hotel lobby bar, we proceeded to order some drinks. I heard a man's voice behind me abruptly say, "Put their drinks on my tab."

It was a very sultry Australian accent. I turned around to see who it was. Oh boy, I had hit pay dirt. He was probably in his early thirties, so I knew he wasn't a player. It turned out that he was one of the coaches and he was cute! He was about 5'10, so he wasn't really too tall. He was taller than I was — which was key — and he had brown hair and brown eyes. Tammy and Louise grabbed their drinks and ran off to go-a-hunting!

The guy's name was Roland and everything he said was funny. He was so animated, so I knew this was going to be a fun-filled evening. Roland gathered two more of his buddies for Tammy and Louise; and we all headed off in a cab to one of the nightclubs nearby. Even on a Sunday night, the place was jam-packed. Hookers and Ho's everywhere! I'm sure the other girls thought the same thing about my friends and me. I watched Roland and his friends drink beer after beer, sometimes even mixing in a few shots. Not once did they seem, or act, drunk…it was incredible. I'd never seen anything like it: then, or even since! Usually, by now, any normal man would be lying in the bushes somewhere naked and comatose, if he had consumed what these guys were consuming. I was so obsessed with watching him to see if I could catch him slip, and slur, a word. I noticed that he was starting to look at me weird while he was talking to me, so I made myself stop being a freak about it all.

Two more hours had passed, as we danced, and he continued to drink. Fuckin' A! I'm in shock. This fucker was still standing upright and not acting like an orangutan! We closed the club down. Tammy and Louise wanted to go back to the hotel and get in the hot tub. Of course, every man in sight agreed wholeheartedly. Louise was FINALLY going to get laid, so she ran past us like a locomotive to flag down a cab. Let's please put the bitch out of her misery! No one had a swimsuit, so we all jumped in with our underwear on; is this legal to do in a hotel? I had stopped drinking a long time ago because my mother instinct had started setting in. We were with men we did not know and Tammy and Louise were shit-faced. Roland was starting to get real touchy feely, and now I really wasn't feeling it at all because I had quit boozing. He could then sense I wasn't on the same level. He eased up and looked over to where Tammy and Louise were and then said to me, "Don't worry about the girls. They will be okay. They are with decent guys. Those guys know that they are too wasted to make a decision about anything, so will take good care of them. I promise you that." I will always remember how sweet, and kind, he was. That was really fuckin' cool of him to make sure that the girls were in good hands. It was now almost 5 a.m. and I was going down hard like Eddie Murphy when he wasn't funny anymore. Then that thing happened that I had been waiting to happen for three hours: ROLAND ALLLMOST SLURRRED A WOOORD! And he caught himself like a super world champion skateboarder! DAMNNNN!

I was so sleepy that I could barely keep my eyes open. Tammy was passed out on one of the pool lounges. Louise was trying so hard to stay awake while keeping her guy interested; she thought she would lean in, and whisper something to him, and then her head would kinda pitch forward. "Wow, it's time to roll out of this hole," I thought. I then looked at Roland and said, "We girls need to get out of here. The sun will be up soon; and if we are not in a cab in 10 minutes, we will all turn to vapor." He started laughing as I went over and said goodbye to the boys, gave Tammy a light slap on her cheek and pinched Louise on her right arm. "Come on bitches, it's time to go!" Roland walked us to the front of the hotel lobby, through which I could plainly see a row of cabs parked out front. I turned to him and said, "Thanks for an incredible night…had a blast."

He then replied: "Aren't you going to give me your number?" What? He wants my phone number? He lives in frigging Australia. But I was too tired to argue, so he ran to the concierge desk, grabbed a pen and some paper, and I gave him my home and work number. Then he did something that was really over the top: he gave us money for cab fare, Thank God! Because I had no pennies on me and I knew the girls didn't either. Roland helped Tammy into the front of the cab and Louise into the back. The cabdriver was grinning like a fuckin' freak! Roland kissed me on the cheek as we said our goodbyes. "Home, James!"

As we arrived at my apartment twenty minutes later, I noticed that the girls couldn't even speak. Tammy zombied up to the sofa, and fell on it face first, as Louise went to my bed and collapsed. I knew that if we all slept all day — that day — we would be okay for the following day, Tuesday, at work. I went to take a shower and put on my feet pajamas, grabbed Val and crashed next to Louise.

As Tuesday rolled around, I walked into the salon and noticed a new receptionist at the front desk. I could see that Kathy was showing her the ropes; so I didn't interrupt and just went back to get my station ready. Debra came over to me and said, "Did you see the new girl up there?" "Yep," I replied, "Why?" "Well, she seems kinda weird." I then said, "Girl, everybody here is weird!" I then went back to the front to introduce myself and she told me her name was Michelle. She had jet black hair that stood straight up like a rocker, and she wore tons of makeup. She wore about thirty bracelets on both her wrists. I couldn't tell if she wanted to be Madonna, or Billy Idol. We started talking and she seemed pretty cool. I knew I liked her right away. I told her, "We will always be straight — you and I — just don't fuck up my schedule when you book my appointments, capice?" She agreed.

Chapter 7: Remedial Groupies

Michelle, as I soon found out, was obsessed with rock band singers. Her life's dream was to become a rocker's wife and travel. Man, she was delusional, I didn't know much; but one thing I did know was that those rocker guys were crazy. They met so many women on the road that they couldn't remember who was who: unless you were a drop dead gorgeous super model, which Michelle wasn't. Well, on one fine day, Michelle came running into the salon screaming that Billy Idol was comin' to town. This was her chance, she said. "I will meet him and he won't be able to refuse me." "Girl, are you out of your mind?" I said. "If you do that, yes, maybe he will let you on his bus, but when he's done with you, he's going to drop your used up ass off in the next city." Of course she didn't listen, so when Billy Boy came to town she went to the concert anyway. Before she left, I told her, "Call me, or Debra, if you need money for the next bus back." "I won't need anything thing," she yelled back. "I'm going to be the next Mrs. Idol!" "Okay Alice, see ya never," I replied. The whole weekend passed and I made damn sure I didn't think about what was going on with Michelle. I knew one thing, though: they surely were not at a wedding chapel in Vegas.

Finally, on Tuesday, Kathy got a call from her saying that she would be back to work on Wednesday; that she wasn't feeling well. I bet she wasn't. No telling what her ass was involved in. She finally slumped in on Wednesday and wouldn't say a word about what happened on her wedding night with Mr. Idol. Hmmmm…could it be that it NEVER FUCKIN' HAPPENED!! Right before my lunch break, I went up to the front desk and could tell that she was really upset. "Hey Girl, let's go get a coffee, my treat," I said. We went to a little coffee shop in the area, and after I got our coffees she started to unload. "Oh my God, it started out so perfect. The concert was amazing. After I threw myself on the stage and almost broke my pelvis, some roadie guy actually handed me a backstage pass. I knew then that finally I was going to meet my husband to be." As I sat there, I thought, "This bitch is looney tunes!" But I listened politely, anyway. "After the concert, the ones with the passes were ushered to a back door past the stage and into a huge room filled with people and tables full of food and champagne." She went on to tell me that Billy was sitting in the corner of the room surrounded by other whores, of course. She ran up to him and fell on her knees, begging him to take her with him! "You did what," I screamed. "Yeah, I did. I knew I had to be more dramatic than the others." "They didn't throw your crazy ass out in the street after that," I asked? "No, he just smiled and said, 'Okay, love, the bus leaves in an hour; be ready.'" Well, five girls were ushered on to the booty bus and Michelle pushed her way towards Billy. "I think he was kinda wasted," she said. "Ya think," I asked? Anyway, he asked her to perform a certain sexual act on him, if you know what I mean. "YOU DIDN'T!" I screamed. However, she had done it; and when it was all over, he passed out and several hours later the bus arrived at the next destination at a mediocre hotel.

All four girls — except the one that looked like a super model — were escorted by one of the roadies off the bus and to the front of the hotel. He then got back on and it roared away in a huge cloud of smoke! I looked at her and I knew then not to put her down because she had been totally crushed. So I said, "Well, at least you gave it a shot and now…no more rockers, right?" "Oh no," she said, "I've only just gotten started; he's not the only one out there!" I shook my head in disbelief, put up both hands in the air, and we both did the rocker sign with our fingers, yelling out together: ROCK OUT WITH YOUR COCK OUT!!!

It had almost been four months and Robert was on his way to start working part-time on the floor. When he first arrived, he was a lot more advanced than some of the previous assistants, including me; yes, I can admit that. But I'm a Diva; he will never reach that stature! My clientele was growing bigger by the month, and my roommate Frank was almost finished with beauty school. He was dating a guy named Philip who worked with him at the restaurant, so he was hardly ever home. I kind of got the feeling Frank wanted to move in with Philip but was too chicken-shit to bring up the subject. I decided to let him stew over it a little while until he broke under pressure, hee hee...

Another assistant came on the scene the following week. His name was Donny. He was 19 years old and gay. Donny had the laugh of a jackal and a wicked sense of humor to match. You could hear him all over the salon, which was pretty damn funny to me; but it seemed to irritate others, especially the ones who were the butt of his jokes. Tammy, Louise, Robert, Donny and I would sometimes go out together. After the closing of the bars, we would head out to a drive-thru to grab something to eat. We would always have Donny order the food; because after he was done with the ordering, the drive-thru attendant would then ask those words that made us all almost pee on ourselves: "WOULD THAT BE ALL, MAAM???" Then Donny would scream back: "I'M NOT A MAAM!!!!" Boy, we would howl every single time! Because we were around him all the time, we couldn't tell he sounded like a woman; but everyone else seemed to think he sounded identical to a woman.

Donny had a friend named Jared that we didn't see too often but was nice enough. I think Jared was pretty close to his family but had not yet "come out" to them. One Monday night, I got a call from Donny telling me that Jared was going to come over so that they could trip acid. Okay, I will tell you right now: I hate acid. I had two experiences with it: one, when I took it; and, two, when a client came in on it. Do you want to hear about THE ACID EXPERIENCES, BOYS AND GIRLS?

Okay, here it goes, experience #1: Never, ever take a tab of acid after doing crystal meth all night; because — believe you me — you will definitely regret it. That's what Robert and I did one Saturday night as we were leaving the club. Some evil person gave us that shit and invited us to an after party. Til this day, I can never understand how we always could find the after parties. Remember that? How you were so boinked out of your mind and still managed to find the fuckin' place. Anyway, we got there, and people were sitting in a small living room and watching cartoons on TV, okkkkk... I then sat down next to a drag queen who was talking non-stop about his little beat-up Festiva. As I watched him ramble on, I noticed that his stubble was starting to grow out of his makeup right before my eyes. I thought he needed to know that, so I leaned over and told him; and he got up screaming and ran off. Hmmm…maybe that was mean. I then realized the shit was starting to kick in, uh oh. All of a sudden, the Muppet show came on, and muppets were flying out of the television at us, trying to grab our nipples! Robert and I started screaming hysterically. We felt a tap on our shoulders and this tall skinny queen then told us, "You bitches have to leave, you are totally fuckin' up this party." So we left...

Experience # 2: I had this teenage boy with naturally curly hair that would come in maybe three, or four, times a year. He said his name was "X." Yes, that's right, the letter X. Whatever.... He would always pay with Daddy's American Express card. I knew he would smoke out before he came in, but he was a paying customer. I didn't care, just as long as he kept his clothes on. He told me he was going to grow dread locks. "Okay," I said. "That's all good, but make sure you twist them and maintain them so they won't all lock up together and get gnarly." Of course, he didn't listen. Five months later he came in and I thought the zoo had lost one of their animals. X came in with two horns on his head, his ram locks connected together; it was fuckin' nasty. The whole salon was staring as I brought him to my chair. Robert came over and whispered, "What are you going to do with that?" I immediately prayed, "Lord help me!" I knew I wasn't going to cut that shit with my good shears, so I went to the office and grabbed some paper scissors. Then I thought, "You'd better wet this shit down first with at least some shampoo; no telling when the last time was that he did."

I then leaned him back towards the shampoo bowl and he started bleating real loud, like a sheep, and making freaky screaming noises. "What the fuck is wrong with you?" I asked. "I dropped some acid on the way here, I thought you were trying to drown me!" he screamed. "Just relax," I said. "This will be over reaaaal soon." After I wet down the horns, I poured shampoo on them and started working it through with my fingers. Just for a short moment, I thought I was going to throw up, because I felt like I was shampooing some mangy wild beast! I finished and took him back over to my chair as he was still making weird ass noises. Wow, I need to charge this SOB a lot more. I picked up the paper scissors and started hacking my way through the first horn. I could hear people gasping around me. What is she doing? Okay, now the next horn. Good, he now had a short little Michael Jackson afro. Ticket is up front, bitch! So, that's why I hate acid!

When Donny told me what he and Jared had planned, I said, "Do not come to my apartment on that stuff; because if you do, I will not let you come in." So what did they do? Around twelve midnight, I hear my doorbell ringing like crazy. I grabbed my robe, turned on my porch light, and looked out the peephole. Guess who was standing there looking like Trixie and Chim Chim. I opened my door, looked at them and then slammed it George Jefferson style. Goodnight, Weezie!!

When I came home one Thursday evening after work, Frank finally approached me about moving in with Philip. He was sitting in the living room, chain smoking and looking nervous. I guess he thought that I would start crying like we did when Kevin was leaving. I probably shouldn't have held out so long. So I decided to break the ice and go first, "You're moving in with Philip, right?" I asked. He looked dumbfounded. "It's okay," I said. "I'm not going to act like a big sissy again. It is time for us to go on with our lives. We can't live together forever because I don't want to end up taking care of your old ass later on down the road." He started laughing. "Thanks, Girl I was hoping and praying you would understand." "Of course, I understand," I said. "I'm still wearing my big girl panties!" He then told me they had already signed a lease and that he would be moving in about six weeks or so. So then it was just going to be me, and Val, facing the world head on!

The following week, I got a phone call from Kevin saying that everything was going well out in California for him and Michael. Kevin was working in a smoking hot salon in L.A.; and Michael was a waiter at very popular restaurant where all the stars hung out. "When are you coming out to visit us!" he asked. I told him I would check out the flights and would be on my way; but there was one little itty bitty problem…I had never flown by myself before! Miss Ceely is scared! I didn't dare say a word about this to Kevin, though. I just played along like I did when I had my first drink with him. When I arrived at work, the next day, I took a look at the next few months on the schedule to see if I had any free weeks available and I did: the actually week of Thanksgiving. So I knew I would have to work like a Georgia slave if I wanted that week off, cause it was one of the busiest times right before Christmas. When I ran it by Kathy, she quickly approved. She knew that I really missed Kevin and was happy that I had a chance to finally visit him. I was actually thinking, "I can finally get my hair done the way I like it. Kevin really spoiled me!"

Chapter 8: Lbs. and Biscuits

The day finally arrived in which I'd be heading to Cali! Tammy offered to take me to the airport. "Don't be late, bitch, or I'll snatch you bald-headed," I demanded. After arriving two minutes early, and driving into the parking lot on two wheels like Speed Racer, the dumb-ass ran over one of my suitcases, shit! She had been up all night and knew I would kill her if she didn't show up on time. Damn betcha honey, you can definitely bank on that happening. We got to the airport in 15 minutes. She dropped me off with the car running. I didn't even bother saying goodbye, cause she was so fuckin' fried. I checked in, did the luggage deal, and kept my carry-on with me. Never, ever, check your facial products, or makeup, on a plane. You know as soon as you do, someone will steal it, or lose it, and then you are stuck looking like Magilla Gorilla — running through a mall that you don't know — trying in desperation to find your favorite brands! As they called my flight for boarding, and we all corralled together, I realized something: I wasn't even nervous.

The flight was really smooth and we landed right on time at 4 p.m. Kevin and Michael were standing at the terminal when I exited. They were so cute that it suddenly hit me how I missed them so. I couldn't wait to go out and shake my booty with them that night! Tons of hugs and kisses were passed all around before Kevin said to me, "Girl, you haven't gained an ounce; are you eating?" "Yes, I'm eating." Then Michael piped in, "She doesn't have to control her weight by using laxatives like some people I know." Kevin turned and shot him a "go to hell" look before we all made a beeline to the car.

The boys were renting a very pretty condo with huge palm trees and gorgeous landscaping surrounding the property, a vision of paradise. I put my things away in the spare bedroom and went to see what the boys had planned for that night. First it was dinner, dancing, then a drag show, of course. "When are you going to do my hair?" I yelled. "Bitch, that's all you care about, is your damn hair!" Kevin screamed back. "You got that right, Cybil!" I said. "You're the one that started all this perfection!" "Well, I want to show you the salon where I work anyway, so we will do it next week on Tuesday before you leave on Friday." *You see, I never told you guys this, but I wore hair-extensions down my back like a stripper. I had an image to maintain!*

It was Saturday night and we all put on our best. I just love the way a gay man puts himself together. They always have the best smelling cologne. And if they go to a pool party, or any place with a patio, one thing you will never see are corn chips moonlighting as toes pouring out of their sandals; and causing sparks to fly as they scrape along the concrete. One thing I cannot stand is a grown man who will not take care of his hands, or feet. God did not make a man's feet to have the ability to hang from a branch!

We arrived at this ultra hip venue with very high-end vehicles being valeted and obviously where all of the beautiful and rich went to tear it up. As we approached the red ropes, a strange man with a goatee, and a very snooty tootie attitude, looked at us up and down, and then glanced at his little clipboard. Then Kevin abruptly said to the guy, "Ramone, you big Sissy, you know who the fuck I am. Quit trying to be all that and let us in, I need a drink!" Ramone started laughing his ass off. "Girl," he said, "You know I was just playing. I just love to see you pissed off." As they let me in first, I heard Michael say to Ramone, "If you weren't so cute, we would all kick your ass!" *Whew, they were friends. I got a little worried for a second. I didn't want to have to go all ghetto on some highfalutin queen.*

We were seated at a perfect table in the middle of the restaurant, which translated to great freak watching. I began to recognize TV personalities right away, some from recent shows; and I also spotted a lot of "has-been's" too. The food was excellent and the cocktails divine. Free entertainment, in the form of people watching, was spectacular. I could not imagine living in this town, and being an actor, because it looked like you could never stop acting until you were totally alone; how exhausting was that? I got tired just watching fake laughing all night.

The boys wanted to take me to this dance club where we would find anybody who was anybody. It was a mixed club, gay and straight, so the boys hinted: "Maybe you will meet Mr. Man tonight?" *Uh no thanks, I am not in the hunting mood tonight. I just want to take this all in.* We tripped the lights fantastic once again. I loved dancing with Kevin and Michael; they were both so smooth. They didn't jerk around like they had epilepsy, or something! There were so many beautiful men everywhere. After the song stopped playing, I asked Kevin, "What is the deal with all the great looking men?" He then started laughing and said, "Girl, these are the High End Gays. You either have some pennies or you're hot, or both. This place will not let anything less tromp in here. "Don't worry," he said, "the others have a place they can call home…"*Awwwwww....*

My trip was going to end soon. It was already Monday night. The next day I was going to get my hair done; I was so excited. We had shopped, and partied, until I wanted to drop; so I told Kevin that during the last few days I just wanted to relax at the house, if that was okay with him. Michael had to go into work that evening, so Kevin and I decided to rent a movie. A few hours later, the phone rang. As Kevin said hello, we suddenly heard a man's voice screaming from the other end! From what Kevin could make out, it was Michael. He was at a pay phone with some guy trying to steal his leather jacket off his body right then. Kevin started screaming back, "Give him the fuckin' jacket now, let it go!" "No, you gave it to me for my birthday!" "Bitch, give him the damn jacket; don't get stabbed over a fuckin' jacket." More screaming…and then silence. *OH MY GOD, IS HE OK!* All of a sudden, we heard sobbing. "It's gone, I loved that jacket." "Honey, it's ok I will get you another one, now come home," Kevin pleaded, continuing, "Oh, wait a minute, don't hang up, can you go to the store and bring me and Miss Thing some rocky road ice cream?"

Kevin and I arrived Tuesday morning at his fabo salon that looked like he worked in Greece. Statues of men and women were everywhere you turned. Fountains, and waterfalls, and booze, oh my! And, in the background, that song "Venus," by Bananarama, was blaring. Ha, ha, what a choice of music. I think I get it! They had a full bar right next to the lobby. Woo hoo! This is definitely Hollywood, baby! Kevin's station was near the bar, of course, so I gave him the fish eye and he started cracking up. "Girl, you know how I need to keep my nerves calm. That's why I have close proximity to the watering hole. "Yeah, uh huh," I replied.

He immediately started attacking my extensions. I knew they were a mess, because I let one of the stylists at the salon do them. I knew it wasn't the same as Kevin's work. "Miss Thing, did someone put these in while high on meth, or something? This is horrible!" "I know, I know," I said. "Just fix my shit already." Well, after 4 hours of work, I put Chaka Khan, Madonna and Cher to shame. Smoking hot mama is back in the game! "Girlllll, you look beautiful," I heard someone screaming behind me. All of a sudden, Liberace, or I think it's him, came over to Kevin. "Ohhhhh, honey, you have outdone yourself this time, the hair is superb! How long did it take you this time, hummmm 5 or 6 hours??" "No, Grace," Kevin said, "Only 4 hours. I don't have arthritic fingers like you do." Ohhh, ouch, that was a zinger! Then Grace fluttered off. "What the hell was that?" I asked. "Oh, that's the owner," Kevin said. "She is always trying to be messy, but I always put her back in her cave." Afterwards, we went to a little Italian cafe and had a lovely lunch. Even though the setting was perfect, and I was here with Kevin, whom I truly adored, I was actually ready to go home. Thursday was Thanksgiving Day and I was to fly out on Friday. We were all invited over to some "friends" of Kevin: his gay parents Tony and Phil. So I guess that would make them my "gay-grandparents," I was told. Couldn't wait to meet the grand-parents!

On Thanksgiving Day we arrived at Tony and Phil's gorgeous, quaint, and humongous cottage. It looked like something from out of a storybook. A man with salt and pepper hair came running out of the house with an apron and house shoes on, screaming, "My baby boy has finally come home! Phil, Phil, Phil!!!! Make sure the champagne is chilled!" "Will you settle down, God!" "Hey, Honey, welcome home!" Phil shouted. Wow, this was going to be soooo much fun, I thought to myself. "Ohhh, is this the little biscuit you told us about?" *I guess I am the biscuit, how cute is that!* "Hi Michael, darling. Good to see you, sweetheart!" Then Tony looked my way again. "Honey, we have to put some meat on those bones, Kevin!" Tony screamed. "You haven't been feeding her at all, but a bunch of booze — since she's been here — have you?" Michael just kept rolling his eyes and smirking. *God, I how I miss Michael's sarcastic ass ways...*

We were all ushered into the house with Tony talking, and screaming, the whole time. I was laughing my ass off. What a cool Thanksgiving this was going to be! Phil showed us to the guest bedrooms. Kevin told us to just put our things on the bed, as they had a butler that would take care of it all. A fuckin' butler... no way... sweet! Tony was screaming something again in the other room. We all gathered into the dining room and the scenery took my breath away. The formal dining room was already decorated for Christmas! Every inch of the room was covered in beautiful holiday décor; it even smelled like Christmas. "Okay, sit, sit everyone; dinner is ready!" Tony called out. "Phil, where are you!! You better not be eating any more of those pies. I swear, he's been sneaking sweets all day and he wonders where all the EL Bees are coming from!!" "EL Bees?" I asked, "What are EL Bees?" Kevin started cracking up. "He means LBS, as in pounds, biscuit!" Everyone fell out of their chairs on that one.

There was every kind of dish known to mankind on that table. I would catch Tony watching me like a mother hen making sure I was eating something. It was magnificent. After the meal, we went into the parlor room, Tony called it, and had cocktails. We talked about what the plans were for the Christmas holidays. I was sitting in a big green velvet chair. I was so full, and comfortable, that I could barely finish my drink, let alone keep my eyes open. The last thing I heard, as I drifted off, was Tony screaming about the good ole days, when he did drag, and he how didn't need to use any padding…

I was awakened the next morning by men's laughter in the distance. Where am I? I lifted up the covers and noticed that I had silk pajamas on. "Who the hell had undressed me and put these on?" I didn't remember a thing, and I knew I wasn't wasted. I must have been more exhausted than I realized as I spotted a silk robe to match hanging on the back of the bedroom door. Boy, Tony really is amazing, he pays attention to every little detail, I thought.

I walked into the kitchen and noticed everyone was having breakfast. "Morning, Biscuit," everyone said in unison! "Oh shut up," I replied with a giggle. Tony ran over to exclaim, "Honey, sit here. I already have a plate still warm for you. Randolf had to put you to bed last night. Your head hit that pillow like a sledge hammer!" "I know," I said. "That was crazy!" And what was even crazier: where was Randolf? *I knew he was around, but I had never seen him*, I thought.

My flight was scheduled 2 hours from then, and we wanted to get to the airport a little early, since it was right after a holiday. Of course, our bags were packed, ready, and waiting by the front door. *That was the weirdest thing ever; how does that guy do it?* Tony and Phil walked us to the car and helped us with everything. As Tony started to tear up, he kept dabbing his eyes with a hanky. "Have a safe trip," he whimpered to me. "We will miss you! Hey, bring your ass back here this summer; and I won't take no for an answer!" he shouted. We all waved our goodbyes and were off…back to reality.

Chapter 9: Christmas Island

Christmas was approaching rapidly and the salon was swamped. I barely had the staying power to go out and party, but somehow I managed to never let my fans down. My steady clients now had standing appointments throughout the year, so it was close to impossible for me to take walk-ins. I would only accommodate them if they insisted on someone who was experienced. One Thursday, around 4 p.m., Michelle asked me if I would take a man's haircut at 5:00. Since I had just experienced a cancellation, I thought about it for a second and said, "Yeah, why not?"

The client arrived right on time. Though he introduced himself to me, I didn't really pay attention to what he said his name was, because I just wanted to get him started and get it over with. One thing I noticed about him was the color of his eyes. They were very odd — like a demon in a horror flick. I guessed him to be about nineteen years old. I could tell from the outfit he wore that the clothes — from the dress shirt, all the way down to his shoes — were designer threads. After he told me what he wanted, and as I started the cutting process, he started directing me through every section I took. What the fuck did he think he is doing? Just as soon as I would finish a section, he would want more cut off. It was turning into a cluster fuck. This guy was being over-the-top picky; it was crazy! Finally, after about 50 minutes, I told him, "Ok, I'm done with you now. Then I whipped that cutting cape off from around his neck so hard he could have suffered severe whiplash. Then he proceeded to stand in the mirror casually checking out his hair. *Oh MY God, really!* At that point, I unplugged my blow dryer and closed my station down. I then walked off to the back dispensary to freshen up and grab my things. About 10 minutes later, Michelle called me up to the front desk and she was looking really guilty. "What's up?" I asked. "Ugghhhhh, that guy you just did told me he didn't have his wallet with him." I could feel the heat rising up to my chest cavity as she spoke. "And he told me he was going to go get it from his cousin." I could feel liquid nitrogen seeping from my ears and mouth….Then I yelled at her: "YOU LET THAT MOTHERFUCKER WALK OUT WITHOUT PAYING!?! He kept me back there for almost an hour messing with his Tom Jones hairstyle." "I'm soooo sorry. I didn't think he wouldn't come back!" "I know, I know," I said, "but someone has to pay for that haircut; and I guess it's going to be you, sweet cheeks."

Three months later, on a Sunday afternoon, Robert wanted to go down to the gayborhood and have some drinks. We went to a small lounge bar that seemed to play only Whitney Houston, or Dead or Alive, videos. There weren't many people there; which was exactly what we wanted. When we walked up to the bar area, I noticed a young guy talking to a much older man. As I watched more closely, I recognized the younger one right off; it was the rat-bastard that bailed on his haircut. He was a super con, as I could tell he was playing like he was gay so that he could jack that poor old chicken hawk! This was going to be good, finally payback! I turned and whispered to Robert, "There's that guy I told you about who never came back to pay." Robert started getting nervous. "What are you going to do, he asked?" He continued, "Don't go over there and kick his ass. I don't want to get thrown out of here for your bullshit!" "I'm not going to start a bar fight," I whispered back. "I'm just going to wait for the right moment and then strike!" Well, the moment I waited for finally opened up, as Little Miss Pencil Dick strolled over to the men's restroom, I'm sure in order to check himself out in the mirror. I quickly approached the hawk with this immediate warning, "That gypsy you are cruising right now robbed me 3 months ago. I suggest you haul ass now before it's too late!" He graciously replied, "THANKS, GIRL!" before taking off out the door. Then I ran and leapt to my barstool like a super hero. Robert and I watched that dumb ass come out of the restroom meandering toward the bar looking all dazed and confused! Yes, one more for mankind; evil did not prevail!!

I was shocked at how time was flying by. My birthday was screaming towards me like a freight train. While growing up, I never, ever had a birthday party. Isn't that amazing? It wasn't like we were poor and down and out. I knew that the downtrodden gave their kids a birthday party, even if the cake was actually cornbread and the present was a sack full of oranges. I think I saw that happen, once, on the show Little House on the Prairie. I think the gang was more excited about it than I was.

The big day fell on a Saturday; but, of course, we had to start the festivities earlier than that so we partied like we were at Woodstock. Friday afternoon at work, Tammy and Louise grabbed me and pulled me into the break-room. Guess what they screamed? We just got tickets for the Depeche Mode concert Saturday tonight!!! Yeeahhhh, this birthday was going to be off the hook crazy!

So, Friday night, Louise and I decided to go to the club where I was on the guest list. We kind of milled around for about an hour. For some reason, the music was kind of lame and so was the crowd. Louise all of a sudden yelled out, "What the fuck?" And we both turned around facing Charlie Chaplin, or a guy who dressed like him. He was wearing the entire costume; and he thought it was cute to poke Louise on her left butt cheek with his cane. Wow, I was never going back there on Friday nights again. "Hi girls," he screeched. Shit, his voice was weird and he gave us both a business card that read BeeBoo Silent Screen Production. *Freaky Deekie Dude,* I thought. He then said, "Why don't we all blow this joint and go back to my studio? I would like to show you girls one of my films. I also have a fully stocked bar." Well, the booze certainly got Louise's attention, but I was really hesitant about going to his place. I proceeded to size him up pretty well, seeing if we could both take him down, if need be. I guess I could have given him repeated blows, and thrashings, with his own cane if I had too.

We left and followed him in his BMW to a warehouse studio that was five minutes away. Well, he wasn't driving a jalopy, so he was either making money on his films or Daddy was supporting his freaky ass. We followed him to a side entrance and he instantly drew out a huge Count Dracula Castle Key. *OOOHHHH! I don't like this at all.* I was starting to feel really weird. I gave Louise "The Look." She appeared as if she was going to start screaming any minute. What the fuck were we doing? It was like we wanted to die! Now I know how those people in the horror flicks do what they do. You can't help yourself; you have to see it through till the end. In the middle of his floor was a huge old-fashioned piano, with big metal chains draped over the seat. Oh shit, this didn't look good at all. "What would you girls like to drink, hmmmm?" he screeched. I wasn't going to drink anything Ebeneezer gave me. "I'm okay," I said. "Me too," Louise squeaked. He then grabbed a bottle that looked like it had some kind of green liquid in it and tipped it up. He drank straight from it, walked over to an old movie projector and turned it on — while Louise and I were practically clutching each other on a sheet-covered couch. The film started out all grainy and foggy, before moving to the image of a piano. There were two girls sitting on the bench "naked" with huge chains wrapped all around them both and they were both banging away on the keys. *Okay, it's time to rock and roll.* I bolted towards that door like O.J. Simpson with Louise right on my tail. I heard a thud behind me. Fuck! Louise had slipped and fallen on the floor. "Get up now, you whore," I screamed. We ran to the door like two cartoon characters. "Where are my car keys!?!" Louise yelled. I shouted, "How the fuck do I know? Find them now!" We were both shitting our pants; this was fuckin' scary! She dumped her purse out on my lap as we noticed Lurch swing the door open. As he approached the car, we both started screaming even louder. Finally, the keys fell out of a side pocket of the purse. She quickly put it into the ignition. Instead of going in reverse, she went forward and knocked out a corner side of the warehouse. AAHHHHHHHHH!!! Then she got it in reverse, knocking over a big trashcan on the way and barely missing a couple of tomcats. I looked at her and pleaded, "Promise me we will never do that again." All she could do was nod her head in agreement.

As Louise drove me back to my apartment, we were silent the whole way. When we arrived, I got out, whispered goodnight, and she just drove off without saying a word. We needed to be a little smarter from then on, for I did want to live to see my next birthday! The next morning, when I arrived at work, my station was covered with happy birthday balloons. Awesome, this also meant bigger tips because it was my Birthday. I couldn't wait for this day to be over, because we were going to see Depeche Mode! This was actually my first real concert ever, so it was super cool for my friends to get tickets. Donny was going also, so I knew we were definitely going to be laughing the whole night with him. This was Depeche Mode's 87/88 tour and it was to be held at one of the huge arenas in the city. What I loved most about the 80's was the way the cool kids dressed. No one ever copied each other; everyone had their own style. And it showed out full force in the crowd at that concert.

We decided to meet up and get ready at Tammy's place, which was closer to the venue. The only thing we all had in common with our attire was that we all were going to wear our black combat boots with our outfits. Except Donny, he was a little put off at first because he didn't own any. He actually had preppy taste so I jokingly suggested that he wear a pair of Tammy's silver pumps. "Shut up, Bitch!" he shouted. The concert started at 7:30 p.m. with the opening act. We didn't care about the first group, so we decided to walk around the arena and people watch. Every person looked soooo amazing. Coming my direction, was a very pretty girl with blonde hair to her waist. But when she turned her head, in the direction of her friend talking to her, the side of her head that was exposed was shaved completely!!! "Whoa, did you guys see that?" I yelled. "That was out of sight!!!" Suddenly I heard a lot of screaming in the distance. *Sweet, they were getting ready to start.* As we ran to find our section, two roadies walked up to us and asked, "Do you guys want back stage passes for tonight?" "Is Sammy Davis Jr. Black!?! Hell yeah, we do!!!" One of the guys handed a pass to each of us girls. I hurriedly asked, "What about him?" pointing to Donny. "Oh, don't worry, he'll get in with no problem," he replied before turning around and walking away.

Depeche Mode rocked for almost 2 hours! The whole arena was up on their feet as we danced the whole time! Dave Gahan looked hot in his signature white jeans: yummy. Afterwards, we made our way towards the stage, holding up our passes along the way, so we wouldn't be blocked. A guy with a huge beard — and muscles to match — directed us towards a long corridor, bringing us to a door that had a sign on the front that read: Private Party. When he opened the door, I noticed that the room was filled with every costume ever created. I saw Vegas show girls, hookers, bondage wear — you name it — fuckin' fantastic. There were ice buckets with champagne chilling in each one, so we each grabbed a bottle a piece. We saw some of the band members seated around the room. As Dave was walking around, I noticed he was much smaller in person than on stage. It actually surprised me. So when he actually came over to me and struck up a conversation, my evil twin inside started to speak and told him that he appeared larger than life on the stage; but in person it was amazing how that wasn't really true; must be the white jeans, huh?? Rut, roh, I just said a no, no and he looked at me and walked off. *Oh well, I guess I will polish off this bottle and start on a fresh one.*

Then there was a commotion at the door and I saw people with press tags trying to barge their way in, but Bearded Billy Boy yelled out to them "PRIVATE PARTY!," and slammed the door! Wow, this was soooo incredible. We were getting to party where the press was not even allowed in, Fuckin' A! After about an hour, I was starting to really feel the booze and I spotted Tammy talking to David. Donny was talking to the bondage boy band member Martin Gore. And you could hear Donny's laugh all through the room. Louise was talking to some death rocker chick. All of a sudden, Bearded Boy yelled, "OK, PEOPLE, PARTY'S OVER!!!" Two more guys came in and started pushing us out.

Damn, they really knew how to escort you in and out of their world. But we didn't care. We got to party with one of the most amazing bands on the planet! As we were walking to Tammy's car, Louise said, "Hey guys, you wouldn't believe what I did before they kicked us out." She then opened her suitcase of a purse; inside were 4 bottles of champagne, free parting gifts: compliments from me! We all grabbed hands and did our best Vegas Rocket showgirl moves all the way to the car...

Chapter 10: Trannies, Plantains and Festivas

The salon was now starting to take on some dramatic changes. Danny and Debra had been living together for almost 8 months and were planning on moving to Colorado. She loved the outdoors and he didn't care where they went; he just wanted out of the business. Also, the original crew — the old-timers, I guess you would call them, the ones that were with the salon from the very beginning — were starting to fizzle out. Lance was in a serious relationship, which was a miracle in itself. Fredrick started acting classes and was then on his way to New York to storm Broadway; which was perfect for him, because he was definitely that brooding, moody, sensitive actor type. Frank and Philip were planning on moving to Amsterdam. Philip had landed a job with a rubber company that made condoms. That was fuckin' hilarious! So Kathy was on a mission to bring in new meat; but the meat she was hiring was looking rancid. She didn't have the experience on judging if the male applicants were bold-faced liars, and con men, or not. For the women who applied that she brought on, she was pretty right on about it. The men she hired were the ones who brought in the most drama.

The first guy she interviewed was definitely a "no no," but she didn't listen to any of her staff. His name was Derek and he was so fuckin' high on coke during the interviewing process, his eyes were bugging out of his face. It didn't help that his underarms had soaked his dark-green, long sleeved silk shirt: Nasty! He turned out to be a descent hairdresser; but to watch him with a client was oh so painful. He would ask them a question and then just keep on talking. They were never able to reply back. Shit, he had conversations with himself 24/7.

The next Big Worm was Mahmood, who said he had come from New York, but I highly doubted it. The story he told was that his "Uncle owned salons in Manhattan." *Whatever Mary, quit lying.* But Kathy took it all in: hook, line and albatross. He was so full of shit, his eyeballs were swimming in it! Another clue that he wasn't what he said he was, hairdresser extraordinaire, was the fact that he never came up with a cosmetology license. *Can we say: LIAR!!* As we all watched him cut hair, we noticed how he did the same haircut on every woman: remember that bi-level, atrocious style? He would only take women, because he said he specialized in women's cuts. Uh…excuse me…he was too afraid to tackle a man's cut because he knew that when he fucked it up, the man would kick his hairy ass! Mahmood was also notorious for stealing other hairdressers' clients and putting our work down! Ohhhhh, when that started happening, we all got out the pitchforks and the knives; we were going to take this mother-fucker down to in the parking lot after hours. Don't ever fuck with someone's clientele; you will get cut! But one fine, glorious, sun shiny day, the heavens opened and the Lord heard our cries! M&M brought back one of his clients and sat her down in his chair. He started running his fingers through her hair with a very displeased look on his face. "Who did your hair last time? It's awful! Tell me who did this horrible job on you!?!" She then turned her whole body around in the chair, looked him straight in the eye, and pointed at that big beak of his and said those angelic words: "YOU DID!!!"

The next clown behind door #3 ladies and gentlemen is CJ, boooo…boooo! This ass-wipe made it really personal with me from the beginning: the first time his skinny ass showed up to work. He thought he was good-looking; and so did the drunk young whores he gathered in the clubs. But I'm sure when they showed up for their hair appointment, most of them probably couldn't remember what he looked like. And when they saw that he resembled a cross between Fred Sanford and Lamont — combined — their sphincter muscles drew up quite considerably. *But what the hay, right? We were going to receive the best haircut, from the "bestest" hairdresser in the city, right? Wrong!!* CJ used these triple blade shears on every haircut. If you came in with any amount of hair on your head, you bet your bottom dollar you would leave looking a like a beaver chewed it off. Since he thought he was a ladies man, he hit on every female client that walked in the salon. One day, I was walking my client up to the desk to say goodbye. I saw that donkey sitting very close to my next client. She looked up at me in sheer terror. I quietly went over and led her to the smock room. I told her to have a seat and that I would be back momentarily…you know, really professional-like. Then I marched up front and told CJ to follow me out of the salon — away from earshot; then I let him have it! "You ever come near one of my girls again, or even look at them sideways, and I will cut your testicles off with your triple-blade shears and make a stew out of them. Then I'll feed them to the pigs!"

The salon lost two more assistants the past month; so we were down to four, which was not enough for the clientele volume. I used an assistant off and on, but not consistently. I liked the personal touch of doing my own shampoos in the beginning of my career; and my clients really appreciated it. A week later, I saw a very anemic and pasty looking guy about twenty years of age, folding towels from out of the dryer. I introduced myself. As he said his name was Joe, for a second I thought I'd seen him before, but I couldn't place where and I never forgot a face. I asked him, "Have we ever met before?" "No, I don't think so," he said. So I left it alone, but stored it away for the future. I watched him a lot and didn't know why. It was as if I didn't trust him for some reason, but he seemed harmless enough.

One Saturday afternoon, my last client at 5 p.m. had an emergency and needed to cancel her appointment. Michelle wanted to do my makeup, so we sat at the makeup counter at the front of the salon. All of a sudden, Joe came in and mumbled that he forgot something and went straight to the back. Michelle and I were the only ones left and only the cleaning lady was in the back of the salon. Michelle finished painting my mug and I went to the dispensary to grab my purse. Uh oh, something was very wrong. I could tell someone had been in my purse. I opened my wallet and all that was left was twenty bucks. All the motherfuckin' thief left for me was cab fare! I was hot!

I ran to the front and told Michelle what happened; then I called Tammy, and Louise, and had them meet me at my apartment. When I got home, I made myself a vodka cranberry and sat, waiting for the girls to arrive. I just wanted to have a game plan on what to do. Nobody steals from a Diva, and gets away with it, without repercussions. As I started to relax more, all of a sudden it became really clear where I'd seen Joe before. It was a few months back, when I went to grab some hair spray up at the front area of the salon, where all the inventory for sale was displayed. My client Paul had come in a little early for his appointment and as I greeted him, I watched 3 people walk out of the waiting area in a hurry. When I went up to get Paul, to bring him back to get him changed, he whispered to me: "I just saw 3 people grab bottles of products and stuff them under their shirts and walk out." "I saw them too," I said, "but I didn't know what they were up to, though they certainly left suddenly." *Welllll, it was a young man, and two girls, and that man was JOE!! I knew I'd seen that* motherfucker *before, I just knew it!!* He obviously wasn't at home watching the soaps right now, so I had a suspicion that he was scoring some party favors. The girls finally showed up; and I filled them in a little on where I suspected Joe to be. I called Kent to see if that little spider monkey had shown up there; and I was right on! "Girl," he said. "He called me earlier and asked would I give him some stuff and he would pay me back next weekend." Kent then went on to say: "Bitch, I'm not a savings and loan; call me when you get your pennies together! He then called me around 5:30 and said he was coming by because he just happened to find some cash." "Do you know where he was going," I asked? "Yeah, to that gay dance bar, off of the strip." I told the girls the master plan and then ran into my bedroom to put on this wild looking black ensemble I had acquired that actually had a black cape accompanying it. I was definitely in the cape crusader mood.

We drove down to the strip, and found a parking place right away, which was unheard of on a Saturday night. I then knew it was meant to be. I led them as we walked into the place and started scoping it out; he wouldn't be hard to find. Hell, he would practically glow in the dark, he was so white. *Ah hah!! There he is!* As I marched right up to him, he looked liked he'd seen a spook. I'm sure that at least small drops of pee were dripping down his leg about then. I immediately started digging in all of his pockets and found some cash and his little bag of tricks. I then opened the baggy, dumped all of the contents on the carpet, and ground it in with my combat boots. I promptly reached way the fuck back and slapped some living color into his damn face, whipped my cape around and bailed out of there like Bat Girl, with the girls close behind. *Hmmmm, maybe I should consider working in espionage...*

When I came in to work the following week on Tuesday, I immediately told Kathy what had happened on Saturday night. I knew that Michelle had filled her in, to a degree, but I wanted her to hear my side of it. I knew that Joe wouldn't be back to work after being pimp slapped. Kathy then said that things had been coming up missing in the salon: random stuff like note pads, pens and pencils. Even the towels were being taken. *What the hell was he doing with the towels?* Ewww... I didn't even want to know!

After work that day, I got in my car and tried to start it, but nothing happened. As I walked back to the salon, I saw Lance coming my way and I told him what was going on. He told me that he had a client who was a mechanic who owned a shop 15 minutes from the salon; so he called him and we had my car towed in. Lance drove me to the shop and his friend John came out to meet us. He was very nice as he did the once over on the car. Then, of course, I knew what was coming. It had over 100,000 miles on it, so I knew I would have to get a new car soon; and this was something I was not looking forward to. I was aware of the horrific stories I'd heard from clients about car salesmen and what you went through with them. John told me that the car needed a new transmission and what it would cost me was about the same amount of a down payment on a new car. I'd never had a car payment before and I knew I had to really think hard, and go over my budget, in order to avoid getting in way over my head. John suggested that we visit a Ford dealership that was down the street. He knew a guy there named Jimmy who was honest and would take good care of me. So Lance drove me there and we got out and started looking around the lot first before we asked for Jimmy. There was so much to choose from. Thank God Lance was with me because I was so overwhelmed. I didn't even know what color car I wanted. This was all happening so fast, but I needed a vehicle like right then! We went into the showroom and asked the receptionist for Jimmy. About five minutes later, a short little man who resembled "The Penguin" from the old Bat Man series came out to greet us. He walked, talked and sounded exactly like that character. The cigar he was smoking was almost as big as he was!

We introduced ourselves and told him that his friend John sent us over. We all sat down in his office and first went over what price range I was looking at. After doing a few mental calculations of the bills I had, I came up with a figure in my mind. He took us out to the south side of the lot. I knew it didn't have to be fancy, so I looked around and spotted a green Ford Tempo. Okay, I know you might be laughing your ass off about now, at my choice of cars, but that's where I was at the time. It was a midsize car with four doors. It had a cassette player, and pretty much everything I needed. Most of all, it wasn't a boat size like my other car. Jimmy asked me if I had a trade in. I said, "Yes," and informed him the make, and model, and that the transmission was out; it was at John's shop at that time. So, after about an hour of negotiating, Jimmy got my monthly payment down to a figure I could live with. I then signed all the papers and became the proud owner of my first new car. As Lance and I waited at the front of the dealership, while they got my car ready, I turned to Lance and said, "This went so smooth. All I had ever heard were horror stories about buying a car." Lance then replied, "It is all about who you know. Remember that." I mentally stored that little nugget away.

The next day was Wednesday. I had just finished up my third client of the day, and I needed to go to the restroom like yesterday. I ran to the back of the salon and the restroom door was closed. Can you believe there was only one restroom for a big ass salon. Who the hell came up with that fucked up idea? God, I hope they're not fuckin' up the place. Don't you just hate when you walk in to the stall and your nose hairs singe from the stench of someone's shit? People, haven't you ever heard of a "mercy flush?" The spray that sits on top of the toilet is obviously left out for a fuckin' reason! How can someone sit there and waft in the smell of their on feces? Nasty!

As I was doing the pee dance, I noticed that around the corner from the restroom was where the manicure room was located. I heard Kathy talking, and laughing, with some guy. His voice was really queenie and his laugh sounded like some prehistoric creature from the ice age, very pterodactyl. As Tammy finally came out of the restroom, I thought, "Damn, finally bitch!" and I brushed past her and slammed the door. Afterwards, I peeked into the manicuring room and noticed they were gone. I quickly walked to Kathy's office and noticed that the guy she was talking to was just walking out. I only saw him from behind but my little pee brain could not register what I was seeing. When I heard him talk, I swore I heard a man's voice; but what I saw walking out was an entity wearing a woman's navy blue suit with opaque navy hose with black pumps; and the blonde hair was to his shoulders, and kinda stringy.

I knocked on Kathy's office door before I barged in and whispered, "What was that?" "Oh, he's the new manicurist Eric; he's starting this Friday. He has a killer clientele and has worked at the same spa across town for 10 years, but he's moving to this area pretty soon and wants to closer to his doctor. He's uhhhh…." And she paused a little, before continuing, "He's a transsexual and he's going thru the series of hormonal treatments right now." Whoa, I was amazed that Kathy would hire him. *How are the regular clients that come here going to react!* Like I said before, Kathy did not have the hiring skills, especially when it came to the male hairdresser, but now she was going to hire a man who was changing into a woman? Now remember, this was the 80's, so they were called transsexuals, not transgenders, yet. "He also wants to be called Erica, not Eric," Kathy added.

So Erica arrived to work on Friday morning and "he" was busy all day. His clients also loved his new set up, because they had a little more privacy with him having his own room and all. I finally had a chance to speak to Erica alone that day, because I was passing by his room and we happened to make eye contact. I walked in and introduced myself. We hit it off right away, and as I finally had a chance to really look at him, noticed that he was a very attractive man. He started talking right away about what he was going through, and that he never felt comfortable in his body. He always knew that he was supposed to be a woman. When he finally made the decision to do something about it, he felt like he was being freed from prison. My heart went out to him, because I could tell he had suffered greatly as a child growing up.

A few months later, Erica came in screaming that he just got his new boobs. A third of the salon staff ran back to go take a gander at them. I have to be honest with you; I couldn't do it, but I didn't hold it against him. By the end of that year, Erica decided to cut back a little at the salon and then eventually he stopped being a manicurist all together. I never knew what happened to him, after that, but I would think of him from time to time.

One early evening, on a Sunday, Robert and I were shopping down on the strip for clothes and decided that all that shopping was making us thirsty. We went to the same lounge we had always frequented. Over the Madonna video that was playing, I heard that oh so familiar pterodactyl cackle. I turned to see where he was but I only saw a strikingly beautiful blonde bombshell instead. I then asked Robert, "Did you hear that? Doesn't that sound like Erica?" We grabbed our drinks, walked over and were bowled over. It was Erica, but a new and totally transformed Erica! She ran up to us and gave us both a hug; Robert and I were both stunned. He, then a "She," started telling us the story. As soon as she quit the business, and had all of her surgeries, she knew she wanted to start her own skin care line. That business had turned into a multi-million dollar business. Wow, that was so incredible. Of course, I was still in shock over what Erica had done to herself, but I could see she was finally content and happy.

It reminded me of a crack-up story that happened to one of my clients, who went on a vacation to Cabo. Baxter had gone on vacation with his buddy Jack. They were both then about 40 and going on some kind of excursion into mid-life crisis with some R and R "playland" time to clear their brains. They had checked into a luxurious timeshare condo and then gone out for the evening. After leaving a dance club one night very late, Jack flagged down a hot looking blonde driving by in a beat-up Toyota Camry. She had stopped at a stoplight and Jack asked her, in broken Spanish, if he and Baxter could go with her to a decent taco stand somewhere. She smiled and motioned for the two to promptly get in the car. Jack entered the passenger seat up front and Baxter got in the back. As they drove along, Baxter questioned the logic of getting into a car with a total stranger. "Fuck it," he thought. He shrugged, and blew it off, out of deference to Jack. He wanted to help Jack get laid if that was gonna be a real possibility. He would just disappear somewhere if they made a love connection.

They all ended up at a Mexican restaurant that had both indoor, and outdoor, seating. As they exited the vehicle, and began walking up the sidewalk toward the restaurant, Baxter noticed that the attractive blonde was quite tall and walked with decided determination and focus, almost athletic. Jack rushed to keep up while whispering into her ear and carrying on with vain "Spanglish" attempts at flirtation. Baxter traipsed behind them as the odd man out. Baxter admired the slender and rather muscular toned legs that emerged triumphantly from the woman's flowered skirt. It was as if she had been a volleyball, or perhaps basketball, player. She was statuesque — but somehow, strangely, a bit odd looking. Jack was giggling, and smiling, like the tacos would be a mere prelude to a wonderful night of absolute debauchery in an exotic locale with an extremely exotic female. Baxter wasn't exactly sure what he was going to do while Jack got it on with the hot tamale.

Jack was noticeably drunk, somewhat slurring his words and staggering a bit, as he made his way to the table inside — to which they were all seated by the affable and portly host of the restaurant. Jack pulled out the chair for the woman; and the woman smiled graciously, while stroking her long blonde hair in a provocative manner. There was a sneaking suspicion that Baxter couldn't shake. What was wrong with this woman? As Baxter visually scanned the contours and lines of the woman's face, he looked down at her Adam's apple and thought instantly, "That just ain't right!" What should have been a delicate, soft and smoothly kissable anatomical feature was actually rather protruding and bounteous; almost pulsating with each bite that the woman took of her tacos.

Though the noticeable tanned cleavage from her v-shaped sweater was heaving pleasantly, she mysteriously allowed minute traces of taco grease to dribble from her lip, in a rather disturbing, masculine way. Damn! Her forearms were ripped, like a javelin thrower. *"This is a fuckn' man! Motherfucker,"* Baxter realized.

Baxter started to subtly motion to Jack, trying the get the newfound revelation across, but it was to no avail. Jack was consumed with emotion: raw, unbridled lust for this woman, an overwhelming, blinding lust! Suddenly, Baxter had his chance. The "woman" wiped off her chin, grabbed her purse, stood up and sashayed to the women's room to freshen up. Baxter leaned over and whispered to Jack, "Yo, dude, that's a fuckn' man, or some kind of transsexual! I don't think that's what ya want; but, to each his own, I guess…" "No, it's not, what the fuck are you talking about," Jack blurted out.

When the woman gingerly returned to the table, Jack started glaring with eyes that could have pierced her soul. Her eyes became fixed on Baxter. The cat was let out of the bag and that "tranny" was pissed. She tried to lean in to speak to Jack and Jack would have none of it. He abruptly motioned for the waiter to get the bill for them. The waiter rushed over. Baxter dropped some cash to pay as Jack stormed away from the table and out to the front sidewalk. Baxter remained seated while the waiter brought the change. Baxter calmly asked for a "to go" box for the tranny's tacos. Baxter noticed the tranny glaring at him with all the love of a Mexican devil on meth. *Perhaps Baxter's generosity would smooth things over,* he mused.

While Baxter was seated, the tranny stood up, grabbed his/her purse, and stormed past Baxter. While passing by, he grabbed a lump of Baxter's hair and yanked hard. "Ouch, you bitch," Baxter yelled. "I buy you tacos, and that's how you fuckin' repay me.

Unfuckin' believable!" Baxter followed the tranny outside to see whatever other commotion was gonna pop off. *His scalp ached. He could recall only having had his hair pulled as a child by a bully on the school ground.*

Out on the sidewalk, the tranny inexplicably waited for the leftovers to be handed to her from the meal. Baxter reluctantly handed the Styrofoam container to the tranny with one hand, while holding the sore part of his head with his other hand. *Damn, that fuckin' hurt,* he thought. The tranny, not speaking a word, grabbed her leftover box with a sense of entitlement. She started storming down the sidewalk, the heels of her shoes scraping the cobblestone path with all the angst of an otherwise ordinary gender non-specific wonder of nature…and third world surgery.

While Jack hailed a cab, he hurled a litany of insults at the tranny from afar: "You fuckin' bitch. What a disgusting cunt you are for deceiving me! Fuck you! Adios, you freak." Baxter laughed his ass off all the way into the cab. "Trannies gotta make a living, too, homeboy," were Baxter's final comforting words to Jack before they retired for the evening. Jack was scarred for life.

Chapter 11: Added Value

The year was 1988 and I was going to be turning twenty-one years old on Saturday of the next weekend. The whole gang wanted to take me out to dinner to a new Mexican restaurant that night, so we decided to go to our favorite hangout the Friday night before.

When I arrived at work that week, on Tuesday, most of the staff was gathered around the reception area. Kathy saw me and said, "Good, I was waiting for you, and a couple of others, before I gave out the news." She proceeded to say that she had purchased tickets for all of us to the big hair show that was coming up on Sunday afternoon. That was going to be so cool; my birthday weekend was already full! There were going to be a lot of world-renowned hairdressers at this event and one of them was Trevor Sorbie, whose work was amazing.

On Friday night, we all went out and stayed out till almost five a.m. *Oh my God, how was I going to make it through Saturday at work?* But remember those days when we could do that? Now, if I even attempted to pull that kind of stunt on a school night, I would end up in the ER. Robert looked green, and Tammy looked like she was going to blow chow any second. But just like the little soldiers we were, we all got through the day, barely.

Our reservations were set for 9 p.m. that night, thank God! That meant I could take a disco nap and be totally ready and refreshed. Well, I took my nap and I still felt horrible. *What's going on?* Usually, I can bounce back in a few hours and feel right as rain but something was truly amiss; it wasn't going away. After dragging my carcass into the shower, I stood in front of my closet trying to decide what to wear. I was still so foggy. What the fuck was going on? See, I didn't realize it at the time, but my body wasn't recuperating as fast as it did when I was eighteen, or nineteen, years old. The partying was starting to take its toll on "Her Highness."

When we all showed up at the restaurant on time, we realized that we were all broken down. Robert's friend Jackson brought their friend Felicia, who talked incessantly — even to the point of actually having conversations with herself. I could tell this girl had done way too much Crissy, if ya know what I mean. There wasn't much conversation going on. Donny wasn't even laughing and making fun of people. *Wow, are we going to have to hang up our party crowns soon?*

Though I could barely eat my meal, I looked over at Tammy and saw she wasn't having a problem at all with engulfing hers down like Jonah's whale. Jackson was sitting next to me and one of the waiters came over to him and asked if he was finished with his dinner. Before he could respond, the waiter started helping himself, not only putting his hands on Jackson's food, but actually gleefully using it to make himself a burrito. Then, when the burrito was complete, the waiter ran off with it towards the men's restroom! We were all so stunned; what the fuck just happened? I was starting to feel like we were all characters in a bizarre John Waters film. Happy fuckin' Birthday!!!

Shit, I couldn't wait for my "Birthday Dinner" to end! When I got home, I didn't even take my clothes off. I just plummeted headlong into my bed. Whew, the next morning I felt sooo much better. I was thinking those five a.m. excursions were going to start being fewer, and farther between, if the recuperation process was going to be such a beating. The hair show was that day and we were all supposed to meet at the salon to carpool. I know you all remember — whether you were a hairdresser, or not — that, in the 80's, the choice of color was black, black and even more black. So, I decided to jazz it up a little and wear a long black dress with my patent leather black shoes, with the square witchy heel, and a black feather boa to top it all off. *Hmmmm, as I looked in the mirror, I wondered if I resembled a sinister "Big Bird."* Nawwww, it was perfect!

There were about twenty five of us going, so we all piled into different cars. We arrived around 11:30 a.m. and found the place to be in full swing. I saw hundreds, and hundreds, of hairstylists with some of the wildest get-ups on. This was also a time when men wore makeup, so envision a lot of "Oingo Boingo" look-a-likes. I had really come to see Trevor Sorbie, so I asked Kathy was it alright if I looked around a little to see if I could spot him on stage somewhere. "No problem," she said. So Tammy and Louise and I started checking out all of the different venues. There was one platform artist we passed who had a young girl in his chair with beautiful naturally red curly hair. Oh my, is that a Bic lighter in his hand? No way, he's cutting her hair with fire! There's no bloody way any client of mine would let me do that to them; they would kick my ass!

As we continued, I heard a man with a British accent speaking into a microphone. *Bingo! Found him.* Trevor had a beautiful blonde woman in his chair, for whom he was creating this elaborate "Updo." I was mesmerized, while watching his fingers seemingly dance through her hair, and will it to do his bidding. I'd only tried to tackle one, or two, Updo's before; but they had always turned out so stupid looking. And when I watched others do them, they were always so hard and stiff, not smooth and fluid like Trevor's. I knew then that I needed desperately to learn his method, because it was groundbreaking: no more "Quinceañera catastrophies." When he finished, everyone applauded. The woman assisting him, who turned out to be his wife, stepped down with him from the stage. I turned a little to my left and saw Kathy coming our way. She actually went up to Trevor as we followed her like little baby ducklings. She introduced us all and said that she had come in on the tail end of the demo, but when seeing the finished product knew it was magnificent! *You go girl,* I thought. *Spread it on really thick, honey!* He then asked about our salon and where it was located. I told him I had always wanted to learn Updo's, but I would inevitably get lost in them. He then said something that almost blew my g-string off: "Why don't I come and do an Updo class, tomorrow afternoon, at your salon? I don't have to leave till Tuesday morning and I'm totally free." Then Trevor looked at me and said, "Love your outfit by the way." *Oh my God, I don't look like a death rocker bird, after all.* Then I heard Louise pop off, "Well, I thought she was trying to imitate Phyllis Diller!" I could not believe that she was trying to front me out in front of the infamous Trevor Sorbie. "What, no you didn't bitch," I said…"with your Ruth Buzzie looking…" Kathy then screamed, "Stop it, girls! So they made the arrangements and he would arrive at 2:00 sharp the following day.

  I was so excited about that day. Finally, I'm going to be taught Updo's by the The Capo di tutti capi of hairstylist! I arrived at the salon almost an hour and a half early.

Michelle called me to the front desk a few minutes after I arrived. "Could you do a man's haircut really quick before the class?" she asked. "Sure, no problem," I replied.

I went up to a man with Coke bottle glasses dressed in an un-tucked white dress shirt with khaki pants. He was a strange looking bloke for sure, but I'd seen worse. He didn't want to put a smock on; and he didn't want to be shampooed. *Okay, fine, whatever buckeye; what's next, you don't want a haircut, too?* He then sat down in my chair. I asked, "How much off here, and here, etc." He gave me the once over and slowly told me what to do, like I was some retard. So I started cutting and then he let her rip! "I HATE NIGGERS, I HATE JEWS. I HATE WOMEN!!!" I looked around me to see if anyone else was witnessing this spectacle from hell. Hmmmm...interesting: everyone had suddenly made themselves scarce.

He then repeated the same thing: "I HATE NIGGERS, I HATE JEWS. I HATE WOMEN!!!" I looked him dead in his bug-eyes and said, "Okay, crazy ass, you're out of here!" I grabbed my cape from around his scrawny rooster neck and gave it a good Heeve Ho as he instantly started making gurgling sounds. "Awwww, I'm sorry, did I choke you?" I asked. "Get out of here, you freak!" I yelled. *Uh oh, I hope I don't get in trouble for cursing out a client, but that mother-fucker deserved it.* He better be glad that I didn't do my "triple sow cow round house kick to his nut sack!" I was a little taken aback by his behavior. When I crept up to the front desk, he was already gone. Of course, Michelle had a goofy ass look on her face, once again. "I'm sorry girl, he's been here before and has pulled the same thing on the other stylist." "So, I want to ask you a question, Michelle?" "Yes, what is it?" she replied. "WHY DO YOU CONTINUE TO LET THE COCK-SUCKER COME BACK!?!" I stormed off before she could answer.

I had to get myself together and focus. That class was important to me. It was as if the Devil himself wanted to make sure that he fucked up my day so I would be a basket case and not be able to concentrate. Trevor arrived a little before two p.m. and Kathy had him set up at a station in the middle of the salon. He asked if Tammy would volunteer as a model. Her tits were practically in the chair before her butt was, as she literally threw herself at him, oh brother!

As he started checking her hair out and getting a feel of what he was going to do, he said something I have never forgotten to this day: "IF I MESS UP, DON'T LAUGH, BECAUSE I MAY HAVE TO START OVER..." *What the hell did he just say? If he messes up; well, he can't mess up.* He is the HIGH PRIEST OF HAIR!

For the first time since I had been in this business — and, at that point, it had not been very long at all — I'd never heard, or seen, a hairdresser, let alone a male, have humility. I knew right then that I had started to change some, and not be so puffed up thinking that I was all that. He then went on to say: "Let the hair tell you what it wants to do. Don't ever force it. If you don't like it, it's not a big deal, just start over. And for God's sake, don't spray it to death the whole time you're working it, or you won't be able to rework it into another shape." When he finished Tammy's hair, she looked like a supersonic retro model from the 60's; it was out of sight! Now, besides being able to leap tall bar-stools in a single bound, my next conquest would be the most dreaded villain in the hairdresser world: WEDDINGS!!!

About a month later, Donny and I went to go grab some lunch. We started discussing some of the things that were going on in the salon. Actually, we were bitching about what was going on. "Girl, I need a vacation," he said. I thought about it and replied,

"You know, that's not such a bad idea." He then went on to say, "The first, and only, vacation I'd ever taken was with my grandparents and guess where they took me? A nudist fishing trip; it was NASTY girl! Who wants to see their grandparents in the buff, let alone the other old ass fuckers shuffling around the pier? Why do people with the nastiest bodies always want to show them off!?! I can still smell Ben-Gay and Old Spice! Anyway, I need a vacation!" he screamed. "Let's finish eating and go to that travel agency down the street," I said. "I'm sure they have some cool specials going on."

After we ate half of our meal, we started to head that way toward the travel agency. I told Donny about a very groovy hotel that I saw on that show "Lifestyles of the Rich and Famous." It was called the Delano Hotel and it was located in South Beach, Miami. Robin Leach also mentioned that Madonna had one of her birthday parties there.

We walked into the office and an older woman welcomed us in. We told her where we were thinking about going; and she started doing a little search and found the Delano hotel. She said that they were having a travel special going on in two months, hotel and airfare included. That was right up our alley.

I was super excited because I'd never been to the beach before. She then told us we had a few days to decide before we booked the trip just to make sure we could definitely make those dates that were available. I thought it was pretty cool of her to do that, as it would give Donny and me a chance to figure out our finances and our schedules.

When we got back to the salon, I asked Michelle if I could go over my schedule with her to book my vacation time. She squealed with delight! "Where are you going," she queried. "Donny and I are going to South Beach hopefully in two months; that's why

I need to set this up now." We spotted only 3 clients I had to move around, but I knew they would be okay with it. "Oh, this will be perfect," Michelle responded. "What will be perfect?" I asked her? "My next-door neighbor has a travel bear that needs to travel to two more places before it can go back to where it came from." "What the fuck have you been smoking?" I asked. Michelle started to laugh and then asked me, "You never heard of travel bears?" "Ohh…no…enlighten me a bit dear," I answered. She went on, "My neighbor said she got this bear from her sister-in-law, who got it from God knows whom.

Anyway, he came from 4th graders from an elementary school. He's dressed real cute with boots and a hat, and overalls, and he even comes with a backpack with a pad and pencil. And you have to write stuff in his little journal about where he has been and what he did while he was with you. So, if you take him to South Beach with you and Donny, make sure you take pictures, also. And it's a good idea to put a little souvenir in his bag, too." "Oh my God," I said, "that's going to be so cool. I can take Val with us; that way, they can hang out together, too! "Girl, you and that damn penguin of yours," Michelle said to me. She added, "You act like that thing is real!" "He is real," I said! "Have you ever awakened with a swollen eye and thought a bug bit you?" "Yeah, that has happened before," she said. "Well, that wasn't a bug bite, honey. What happened was your stuffed animals gave you a sock in your eye because you left them on the floor and didn't tuck them in properly in bed!" "Oh my God, you are a freak," she screamed, before laughing out loud!

Donny and I got everything in order, in about two days, before I went ahead and booked our trip. We both worked like two Clysedales. Donny was then on the floor part-time, which was excellent, because that way he could make a lot more money. The day of our trip came up fast, but we were all packed and ready. As Tammy and Louise saw us off to the airport, we could tell that they were a little jealous. But the reason I didn't asked them to go was because I knew it would be too many personalities clashing, and I did not want this vacation fucked up. You get three girls, and a gay guy, anywhere together for more than a week, and you've got a holy war!

We said our goodbyes and Tammy drove off on screeching tires. Donny and I looked at each other and started busting out laughing. *Who gives a fuck if she's mad, we're going to South Beach to party with runway models from Europe while they get to see that "Fan Dancer" do his thing near the dj booth again!!!*

Yeaaaah, we were there in South Beach, land of the bold and the beautiful. We collected our luggage and held a cab that sped us off on our way to the Delano Hotel. As the cab driver pulled up front, two hotel bellmen came running out quickly and grabbed our bags. "This is uptown, honey!" Donny whispered in my ear.

We slowly followed the bellmen to the front desk, and I mean slowly. The lobby itself was exquisite; the detail in every piece of furniture was incredible. Donny and I quickly pulled our selves together so as to not look like two country field mice. One of the bellmen escorted us to our room and I couldn't believe my eyes. Everything was the color white! The walls, bedding — even the stereo in the white cabinet — were all white. And, to top it off, white lilies were in a white vase on a table by the window. This was the most breathtaking place I'd ever been too. Well, hell, I'd only been to a small part of California before this, so that's not saying much. But this was definitely on the upswing!

The bellman placed our luggage down; and then he kinda started looking around the ceiling for dust or spider webs. "Oh shit," I thought. We need to tip him! I hurriedly grabbed my bag and pulled out some cash and handed it to him. He said, "Thank you," smiled and skipped out. When Donny came out of the bathroom, we looked at each other then ran and jumped on our beds as hard and fast as we could! *Time to get this party started, Bitches!!!*

I had, of course, brought "Thunder Pussy" with me on the trip. Though I had packed it away with Val, and Travel Bear, in my carry-on, I decided to wear a very sexy mini dress out that night. I wanted to scope out the crowd first before I let them have it with "My Haute Couture"! Donny, of course, dressed as his usually preppy self, but that was okay: he looked smashing. We walked to the concierge desk, which was a site in itself. The desk looked like something from the Victorian era; and sitting behind it was a tall and beautiful blonde boy. He flashed his pearly whites as we approached him as we asked him about the eateries and clubs in the area. He gave us a tip of a swanky restaurant bar right down the strip that we would love. He mentioned two clubs that were nearby the restaurant, so that if one wasn't to our liking, we could just hop over to the next one. Great! As we thanked him and started out, we were both starving by this point and very, very thirsty.

The restaurant was in full swing with tons of people of every ethnic background who were mostly in the bar already tying one on. *Looovvveee it!* So we didn't have to wait long for a table. The hostess sat us in a booth towards the back of the place, with excellent people watching from that angle. I was hungry for something Italian (I'm talking about food, hooker!) But I knew if I gorged too much, I would look four months preggo in that dress, so I decided to order a salad with everything they could possibly slam on it. *Hmmmm... the apple martini's sound delish, never had anything like that before.* Donny ordered a burger and fries. *Fuck! that looked sooo good! Oh well, I would just sit there and eat my rabbit food while letting the bartender keep pouring those Martinis till his arm got tired.*

After we finished our dinner, I was really starting to feel the Martinis. Donny's eyes suddenly got real big, as he proclaimed loudly, "Girl, there is a big ass cockroach right to your left on the back of the booth!" People next to us turned around as I flew the fuck up out of my seat and started attacking that mother with my napkin! *How fuckin' gross is that? They have cockroaches for patrons here!!!*

The manager came running over to see what the commotion was about and he saw the monster roach scurry to the next booth. Nasty! Then, it disappeared into the bowels of the establishment to one day return again and harass the next unsuspecting Diva! The manager apologized over, and over, before speaking those oh so magic words: YOUR MEAL IS ON ME! WEEEEEE, more Martinis! Well, after about three more of those bad boys, I realized I had made a very big mistake. I could barely get up from the table, dammit! *Now I can't go out, hell I couldn't even walk...let alone dance. I was sooo pissed off at myself.* Donny was being very sweet about the whole thing. He kept saying, "You didn't eat enough food honey. I will just get you to the room and you can sleep it off." "Whatttt about youuuu?" I slurred. "I will be fine," he said. "You just need to go to sleep." *The last thing I remember that night was slamming into those beautiful lilies and watching them go crashing, vase and all to the floor, or was it the other way around?*

Ughhhhh....I woke up with the taste of apple in my mouth. Ughhhhh..... I like saying that; it seems to make me feel better. Ughhhhh....what was I thinking? I never drink martini's, especially fruity ones. I laid in bed trying to gather my thoughts about the evening, then turned over to my right to see if Donny was awake. *DONNY WASN'T EVEN IN THE FUCKIN' BED!* Wow, that hooker didn't even come back to the room after he dropped me off. I then starting singing to myself...♪ A whoring we will go.... A whoring we will go... Hi Ho... something or other... A whoring we will goooo♪ That little hussy! Mama ties one on and turns her back for the whole evening; and he goes prowling around South Beach like some sex-crazed iguana. God, my head was pounding. I was so sick that I couldn't even throw up; now ain't that a bitch! I shuffled to the bathroom to brush my teeth and started gagging when the toothbrush glided over my tongue. Ughhhh...I hopped in the shower and just stood there like a statue. After the shower I was feeling better enough to choose what I was going to wear to the pool. I put on my sparklie white bikini — with the sarong to match — and my cute little sandlettes that had a small heel so I could walk around and not look like I just came out of the bush. My hair actually looked pretty damn good, the after-morning wild look; so I just shook it out more to make it bigger. It was around 11 a.m., and as I walked past the dining area I could smell breakfast. Gack, I started walking faster before I puked from that bacon smell!

    I came to the edge of the courtyard and just stood and looked out at the pool area. Wow, magnificent! There was furniture outside on the grounds that looked just like the inside of a gorgeous house. There was a queen size bed, a full-length mirror, and chairs. Suspended in the middle of the swimming pool was a bistro table with two chairs, and you could hear funky club music coming from all areas. I sashayed over to a group of lounge chairs on the other side of the pool and passed by cabanas with curtains that allowed for more privacy for the lovers. The sunshine felt so good, my headache was starting to go away. I found a lounge that faced the whole area so I could people watch while dozing off and on. I passed two men who were reading newspapers on lounges next to each other; I'm sure they are together, I thought. I placed my towel down and put my bag next to the chair, sat down and got out Val and Travel bear. I then put Val's Speedo on and I sat them in a chair together, got out my camera and took several pictures of them. I could feel someone looking in my direction; it was the couple I had passed. Oh, yeah, I guess this would seem strange to some people: seeing some chick taking pictures of stuffed animals. Perhaps putting clothes on him could draw some attention pretty quickly. One of the guys then asked me, "What are you doing?" I started laughing and told him the story of the travel bear. He smiled and replied, "I never heard of such a thing." "Me either," I replied, "this is a first for me, too." He introduced himself. His name was Andreas and his friend's name was Bruno. They were from Germany and this was their first time to South Beach. This was my first time, too, and I then told them what happened to me the previous night, and that my friend who had come with me had gone awol. I hadn't seen him sense. "I'm sure he's ok," Andreas said. "This place has a way of making people get a little wild and crazy." I was thinking, *Hmmm, Donny could get wild and crazy at a grocery store.* Andreas was definitely the friendly talkative one. He elaborated by telling me that he was a model and was putting himself through dental school. And boy…he was super good-looking. Bruno seemed annoyed that I was around. He kept looking at me over the top of his designer sunglasses. So I then said, "Well, I won't bother you guys much longer, I'm going to go to the bar over there and grab a Bloody Mary." *Did I just detect a disappointed look from Andreas? Aren't they together? Ah hell, another sugar tank to try to figure out!*

Chapter 12: Don't Throw Away a Perfectly Good White Boy

I grabbed my wallet and headed to the outside bar. While walking over the cobblestone sidewalk, I noticed some workers fixing the sidewalk on the opposite side. I wasn't paying attention to the fact that I was now on a slippery slope. Before you could say, "Stop in the name of Love," one of my heels got caught in the stones and I fell face down IN FRONT OF THE WHOLE POOL AREA! I heard people running towards me, "Are you all right!?!" I then felt big strong hands start to help me up and I heard Andreas' voice say, "Here, let me help you." The pool manager then ran over; he was freaking out! I then realized what the situation was all about. Someone else must have fallen out here before my blunder and that's why they were desperately trying to repair the other side, before they got a law suit slapped on them. I checked myself to see if I had any scratches. I told everyone that was hovered around me that I was fine, no problem. "Just get me a Bloody Mary, please!" Andreas walked me back to my lounge chair and held my hand while I sat down. Wow, too bad he's gay, he is a sweetie pie! He seemed pretty concerned and I then told him, "Look, thank you so much, but I don't want to interfere with you and Bruno's time together." "What are you talking about?" he asked. Aren't you guys together…like a couple? Andreas started laughing, "Nooooo," he said. "We are friends. I'm not gay!" I then heard a slot machine in my head: Cha Ching, pay dirt!!!

Finally one of the cabana boys brought my drink over. Andreas then decided to order the same thing after saying that he had never tried a Bloody Mary before. So I let him have a taste of mine while his was been prepared. I think that finally did it for Bruno, as he stated something abruptly to Andreas in German, packed his little man purse, grabbed his reading material and left. "Is he alright?" I asked. "Oh, don't pay attention to him, he can be a big baby sometimes. He's not very social, is all."

So Andreas and I spent the whole glorious afternoon together. At one point he got up to jump into the pool and it was amazing to watch him. This mother-fucker was "a tall Glass of Water!" *In other words, he was fine!* He got out of the pool, went to the outside shower and rinsed himself off, then cat-walked over to the full-length mirror to check himself out. Then he modeled his way back. You could tell he wasn't trying to show off; he actually just naturally walked that way! He saw me smiling at him when he came back. "What?" he asked. "Oh nothing," I said, "just enjoying the view…"

After a while, I realized that I had totally forgotten about Donny! I couldn't believe he hadn't come back yet and then I was more than just a little worried. It was almost 5 p.m. The entire day had practically passed and that clown was nowhere in site. I called the room several times to see if he had made it back there, but there was no answer. I tried not to imagine him dead somewhere in a dumpster. A few days might pass and the trash men would come to empty it out. Donny's body falls into the back of the truck, one man will look at the other and say: "Someone threw away a perfectly good white boy!" My thoughts were interrupted with Andreas asking me a question. "What? What did you say," I asked. "Would you like to go out with me tonight: dinner and the disco maybe?" *Oh my God! This beautiful, amazing Adonis was asking me on a date!*

"Yes, that would be very cool!" So I gave him my room number and he said he would call before he arrived. I was on cloud 120. I was going on a date with probably one of the hottest men in South Beach! Shit, I hope Donny is having a great time — wherever he's at — because I'm not going cancel this date for anything, or anybody!

    I went to the room and set my alarm for an hour later so I could take a nap, because Andreas was going to call me around 7:30. I'm a very light sleeper, so when I heard someone at the door I turned over and sat up right away so I could get an up close and personal look at the spectacle that was getting ready to grace me with his presence. It was Donny. "Oh my word, where are your clothes?" I screamed! "Girl, it was horrible!" Donny answered. "Well make it quick," I said. "I have a date in less than an hour. While you left me alone while you prostituted Miami, I met a super model from Germany, so go on tell me your story." "After you passed out," he began, "it was still early, so I went down to the hotel bar to check it out and it was happening. I sat down next to this guy and we started talking. He said he was from Spain and was visiting friends here in Miami. And girl, you know how I have a soft spot for the Latin boys!" "Honey, you have a soft spot for any warm body if the wind blows in a different direction." "Shut up bitch and let me finish!" he shouted. "Well, keep talking; I have to start getting ready." He continued saying that this guy, whose name was Fernando, invited him to a party across town. Fernando had a car, and Donny definitely had the time. They arrived at this house and Donny had a few more drinks before they left the bar, so he wasn't paying much attention to where he was being taken; and he didn't remember how long the drive was to the party. The place was packed with salsa music blaring all around, and filled with men. They walked through the house and went out back, where there was a huge pool. The host of the party was standing on the deck. The host leaned over and whispered to Fernando. Fernando then looked at Donny and asked him if he wanted to do a hit of acid? "Oh noooo, you didn't?" I groaned. "Yes, I did girl, you know how I can't resist that stuff!" "Well, you should have resisted it then," I admonished. "You don't know anyone here, or what they make that shit with, or where they make it!" I know, I know, let me finish," he said. "Anyway, I took it...and the last thing I remember was dancing on the deck with Fernando and a bunch of hot guys. I woke up on the floor in the dining room and my clothes were gone: some freak stole my clothes! Only thing left on my body was my undershirt and my Bvd's." I then started laughing hysterically! "So then," he went on: "I remembered I had left my wallet here in the room, so I had no fuckin' money! No one was in the house but me. I didn't know where the fuck I was, so I grabbed my undershirt, synched it up and tied it between my legs, and made a "Man Jumper!" At this point, tears were streaming down my cheeks I was laughing so hard. He went on to say: "I then tip-toed through the house, out the front door, and started walking through this scary ass neighborhood - you know, the kind of hood where wild dogs run rampant through the streets. I finally saw a convenient store, and of course, not one person could barely speak English or understand what the fuck I was saying. So I "sign-languaged" the use of a phone and the man behind the counter handed me a cordless one. I dialed the operator and got the number for the Delano and called our room, but you weren't there." "Yep," I said, while putting on my mascara. "I was at the pool with my boyfriend." "So I then saw a phone book across the counter, on a bottom shelf, and motioned for the guy to hand it to me. I found a cab company and told them where I was and I waited outside the store on the curb with the rest of the bums: who, by the way, were laughing and pointing at me.

You know when you've hit your bottom when homeless guys are laughing at your sorry ass! And girl, I have to tell you, even the bums here in this town are hot with bodies of death!!" "Oh shit," he then screamed. "I completely forgot about the cabbie; I need to run down and pay him!" "Well, put some pants on first!" I ordered. Suddenly, we were interrupted by the telephone ring. He ran over to grab it before I could, then smirked and handed it to me, saying, "It's your boyfriend….."

As Donny headed out to pay the cab, he turned around and said to me, "Have fun, girl!" "I sho' will, Mr. Man," I declared. Andreas asked me if I was ready, and I said "Sure, come on up." I decided to wear this mini-dress that Tammy, and Louise, and I would rotate wearing. It had the same colors as the "Life Saver" candy wrapper, hence: The Life Saver Dress. I wore it with a beaded bag and stilettos to match. Suddenly there was a knock on the door; my sweet prince was there! *Oh my God, he was beautiful!* He even had flowers for me. I'd never gotten flowers from anyone before. How sweet is that? And to top it all off, his outfit was slamming! Brown leather pants that hugged his little bootie, with a gorgeous man blouse on, whoa! And I could go on and on about the shoes; he was perfection!

He asked me what kind of food was I in the mood for, and I then realized I hadn't eaten anything except the bar snacks at the pool that afternoon. No wonder this dress wasn't as tight as it usually was. I think I lost five pounds in two days, woo hoo! Donny suddenly burst into the room like a Gay Bat Man all out of breath. "Really?" He practically ran all the way back to the room so he could size Andreas up and stare at his crotch. I grabbed a pillow and threw it at Donny's face. "Quit that!" I said. I introduced them and Andreas just winked and smiled at me. He then asked Donny "Would you like to come along, or do you have any plans?" Donny knew that if he said yes, I would beat his faggot ass to a pulp. So he graciously declined and told us to have a great time. He had actually just gotten a date himself when he ran down to pay for his cab. *Oh man, was this guy the "Ever Ready Bunny" or what? Doesn't he ever shut down?*

Andreas asked me what kind of food was I in the mood for. *Anything at this point, I'm starving.* So we walked about a block from the hotel and spotted an Italian place with outside seating. "How about this place?" he asked. "Perfect," I replied. They seated us right away and I made sure to order my usual cranberry and vodka, no apple anything for me! And I made sure to drink lots of water and eat plenty of bread that was brought out right away. I will not, I repeat: I will not…get wasted on this date! Andreas was sooo much fun. He told me a little about his upbringing. His father was a plumber and his mother was a homemaker. I asked him who he took after in his family, his mother or his father. He said, "Neither, I actually resemble my mother's sister." I told him a little about myself, where I worked, how long I'd been a hairdresser, etc. And he seemed to hang on to every word I said. He actually seemed interested in what I had to say, not like the last date where that mother-fucker went on and on, then finally ended up talking about ice cubes. I knew that wasn't right! I couldn't eat very much because I think my stomach had shrunk the last 48 hours, so Andreas suggested that we at least share a little dessert.

After the meal, I asked him, "Okay, are you ready to show me your disco moves?" "I'm ready and willing," he said. So we walked a few more blocks and saw a huge crowd of people standing by a club with red ropes. "Ohhh, I like these kinds of places," I told Andreas. "Why?" he asked. "Well, it reminds me of the place my friends and I frequent back home. And I know you and I will get picked to go in for sure!" He threw his head back and laughed. *Damn, he was hotter than fish grease!* He grabbed my hand. *Whoa…whoa, I just got butterflies in my stomach.* We pushed our way to the front of the line. At the door, with a clipboard, was a tall-blonde drag queen with glitter eyeshadow on and glitter lips to match. Andreas then shouted something to the drag queen in German, and she came down the steps, unhooked the red rope and let us slide in. I was shocked! "You knew that drag queen," I asked? He then replied: "Believe it or not, I met him in the hotel lobby bar the night before. He handed me his business card and it turns out that he grew up ten miles from where I was raised!" *Now is that crazy or what, to meet a drag queen who grew up in Germany and now lives in Miami?* Go figure.

    As soon as we walked into the club, that song "I Will Survive" by Gloria Gaynor started playing. "Shall we?" Andreas asked, and we ran to the dance floor and lip-synced and danced to this song! We were having such a blast that I forgot to even order a drink; and you guys know, by now, that is not my MO. I think we were on that dance floor for almost two hours. The club played all of the best disco hits as Andreas danced like a dream. Before we knew it, it was three a.m. Crazy how the time just took off like that! Andreas had to leave for Germany the next afternoon, so we decided to leave the club and walk around for a bit before heading back to our hotel. We walked arm in arm down the strip watching all of the people still out and about. Finally we arrived at the hotel, and I suddenly remembered the travel bear. I had the most perfect idea: I asked Andreas if he would consider taking the penguin to Germany and snapping a few photos. Then, would he send him back to the address that's in his journal, because that would be his last and final frontier? He was only so happy to do it and he told me that he would definitely contact me when he returned. "Perfect," I said. He walked me to my room. I opened my door, grabbed travel bear and handed it to him. Andreas leaned down and kissed me on both cheeks, said he had a wonderful time, and said goodnight. I know what you nasty monkeys are thinking! You're suspecting I left something out! Well, I didn't. It was a very respectful date with an amazing guy; and that's the truth, Ruth. Hmmmm… "The Whoremonger" didn't make it back again that night. Well, I knew one girl who was going to have "sweet dreams" and her name ain't Annie Lennox!

  I woke up the next morning in that beautiful hotel fully refreshed. I turned over to look at the clock and it was 9:30 a.m. I then heard the door ease open and there she was: Miss America! "Don't even tell me what you did last night," I told him, "just as long as you had a good time and I can see you escaped with your clothes this time." Donny then laughed and headed toward the bathroom. I lay in bed while he showered the party scum off his body, and I started reminiscing about last night. I had such a blast, I didn't get wasted, and I acted like a responsible adult. I was pretty damn pleased with myself! We had one more full day, and night, in South Beach and I really wanted to spend it with Donny. We decided to have some breakfast in the dining room first and then head out to the beach, as we both needed to definitely work on our "high pro glow! When we arrived at our destination, it was filled with families with their screaming ass kids and couples groping each other with their tongues down each other's throat. Ughhh, that's the last thing I want to witness on our last day here; or any other day, for that matter. We headed down the beach quite a ways. In the distance, I spotted three rainbow flags blowing briskly in the breeze. "That's where we need to be," I said to Donny as I pointed in the direction of the flags. After putting our blankets down, and getting somewhat settled, I saw three young men walking through the mass of people. One of the men had something in his hand directed right at some women who were lying topless. Shit, it was a video camera; that is so fuckin' uncool! As the guys got closer, you could tell they were of college age, laughing and giggling like little bitches. When they got closer to us, I looked them all in the eyes, gave them the go-to-hell look, and they ran off cackling like a bunch of retards. And you straight men wonder why girls won't give you the time of day most of the time. Hmmm....could it be your actions maybe, hmmmm? I then spotted a quaint shack on the beach that rented out little cabanas, and I pleaded with Donny for us to get one. He reluctantly agreed and the guy set us up in the most prime spot, where we were getting ready to witness the sitcom of the summer, entitled "The Gay Chronicles!"

There were tons of men — hundreds of them — lying on blankets, frolicking in the ocean. Let me do a quick run down on the cast: a) your "High End" Gays; b) the cute ones that don't have a lot of money but do ok; c) the morbidly obese ones that have money; d) the body builder ones that are beautiful to look at, but their penises have disappeared from doing too much juice. And last but not least, e) the "Annoying Nellie Little Queen" who never has a steady job and spends his every waking moment mooching and pillaging every person he runs into. Also, his best magic act is somehow showing up at private parties he was never, ever invited to. This, and more, was all that we were witnessing on the beach that day.

I turned to my left and saw an older, dark Greek-looking Adonis walk over to two blonde muscle bound guys. As he walked over, every man on the beach followed his every move. He then introduced himself to: we'll call them Hans and Frans. He extended his hand out to them, smiled, and they all greeted each other with gales of laughter. *Oh, this is going to get good,* I thought. I looked over at Donny to see if he was enjoying the movie too, but he had fallen asleep with his mouth wide open. Adonis then handed the boys a business card, smiled, and walked slowly back to his towel so everyone could get a gander at his "cooter cakes." Shortly after that, a younger blonde guy approached the Adonis and asked him to rub some tanning oil on his back. The Greek statue hesitated for a second; but he graciously obliged with a very bored, uninterested look on his face. The blonde could obviously sense that Adonis was annoyed, so he took his bottle back and slumped back to his playpen. *Wow, if he doesn't stick that lip in soon he's going to get sand all over it,* I thought to myself. I then heard someone singing that Madonna song "Like A Virgin" really loud. *Oh boy, honey, you don't look like you were ever a virgin!* It was a pale, skinny little Queen with earphones on singing off-key at the top of his lungs. Ohhh, nooo, he's not going to sit there, is he? Oh no he didn't…but, oh yes, he did! He planted his sorry ass right next to Adonis! Oh, this is getting better by the second! The virgin then took off his earphones and started talking to Adonis. He talked and talked and talked while the statue never responded. Oh my God, I was getting embarrassed just watching the guy make a fool of himself. Finally, Adonis had had enough. He got up, picked up his towel and as he walked past Virgin Boy…No way! I can't believe what I just saw: as he walked by, his left foot kicked a small amount of sand that went flying towards Virgin Boy's mouth. *That was fuckin' awesome, oh my God!* Adonis then headed down to where Hans and Frans were, and placed his towel down right in the middle of theirs, allowing them all to enjoy the rest of the afternoon. Whew, what a dramatic ending! I was so worn out after watching that I decided to just lie back and listen to the crash of the waves and watch some seagulls tear into something that resembled a hotdog.

What a great day Donny and I had spending the whole afternoon on the beach relaxing and people watching. Finally, around 5:30 p.m. we went back to our hotel room to shower and change for dinner. As I entered the room, I saw that the red message light on the telephone was blinking. I went over and pushed the button and the message was from "My Man" Andreas. He had called the room right after we left for the beach: dammit! He said that he had a wonderful time last night and that he had packed Travel Bear safely away in his carry-on. And that he would take very good care of him. He also went on to say that he had a photo shoot that was set up as soon as he arrived home. So after the shoot, he would contact me and fill me in on when he was going to send the bear back. What a sweetie pie! After I hung up, I told Donny about the message Andreas had left and how nice it was, to which Donny callously responded with fart noises he made with his lips. You're so fuckin' stupid, I told him! Our flight was scheduled to leave at 11:30 a.m. the next morning, so we were going to have a nice quiet dinner and then come back to our room to pack our things. We ended up at a Cuban restaurant that was about five minutes from the hotel. Since it was an early Sunday night, there was not much going on. One thing I noticed about South Beach was that there was a party going on all the time, but always later in the evening. Things really don't start hopping till 11 p.m. I could never live here for the fear of just burning out from such a fast paced party scene. Our meal was different but very good. Donny and I had never experienced the Cuban cuisine and we were both pleasantly surprised. But after that meal I couldn't wait to go to sleep. I decided to check in early and then pack the next morning. Donny decided he was going to watch TV while he packed. I fell asleep to the opening theme song of "Miami

Vice." As I drifted off, my thoughts turned to the realization that I totally despised that show; how could he watch that shit?

Chapter 13: Let's Get Physical

Well, Donny and I made it back home and I was booked solid. As I looked at my schedule for the week, I noticed that Michelle had barely given me a pee break, let alone a lunch break. She had me working like a ten dollar whore! I told Michelle that I met a gorgeous model on the trip and that he took Travel Bear back home with him to Germany. "Ohhhh, that is perfect," she exclaimed, before adding, "those kids are going to be so excited when they see all the pictures of his travels." *Yep*, I thought: *especially the one I took of Val sitting next to him on a lounge chair in a Speedo, ha!* After my first day at work after the trip, I couldn't wait to get home and relax. I needed to unpack my luggage and do laundry; I was down to the ugly uncomfortable t-backs now, ouch! I threw down my purse and keys on the coffee table, grabbed the remote to turn on the TV, and went to the kitchen to make a Cranberry Vodka.

While making the drink, I realized that the sound was up way too high. As I hurriedly took a sip, I heard the words "Travel Bear and drugs" from the newscaster. What the hell!!! I ran into the living room and stood in front of the television in total disbelief! The camera had a close-up of Travel Bear on a table gutted wide open with a bag of cocaine lying beside him. All of a sudden, I heard a wheezing sound coming from the couch. Oh no....I looked over and Val had his flippers covering his beak. He was hyperventilating, so I quickly grabbed a small paper bag and placed it over his beak so he could breathe into it. "Don't worry, Val," I said. "It's going to be fine. I don't think that is our friend; it may be an imposter, a look-a-like." *There has to be some mistake,* I thought. *Andreas would have called me if Travel Bear didn't make it back with him.* Wow, that is really, really going to be awful; those kids are going to be so upset. Then I remembered: *I never got Andreas' info; he only had mine. Dammit, I needed to find out now!*

I had just started to unpack and get the laundry started when my phone began to ring. I hoped it was not someone calling me to go out tonight, because I wasn't in the mood. "Hello?" I answered. I could hear a slight pause for a second on the other end; then I heard that smooth, lovely voice: "Hi, it's me, Andreas." *Thank the Lord! Thank the Lord! I knew I would not be able to sleep tonight if he hadn't called me.* "Andreas, is Travel Bear with you?" I asked. Then I went on to explain what I saw on the news 30 minutes prior. He replied, "Oh yes, he's sitting right next to me now. I took him to the photo shoot with me. At first, everyone thought I was out of my mind when they saw me with a bear. But then I explained the whole situation, and you wouldn't believe it. The photographer took several shots of him; and he will downsize them so I can put two of them in his backpack." That was sooo out of sight! I looked over at Val and caught him with his beak stuck down in my glass gulping my drink. "Stop that," I whispered. "Oh Andreas, thank you, thank you so much for taking care of him," I offered. Andreas then said that he would ship him back in a couple of days, and would attach his address to the photos, so the kids could contact him after his arrival. We spoke for a few more minutes after that, about his classes starting up again for dental school, and my job. We both knew we would probably never see each other again; but we were somehow both comfortable with that; and it was okay because it was better that way…But who knows, huh?

The next day, I came in later in the afternoon. I needed to finish my laundry and get things in order after being gone for a week. I went in and started setting up my station. Robert was escorting one of his clients to the front desk. He then leaned over to me and asked, "When is your first one?" "In about 20 minutes," I replied. "Okay, I need to run something by you in a sec," he said.

He came back and sat down at the empty station next to mine before letting out a big sigh. "What's wrong with you; did you miss your 'Bubbala'?" I crooned. "No, I didn't," he smirked back. Whatever I said, I know you all too well. What's up? He finally spit it out: "I need a change," he said. I feel like that all I do is work, party, and sleep." "And don't forget shopping, too!" I added, laughing. "Yes, shopping too, but I'm bored with all this. I think I need to start working out." "At a gym?" I asked. "You're really serious about this, aren't you?" I queried. "Yes, I'm serious," he answered, adding: "I think we need to do it together so we can inspire each other." "Okay, that's all good and everything; but where the hell are we going to go?" I replied, adding: "I know you don't want to go to the bodybuilding gyms, because you would be too intimidated around those guys. Plus, there is a lot of screaming and moaning going on in those places which would be too fuckin' distracting." "Yeah, you're right. Hey, don't you have a client who owns a personal training gym?" he asked. "Oh duh…I totally forgot about Ajay!" I shouted.

"The building, from which he offices, is right down the road. It's practically walking distance from the salon." "Great, call him and set up an appointment for the both of us to talk to him about getting started. I'm ready to put some muscle on these arms of mine," he said. "Yep!" I replied, "that way, your body will finally even out with that cranium of yours!"

Okay, I'm going to now break the situation down to you, folks. Robert had never — I mean ever — worked out a day in his life; and he never played a sport of any kind in high school. So this was going to be a Guinness Book of World Records feat. I, on the other hand, at least played baseball, softball in the summers, and then ran track in junior high. I didn't say a word, though, because I never discourage a friend who wants better changes for themselves. I'm all on board about that! Around 3:30 that day, I had a ten minute window between clients to set up a consultation with Ajay. His secretary answered and put us down for 11 a.m. the following week on Thursday. That was perfect, because if we wanted to go out that weekend, we would have plenty of time to regroup.

I kinda got a little nervous while I was setting up our appointments, but I wasn't going to tell Robert that. You see, I have to give you guys a little background scoop on Ajay: Mr. "owner/personal trainer/masseur and 'behind closed doors' perve." Let me explain a little more in GREAT detail. I'd heard rumors around the salon that Mr. Ajay — during his massage sessions — gave women more pleasure than they bargained for, with a money-backed guarantee! Somehow his fingers did more walking than a Southwestern Bell telephone ad, if you catch my drift. Anyone who doesn't is as dumb as a post! Every time Ajay would come in for a haircut, he would always suggest that I come in for one of his massages. I just wasn't feeling it. Now, if it was Scott asking me…well, you can just use your imagination! He was also very nice — with a great sense of humor — and he looked like your typical body building guru from the 80's: heavy blonde frosted hair with a Chippendale haircut to boot; super tight spandex pants, or shorts so fuckin' tight you could see the whole outline of his bulbous bird. And the grand finale: those oh-so-lovely "Olivia Newton-John off the shoulder" brightly colored workout tops. Let's get physical, you cheeky monkeys!

We arrived at our appointment thirty minutes early, which was perfect because the receptionist handed us paperwork to fill out. Damn, this place was serious! But that was exactly what we needed, so we would show up and not wimp out. Just about the moment we were almost done, Ajay walked out with one of his clients and the guy looked like he was going to vomit all over the room. I turned and looked at Robert, thinking just for a second that he was getting ready to bolt from the room after seeing that guy's face. Then Ajay slapped him on the back real hard and said, "You'll be okay, cowboy; next time, you won't drink so much beer the night before a session, huh?" The guy slowly shook his head back and forth, which meant "No." Then, without warning, he ran towards the restroom, swung and slammed the door open with his right shoulder and promptly sprayed green vomit all over the sink! Ajay then looked at us and laughed, saying, "I'm glad you witnessed that just now; many have tried and all have failed!" Robert and I laughed nervously as I made a mental note to never have a session booked after a Sunday night!

Our first workout sessions were on the following Tuesday morning at 10:30 am. Robert picked me up at my apartment and he walked in looking like Jack LaLane. But I didn't laugh at him, because I felt like "Sheena Easton." *My baby takes the morning train...* I could tell Robert was nervous, so I decided not to joke around and just keep my mouth shut. We checked in at the front desk. The way the place was set up involved six private workout rooms, so no one else but you could see you drop the free weights on your foot; or throw up in the metal bucket that was positioned in the corner of the room near the window. Ajay had five personal trainers on staff and each week they would rotate; that way you got a different trainer every week. It was a pretty nice operation and the clientele were all much older, and more established, than Robert and me. It was a little expensive, but it was well worth it. Plus, we could afford it! Ajay didn't train either of us our first day. I got a guy named Marcus and Robert got Devon. As we were led to our individual padded cells, I looked at Devon and said, "Now be gentle with that delicate flower," before he abruptly shut the door!

Marcus then led me to our room. Man, this place had every type of equipment ever made and I didn't know how to use over half of it. I'd been in gyms before but this was all state-of-the-art, new and improved stuff. He started me on the stationary bike for a six minute warm-up, then some light stretching. I had written on my forms the week before that I wanted to build a little muscle because I was so skinny. And, back in the 80's, a muscular girl was a sexy girl! Then he led me through a series of strength tests to see where I rated. Even though I was skinny, I was still pretty strong; and he was pretty happy about that, I could tell. He wasn't dealing with some weak-ass chick that would be a crybaby upon breaking a fingernail.

We then moved on to a series of back and bicep exercises. *Okay, now how many reps were we going to continue to do there?* Then he had me start doing jumping jacks in between the sets before throwing in some strenuous abdominal workouts. *Oh my God, this is fuckin' hard,* I thought. *I won't give up...I won't stop.* I tried to think about anything except the pain and the agony. I tried picturing Muhammad Ali in that movie "The Greatest." *Shit, that's not working. I'm not a fuckin' black guy; that's a boxer, Uggghhh!!!* Finally, the hour was up and I collapsed on the floor like a slinky toy all twisted up. "You did great!!" Marcus yelled. I got up and rectified my brick house shorts that had somehow crawled up my ass crack during that last set. I held my head up high as I walked back towards the reception area. Robert hadn't made it out yet, so I ran to the restroom to pee and check my face out in the mirror. *Oh my God, my ponytail was all jacked up!* I looked liked I'd been in a prison fight. As I got myself together, Robert was walking out kind of in a sideways manner. "Are you ok?" I asked. "Yeah, I'm good. Just get me to the car before I start crying like an old woman!!"

    Wednesday, after our workout session, the soreness was pretty intense; but on Thursday I thought I was going to have to take Robert to the emergency room. He said that he tried to sit on the toilet to take a crap and he couldn't bend his knees to sit down, so grabbed the shower curtain as he came tumbling down to the tile floor. "Look!" he shouted, "I think I'm allergic to working out because my whole left forearm is swollen." "That's probably from you taking that fall in the bathroom, you big dummy!" I exclaimed. I went on to say, "We are not quitting; we have put down huge down payments that I don't think we can get back now. It will get better with time, give it a chance; you've never done this before in your whole life." Our next session was scheduled on Friday at 5 p.m. after work. *Thank God. That way, I could go straight home and sit in the tub. I didn't tell Robert this; but I was so fuckin' sore that even my teeth hurt!*

That day, one of my clients came in who, to be honest, had worked my last straight nerve. I know every hairdresser reading this has had, or has, a client who wants to be your best friend. You know that something sinister is lurking behind that motive, and all you can come up with is the obvious: that they want their hair eventually done for free. But you know that is not the case and you finally give in and befriend them. When it's all said and done, they have practically tried to take your life over and become you. You have to pretty much take on a totally new identity and move to Guam. Well, I guess that's bit of an exaggeration; but I know I'm pretty damn close.

I will not use her name or even make up one, because there are so many crazy bitches out there that have done some fucked up shit to their hairstylist. I will just call her Single Crazy female, SCF for short. SCF was a walk-in client that worked in the area. She was a tall, and pretty, woman about four years older than me. She had beautiful thick wavy hair that she wore long; but said she really preferred her hair short, which she thought was more flattering for her. So eventually we started going a little shorter each visit so she could get used to it once again. She totally loved my work and I enjoyed doing her hair; but every time she would come in she would always bring up the topic of us going out on the town. Though I wasn't a party snob, by any means, I knew she didn't, and wouldn't, fit into my inner circle. She was way too uptight about her looks. I knew she didn't wear costumes but she was fond of that top forty party girl look; and that was okay, just not on my turf. Also, she was always looking for a man to do somethin' for her, to take care of her, or whatever, and I would always think: *What are you going to bring to the table to be taken care of like that?* But I never said I word. I finally broke down and went out with her to a couple of clubs, but the music was disgusting. I did not want to hear A- Ha's "Take on Me" because you couldn't dance to the shit at all. Then the lame-O DJ would get your hopes up when he would crank out The Pet Shop Boys; but he would play the one song you could not stand, it was insane! My music of choice was, and still is, House music but I will touch on that subject later. She was also involved in a newspaper ad dating service. Back then, you could meet the opposite sex in a want ad and they would set you up with a separate voice mail, so the potential Wack-a do's didn't know your real phone number. SCF kept pestering me to do it, and I noticed she hadn't found her Mr. Right on there yet. So why was she so gung ho on me doing it? Oh I forgot: *Misery loves company* was her motto.

One day, SCF double dared me to do it and I said, "Okay, I will. She wrote my ad and everything. We put in the ad that I wanted to meet men who were between the ages of 22-32. Guess the ages of the Cyclops who answered my ad? There were a handful of youngsters, but it was mainly the *Nearly Dead and Decrepit Sleestaks,* because the majority of them looked like they came right off the set from that show Land of the Lost. They were so blinded by the lust of a younger woman that they just bypassed right by that detail. We're talking 42-72: YUCK! The first guy that I talked to was special. Once I told him that I was a hairdresser, he immediately started asking me questions about the pimples on his nose! "Ahhh, Honey," I told him… "I'm not an aesthetician, so I can't help you in that department, or any other department for that matter." Strike 1! The next joker was the type that still lived in his high school glory days. You're 30…so move on!! He said he looked like some actor on TV. Lordy, Lord, please don't tell a woman you look like an actor. Because you always look like a parody: a feeble or ridiculous imitation of the actor, the cartoon version, you nimrod! Strike 2! There were many, many others, some of whom I had never even seen their mugs in person. The last one was one I actually met at a neighborhood gym; and, yes, he used the celebrity look-a-like thingy again. He said he looked like Sting from that group The Police. Let's say he looked more like he was Stung! Though he was more swollen, and puffier, than Sting, he did tell the truth in one area: he was about the same height as Sting and he had blonde hair. So he wasn't a total liar!

When we met that afternoon, the workout outfit he wore was completely white, with his t-shirt tucked in these extremely tight white shorts. You could see the whole outline of his Mr. Peters! When I spotted his ass in the gym, I marched right over to him. The first thing I said was, "Pull that shirt out and cover up your dick; nobody wants to see that while they're lifting more than their own body weight!" He turned out to be a nice enough guy, but there was just nothing there between us and we simply parted ways gladly. So I'd had more than enough of the ad and so had SCF! When she came in that day, and asked me if I wanted to go out again soon, I told her "No thanks; and I'm also done with the ad, also." Of course, she was in shock, but I didn't give up this time. Later that evening, she called me to harass me one more time and I finally let her crazy ass have it! I told her "I have a fuckin' life and it's not all about meeting some ugly, desperate goober!" Whoa, she didn't take that too well and hung up on me; but I knew she would never book another appointment again — which was exactly what I wanted to happen. I got off pretty easy; most of you did not, but when you get that small window of opportunity, seize that moment like a Rottweiler on a bunny rabbit!

Chapter 14: Hierarchy of Breeds

Donny approached me in the break room super flushed and excited. "Girl, guess who is coming to town in concert?" "Who, Cher again?" I asked him. "No, I wish, but I saw her last year and she was hot!" Donny exclaimed. "Madonna is coming in May and we have to go see her!" he shouted. About that time, Tammy and Louise showed up, with Louise asking, "What has his panties all in a knot right now?" "Madonna is coming to town and he wants to go." "Hey, that would be pretty cool. I heard that her costumes are incredible!" Tammy said. "Well, that's that, and Miss Thing, since your birthday is coming up, we will all chip in and buy your ticket as your birthday gift," Donny said. "You cheap bastard. What if I don't want that for a gift and I want something else!" I said. "Tough titty, because that's all you're getting!" he yelled.

Madonna was definitely the talk of the music scene at the time. And still is to tell you the truth. I was into her music, and her look, while in high school, but pretty much let it all go by the wayside once I hit the club circuit. But, of course, if you're a Diva, or Fag hag, you will never escape the Madonna craze. Also everywhere you went — whether it was a mall or a grocery store — you would always spot a Madonna drone! Okay...Okay, I will admit, I did wear several bracelets, and watches, on my arm for about thirty days and then quickly figured out that I looked Mr. T. Her concert was titled *Blond Ambition Tour*, which I thought was pretty clever and cute. Donny made sure that I put the date down in red ink on my calendar at home, and on the appointment books, so I wouldn't dare forget. *God, the way he was carrying on, you would have thought that the Queen of England was coming to perform some off the wall break-dancing and pop-locking moves!* I thought.

The appointed night finally arrived. We all decided to take a cab because we had a feeling that this venue would be swarming with wall-to-wall Madonna "wanna be's." When we arrived, it was more congested than we imagined it would be. Everyone was dressed like Madonna. At one point, I thought I saw a couple who had their little boy, who looked to be about 7 years of age, dressed just like Madonna! *That was fuckin'* insane! I thought. It was a pretty big stadium and we were all pretty turned around on where our seats were located. So Tammy found an employee who directed us to walk the opposite direction from which we came, informing us that an attendant would guide us to our row of seats. *Whew, thank God I wore TP, and my combat boots, since we were forced to do a little cardio before this event began!*

We were quickly taken to our seats before the stage light show triumphantly began and industrial-sounding music kicked in. The dancers slowly crept out onto the stage as the crowd went wild. Madonna kicked off with *Express Yourself* while descending a long staircase! The crowd went even wilder. *Amazing, this was actually a pretty good intro,* I thought. Everyone was pretty much on their feet, which was fine with all of us, but there was beginning to be one small problem starting to unravel. Standing up in the row right in front of Donny's seat was a mountainous black drag queen; and accompanying him to his right was an Amazon type blonde chick that was NOT dressed like Madonna. That drag bitch was sporting the bondage ensemble from head to toe: you go girl! The problem was that "Miss Mastiff" kept flicking and waving her feather boa all over the place, hitting Donny in the face with it, not even once turning around to see if anyone was behind him. How fuckin' rude! Finally, by the third song, Donny had had enough of the boa submarine in his mouth. He lightly touched "Mable Mastiff" on his bulging muscular shoulder and asked; "Could you please watch where you swing that thing? It's been hitting me in the face for a while." Uh oh, M&M was not pleased that he was being interrupted from his good time! Then his Preternatural Ally turned around and started yelling at Donny! *Whoa, what the fuck is this, who the hell do they think they are?* I thought. Let me reiterate that I was reared by drag queens and was taught from the very beginning on how to deal with a black one. Here's a short lesson, and summary, on the subject called: "The Gay Hierarchy":

A) The Black Drag Queen: A straight white female, or male, will never be able to fight verbally with this type; they will be shamefully ridiculed in front of all their friends and loved ones.

B) The White Drag Queen: This type can verbally and physically fight the Black Drag queen and sometimes is even victorious! How do I know? I've witnessed it with my own vodka goggles.

C) The Black Gay Man: This type is fine until the bronzer perpetually disappears. When he discovers it missing, that chandelier starts to swing, honey; and it is becomes a scene out of that movie which I call: The War of the Black Roses. Ooooh, it's a thriller!

D) The Hispanic Gay Man/The White Gay Man: These mother fuckers have been fighting their whole lives to survive, oh yes they can take him down no problem!

E) The Black Girl: No problem here, because that's who they're trying to portray, silly!

So I hope this has helped everyone to think, before you act, when this type of circumstance occurs. Donny immediately ripped M&M a new asshole. I can't, to this day, remember and repeat what he told him. But, of course, I couldn't let my "Gay Pride Partner" partake in the festivities alone, so I had to dive in myself. "Uhhh, look Florida Evans, why don't you and J.J. shut your fuckin' pie holes and get a hold of that cheap J.C. Penny duster you think is a boa. Straighten that wig of yours, and turn the fuck around, before I call "Miss Betty Blue with a Brooch" over to escort your Black ass out of here!!!" I yelled. Ooooo, Weeee! M&M and J. J. both snapped around like two privates in boot camp and promptly followed my immediate orders.

Donny, Tammy and Louise all turned and looked my way in disbelief as I danced out the "running man moves" to ♫ Where's the Party♫

Chapter 15: It's a Spiritual-Love Thing

Our workout sessions were getting a little easier. *Well, at least we could stand up right and our knuckles were not bloody anymore from dragging the ground.* Robert was so proud of himself then as he actually had started to develop some pecs. "Watch out now," I told him. "If you're not careful, we will have to make a visit to Victoria Secretions and get you fitted for a B Cup."

A girl named Susan, who worked as an assistant at the salon for about 6 months, realized that she could not do that type of work; she hated it! Wow, she was fuckin' brilliant and I didn't know it at the time! I actually started doing her hair before she left and we stayed pretty tight. She came in for a cut and she told me that she had just gotten engaged to be married. How exciting, this was the first friend I knew that was going to take the plunge. She then asked me something I wasn't expecting: "Would you do the hair for my wedding?" Before I gave any thought to what she'd just asked, I said "Yes!" which totally surprised the hell out of me! After the Trevor Sorbie venue, I tackled a few homecomings, and proms, but this was the big league. She started giving me the details and I immediately started writing it all down: just her, her two sisters, the bridesmaid, mom, and one flower girl. That seemed pretty simple and easy enough. The wedding was going to be in ten months, in October, an ideal time because the weather is still beautiful.

I put her on the books for the practice run and the day of; and that was that: my first wedding. I didn't know whether to be excited, or petrified. Actually, I felt hollow inside, like I sensed I was getting ready to be pulled into another dimension: THE TWILIGHT ZONE!

The glorious day finally arrived. The wedding was to start around two p.m., so I didn't have to get up super early. I was going to do the girls at the bride's' mother's home; and she lived pretty close to the salon. That was a win-win! Since this was my first wedding, it pretty much became the prototype of how I continued to conduct the rest of them for many years to come. I never packed my travel bag the night before — always the day of the wedding — because usually after a long day at work, if you try to prepare for something like this at night, you could forget something huge, like your blow dryer. I arrived at the house forty-five minutes before starting time and discovered that everyone was there, which was key. So we're off: I did mommy, then the sisters, and the bridesmaid. Then I threw some rollers in Susan's hair, the flower girl's, and finally finished the bride. It was amazing; it was like I was born to do this! They were going to do their own makeup, something I had never wanted to get into: painting a girl's mug. Girls can be really delusional when it comes to the war paint. What made this day so easy was the fact that I knew the bride and she was a great person to be around. Susan loved my work; she was ecstatic! Her Mom handed me the check, I packed my bags, and left. This was sooo cool. I had the whole rest of the Saturday afternoon off! I could really get used to this, for sure!

After a few months of the wedding gigs, my reputation started to spread around the wedding circles like wildfire. I started getting tons of referrals from brides I'd done previously; I have to tell you, it really amazed me. I was already booked at the salon during the week but now the weekends were starting to fill up with weddings. Uh oh, this was starting to interfere a little with my playtime. I had to start figuring out a way to arrange some time for me! For months, pretty much all of the brides and their families were pleasant enough, but then the monsters gradually started to filter in. You just never knew who in the wedding party was going to be the Beast of Burden.

  I'd already conquered the "mother living vicariously through the daughter" species right off the bat; you know what I'm talking about? The Mummy, and Mummy of the Bride. But after a while, I started to encounter other very strange and disturbing phenomenon in these little Cabaret of Horror venues. Now, there are shows on television called Bridezilla, or Dial-a-Snatch, etc. I won't watch them because I'd already been through the fire first hand! After a while, I'd met every type of bride that walked planet earth. I think I even did the Lochness Monster, and her family, too. And what I loved most of all was that one bridesmaid who wanted you to cater to her like she was the one getting married. Sit down and shut up bitch! This is not your video!!

  ♫ Life is a Cabaret....♫

  I made it through another Saturday. I was so worn out that I did not want to even think about putting on a costume and going anywhere. I checked my messages when I got home and discovered that Andreas had called to tell me that Travel Bear made it safely home! He also said that one of the teachers attached a note inquiring about what the penguin was wearing at the pool. Rut Roh, naughty teacher was looking at Val's bum! And what? A message from Kevin. Sweet, I hadn't spoken to them in a long while, but I was so tired from work that I just wanted to lie down for a second.

Shit! I woke up and looked at my wall clock in the living room; it was 3 a.m. I'd fallen asleep on the couch fully clothed! It was starting to get a little chilly outside; so I changed into my feet pajamas (sexy) and got ready for bed. I woke up around 9 a.m. to the sound of my doorbell ringing. *Who the hell was that?* I looked out the peephole and it was Donny staring right back at me. "I can see you looking out, bitch!" he screamed. Open the door; it's colder than a witch's titty out here! "How would you know what a titty felt like?" I asked him. "What's going on?" I said. "I had this great idea and I wanted to run it by you before the week got started, so we can plan for it now." *Oh no, what now?* I thought. He went on: "You know how we all love that show 'Knot's Landing,' right?" "Yes, we all love it!" I quickly replied. "Well," he continued… "I think we need to have Knot's Landing 'get togethers' at each other's apartments and each person bring a dish or something." "Hey," I said… "that's a great idea. How did you come up with that one; did you lay off the weed this weekend?" "Whatever, girl, I always have great ideas. So, I thought we should maybe start the first one here at your house, hmmmm? What do you think?" "That's fine," I said. "And it's up to you to tell the gang, since it is your thing, right?" "Yep, I'll get right on it." *This was cool; we could finally have one night a week just relaxing at each other's pads.* I know everyone remembers that TV series Dallas; well, Knot's Landing was a spinoff from that. Our parents were more into Dallas than we were. This was going to be fun! Hmmmm...maybe I will make turkey burgers for everyone. Ground Turkey had become the rage then, a super healthy meal they were all going to love!

Thursday rolled around and everyone showed up about an hour early. I noticed that there was more booze brought over than food. I wasn't too sure about the turkey burgers, which seemed kind of dry; they actually looked like something a Saint Bernard would drop in your yard. Okay, so I wasn't Julia Child. Hopefully, they would start drinking and not even notice how disgusting the cluck and purr burgers really were. The show finally started as the kitchen counter became a buffet line, with everyone all talking at once and Donny starting to get po'd. "Shut the fuck up!" he screamed. "I can't hear the show!" Then everyone would bring it down a notch. It wouldn't be five minutes later that they would all start talking again; this was not a good idea.

Then I heard what sounded like choking behind me. Robert glared at me and scolded me with, "Girl, what did you put in this burger to make it so fuckin' dry, more dirt!?!" "Ha, ha, Don Rickles," I said. "I know they're pretty bad, huh?" I added. I then saw Tammy and Louise dump theirs in the trash, not even bothering to conceal their dislike! "Okay, Okay, I will order you mongoloids a pizza; happy now!?!"

I rummaged through one of my kitchen drawers and called up the pizza place. Just when I finished making the order, we all heard a loud sound coming from the parking lot outside. Everyone practically killed each other trying to get outside to investigate what had happened. I looked to the direction of the security gate and saw a big Cadillac that had crashed through it and obliterated its entire front end. Suddenly, a guy rolled out of the car, and onto the pavement, as a huge billow of pot smoke erupted from the vehicle. Where was Puff The Magic Dragon when we needed him? And you wouldn't believe how the guy was dressed; it was right out of that pimp movie "The Mack!"

About four cop cars came screeching in and The Mack took off running with his purple fur coat flying behind him. *Oh My God, this was way better than Knot's Landing!* The cops tackled him to the ground and a huge baggy of white powder fell out of his coat. We all looked at each other knowingly, thinking the same thing: *Did Betty Blue see that little bag of gold just materialize?!* Yep, they sure did. One of the officers picked it up. They handcuffed The Mack, placed him in the squad car, and took off. I figured a wrecker service would take care of the car later that night. We all stood there mesmerized on what had just so strangely taken place.

The pizza guy showed up, and I ran in to grab some cash to pay for it. When I came back out, the pizza guy was inquiring about what had just happened. He then walked over to the pimp car, sat in and fiddled around a bit, then pulled out the cassette player before getting into his VW Bug to speed off! Wow, I can't wait till next Thursday!

After the Thursday night live showing, we all wanted to call it a night. Everyone left at around 11 p.m., so I decided to call Kevin to see what was going on with those two. Michael answered the phone and it was so good to hear his voice. He started in right away saying that they were planning on moving back and he was counting the days. He was so ready to get the fuck out of California! "Yay! This is great news!" I said. Then I heard Kevin in the background: "Hey, I want to tell her the details. Give me the phone! Hey, Miss Thing. Yes, Mama is coming back; you know how I am about staying in one place too long!" He went on to tell me that he had already spoken with Kathy and gathered all of his clients back; so they would be arriving in thirty days. What I really admired most about Kevin was that he could lapse into a hairdresser breakdown, leave his clientele and everything else behind, and simply start over without even flinching. He was never bound to a person or any material thing. It was unreal. To this day, I've never witnessed anything like it in the hairdresser industry.

Work was busy as usual. The wedding traffic had kind of slowed down because the holidays were approaching rapidly. So that meant I had a little more time to go out and shake my rump shaker!

Like I mentioned before, my music of choice was, and still is, house music. The party scene was starting to shift in a different direction. Our favorite club was starting to wind down, due to the second drug bust, and they were starting to just let any ole' thing party there. You could tell that meant desperate times were a-coming; and if it shut down, where the hell were we going to go? There were other places that were available, but once you're used to a certain place that has a vibe you like, it's hard to stray from it.

For those who don't know what House music is, it's a style of electronic dance music that originated in Chicago, Illinois in the early 1980's. It was initially popularized in mid-1980's discothèques catering to the African-American, Latino American, and gay communities; first in Chicago circa 1984, then in other locations such as New York City, New Jersey, Toronto, Montreal, London, Detroit, San Francisco, Los Angeles and Miami. Eventually, it trickled down all through the United States. House then reached Europe, and since the early to mid-1990s, it has infused into mainstream pop and dance music worldwide. What I had heard was that the term "house music" may have had its origin from a Chicago nightclub called The Warehouse, which existed from 1977 to 1983.

Of course, in the salon we were forced to listen to top 40 dribble because Kathy had no taste in music; so that is what she blared out of the speakers from the radio at work, especially on a busy Saturday. Most of the staff would be freaked out because the music was so tired. It was definitely so hard to be creative under that earsplitting force that, after a while, I started to get a little concerned that we were turning in to alcoholics.

Soon, after the workday was over, at least five of us would fly down to the neighboring watering hole and do several shots of tequila. The tequila was our antidote to the anxiety attacks we were experiencing from hearing the same damn Air Supply song every hour on the hour.

Two weeks later, my client Dane came in for a cut. He started filling me in about this huge warehouse that was going to host several DJ's. The admission was only five dollars, but he would give me several passes to get in free. Dane worked in the club scene promoting up and coming DJ's, so he knew all the 411 on the circuit. This was great, as there was finally a place we could go where they would not be afraid to play house music. Dane then told me that it was going to happen on the upcoming Sunday. Oh no! I remembered that we had a workout session scheduled for the following day on Monday. Oh well, my fans expected to see me and I wasn't planning on disappointing them!

Chapter 16: That Queen Had Balls

Later on that day, I finally had a chance to tell Robert about where we were going to trip the lights fantastic Sunday night. "Good," he replied. "It's time to move on, cause that DJ at the club is playing the same shit weekend after weekend." And, to make matters worse, the asshole would get offended if you asked him to play a certain song. I swear he would purposely play the worst mix ever just to shut us both up and get us away from his booth!

Sunday night we headed off to our new discoteca and we couldn't find the fuckin' building. It was supposed to be in the downtown area warehouse district but the buildings all looked the same. We were driving around for almost forty-five minutes, and Robert was starting to get really pissed. I knew to try to keep calm and not turn into the moo-moo-bossy cow co-pilot placing herself at risk of being violently thrown out of the car in this seedy neighborhood. Robert had the type of personality where you never knew what he was going to do next to you, or anybody else. He actually was a pretty good prankster; and, guess who always got the brunt of it?

One summer, the June bugs came out in full force. I hate those nasty things. They are supposedly blind, so when they fly towards your hair, or face, you practically go ballistic trying to avoid becoming their landing pad. And, after they make their mark on you, they seem to have some type of adhesive to their grimy little feet; so they can hold on to you while you dance in the middle of a parking lot like Sammy Davis Jr.! One evening, I asked Robert to pull into a suspect-looking gas station, so I could buy some cigarettes. I didn't pay attention to what was swarming all around the place, but Robert saw them coming. As I ran back to the car, screaming my head off in terror, he locked the fuckin' car doors so that I couldn't get back in; isn't that horrible!?!

Suddenly, Robert turned down a non-descript alleyway and we heard base thumping in the distance. There it was, with no sign, lights, or anything telling you what it was: just some dark and ominous building with hundreds of people standing in line waiting to get in. We circled the building and, after quickly locating a really unsafe parking spot back behind the building, parked the car, got out, and ran like hell towards the front door of. Thank God! When we arrived, Dane just happened to be standing on the sidewalk. "Hey Girl," he shouted, "I didn't think you were gonna show!" "We got kind of sidetracked," I replied, adding, "This place was a bitch to find but it seems like these people didn't have any problem at all." "Follow me," he commanded. "I will take you in through the side door." We walked in to discover that the place was massive and the music was the best ever! People were dancing everywhere. The place was just one huge dance floor. What I loved most about house music was the fact that it brought everyone together. There was no hate or strife; it brought all ages, colors and nations together. There was a makeshift bar where they sold vodka and orange juice in plastic cups; and it was the cheapest vodka ever made, but I didn't care. Robert and I danced forever. Each DJ that performed had their own groovily smooth sound and they were all phenomenal. We didn't leave that place till 4 a.m. and it was still bumping as we walked to the car. Our workout session was at 10 a.m. that morning. All of a sudden I got a vision of the guy we saw the first day throwing up all over the bathroom. *Nahhh, that won't happen. I will be able to handle it.* Besides, I danced most of the alcohol off anyway, right?

Stupid, stupid, stupid I hate myself! My head was exploding into a billion pieces! I got up, ran to the bathroom and lost my cookies. Dammit! I had to be at that gym in less than an hour! I will never drink cheap ass rotgut vodka again. I'm an Absolute girl; always has been, always will be!

I could hear the phone ringing in the bedroom and the recorder immediately picked up. "Hey Miss Thing we're back, we just landed! I will call you as soon as we get to Steve's house, love you!!" *Oh shit, I totally forget Kevin and Michael were moving back that day. I was all kinds of fucked up!* This was not good; this was not good. Thank God Robert wasn't picking me up that day; maybe I could get there and finish before he did so he wouldn't see that I was still fucked up like polio! Oh my God, I was so nauseous I could barely see straight. I reached into one of the dresser drawers and grabbed some shorts and a t-shirt that were the same color. At least I won't go in looking like I belong under the big top in ring 3. Whenever severely hung-over and in doubt on what to wear, always do the same color from the neck down; you won't regret it.

I arrived at the gym ten minutes early; how did that happen? Marcus was in line to train me that morning. *Whew, praise the Lord for His Mercy!* A few weeks prior, Marcus was spilling his guts to me during a session about his girlfriend and the problems they were having. I knew that he had been on a drinking binge ever since, so I was secretly hoping that he was hung-over that day, too! There was no one at the receptionist desk and Ajay was nowhere in site. So I sat there trying to swallow, and breathe, so I wouldn't get sick again. Hmmm, something was very, very wrong. Marcus still hadn't shown up; and where the hell was Robert? It was then 10:20 a.m. The phone started to ring and the recorder picked it up after the fourth ring. "Hi, this is Robert... I know I had a 10:00 am appt....but I'm obviously not going to be able to make it in..." *No fuckin' way I'm going to kick his Snuffaluffagus ass!* I had dragged my beat-down body all the way there and he didn't even make an effort. I really couldn't care less where the fuck Marcus was. I grabbed my workout bag, reached in, and pulled out a bottle of Gatorade. I took a couple of sips…hoping I could keep it down. I booked it down the hallway of the office building, got in my car, and squealed off. All I wanted to do was to lie back down in that bed and not resurface for a few hours. Plus, I knew that Kevin and Michael were going to want to get together that night; and I really had to be mentally, and physically, capable of handling those two. It had been a very long time since we'd seen each other and I needed to be up to par, for sure.

When I arrived home, I stripped and dove into the bed to sleep for six hours. I lay in bed after I woke up, pondering a few things. I was really going to have to re-think this partying and workout schedule, because the two combined just might kill me. I rolled over, picked up my phone, and dialed Robert's number. *Let's see if Mr. Sneaky Snake will answer.* Nope, he will be in hiding for the remainder of the day, I suspected, so no use in stalking him. Hell, I didn't blame him. When you have an appointment with someone, you just don't cancel unless you are on your way to the morgue; and I guess he was on his way. I got out of bed, went into my living-room, and saw the light blinking on my answering machine. It had to be Kevin calling after they arrived at his friend's house. Yep it was him: "Hey, we made it. Where the hell are you at this time of the morning? It's Monday. I know you're not at work, so call me! Steve's number is 555-5555. We want to see you tonight!" Steve was a guy that Kevin met on the gay volleyball circuit and he was out of his mind. What I mean by that is he would do anything for shock value, to get a reaction out of someone. The few times I would go over with Kevin to visit, Steve would have his VCR ready to start playing porno movies as soon as we walked in the front door. Kevin would then scream at him to "Turn that shit off! Are you fuckin' crazy? It's the middle of the afternoon, so why do you have that on when you know we are coming over." Then Steve would just hold his stomach and roll around on his couch laughing hysterically. I never understood why he thought that was so funny. I guess our reaction was the appropriate one. I wondered, did he pull that same stunt on Kevin and Michael when they arrived this time?

    I called and Steve answered: "Hey Miss Thing, the Girls have been waiting for you to call back. Did you have a hot date last night, or something? Did you finally have to kick him out of bed?" "Steve?" I implored… "is sex the only thing that you think about day and night?" "Yes," was his emphatic reply. Kevin grabbed the phone and hit Steve in the process. How do I know that? Because I heard Steve yell, "Owww, girl, that hurt!!!" "Hey, what have you been doing?" Kevin asked. "It's a long story," I said. "I may tell you later, if I'm up to it. What are the plans for this evening?" I asked. "Steve told me that Jade was performing tonight and we haven't seen her forever. How does that sound to you?" Kevin queried. *To tell you the truth, it didn't sound appealing at all. Oh my God, I thought, really all I wanted to do was go have dinner and then crawl back in my Diva Cave; but you know how you are when you are young: nothing can stop you from making an appearance somewhere. It's like you have this strong inclination that the one time you don't show up at an expected venue, you would miss out on some event of a lifetime. I think you might call that "freakish paranoia," because later on in life, as you get older, people really don't give a damn if you show up or not.*

Jade was this really, really tall drag-queen who would swing his beer bottles on stage as fast, and hard, as he could during one of his performances; and you never knew when it was going to happen. You could look down, or turn to a friend, and in a split second you would see liquid splatter into some guy's Scary Curl sitting by the stage! Actually, that's fuckin' funny; because it then looks like he added more activator to his do. Jade also had a very peculiar way of speaking. Kevin would always imitate him at home when we lived together. He actually sounded a like a cross between Fat Albert and Mushmouth. It was crazy sounding. I never really understood a damn thing Jade said, but he was very nice; and I didn't ever want to hurt his feelings. So, I would just smile and laugh when Kevin did. Kevin said it took him almost a year to figure out what the hell he was saying. Jade, by far, was the most dynamic performer I'd ever seen. The bitch was fierce. He loved to go on as the last act and his signature number was dancing and lip-syncing to Donna Summer's "Last Dance." Very catchy, huh? This also served as a warning for what was to transpire.

I'd never seen a man who wore a size 14 pump dance the way he did. Plus, he was over 6'5 in those things. To see him glide across that stage, and move the way he did, you were at a loss for words. So I knew to suck it up and not complain about going because we would have a lot of laughs and a good time. I suddenly had a stroke of genius, asking Kevin if would they pick me up, instead of me meeting them, and he readily agreed. Then, I quickly called Michelle and asked her when she was scheduled to go in the following day. Would she move all of my customers down for later time slots if that was possible; if not, maybe switch them to another day. I knew that it was going to probably be another late night. Knowing that it was the first time I'd asked her to do something like that, I also knew that it would be the last time. I didn't want to make it a habit of partying being a priority over work. That's when you knew your ass was going down to China town!

The boys picked me up at 9:30 p.m. and Kevin said they had to make a quick stop to pick up some party favors for the night. "Tonight!?!" I asked. "This is a school night, right?" *What the fuck was he thinking, anyway?* I knew that partly he was picking it up for Jade, who had a major addiction to cocaine. But this was strange. Had Kevin somehow picked up some nasty habits while living in California? I thought so, and a very dangerous and expensive one, too. I just sat in the back seat and shut my mouth right away. I knew Kevin was not in the mood for a lecture. We arrived at Kent's house and walked around the back towards his backyard. Kent did not like anyone knocking on his front door; he said that it just made the hairs stand up on his chiny, chin, chin. That was the giveaway that it was not a regular customer, but Miss Tilly herself coming to blow this little operation wide open!

Kent was sitting on his patio, smoking a cigarette in an aquamarine colored bathrobe with slippers to match, looking like a gay Hugh Hefner. "Greetings, my friends, have a seat and take a load off those dogs!" he declared. "We can't stay long," Kevin said. "Jade goes on in about thirty minutes and she's going to want a little pick-me-up, beforehand." "I understand, girl," Kent said, before shuffling into his house to bring out a huge bag of powder. I was starting to get a really uneasy feeling in the pit of my stomach for the first time ever. I started picturing us being stopped by the cops and all of us going to prison for a thousand years. Why was I so paranoid? Well because: THIS WAS FUCKIN' ILLEGAL! All of a sudden, I had a conscience of what I was partaking in. Hmmm…maybe it's because I was no longer a teenager and I was starting to consider the outcome of the choices I made. Naaah, that's not it.

Kent then put out a line for everyone and the rhinos went to town. I only did half of what was put out for me, knowing that I needed to be totally coherent that night. We then headed out to the bar. All of them, including Steve, were talking like a bunch of magpies. I looked over to my left and saw Michael opening the bag and trying to sneak more coke out. Then, something happened that you only see in the movies. While Kevin was driving, he suddenly decided to slam on his brakes so he wouldn't run a red light; and that magical Leprechaun baggie went flying out of Michael's hands and landed on the carpeted floor-boards. We both screamed like we were in a haunted house! "Oh, my God, oh my God!" Michael screamed!

Kevin pulled the car over and Steve got up on his knees to look at what was going on before starting to scream, "Girl, what have you done!" Kevin then reached into the glove box, pulled out a Mapsco, and proceeded to hit Michael in the head several times before handing it to him, saying, "Scoop as much of it up with this, you stupid Bitch!" It was total mayhem.

I felt something sticking me in my butt. I reached behind me and saw that it was a teasing comb. So, I took that comb and started scraping the rest of the blow towards the bag. *This was fuckin' insane. Now, I really want to go home!* Steve was trying to calm Kevin down because he was so mad. He finally got him to settle down before we reached our destination. When we walked into the place, I felt so detached from it all, like that character "Carrie" in the Stephen King novel. Jade came barreling up and motioned for us to follow him to the back dressing room area so that he could get his fix before introducing the other acts. I just walked around looking at all of the bronzer, and makeup, scattered around the counter and touching the different wigs he had mounted on the Styrofoam heads. *I just couldn't seem to get into it.* I was trying to have fun, but it was such a major effort to do so. Finally, Jade did his thing and of course the crowd loved it; but the boys wanted to still stay out while I wanted to get the fuck out of there. Then, it finally hit me like the smell of mayonnaise! I think my days of the "Reigning Champion Fag-hag" were over. Don't get me wrong. I loved the gays, but something in me had changed and it was like I was getting bored with it all. Once I knew that they were in high-gear, and were not planning on leaving anytime soon, I leaned over and whispered to Kevin that I was going to take a cab home. He looked at me a little surprised, but he just smiled and gave me a hug before I darted out of that mother-fucker!

I got home around 1:30 a.m. and checked my machine to see if Michelle had left a message about my day tomorrow. Sweet, I don't have to be there till 1 p.m. Thank God! Things were going to start changing from that point on. I knew, for the time being, that partying would be a part of my life, but I had to really concentrate on work. You see, I didn't have a Mommy or Daddy I could call up and bail me out, if I fucked up! If I messed up, it was all on me, baby! I woke up the next day, which was Tuesday, and I decided to go for a walk in my neighborhood, something I had never done. I was too busy blowing, and a going; never was I stopping to smell the roses, or the grease, coming from that Burger King down the street.

I walked for about a mile, or so, and saw a small workout gym that was nestled between a shoe repair place and a Jewish deli. *Pretty interesting,* I thought. I wondered what the membership there would cost. I knew it wouldn't cost nearly as much as what we were paying at the time. We had been steadily going for a few months; and I sensed that Robert was pretty much over it. But I wanted to continue on and I think I pretty much had learned all I could from those trainers. It felt like it was time for me to step out on my own. Ladies, I then knew the secret of preventing "hail damage" from forming on my butt and legs! I walked in and noticed, standing behind the desk, eating a protein bar, a huge muscle-bound Viking. When asking him about the gym rates, he handed me a small brochure and asked me if I would like to take a tour of the facility. "Yes, that would be great," I replied. It was much smaller than the personal training gym and a little on the raw side; but it was full of amazing equipment. I started checking out the patrons; and, boy, this was going to be a great incentive to make keeping fit a big part of my life. Almost every person was in top-notch shape. They all looked like they did ads for muscle magazines. I couldn't stop staring at the women, some of whom were way too muscular for my taste; but the shapes of their legs were absolutely gorgeous. Knowing that this would be a great move for me to make, I walked back to my apartment and got ready for work.

When I got to my station, I could hear Robert talking to one of his clients at the shampoo bowl, so I made a mental note to approach him about the other gym. I really knew that he wouldn't want to transfer to that type of place, but I would at least be polite about it and ask him anyway. Robert was my buddy, and if working out wasn't something we were both interested in, there were definitely other options. I was super busy that day because of the re-arranging of my schedule, so by the time Robert and I had a chance to talk to each other, it was almost four in the afternoon. Sitting in the break-room alone when I walked in with some food, he looked kind of embarrassed. "Hey, don't worry about yesterday. You actually have a longer drive than I do; and I was so fuckin' sick that I could barely see straight. And, on top of that, Marcus didn't show up for my appointment at all. I think he really drank like a sailor the night before," I told him. Robert then replied, "Honey, I had the worst headache ever in my whole life, cause that vodka was sooo shitty!" "Yep, that's what did it," I said. "From now on, can we maybe have a nice dinner out before we paint the town pink?" I asked. "That way, it won't hit us so hard, because we will have something lining our stomachs," I added. He totally agreed with me on that one. I then started relaying to him about the smaller gym I stumbled on and, right away, he said "Nope, I'm done, but thanks for asking me." Then Robert perked up and said, "Oh yeah, I've been wanting to tell you where I went yesterday when I could finally leave the house. A while back, Jackson had mentioned to me that Felicia took him to a vintage clothing store that has tons of boots, and gloves and hats: all kinds of accessories for men and women." "Wow, that is so cool, when do you want to go?" I asked? "How about this Friday?" he said. "That way, we may find something for Saturday night!" *That day, after our conversation in the break-room, our relationship started to change a little, too. I think we both sensed that we were about to start doing our own thing with other people. But we just let it ride and take its own course.*

Chapter 17: Celebrity Hooker Like

I joined that gym in my neighborhood and I ended up really liking it a lot. What I got a kick out of mostly were the signs that were strategically hung all over the gym, which read something like this: YO MAMA DOESN'T WORK HERE; SO RE-RACK YOUR WEIGHTS!! I took a few guests with me, but they seemed to only be a distraction. Donny complained the whole time and Tammy and Louise just gawked while hitting on the men there. I kept telling them, "This place is for people who are really serious. This is not a night club!" But they wouldn't listen; so finally I just started going there alone, and really early in the morning, because neither of them would workout at 5 a.m. Ha!

One Thursday, I decided to break the normal routine and workout at 5:30 in the afternoon. That was "back and bi-cep day," which I loved, because it was super easy for me. Now remember, the people here were pretty serious, so I didn't pay much attention to what was going on as far as people hooking up with each other. It was really crowded, because it was right after work, the "happy hour," as I called it. But I could feel someone, or something, staring at me, so I would look around quickly to see if I could spot him, or her — or whatever it was — but there was nothing.

I went over to get a drink from the water fountain. When I turned around and looked up, there was a guy standing in the very back of the gym near the squat leg-press machines. He wasn't very tall, but he wasn't the size of a troll doll, either. He had medium to dark brown hair and, from the looks of where I was standing, he had a nice physique, too. But the one thing you are going to flip a wig over is the person he looked like! I'm not just talking about resembling just a little; or that if he turned to the side, he faintly resembled. For a split second, I thought it was him, but then no one else seemed to give a shit, so I figured it wasn't the real guy. Ok, are you ready for me to tell you who this guy looked like? You can barely stand it, huh? All right, brace yourself! HE LOOKED JUST LIKE FUCKIN' TOM CRUISE!!! Okay, I will admit that I was never really a big fan of the guy, (no offense, Tom), but to actually see his twin was such an unreal experience. We all know that everyone has a twin: doesn't matter if it's Fred Sanford, or Marty Feldman.

He started grinning and walking towards me. I could see that his eyes were blue and, from what I can remember in pictures, Tom Cruise's eyes are green. Anyway, he sauntered over and introduced himself, telling me that his name was Bobby. I told him my name and then launched into what I'm sure he had heard for about three years. "Do you know who you look like?" I asked. He started laughing. "Yeah, yeah, I know," he said. He continued: "I've never seen you here before. Are you a member?" "Yes, I just joined a couple of weeks ago but I normally come in around 5 a.m." I answered. "Ohhh, okay," he replied. We talked for a few more minutes. I told him that it was nice to meet him and that I was going to go and hit the treadmill for about thirty more minutes before getting out of there. "Oh, I will join you then!" he declared. "What is he doing," I thought. *Is he interested in me, or something?* You have to bear with me a little, as I can be a little slow in this department, especially after being reared by drag-queens.

So Bobby got on the treadmill next to mine and we both started running at a steady pace, but not so fast that we wouldn't be able to speak to one another. He was pretty damn funny, very quick-witted, which I liked. He kept complimenting me on my shape, hmmm... this is getting wilder by the second. Thirty minutes were over in no time, so when I grabbed my workout bag, Bobby offered: "Hang on a minute, let me get my stuff." He walked me out to my car and proceeded to ask for my phone number. Wow! I was being asked out by a Tom Cruise clone! I opened my trunk, took my purse out and rooted around for a pen and paper. Then I wrote it all down and handed it to him. "I will call you tonight," he gleefully exclaimed, before adding, "Maybe we can do something this weekend if you're free." Then he walked to his car, got in and drove off. I was still standing there looking like Marty Feldman, so I hurriedly got in my car. While driving home, I didn't remember if I stopped for red lights or stop-signs, small children or animals.

After I left the gym, I had to go by the grocery store, as I needed to start keeping edible things in the fridg, and in my cabinets, not just booze. I couldn't stop thinking about Bobby calling me. Thank God for answering machines. I know many of you can remember back in the day. If you weren't home to get that important call, you didn't get the call. Just when you're trying to get your keys out, and open the door, you could hear the phone start to ring; plus, you had to pee like a racehorse. So you bust in the door like Lou Ferrigno, running like a wild person to the phone; and while grabbing the receiver with way too much brute strength, the heavy paper weight base falls on your foot and you hear the steady dial tone on the other end! Fuck!!! I already had a list of what of I needed, so I was in, and out, in no time.

I got home around 8:30 p.m. and, of course, the light was blinking and there were two calls. The first one was from Michelle saying that she wanted to talk to me first thing tomorrow morning. She said that a client referral had inquired about me maybe doing their wedding the following month; but I was pretty booked up, so she needed to speak to me and see what we could come up with. I really loved Michelle. She was so efficient and she always had my back and took care of me!

The next call was from Bobby. *Boy, he really wanted my "cooter cakes" for sure!* I quickly put my groceries away, then made myself a cocktail, and called him back. He practically answered on the first ring, damn! "Hey, I went by the store before coming home and just got your message," I said. "No problem," he replied, "I really had a nice time talking to you today. I normally don't talk to women in that gym, mainly because most of them come in with their 'roided up' boyfriends. Or they are more muscular than I am; and that kind of creeps me out a little." We both laughed at the truthfulness of that statement. So he finally asked, "Would you like to go out sometime this weekend? Actually, tomorrow is Friday and I know we just met today, but if you can do tomorrow night, that would be cool." *Sure, why not?* I thought. *That way, if Robert wants to do something on our usual Saturday, that would be perfect!* "No, tomorrow night is fine with me," I said. "Great, do you like Mexican food? If so, I know of a really good place with excellent margaritas," he piped up. "That would be great," I answered. "Okay, give me your address and I will pick you up at your place at 7 p.m." After I hung up, I looked over towards the couch and saw Val giving me a disapproving look while shaking his head. "What?" *It's just an innocent date!*

The next day, Michelle grabbed me as soon as I walked in the door and we figured some things out in my schedule to accommodate this particular wedding. "How do you pronounce this Bride's name?" I asked her. "I don't know," she replied, "I guess after you call her you, can ask her." "Yeah, thanks a lot," I said. I quickly made the call to the bride and she seemed pretty nice on the phone. Her accent was a little heavy, but I could still understand her pretty well. Her family was from some part of the Middle East but they had moved here to the states about two years ago. She then went on to say that I had done her cousin's hair last year and she loved my work! *Well, that's good. At least she'd seen what I can do, which is definitely a plus.*

Kevin entered the salon while I was on the phone with the bride. I noticed that he looked kind of puffy. I'd never seen him look bad before, but he was his ole' chipper self, so I didn't ask him about what they did Tuesday night. Something told me that he was starting to do the nose candy during the week; but I didn't know how to approach that subject with him. I feared that he would probably curse me out and tell me to mind my own business. Actually, that's exactly what would happen, so I kept quiet about it. It didn't seem to affect his work. He was still as talented as ever and his clients simply adored him. That afternoon, I went back to the break room to grab some towels and Robert and Kevin were talking and eating. So I abruptly butted in and exclaimed: "Guess what, hookers!?!" They didn't respond. They just kept looking down at their food. "Excuse me!!!" I said. "Guess What!?!" "What!!!" they both screamed. "I have a date tonight, with an incredible looking guy!" "Girl, have you been hallucinating again, thinking those strung-out whores on the strip you meet are now datable?" Kevin interrogated me. "Ha, ha, hell!" I shouted. "No, this is totally legit, Robert. I actually met him at that gym yesterday afternoon." "Well, that's cool," they both chimed in unison. "Where are you guys going?" Robert asked before adding: "I hope he doesn't try to pay with a coupon!" Then they both started cracking up. "Okay, okay," I said. "I'm not giving you fuckers any more details. I can tell by the green slime that's seeping up through both of your eyeballs that you are seething with envy! The Diva is leaving." I added, before whipping my head around and catwalking out.

I finished my last client that Friday around 5:45 p.m., then raced home to get ready for my date. I was pretty excited, because this time I knew what the guy looked like and decent conversation had already taken place. So, hopefully, there would be no surprises. Maybe I was being a little too trusting. *Maybe I should have told him I would meet him at the restaurant, so I would have my own vehicle just in case he turned out to be a chronic nose-picker or a tooth-sucker.* Shit, I needed to quit thinking about it, cause my imagination was starting to run amuck! I decided to wear a cute blue jean jumpsuit. I turned on my stereo and popped in "Heart of Glass." Blondie, eat your heart out sister, Mama's back in town!

I threw hot rollers in, put on a little makeup, and by the time I finished teasing my coif, the doorbell rang. Wow, it was already 7 p.m. *Very impressive, he's on time to the very second!* I skipped halfway to the door, then slowed down, so I wouldn't open the door snorting like a mare in heat. "Hi Bobby, come in," I said. "Man, you are right on schedule." He laughed. "I know," he said, "I cannot stand being late or, even worse, people who think that not being on time is normal. It's one of the most rude behaviors," he admonished. *I like this guy's way of thinking,* I thought. "You look great," he said. "Thanks, so do you," I replied.

Bobby escorted me to his car, to which he referred later as being gift from his grandfather. It was a black 1980 Fiat, totally suiting him. "Our reservations are for 7:30 p.m.," he said. We arrived there about five minutes early, but they could seat us right away. It was a happening place, with a mariachi band playing and the main guy swinging his hips around like Elvis.

The waiter came and we both ordered their famous margaritas. I was not a big fan of this drink, but I had to admit that it was pretty damn tasty. *I suddenly remembered: don't go fuckin' crazy with the tequila, cowgirl.* This is the first date and you don't want to end up like one of your friends, Ricardo, who finally had his chance to go out with this guy he liked. He ended up drinking way too many martinis because he was nervous. Then his date suggested that he not slam down so many, so fast, before dinner. Ricardo retorted with several explosive curse words towards the confused chap. Finally, he was reduced to throwing up in the restroom and crawling out of the window — while the date was on the other side of the door inquiring if he was alright. *Yep, don't want to go there tonight, no sirrreee...*

Bobby had a very cute personality. I noticed that every time he would make a comment about something, he would immediately say: "Huh." He would then wait for your reaction, after which he would continue talking. He was a pretty quirky dude, but funny as hell; and I tried not to stare at him like I was star-struck. But he looked so fuckin' much like that actor!

The food was awesome. I would totally return to this restaurant, for sure. Bobby then said that he had a surprise for me after dinner. The guy actually had something else planned besides sitting on my couch talking about the shape of ice cubes. Bobby paid the check and didn't even break out a coupon, either. "Where are we going?" I asked. "I'm never going to tell you, so forget it," he said while laughing. "It's just down the road." In the distance, I could see bright lights twinkling in an arch-like shape. Then I could hear what sounded like motorcycle engines running. He was taking me to a Putt Putt Golf park that also had racing cars. *I loved that shit, how cool was this!!!* We ran towards the entrance like two ten-year-olds, first playing "putt putt," for which we both sucked. Then we raced cars for over an hour. By the time it was all over, my voice was so hoarse from yelling. It was almost 11:30 p.m. and I had a very busy Saturday; so I knew I had to hit the sack as soon as possible, though I really didn't want this date to end. Bobby drove me home and walked me to my door. He leaned over and gave me a sweet soft kiss and then said, "I will call you tomorrow, sleep tight." All of a sudden, I just levitated right through my front door and floated into my bedroom.

 I was so busy the next day, which was Saturday, that I barely had time to breathe, let alone eat. Robert, being a peach, ran to grab some Tai food for me, and he left it wrapped in the bag on the table in the back room. By the time I finally got around to eating it, some "Jive Turkey" had already plunged into it and was gracious enough to leave me only half of the food in the bag. Now, who the fuck would eat someone's lunch, whose name was clearly written in red marker on the paper bag? So, I took about three or four bites, then a swig of Coke a Cola, and went back to the battlefield. I was so glad that I had gone to bed at a reasonable time the previous night.

 I heard Michelle on the intercom announcing that I had a call, so I ran to the phone and it was Bobby. "Hey, I know you're probably busy, but just wanted to say hi." "Hey, thanks," I said. "Yes, I'm swamped, but it's good you took me away from it for a sec." "Would you like to workout with me on Monday, let's say around 5:30?" he asked. "Yeah, that would be great," I replied. "Okay, nice, have a great weekend and see ya on Monday," he said. I told him bye and then I ran up to greet my next client.

After work, Tammy and Louise asked me if I wanted to go and have some drinks. Actually, what I really wanted to do was sit on the couch with Val and watch something stupid on TV. *I never watched the idiot box, so this would definitely be a treat,* I thought. "You never do anything with us anymore," Tammy whined. "I know, it has been a while," I said. "I have a wedding coming up in two weeks after I'm finished with that. Let's go boogie oggie oggie."

We had planned for the next Tuesday for the bride to come in for a practice run and it was going to be only a few in the wedding party. I found that to be very strange for her culture; normally, everybody is participating somehow. But this one only consisted of the bride, the mother-in-law, her two daughters, and the sister and mother of the bride.

On the day of the wedding, I was to meet them at the hotel. The bride had a huge penthouse suite she was staying in, which meant I had more than enough room to concoct some massive beehive…just kidding. From the very beginning, I made it a point to really be mentally, and physically, rested up for those hotel weddings, because there was always so much going on at once, that someone had to have their wits about them. I had a few days to get prepared for that wedding.

Robert was still working on a client, as I was getting ready to leave for the day. I went up to him and told him I was going to be settling in for Saturday night. He started laughing and said, "I'm going to put this one down in the record books," because he actually had plans to go out with his parents: unusual for us both to have alternate plans to going out to party. "No way," I said. "That's crazy!" "Yeah, I know!" he replied.

I went home to put on my foot pj's, made popcorn, and poured glasses of wine for Val and me. He had to have his own so that he wouldn't be sneaking sips from mine! We kicked back and watched episodes of All In The Family and Maude. That Maude character was a bitch; I loved her! I decided to turn in early. I did not want to be awakened in the middle of the night from a drinking and dialing friend; so I turned my ringer down on my phone and adjusted the sound on my answering machine.

I woke up around 8 a.m. I don't remember ever sleeping like that since high school, probably because I wasn't partying back then. Slamming down beers in a parking lot, while sitting on top of friends' cars, never sounded appealing to me, at all! I got showered, and dressed, and then started doing chores around the house. As I passed through the living room, I noticed the light blinking. Oh, I had forgotten to turn everything back on from last night.

The first message was from Kevin, saying that Jade was in the hospital and that he was really bad off. Kevin had told me a few weeks back that Jade was HIV Positive: that he had Aids. I had heard that the Aids virus was first discovered around the year 1980 in the United States. So then it was 1988 and a lot of the people still did not understand much about the disease. Everyone was just afraid that they could catch it from kissing someone or from a toilet seat. Not too many people had a clue about what was going on at all. I called Kevin at his house but there was no answer. I figured he was probably at the hospital with Jade. Wow, this was really a shocker, because this was the first time I'd known someone personally who was that sick and with something for which there was no known cure. I continued to clean my apartment and made a quick trip out to the dumpster to throw at some trash.

When I came back, my answering machine light was blinking again. Maybe it was Kevin with some news about Jade's condition. Nope, it was Mr. Robert. "Hey, what's up? Did you ditch your parents last night and decide to go out after all?" I asked. "Nooo, and thank God we didn't go to the club last night; you wouldn't believe what happened! Jackson just called and said that there was another drug bust that went down. This was the second one in 2 years!" "Did Jackson go, too?" I asked him. "No, he didn't, he ended up in the gayborhood, instead."

He went on to say that there were so many pills, and baggies, on the floor that you could've opened up a pharmacy out of the trunk of your car. Vice cops stormed the place around 1:30 a.m. and forty-six people were arrested. I asked if Kent was there that night and did he get caught with that big ass designer purse in plain view? "I don't know, but Jackson is getting all of the details; you know how he loves to stick his nose in everyone's business. So I have confidence that I will find out more than the cops know in about an hour. I will call you back when I get more details." *Wow, this was a crazy Sunday morning: first Jade and now the club!* I wanted to sit down and have a drink, but it was only 11 a.m. I refused to have a drink that early because that's how it starts. You take a little nip to take the edge off after hearing bad news; and in a year you are drunk before 9 a.m. and babbling incoherently to your imaginary cat!

Chapter 18: Bitchin' Laws

Monday was my day off and I'd finished all of my housework the previous day, so I wasn't quite sure what I was going to do that day before I met Bobby at the gym. About thirty minutes later Robert called to see if I wanted to check out that vintage store. "Yes," I said. "That would be great. What time do you want to head out there?" I asked. "How about if I pick you up in an hour," he said. "Cool," I thought. *This was going to be so much fun, I'd never been to a vintage store before.* And no, going to Goodwill with your mom back in the day is not the same experience! When we pulled up to the place, it looked like something from a children's storybook. The store was actually a small house; when we opened the door, an old-fashioned bell rang to let the proprietor know that he had patrons. We heard a man's voice in the very back of the store saying "be right with you!" A guy that looked like he was in his early 50's popped out from behind a clothes rack filled with men's suits. Oh my. I looked at Robert and he grinned back at me. This man looked exactly like that guy Mr. Drummond from the show "Different Strokes." Wow, this was going to be fun! He had those bugged eyes and the same voice as that character: fuckin' crazy! "We just want to have a look around your store." Robert mentioned that a friend had told him about it. "Okay, that's fine, that's fine," he said. "My name is Phillip; and if you need anything, just holler." *Oh my God, his name is*

Phillip; wasn't that the name of the guy on the show!?! This place had clothing from every era from the 1920's on. But one thing Robert and I both noticed was that the size of everything was sooo tiny. I would try on a pair of gloves and could barely get them on. We were not that big. I certainly wasn't, but those people had to have been super duper tiny. Robert tried on different types of hats and they all just sat on top of his melon ball. I started laughing my ass off when I saw that. I then went to the left of the store where all of the 1970's merchandise was and POW! I found the one item that I was born to have! They were "GLOW IN THE DARK ORANGE GO-GO BOOTS." Awesome. I ran over to scoop them up, sat on a footstool, took of my boots and then started struggling to put them on. *Fuck, how do I get these on?* I thought. "Robert, come here. I need your help," I yelled. "Those are cool," he said. "Yeah, they are, but the boot is like made of some weird rubber inside, or something, and they don't have an outside zipper," I clarified. Then Phillip must have heard all of the commotion. He peeked around the door and said, "Oh honey, let me get you some talcum powder; that's the only way those puppies are going on!" He ran off and quickly came back with some baby power, sprinkled a hefty portion on my legs and feet; and then I shoved my foot in and inched them up my leg. Glorious, they were glorious! I could barely contain the joy I was experiencing that moment, while wondering, *how would these go with Thunder Pussy!?!*

    Robert and I finished our shopping and then grabbed a quick bite to eat. He then dropped me off at my apartment so I could get ready to meet Bobby at the gym. When I arrived, he was already there on the treadmill. "Hey, how long have you been here?" I asked. "Only about ten minutes, not long," he said. So I got on the treadmill next to his and started doing a little warm up myself. We talked about our weekend and I told him about Jade and what happened at the club. "Wow, that's crazy!" he said. "Yeah, for sure, but on a lighter note, my friend Robert and I went shopping yesterday and I found these amazing boots; I can't wait to break those babies out!" I exclaimed.

When we were just about finishing up, Bobby asked me if I wanted to maybe grab a burger somewhere. "Sure, I'm game," I said. I followed him to a little place about three blocks away. At this little eatery, you just gave your order and they would bring your food out to your table. Even though I hadn't known Bobby for very long, I could tell he was acting a little nervous. He was laughing hysterically at everything I said. Now, I know I'm funny; but not that fuckin' funny. And how do I know that? Because some "dickweed" thought it was a little tidbit of information I needed to know about my personality. As he sat across from me, laughing like a crazed hyena, I started to wonder *what the fuck was he doing?* Then, the question finally slipped out of his mouth that revealed what was making him act so whacked out: "Hey, would you like to come over to my place and watch some TV or something?" Ohhhh, it took a while for it to sink in (and no, I'm not a blonde) but I then realized why he was so fidgety. "Sure, that would be cool," I said.

So I followed him to his apartment. When I stepped inside, I asked him where his bathroom was. I was schooled by Kevin that if you ever go to a man's pad, you better make damn sure what his bathroom looks like right off the bat. Look to see if there's anything crawling around any part of that room, or if there is something that has settled in there that has fur on it, but isn't a rug. If any of that should happen, all of a sudden start faking severe menstrual cramps and bolt. Because if the mother-fucker won't clean his bathroom, then what else doesn't he clean; comprende!?! *Oh, thank God, it's clean!* I

180

pulled back the shower curtain, looked around in the corner, and on the sink. Nice: the mirror wasn't sprayed down with toothpaste particles, either. He has definitely passed the test.

When I came out of the bathroom, Bobby was at his kitchen bar, with a bottle of wine, and two glasses, already out. *He is not wasting anytime,* I thought. He came around to the other side of the bar and started pouring some in the glass next to me. I looked down and noticed that he had taken his shoes off. Good, he doesn't have talons posing as feet, excellent! Now, I know what you guys are thinking about right now! You're thinking, "Wow, she is one picky bitch!" Well, I know one thing: you put up with a few things like nasty bathrooms and fucked up feet, and you will tolerate almost anything. This, of course, results in going to your hairdresser, and bitching, for two to three hours about your plight.

The wine was very good and — as I was telling him about the wedding I had coming up the next weekend — Bobby suddenly leaned over and started kissing me. He then led me to his couch as we continued kissing and groping each other like two caterpillars. Then, all of a sudden, Bobby started getting really excited and he started kissing me harder. All of a sudden, it was like he couldn't control his saliva; and it began to feel like I was being kissed by a circular water hose sprinkler dribbling all over the place. I began to get nauseous and totally grossed out. I think he could sense me pulling away a little as he looked at me and asked, "What's wrong?" Oh boy, I couldn't hurt his feelings because I really liked him, and I was by no means an expert on kissing. But I didn't think I could continue letting this Labrador retriever continue to have his way with me. I "knew" that if you were getting physically sick to your stomach from someone kissing you, that was fucked up! "No, I'm okay," I said. "I just think we need to cool it a little. "Okay, I understand," he said. *Shit, I hate when this happens, as it's so horribly awkward, but I couldn't continue to go on another minute.*

I got up and grabbed the bottle of wine and our glasses, filled them up and told him: "Hey, let's watch some TV." He took his glass and then turned on the tube. Thank God Magnum P.I. was on, because it seemed to perk him up a bit! That's why till this day I have always loved Tom Selleck; because he always seemed to come to the rescue in a pinch with his fine ass!

At 8:30 a.m., I arrived at the hotel about 30 minutes before the sister and the mother of the bride were supposed to arrive, so I would not be rushed. They were staying in a separate room from the bride's suite, so I was going to have to pack up all of my things and move to the bride's penthouse suite to do the rest of the wedding party. So you know, of course, I had to charge extra for that.

Finally, it was 9 a.m. I was sitting in the lobby of the hotel so I could spot them right away. Then it got to be 9:30. This was not looking good. I knew that in certain cultures being late was readily accepted; however, in my world it was bullshit! I waited another 15 minutes then saw a phone booth across the hall near the restrooms of the lobby. After looking up the bride's number in my appointment book, I dialed it and the phone just rang, with her never picking up. Shit, that fuckin' blew! I knew I had to at least wait for the bride to show up; plus, she had already paid me in advance the night before. So, I had to make a decision on what to do soon. Guess how long I sat drinking water and coffee at the hotel bar? Go ahead, take a crack at it! Three miserable, horrible stinking hours! I was livid! I knew then that if the mom and sister finally showed up, I would definitely do them, and the bride — then one other person. I was scheduled to do six, but there was no fuckin' way I was going to stay and do the whole party. There was not enough money you could offer me to stay, because by that time I wouldn't have any creative juice left.

Finally, at 1 p.m., the mother and sister came running into the lobby looking around frantically. I quickly came over and introduced myself. The sister began apologizing right away. Though the mom couldn't speak English, by the look on her face I knew she, too, was upset. The sister explained that the person who was supposed to come and pick them up at the bride's house never arrived. They had never been to this city before and had just arrived the previous night. *Wow, that was pretty shitty of someone who was given that responsibility to avoid owning up to it.* So the sister told me to just curl her hair — she would do the rest herself — and just take care of mom. They were both very gracious women, which I have never forgotten. I finished them both in about forty minutes, then called down to the front desk to see if the bride had checked into the penthouse. I was told that she had arrived, but I had to be escorted there by a bellman because it was on a private floor. The particular hotel was a little older, but it was very posh.

When the bellman opened the double French doors to the room, it looked like something out of a foreign film. It was absolutely stunning; every inch of the room breathed perfection. The bride came out wearing one of the complimentary bathrobes. She looked like she didn't really get much sleep, which, of course, is a "No No" for a bride. She proceeded to tell me how she was up till two a.m., and then slept till twelve noon, at which point she finally received my message. I asked her what had happened:

why did her sister and mom show up so late? "Well," she hesitated a bit, "My soon to be mother-in-law was supposed to come by the house and pick them up and bring them here to the hotel; but she never showed up. And when I woke up, she was at my house getting all of the dresses together. So I inquired about how it went this morning, and she said: 'Well, I didn't feel like taking them, so I had my son pick them up instead.' I was so angry at her, but she likes to argue, so I knew not to take it any further." *Now, ain't that a pip!* I thought. The bitch-in-law was the one who had my happy ass sitting at a hotel bar drinking coffee. Huh!?! Okay, well, she messed with the wrong Diva, honey! Because I was going to win this mother-fuckin' round! Ding!

  I started putting rollers in the bride's hair and just as I was beginning to start the transformation, the troublemaker showed up with her two young daughters. "Ohhh!" she squealed. "When will you be done with the beautiful bride? My daughters and I will be next in line, no?" "Nope," I said. "I'm only doing one more person after the bride; and do you want to know the reason why?" I asked. "Because I sat in this lobby for three hours!" "You can't do that!" she screamed back at me. "Oh, but yes I can, do you want to pay me an extra $1000 for my time? Of course you don't," I said. "So let me repeat, I'm doing one more and I'm done for the day; got it?" She then proceeded to mumble under her breath and do the pouty dance, so I turned to her and said: "If you say one more word, I'm leaving after the bride!" The bride just sat there stunned because she had never seen anyone shut that woman up.

  Then another woman flew into the suite with a chair, and a huge travel bag on wheels, singing at the top of her lungs, "I'm here!" *It was the makeup artist. Thank God: another warm body to buffer this insane atmosphere!* She came over and introduced herself to me, "Hey girl, I'm Sandra. Do you have everything under control?" And before I could answer her, she went on a tangent and started talking to the bride. This woman talked non-stop, and then she talked, and talked, and talked, never taking a breath or even swallowing. That's not fuckin' normal!

I once had a client who would talk like that for two hours. By the time I was finished with her, my head was pretty much hanging down from my shoulders because she had decapitated me. One day, while she was in full force, she started choking and coughing violently. "I think I need some water," she screeched. I then scolded her, "I think you probably need to shut up for a second; what do you think?"

After doing the finishing touches on the bride, Sandra came over and put something in the bride's hand. "This will help you relax a little, honey," she said. *Oh nooo, what the hell did she give her!?!* I then turned to the Bitch-in-law and asked, "Okay, who is going to volunteer to be next? Because, after this, I'm gone!" You see, the mother-in-law was probably in her early 50's, but you could tell that in her "heyday" she was a raving beauty. She had a very fair complexion, with beautiful strawberry blonde hair and green eyes. So, this whore was used to getting everything, and anything, she wanted. The sweet daughters then said to their witch mommy, "It's okay, mother, you can get your hair done, we don't mind." And she then sauntered over, plopped down, and blurted to me, "Make me look like a movie star!" I almost said, "Which one?" As I pictured Bea Arthur, I sprayed her hair down with a water bottle and blow-dried the living hell out of it. I put big rollers in, then teased and backcombed it, sprayed it with a stiff-ass hair spray, and abruptly announced, "You're done, Sweetie!" She was so mad at me that volcanic ash instantly erupted from the base of her neck! I packed my implements, and supplies, and turned to look at the bride to say goodbye; and… oh shit, she was going down for the count! Whatever Sandra had given her was taking effect in a major way. One eye was open as a steady stream of drool was running down to her robe! *God, this was terrible; this bride was not even going to make it out of the hotel room!* But that's not my problem. "Sayonara," strumpets!!!

I ran out of that mother-fuckin' hotel like I was on fire! I couldn't wait to peel my clothes off and take a shower. That day really beat the shit out of me; I was so mentally and physically spent. I might have needed to reconsider doing the CJ's (which in layman's terms means: Camel Jockeys.) All right, all right… don't get your Christian panties all up in a wad, or your liberal jockstraps twisted in a loop-dee-loop. You know what I'm talking about, when you are dealing with certain people, from different backgrounds. You have to make some major decisions about dealing with some of them in the future, especially the ones who want you to do their hair, rub their feet with oil, and administer a butt-wax treatment for twenty bucks. Yeah… right! You're in America now. No one over here is going to let you nickel and dime them to death after they see you chariot up in your Rolls Royce.

Before I went home, I decided to run by the salon and drop off my supplies first; that way, I would be set up for Tuesday morning. Robert was just packing up his bag when I walked in. "Hey!" he shouted. "I was just getting ready to call you. How was the wedding party?" "Uhggg, first let's go have me fitted for new shoes, because my dogs are barking; and then put my tired ass to pasture," I said. I added, "The bride was cool, but her mother-in-law was a piece of work. I'm too tired to tell you the whole story, so what's up with you?" I asked. "Well, are you up for going out tonight?" he asked. "No way," I said. "You would have to prop me up with a stick in my back like a paper doll; I wouldn't last 30 minutes out." "Okay," he said, "I'm probably going to meet Jackson. Anyway, he came by the salon today and told me that no one we knew had been arrested during that drug bust." "Oh, thank God," I said, "and what about Kent?" "He was having a party at his house that night, so he was safe and sound." "Okay, have a good time," I replied, "I will probably talk to you tomorrow."

Robert left and I started putting my things away, then checked up on my schedule for the upcoming week. I arrived home around 6:00 pm and it was so strange how I was beginning to stay home on Saturday nights. I didn't even want any alcohol. *Wow, Mama is growing up, for sure!*

I was awakened the next morning with my phone ringing like crazy. *Why was the answering machine not picking up?* "Hello," I said, "this better be important!" "Hey Girl, I know it's early." It was Kevin and he sounded awful. "What's going on?" I asked. "Jade passed away this morning around 1 a.m.," he mournfully said. After Kevin spoke those words, I felt like I had been sucked into a vacuum. "What?" I stammered. "He's dead?" "Yes, he had complications from pneumonia," He went on to say that Jade really didn't have any family: only his mother, and she was elderly, with limited funds. So he was going to try to rally up all of Jade's friends to see if he could collect enough to give Jade a proper funeral. *Oh my God, this was too much,* I thought, as tons of emotions came bubbling up inside me. "I will call you later about the arrangements that are made. Most likely the funeral will be during the week. I know you may not be able to take off from work, so don't worry about it. I will totally understand," he said. "I have to tell you something else as well," he continued. "Michael and I are splitting up." "What!?!" I screamed. What is going on? What did you do?" "What do you mean, what did I do?" he yelled. "This was starting to come to a head after we moved to California. Anyway, I will talk to you later about it. I've been here at this hospital for days and I'm dead tired. I just wanted to tell you a little of what's going on, because Michael already moved out. Talk to you soon. Love you," he said. "Love you too," I said. *Waaaaaah!!! I just wanted to start balling like an infant; this was too much to bear!* I crawled back under the covers and pulled them over my head to shut out every feeling, and thought, I was having at that moment. *I'm going to stay in this bed forever, I will cancel my week and stay in my apartment drinking booze and smoking cigarettes!* As the phone started ringing again, I thought, *Oh nooo, more bad news.* "Hi, it's Bobby, are you busy?" All of a sudden, I felt there was no need to wallow in sadness and despair. Amazing how when the opposite sex comes a calling, all of a sudden that sparkly rainbow breaks through your window and everyday feels like a holiday; and you are just living the dream!

    Bobby called to see if I would like to meet him at the gym again the following Monday. I really wanted to, but I didn't really want to go to his apartment again. How was I going to break it to him, if he asked? *Damn, I don't need this kind of aggravation right now,* I thought. I knew I could not endure another kissing session that made me feel like I was in a severe thunderstorm. But I completely enjoyed his company and I liked everything about him, except his kissing skills. *Was I becoming a smoocher snob?* I told him that I would meet him there at 5:30 p.m. again. "Great," he said. "And if you feel up to it, I know a great Chinese place a few blocks from there." "Okay," I said, "that will work for me." I knew that I was going to have to say something at the restaurant. I couldn't string him along forever. That wouldn't be right, at all, to treat him that way. I may be a Diva, but I do have a heart, you know!

My Tuesday at work was kind of strange. I had a "no show" and it was a regular, so I hoped she was okay. I asked Michelle to call her and leave a message, making sure that everything was all right on her end and that the "receptionist" hadn't screwed things up. Ummmm…not pointing any fingers; I just wanted to follow up. *Oh well, I guess I could go shopping, or get something to eat.* As I was walking away from the front desk, Kevin ran up to check on his next client, who was obviously very late. The client walked in with her big boobies stuck out, acting like nothing was wrong. "Girl, you are twenty minutes late!" Kevin barked. "Oh, you can still take me, can't you? It won't take long. All I need is a little shaping up," she purred. "LISTEN CANYON CUNT!" Kevin screamed. "My time is valuable! I will not let you, or anybody else, run me behind all day. Now you're going to pay for my time and then get the fuck out of here!!!" You could hear gasping and snickering all around. She sure as hell paid for the time. With her voice barely at a shaky whisper, she made another appointment, then turned to Kevin and said she was sorry and scampered out. *Oh My God,* I thought. *Will I ever reach such great heights of authority as this?* Kevin then turned to me and said: "Come on, let's go have lunch; we need to talk anyway." I knew he had to talk, especially after having just let his client have it. We walked down the strip to an Italian place and he immediately ordered a vodka seven. *Wow, this was going to be a heavy convo,* I could tell. I ordered a Dr. Pepper, because I didn't have the faith to swig down a vodka cranberry during working hours.

Chapter 19: Dark Side of the Rainbow

I suddenly recalled a memory of a time that was the first, and last, time I did something super stupid while on a break. I had let Donny talk me into smoking a joint with him. I have to tell you, I hate marijuana. All it does is either make you crazy, stupid or hungry; and if everything is going right for you at the time, you can accomplish all three of those traits in about three minutes. I only took two hits; and when I came back to the salon, I had a new flat top client waiting for me. I screamed silently in my head, or did I scream out loud, uh... can't remember. I turned to the poor manly man that was going to get a real chop job, if I didn't excuse myself first, and go running around the block for 15 minutes. I do think the brisk sprinting around the block several times seemed to help a little, because it only took me 45 minutes to do it, instead of my normal 30 minutes. Plus, he didn't seem to mind; and I knew this, because his elbow maintained contact with my pelvis area.

Oh shit! I got lost in thought while Kevin was talking! "Anyway," he said; "I knew that he had met someone else, I could sense it. He started working out every day, staying late at the restaurant when he never use to do that before. I think he was messing around with the owner's son who by the way has massage hands and feet and is around Michael's age. I guess he got tired of my old ass!" "What are you talking about!?!" I said: "You're not old!!" I really wanted to bring up to Kevin his excessive coke usage, but I just couldn't do it. It was like it had been so instilled in me to never cross the boundaries with a friend that's older than me. But I will let you in on a little secret: I couldn't cross that boundary then, but I can, sure as fuck, do it now if an old bitch gets out of line. Kevin went on to say that he only wished the best for Michael. He reached for his wallet, took out a piece of paper, and handed it to me. "Here is his new number at his place. I want you to continue to keep in touch with him; he loves you very much. Oh yeah, one more thing," he said. "Jade's funeral is tomorrow; I already looked at your schedule and you're swamped." "Yes, I am booked solid all day, but I want to give you some money to buy Jade's mom a nice arrangement." I then handed Kevin $100.00. "Thanks girl, I really appreciate this. You know I really miss that Ghetto bitch," he said. "She was my true, blue 'Soul Sissy'." And that was all that was said about that and we finished our meal in silence.

I felt like Dorothy in "The Wizard of Oz" because the week flew by just that fast. It was already Saturday. After another crazy workweek, I was ready to get loose! Tonight was the night to debut my orange gay day-glow boots that were just about ready to high step it out of my closet. Robert was going to meet Tammy, Louise, and I out later, as he had some event he had to go to that one of his clients was sponsoring. We were all going to another warehouse party located downtown, hopefully one we would be able to spot a lot faster. Tammy actually had a pretty good sense of direction for a chick; Louise and I were fuckin' clueless when it came to that. Thunder Pussy and the orange boots did not look right together at all: hideous! So I just wore a black turtleneck with a black mini skirt; then I added a black and orange box purse that a client had given me for Christmas. Very, very cute and sexy: I could dance all night with no restrictions. I told the girls I would be at their place around 10 p.m. To tell you the truth, I really didn't like going to their house because they had a next door neighbor name Claude who was always playing loudly with his rock band in his garage. The name of the band was called "Ass Juice." Yep, you're not mistaken; this is not a typo. That was really the name. Their music stunk about as bad as that name did, too. The few times I'd seen Claude he was always high on coke, and the most annoying person to be around even when he wasn't on it. He would bring up the most fucked up topics of conversation and you could never get a word in because he was talking ninety to nothing. I would get so aggravated that I would just shut up and try to ignore his dopey ass.

Tammy and Louise's parents bought that house for them, so all they had to do was pay the utilities. But one day they seriously thought about moving out when Claude, high on "toot," suddenly emerged at the doggy door and started squeezing and humping his way through it. He scared the living shit out of Louise, who was in the kitchen at the time it happened. She was just getting ready to place some dough on to a sheet to bake cookies. With the reflex of a ninja, she threw a spatula at his noodle and began to repeatedly beat him with the cookie sheet until he slithered back out like the freakish ghoul he was. Tammy came running in to the kitchen when she heard Louise screaming right at the time Claude was making his spine-chilling exit!

When I arrived at their house, Claude's lights were on but no noise was coming from the garage. Great, hopefully we would get out before he showed up. The girls were all dressed and ready to go, so we headed out. It only took Tammy 20 minutes to find the place; she was incredible. Of course, the place was packed and we started scoping out the crowd to see if there was anyone we knew personally. Then, from out of nowhere, we heard this Darth Vader/James Earl Jones voice behind us saying: "Hi Louise…I didn't know that you were going to be here tonight." We all turned around and saw that it was that super creepy dude obsessed with Louise. Like I said before, everyone in our scene pretty much wore costumes out, some a little on the freaky or quirky side. But this guy actually wore a Darth Vader one. Of course, he called himself D.V., but Louise called him V.D. He always seemed to materialize in the most obscure places. This wasn't even his type of gig. He normally preferred those Top 40 clubs; in fact, that's where he accosted Louise in the first place. Louise then replied to V.D, "Of course you wouldn't know I was going to be here, because we don't talk!" He started laughing and breathing in that bizarre voice. Wow, was he a loony toon or what? "Are you girls on the list?" he asked. "Well…actually no," I said. "I was hoping I would see my friend Dane but couldn't spot him anywhere." "Well, tonight is your lucky night. My baby brother is the main headliner tonight, so I can get you 'foxy ladies' in. But if I do, I have only one request for Louise." *Did he just say "foxy ladies?"* Tammy and I started laughing, as Louise started shaking her head and spoke up, "Fuck no! There will be no fuckin' request granted from this one!" "Oh, come on girl, he's not asking you to suck his dick or anything, or you better not be requesting that V.D." Tammy said. "No, no, all you have to do is let me dance with you for at least three songs and then I will go my merry way happy and content." *God, this mother-fucker was creepy.* "Come on girl, it's only three songs!" I said. "Yeah, but those house music songs last ten minutes a piece," Louise replied. "Okay, Okay, this is going to be so fucked up," Louise shouted as we walked up front through the massive line of people near the front door.

Of course, the music was pumping and V.D. ran and got us some plastic cup vodka and orange juice, though I knew not even to go there with that. I had actually brought some crissy with me, so I knew if I did just a little of that, and not drink that rot gut swill, I would be terrific. I heard Tammy laughing, so I turned around in her direction to see V.D. swinging that cape around Louise. She was so fuckin' pissed. My sides were starting to ache from the deep belly laughing I was experiencing from that visual. I had a habit of either dancing around my purse or sometimes (and I know this sounds stupid) I would actually place it in a dark corner of a club and just kind of keep my eye out for it, never venturing out to far from it.

Well, later on that night, after Louise finally broke free of her captor, I noticed three girls rummaging around in a black box. Fuck, that was my black box! I ran over and yelled as loud as I can: WHAT ARE YOU HOOKERS DOING!?! Then I raised my right hand back as far as I could and did a Three Stooges slap across Lanky, Swanky and Sleezy's faces! They were so fuckin' fried from their party favors — with their eyes bugging out of their heads — that they couldn't even react to what I just dished out to them. I grabbed my purse from their nasty little mitts and went back and found the girls.

We practically spent the whole night dodging V.D. Yep, he didn't keep his promise. He remained a dark force in our path the whole night. But one positive thing did happen for Tammy: V.D.'s baby bro took a liking to her and Louise was steaming mad over that hook up. All the way home, Louise said we owed her big time! Tammy chimed in, "Maybe you should have given him a chance. Who knows, he could have had something amazing underneath that cape!" We all made gagging sounds to that vile image! Then it hit me, all of a sudden, like a baseball bat! Where the hell was Robert? With all of the commotion, we didn't realize that he had never shown up!

When I returned home that night, I ran over to my machine to see if Robert had left a message. Nothing! "Wow, this was not like him at all," I thought. I called his house, but his answering machine picked up right away. I left a message for him to call me as soon as he got in, just a little concerned that he hadn't shown up that night. It was 4 a.m. on Sunday, so he probably had his ringer turned off. I didn't think about how late it was. I finally dozed off around 5 a.m. and woke up at 10 a.m. I went to the machine again, and there was absolutely nothing! Where the hell was he, anyway? I called and left another message, by this time really not knowing what to think. *Had he been murdered, gotten really wasted, and flown off a bridge?* My mind was racing out of control. *Get a hold of yourself. He is a grown man. Everything is okay, maybe he met someone? Naaaah, that couldn't be it at all, because he's too fuckin' picky.* This kind of reminded me of some of the few occasions in which I would go out with Kevin and Michael, before they broke up, and we would meet some of their friends out. We would all be having a good time, and then the clock would strike 1 a.m. Then it was like every single male, or the ones that played like they were single, started out on the prowl. You could cut the testosterone with a chainsaw. And all of the girlfriends, fag hags, or whatever your title was, stood there holding their purses, and drinks, in a corner watching the roping steer rodeo. I know I'm exaggerating a little, but we girls all know that we have a special place in a gay man's heart; though there are those times when you have no place in their world. Robert was pretty much on the gay/straight fence, but we both knew he leaned more toward batting for the other team. It's like deep down I really knew that Robert had actually met someone that night and "everything between us had instantly changed."

Monday rolled around. Alert, Alert, homosexual missing in the mid-cities area, I repeat!!! Ah fuck it, I'm not calling anymore like a worried mother hen. I had shit to do that day. Plus, I had to meet Bobby at the gym later that afternoon. I did some light housework, and accomplished a few errands, before meeting Bobby promptly at 5:30. He was already on the treadmill when I arrived. Everything went pretty smooth with us working out together; it was like the other night never happened. We went to grab some pasta, and a glass of wine, afterwards. While we were waiting for our meal, Bobby actually brought up the touchy topic. "You know," he said, "about the other night, I think I kind of made the moves on you too soon. And I want to apologize for that." *What was I hearing?* He was actually sorry. *Man, now I really feel like a piece of shit for what I was thinking. Okay, Okay,* I thought, *choose your words carefully; the guy is putting it all out there!* "Bobby, don't put the blame all on yourself. Hey, I was participating too. I wasn't kissing your couch back." We both started laughing and that totally broke the weird vibe that started to hover over us. He went on to say, "Let's just see how this goes and let it take its course without trying to make something happen." "Agreed!" I said. Whew! All of a sudden, I could hear that song by that rock band Queen; ♫ Another One Bites The Dust, Another One Bites The Dust ♫

Chapter 20: From Gluttony to Transmology

I came to work on Tuesday and went to the front desk to look at Robert's schedule for that day, noticing he was marked out till 1 p.m. Yep, he had met someone for sure, as I knew he wouldn't move his schedule around for his mama. At 12:30, Robert tip-toed in looking like the "Cheshire Cat." I was blow-drying my client at the time and I just let the "high beams" from my eyes follow him to his station. A couple of hours later, I came out of the restroom and noticed him standing by the door. "Hey, do you have time to talk right now?" he asked. "Yep, my next one is in twenty minutes," I said. I followed him down the hall to one of the manicuring rooms that happened to be empty at the moment. "I met a guy Saturday night and we spent the whole weekend together, and even yesterday," he said. "Yeah, after I never heard back from you, I pretty much knew that had happened. What's his name?" I asked. "His name is David, and I really want you to meet him soon." "What date is the wedding?" I asked. "Ha, ha," he replied. "You will like him and I know he will like you. He is funny and loves art and shopping. We have so much in common," he added. As I stood there listening to Robert, going on and on about this guy, I had to really get myself centered to actually start feeling happy for him. I guess I was a little perturbed at the fact that the motherfucker never called me back that time to let me know he was okay. But love is bliss, right!?! *Or is it blindness?* "How about it if we all go out to dinner this Friday night?" Robert requested. "Okay, that will be fun," I said, as I tried to muster up a fake ass smile. I kind of went through the rest of my day in a funk, not hearing a damn thing any of my clients were bitching or talking about. All I could ponder was Robert and David sitting in a tree…

Robert suggested that we meet at a little French Bistro near the downtown area, so I put on my faithful little black dress, pulled my hair up in a 1960's pony-tail: "Oui, Oui!" Reservations were set for 8 p.m. *Hmmm, I know what this means. After we have dinner, we will all be going our separate ways. I won't be able to tag along afterwards to the gayborhood.*

I arrived about ten minutes early and was seated at the bar, so I could spot them head on as they entered. I wanted to be the first to get a gander at him before he could get to me. When they arrived on time, I hopped down from the barstool to greet them. I ran over to give Robert a hug and…*ohhh, did I just see a flicker of dislike in David's eye? Yep, I sure as fuck did!* I could already tell this was going to be fun. *Where the hell did I put my sword?*

The waiter came over to take our drink orders. I wanted a Vodka martini, but David interrupted, and started ordering a bottle of wine for us. Ok, Ok, I will go with that. I can see that "she" likes to run shit! I then asked David what he did for a living; and he told me that he worked as an art dealer downtown. Well, that's cute, I thought. "That's wonderful," I said, "You must really enjoy it?" "Yes," he replied, "I get to work and hangout with all the right people." What the fuck does he mean by that, "all the right people?" I looked over at Robert and he was sitting there looking like a geisha girl: so prim and proper. *Why the hell was he sitting like that? He never sits like that!* Oh my, he has already taken on some of Poindexter's personality; how the fuck can you take that on so quickly?

Throughout the meal, every time I would make a comment about a particular subject, "Ole Monkey Balls" had to one up it. I wanted to slap the gay out of him!! I have been replaced by a "Nellie Know It All!" At that moment, I knew that my friendship with Robert had been severed, and that his boyfriend was a major stuck-up dick. *Why was he with him? This guy wasn't even funny!* Wake up and smell the "boy butter!" I wanted to scream, but I sat there and used everything I had to not spit venom across the table. Okay, just one more thought.... Bitch!!!! Now I feel better.

When we finished our meal, Robert said they were going to go to that piano bar on the strip. "Great," I said, "it's a very nice romantic place." And they both gushed at each other like two parakeets in love. *God, was I jealous? Yes, I think I was. Get a hold of yourself, girl,* I thought. This was not a time to think about myself (well, it was, and it wasn't). It's not all about me, me, me. I was really experiencing for the first time ever to be truly supportive of a friend — even when that meant maybe not ever having what you had before ever again.

Things were definitely different now. I only saw Robert at work now. Those two were joined to the hip day and night. Bobby and I were seeing less of each other, both knowing that it was going to fizzle out after the first tongue bath incident. And, of course, the whole gang was starting to disperse into different fragments. Tammy was in a hot and steamy relationship with V.D.'s brother. Donny and Jared had finally moved in together and were renting a place way across town. Even Michelle had finally met someone and HER NAME WAS MARY!!! That explains all of the very bad encounters and decisions she made when it came to the opposite sex. So guess who was♪ left to their own devices♪? Me and Louise!

After work on Saturdays, Louise and I started having wine at a local hotel bar. A lot of the people who worked around that area would frequent the place, too. The hotel bar didn't have restrooms, so we would have to walk down a long corridor passing wedding receptions, and parties, that were being held in the different banquet halls. After a few months, Louise and I got really tired of that bar food, as most of the choices on the menu were pretty fattening. So we were really limited on what we would order. One day, we were sitting there pondering whether to leave and go to a real restaurant or…"Are you thinking what I'm thinking?" Louise asked. "I think I know what you're thinking," I answered, "and let's do it, because I'm starving." We crept down the hallway and came upon a banquet hall that was packed. "Okay" I said, "we gotta make sure that it's a buffet, and not reserved tables, or we are going to be so fuckin' embarrassed to be kicked out of this place."

We scanned the room like two detectives. *Yes! A magnificent buffet with everything you could imagine and much, much more.* We were dressed nice because of work; so that's why we could get away with sneaking in, in the first place. We grabbed one plate each and headed straight towards the meat carver, then the cheese…*Oh yeah, and the rolls: gotta have some rolls.* "Why didn't we think of this sooner?" we both whispered. There was free food and booze, we didn't know a fuckin' person there, and they are all so looped they were not even paying attention anyway. As far as I had known, I'd never heard of anyone who crashed receptions until a movie came out much later about two guys crashing weddings. So we were definitely way ahead of our time.

We didn't go to pick up men. As sex-starved as she was, Louise only wanted food and drink. We continued on with our excursions every other Saturday, trying not to be too obvious to the staff that worked the banquets at the hotel. We got so good at it that we knew which ones to crash and which ones to avoid like the plague.

Rule #1 for Reception crashing: never crash a wedding from India; you will be spotted as soon as you hit the threshold. Rule #2: Never crash an African American wedding; the Sistas will personally escort you out, because the brothers will be on you like gravy on grits! There has to always be a big mix of ethnic backgrounds for happy grazing to be able to take place. We kept this deal up for three full months, all summer long. I had to work out like a fiend to keep the weight down! Our eyes feasted on a beautiful reception with a big band playing and a singer that sounded like Billy Holiday. Whoa, we had to take that one down! Louise and I made the usual rounds: smiling and nodding, making sure we didn't know a soul there. We grabbed the big dinner plates and began to pile on huge amounts of appetizers. Suddenly, we felt a hand on both our shoulders and a man's voice whispered to us: "Hi girls....you don't know a damn person here, do you?" Louise had about half a ham shoved in her face and started choking. I kept looking down at my food pile, praying to the Lord in heaven that this "rat bastard" would disappear into a hole in the floor beneath him. Louise regained her composure and saw that it was one of her clients. He then gave us a shit-eating grin, winked and said: "Don't worry, I won't say a word." He then reached down to grab a glass of champagne and walked off. After we were finally caught, it totally took the thrill out of it all. *Shit, that is what made it so much fun in the first place! Now, what were we going to do?* "Eat and drink up girl," I said. "This is our last rodeo!"

Louise and I were now kind of in limbo after our cover was blown a few weeks back. So, on one Wednesday evening, we decided to hang out at her place and watch a movie on TV. I brought the wine and she furnished the snacks. I also brought Val with me, which seemed to make Louise a little annoyed. "Why did you bring that penguin tonight?" she whined. "Because he feels good to hold and he's my son," I replied. "That's fuckin' weird; it's material that is stuffed with more material. It is not real!" she quipped. "Where is your compassion for the stuffed animal kingdom," I asked, "Are you that heartless?" She knew to just shut the hell up and find a movie. We came across Yentl, with Barbara Streisand. I'd rather slowly pour acid into my own eyes than watch a musical! I can't stand it when, just as you're getting into the movie, they decide to break out with a song. Drives me up the fuckin' wall. I can never finish watching those things. *Those horrible, hokey show tunes, yuck!* But Louise was head over heels for musicals, even watching the movie "Grease" every week. So since I brought Val with me, I knew this was a major compromise. Actually, the movie was pretty good: a woman posing as a boy to have a different life for herself. Interesting…do I detect a new idea approaching?...indeed, I do…!

After the movie was over, I followed Louise into the kitchen and asked her, "What is the rat bastard's name who caught us at that wedding reception?" "His name is Lawrence, why?" She asked. "Because he looks like he's about our size and I have an idea." "Our size for what?" she hesitantly asked. "I was thinking, maybe you could inquire about us borrowing a couple of his suits, so we can cross-dress and experience how the other half lives." "Did Kevin put your weaves in too tight this time, girl?! That is crazy, how are we going to get away with that?" "Well, I think it would be easy. First

202

thing is to wear no makeup and slick our hair back into tight ponytails. I'm going to have to figure out how to do mine legit so I won't resemble Rick James; but I guess I could go by his first name. And we both have husky deeper voices, especially after talking non-stop all day on a Saturday." By this time, Louise was really cracking up! I continued, "Oh, and you are going to have to bind those vivacious ta-ta's down, so you won't look like a man going through the change." "This is actually going to be fun!" Louise screamed. "Lawrence comes in this Friday, so I will give him a call on Thursday so he will bring the suits with him. He will really enjoy this, because he's kind of one of those freaky dudes. And I know he's going to want a picture of us," she said. "That's okay," I replied, "we'll give him a picture all right!"

Lawrence brought in two nice designer suits to Louise on Friday. Throughout his haircut, he couldn't stop laughing and talking about what we were going to do. He kept giving me the nasty look every time I walked by, creepster! Louise and I decided to head out on the town Saturday night, to a different hotel bar across town, so as to hopefully not be spotted. Getting ready for the evening was a little more difficult than we anticipated. Louise's boobies were bigger than I realized! I thought, for a moment, that I was going to have to use industrial duct tape, but eventually we got everything under control. "Oh shit, maybe we should have gotten some fake mustaches!" Louise said. "No girl, we don't want to look like two "Mammoni's" straight off the boat from Sicily." For those of you wondering what a Mammoni is: "Mammoni," in Italian, means mama's boy. It is just as unflattering there (though they take less offense) as it is here in the US. "More than half of the single Italian men in Italy still live at home," I said. "Oh, okay," she replied. We stumbled onto a beautiful older quaint hotel in an area of town where there was a lot of old money. "This was going to be even better," I told her, as the valet came out to take the car. "Why?" she asked. "Because, most likely, we're going to meet a lot of very rich women there. Which means: they will be fighting over each other to buy our drinks!" "Oohhh, great," Louise exclaimed. As we walked into the lobby, Louise was in front of me; and I saw, for a split second, that she needed to concentrate on her walk. I skipped up to her and grabbed her arm, saying: "Hey, remember, you are a man now, so quit walking like a fag!" "Oh shit, I forgot," she said! We both started giggling uncontrollably after that statement. "Dammit, I can't stop laughing," I said. "Me neither," she replied. "Okay, okay, let's take a deep breath and get a hold of ourselves," I added. We straightened up, cleared our throats, and walked into the bar. *Why, it was sooo gorgeous: the lamps, rugs, and chandeliers. Oh crap, quit looking at the décor,* I thought. Man, this was harder than I realized, acting like a straight guy. Maybe we should have done the gay guy thing instead; it would have been a hell of a lot easier! We sauntered on up to the bar, as Louise was trying so hard to control her walk that she looked like a gimp! We sat down quickly and the bartender came over and asked, "What can I get you guys?" Oh my God! Louise and I both looked at each other, thinking the same thing: *he thinks we are guys!* Holy shit and shine ola! I lowered my voice a tad and spoke up, "I will have a vodka martini, shaken not stirred." Louise started laughing hysterically; so I reached down underneath the bar and squeezed her left thigh super hard, which made her yelp like a puppy. "I will have the same," she responded. As the bartender walked away to make the drinks, we leaned in together and whispered to each other, "Can you believe that this is working?" When noticing some older gentlemen smoking cigars, I said to Louise, "We need to get some of those to make it really convincing."

So I walked back into the lobby, found the gift shop, and purchased the biggest cigars they had. When I got back to the bar, I noticed that Louise was surrounded by two women. *Shit, that didn't take long at all.* I slowly walked to the bar when, suddenly, Louise spoke up, "Hey ladies, this is my friend Rick." I almost lost it right there, because I immediately had an image of Rick James singing that song "Mary Jane" on the show Solid Gold! "Hi girls," I said, "nice to meet you." I extended my hand out to them. "Wow, your hand is so soft!" one of them charmingly remarked. "Well," I answered, "I'm a firm believer that a man should take care of himself. There is no crime for a man to lotion up his hands and elbows." I looked at Louise and she was trying her damnedest not to spew her martini all over everyone, as she wanted to laugh so hard. One woman was a red-head and the other a brunette: both probably in their mid- forties. The red-head's name was Susan; and Barbs was the brunette. They were buyers for furniture showrooms and were only in town for market through the following afternoon. "So, are you guys staying at the hotel?" Susan inquired. "No, no," we both answered, "we had a client meeting nearby and decided to come by and have a drink." "Ohh, really!" Barbs got more interested, asking, "What do you guy's do?" *Oh shit, Louise and I never got around to discussing that part.* We couldn't say that we were hairdressers, because then they would want to talk about their hair all fuckin' night. Not in the mood, Mary!!! "Uhhh...Uh...,we are in the Bidet business," I said. At that moment, both women looked at each other. I could tell they didn't know how to respond to that one. Louise suddenly ran out of the bar because she couldn't hold back the laughter in longer. "Yes," I continued... "we specialize in the most elaborate bidet's ever manufactured." "Oh, that's very interesting..." they said. "Well, on that note, can we buy you guy's your next drink?" Barbs asked. "Well, that is so kind of you," I said. By that time, Louise had come back in. "Hey Vic," I said, "the ladies want to buy our next round!" So we all sat and laughed and joked, while Louise kept choking on her cigar. Finally, after about two hours, I noticed that Susan and Barb were getting sloshed; and Susan started getting touchy feely…so was Barb. "Would you guys like to come back to our room for a night cap?" "No!" Louise suddenly screamed! "Uh, I meant 'thanks girls' but we have to get up really early tomorrow morning. I want to thank you lovely ladies for a magnificent evening! Bye, Bye, now!" We ran out of there like cheetas after a gazelle! The valet guy bolted to get the car. I could not stand my hair pulled back in that Slick Rick pony-tail any longer, so I took it down and shook my hair out. Louise did the same to hers. After the valet guy pulled up and got out of the car, the expression on his face made our whole night. He looked like he'd been scared out of a bush when he handed the keys to Louise. I could then hear in the distance Barbara Streisand belting out ♫ The Way He Makes Me Feel….♫

  The following week, Tammy and Louise started bringing up the subject of getting their belly-buttons pierced. I personally didn't know what to think about that. I'd only seen a couple of girls that had it done, and it did look pretty cool, but I tried not to visualize how big that needle would have to be to go through that much skin, yikes! The girls wanted to get it done in the afternoon before going to a pool party we had all been invited to. The guy having the party name was Trenton. Trenton and I met at the club. I'd seen him there before on several occasions. But, on this particular night, I noticed that he was wearing the exact type of harness I was wearing. That pretty much broke the ice. After I approached him, and introduced myself, he said that he already knew my name.

We grabbed our drinks, went to the uni-sex lounge restrooms, and talked for almost an hour. Trenton was very attractive, with beautiful brown hair and amazing blue eyes; and, of course, he was gay. Being one of the wildest, funniest mother-fuckers on the planet, he became one of my best friends for life. After work, I decided to go with them, so I said, "Hey, I will drive you guys there." "Wow, that's cool," Tammy replied. "No problem," I said. One thing I forgot to mention about the girls was the fact that they loved them some WEED! I don't mean just a hit every once in a while; they could smoke that shit all day. I've seen guys who could smoke like that — Donny being a prime example — but never girls.

So, as we headed out to the Pierce Factory, I had barely pulled out of the parking lot when Tammy began lighting up a joint. Then, all of a sudden, I did something that I'd never done before, and haven't since while driving a vehicle. "Let me have a little of that," I stated. "What!" they exclaimed, in unison. "You hate po!" "Well, I'm only going to take one, or two, hits." I discovered that was way too many for me. As I headed down the freeway, all of a sudden I started getting a tingly sensation in my hands. *Hmmm…that's not a good feeling, when you're gripping a steering wheel.* The radio was blaring Cindy Lauper's "Girls Just Wanna Have Fun" and the music was soo fuckin' loud! All of a sudden, the freeway disappeared; all I saw was big, white fluffy clouds…*Oh shit! Is that Mother Teresa holding a pink poodle walking in a field of ganja? Shit, shit, shit, I'm way too fuckin' high. What the hell is in that stuff?* I couldn't tell the girls that I had lost all control, so I calmly asked them: "Hey, can you guys refresh my memory on where that place is located again? You know how I am with directions." "Yeah, that's for sure," Tammy said. Tammy started giving me directions, when suddenly I experienced a hallucination of Mother Teresa on a cloud; and then Mother Teresa running off with the poodle. Man, that was some crazy shit! I felt like the car was only going 20 miles per hour. When I looked down at the speedometer, I realized that I was going the speed limit. I HATE WEED!!! When I finally got us to our destination, I reached up to wipe away the beads of sweat from my brow, so the girls wouldn't see how whacked out I was.

We walked into the piercing place, which was empty. We were the only customers inside. Being a Saturday afternoon, for most people it seemed that going to this shop was not high on their priority list. That New wave post punk band "The The" was screaming from the speakers positioned up in the corner of the ceilings. Menacing gargoyle statues stared down at us like they were ready for feasting. The guy that owned the place name was Stanley. He had dated one of Tammy's girlfriends. Stanley bounced out to the store front to greet us. "Heyyyyy, glad you could make it," he drawled. "So, are all three of you getting done today?" he asked. "Just me, and Louise," Tammy replied. "Ok, ok, well come over here and choose which rings you want first." *Wow, there were things in that case that I never had a clue you could use for piercings.* Ouch! I could tell the girls were getting a little bit nervous, so I started looking, assisting them with choosing.

My eyes suddenly landed on a simple silver ring with an off black ball arranged in the center of it. "Oh, this one is very nice," I said. "Oh yeah," Stanley agreed, "this one is our basic ring, but the most popular one." "Ok, I will go first, then!" I told him. "What? You're going to do it, too?" the girls gasped. "Yep, I can tell both of you are shitting bricks, so I will test the waters first." *Man, this weed made me feel invincible; empowered all of a sudden, or just plain dumb!*

I walked over to Stanley's examining table and stared straight up at Mr. Gargoyle. Then, Stanley, with his gentle bedside manner, said: "Wow, it's kinda hard to believe I've made a living poking holes in people." Then, after sanitizing my belly and the rhino needle, ZOW WEE! I suddenly felt warmth that permeated from my belly to my ears. Oh my goodness! I felt like I was on fire. And then it was over. *Hey, I didn't even scream, or cry, probably because I went comatose for three seconds.* "You did great!" Stanley said. "Ok, come on down. Who's going to be the next in line?" Tammy slowly walked over to the table and, looking at me, she said, "Wow, you didn't even flinch; it's not that bad, huh?" Then, she screamed like she was being tortured. I saw Louise walk back into the shop. I think she had gone out to smoke a little more just to be able to cope. When it was Louise's turn, she was so stoned that it looked like he was piercing a blow up doll; totally no response. But we looked hot, hot, hot! "So, what do you girls have planned after this?" Stanley asked. "Oh, we're going to a pool party," I casually answered. "Well, you bitches better not dare get in that pool — with all that bacteria and piss and shit floating around. You have to keep that area cleaned at all times, I'm giving you all a bottle of this cleaning solution to ward off infection." *Well, that's fine,* I thought. *What chick gets in a pool at a pool party, anyway, huh?*

Chapter 21: Pity Party for Two

When we arrived at the party around six p.m., it was packed. This was the first time I'd been to Trenton's house and it was very nice. We already had our swimsuits on under our shorts, and we wore our bikini tops, because we had been prepared for the piercing place and the party! As we approached the other partiers, everyone started staring. *What the hell are they looking at?* I thought. As I whispered this thought to the girls, Tammy promptly replied, "Well, we are the only girls wearing thong bikini's and stiletto high heels to a party." "Oh yeah," I said, "that totally explains everyone stopping in their tracks, and the fact that our bellies were pierced was a major factor too." As Trenton saw us approaching, he screamed from his upstairs balcony, "Hey girls, come up here!" We waded through the wave of onlookers and, as we passed, several other girls gave us the "go to hell -jealous- dagger stare." Love it!!! With house music blaring through the whole house, I knew that Trenton would only have the best music playing. "Hey," he said, "I want you to meet my aunt, and she is "X'ing" her tits off right now. Do you want to do some?" Of course, Tammy and Louise were salivating at the idea. I think I loathed ecstasy almost as much as weed. I really only liked crissy because I could control it much better. The pill form of X was something I took only a couple of times and all I wanted to do was throw up violently with my arms flailing behind me: fuckin' horrible. So I declined on that, but I asked him, "Do you have any crissy?" Of course he did. Trenton's aunt was very sweet she was much older than we were, probably around early 50's, wow she's a trooper and everything, but I'm not going to be "X'ing" my tit's off when I'm elderly, sorry! Trenton kept going on and on about how good we looked: "You bitches look hot; everybody is freaking the fuck out!"

Then we heard that voice we only hear in random off the wall places: "Hey, foxy ladies…" Oh my God, we all turned around and V.D and Baby B. were standing right behind us. "Tammy, you told this mother-fucker where we were going tonight! Dammit, all you can think about is yourself!" Louise was getting very upset, so I gently grabbed her by the arm and said, "Hey girl, I know what she just pulled was pretty shitty. But let's not cause a big scene, huh? Trenton is being very cool and sharing his party favors. Hey, tell you what: I will hang out with you and V.D and… who knows? Let's get to know him a little. And you did just pop the love drug, so calm the fuck down and enjoy yourself," I added. That seemed to help a lot: my saying that I wouldn't leave her with "nut boy."

Trenton came over and asked if everything was all right? "Yes, everything is fine, uhhh, I want to introduce you to uh…V.D., what is your real name anyway?" "My name is Hamlet…" he said. "What?" we all spoke in surprise. "Yes, it's Hamlet," he answered. Hamlet wasn't wearing his Darth Vader mask, but he had a masquerade ball mask on tonight. Hamlet? Trenton asked, "Why don't you take off that mask, honey? It's fuckin' weird." And what do you know he took it off, and I heard Louise gasped next to me. Uhhh… Hamlet was fuckin' hot! He had these amazing ice blue eyes like Paul Newman.

Whoa the brakes, cowgirl! Next thing we all knew, Louise had her arm hooked into Hamlet's and she was steering him clear away from us. "Let's dance!" Trenton yelled. Then we all turned his living-room into a dance floor and partied til the break of dawn.

Trenton's party was so much fun! We headed home around twelve midnight. I dropped the girls off at their house and then drove to my apartment. I was still pretty wide awake because of the speed, so I grabbed a glass of wine and watched TV before finally dozing off on the couch. I needed to break this nasty habit of falling asleep in my clothes!

I woke up a 5 a.m., stumbled to my bathroom and got myself ready for bed. I slept till 1 p.m. the next day, which was Sunday. *Wow, I really felt like a loser.* Do you remember those days of horrendous guilt when waking up the next morning after partying and feeling like you were the princess of loserville: that uncanny feeling that you were going nowhere fast? Yes, the coming down stage from crissy was the worst ever. ♫ Crissy crack corn and I don't care, crissy crack corn and I don't care♫ I loved the way it made me feel during the experience; but, afterwards, you just wanted to fling yourself into traffic.

I rolled over in bed and grabbed Val, hoping that he would at least give me some words of encouragement; but he was still asleep — and snoring, on top of that — which was pissing me off! Then, the phone started ringing. *Ughhh... I fuckin' ache all over, crissy kicked my ass!* "Hello?" "Hey girl, I have a surprise for us!" It was Louise. "What, have you and Hamlet planned your engagement party already?" "No, sour puss, hey maybe you shouldn't do that crissy stuff. You maybe need to switch over to ex or weed; that way, you won't be so grouchy the next day." "Oh, whatever!" I said, "what's this surprise, anyway?" "Well...," she went on to say, "my parents have a condo in South Padre island, and they were supposed to go for four days, but Daddy has to go on a business trip that week. So he called me to see if I wanted to go and take a friend with me." "Super cool," I said. *This is exactly what I needed,* I thought. *I need to get away from the partying a little, and get some R&R.* "Count me in!" I said. "Okay, cool," she said. "I will give you more details and we can go over our schedules with Michelle on Tuesday." "Okay, great, talk to you later," I said. *Wow, this was exactly what I needed: a sabbatical that was totally paid for!* Okay, call me stupid, but I didn't think to check on the status of the place, and what might have been taking place before we arrived. I knew I needed to talk to Kevin about certain feelings I was having. So I called him that afternoon to see if he would meet me for lunch. We decided to meet in the gayborhood at our favorite hamburger joint.

    Kevin greeted me with a big huge and then he asked, "What's going on with you Miss Thing, everything going alright?" I then began to spill my guts out about how I felt like I was spiraling out of control, like that character from "Breakfast at Tiffany's": Holly Golightly. "Yes, work was going great," I said. "I'm steadily busy all of the time. But I feel like I'm not accomplishing anything, just working, partying and shopping. Like there is no substance in my life!" "Girl, did you do speed this weekend?" Kevin asked. "Yeah, why?" I asked, nonchalantly. "You're just talking out of your ass right now," he said. "You are doing great. You have single-handedly built, and maintained, an amazing clientele base in such a short period of time and at such a young age. You are way ahead of the game, so quit beating yourself up and start being thankful for what you have!" Zing! Kevin really knew how to hit it home with me! All of a sudden, it was like I totally snapped out of my pity-party for one attitude. *So just try to stop being Miss Control Freak and enjoy every moment that you have.* Boy, I was really thankful for that revelation at just the right moment! I then told Kevin about the trip to South Padre, and he said, "Good, go have a great time and stop worrying about stupid shit!" As our food finally arrived, we just sat back and enjoyed that beautiful Sunday afternoon.

The day of our trip finally arrived, and guess what: This time I wasn't going to take Val along with us. I knew that I would really be pushing the envelope of Louise's patience if I did. I really never understood why just the very presence of Val in a room would drive my friend up the wall!

After we made it to our destination, we took a cab to the condo. Louise told me as we were on our way there, "You're really going to like the way my Mom decorated the place. It has a very 'Andy Warhol' eclectic theme to it," she said. "Cool, totally right up my alley," I said.

The cabby parked right in front of the condominium complex. After he helped us with our bags, we paid him and he took off without saying a word. Wow, what a great welcome that was! This place was beachfront property. It was fabulous; I loved it! We unpacked our things and then decided to go grab something to eat. After that, we would come back and take a disco nap.

We walked down the strip and stumbled upon a little seafood place, packed to the gills! As we approached the front entrance, there were tons of people milling around, obviously waiting to be seated. Every few minutes, or so, one could hear the hostess screaming on the intercom the names of the next famished patrons. This brought to memory a joke Jade had told me that he played on a restaurant hostess — and the entire restaurant — one night when going out to dinner with a friend. So I whispered to Louise my idea and she responded with, "No way, are you really going to do that?" "Oh yes, I see this as an opportunity of a lifetime; plus, no one knows us here!" As we approached the hostess station, I noticed that the girl taking down names was very young, so I knew this would go over like butter on a hot roll. She would definitely not catch on at all. She asked for a name and I then replied: "Last name Pity." "Pity," she said. "Yes, P-i-t-y, Pity. "Okay, and how many are in your party?" she asked. "Just two," I said. "Okay, it will probably only be about a ten minute wait, since you don't have a big party." All right, that's perfect," I said. Louise turned beet red trying to conceal her laughter while I just stood there looking around at the crowd so I wouldn't lose it myself. Then the moment finally arrived, "PITY PARTY OF TWO, YOUR TABLE IS READY... PITY PARTY OF TWO: YOUR TABLE IS READY!!!" While everyone in the restaurant started screaming with laughter, I looked over at the bar and witnessed a man spewing beer from his mouth all over his wife's face!" The kitchen staff ran out — with their utensils in hand — roaring with laughter. The bartender then came over to us and said, "Your first round is going to be on me; that was fuckin' hilarious!" Louise leaned over to me and said, "What a great way to start our vacation!" I totally agreed...

After Louise and I were finished with dinner, we were both extremely ready for a nap. This was a two-bedroom condo, so I went to one room, and Louise went to the other. As I was walking off, I told her I would set my travel alarm for an hour from then, which would be 9:30 p.m.: just enough time to take our time getting ready, but not be out too early.

We hit the strip at 10:15 sharp, and as we strolled along the strip, we heard a band playing a few yards ahead. "Let's stop by that place," I said. "And if it's lame, I'm sure we can ask someone there what else is happening down here." Louise readily agreed. The place kind of resembled a juke joint somewhere in New Orleans. It was a misshapened shack with party lights strung haphazardly all around. Raggedy picnic tables sat to the left of a worn-out wooden deck of a dance floor; and there were people bumping, gyrating and grinding to this incredibly horrendous music coming from the stage. All of a sudden, a song I'd heard on the radio before, that still haunts my dreams till this very day, started playing: ♫Clean shirt, new shoes, And I don't know where I am goin' to. Silk suit, black tie... I don't need a reason why♫

Chapter 22: Hi Fi Mama

Oh no! I thought, *is that fuckin' ZZ Top on the stage? Shit, what the hell? I can't dance to this crap* (No offense, ZZ). Louise and I saw a couple sitting near where we were gawking. I leaned over and asked if there was any other place besides where they would play club dance music. "Well," she said, "there is a place down the street that does, but only on Saturday nights. Tonight is western night." Louise went on, "Well, let's a least get a drink, and after a few, we won't mind it as much. I actually like it." *I would have to drink moonshine to be able to block this shit out!* I thought.

We went to the bar and I ordered a Cranberry Absolute Vodka, while Louise ordered a screwdriver. Man, those people were really getting after it on that dance floor. While watching them, I felt like I was observing some unknown tribe in New Guinea. I slammed the first drink down and then ordered a double for the second round.

By the third drink, the music was actually sounding pretty tolerable. As psychotic thoughts rolled around in my brain, I saw a man standing on the other side of the dance floor looking right at me. He smiled, and then I smiled back, and he motioned that he was going to come over to where we were. Then I watched him roll away...he just rolled away from where he was standing. Oh my God, did someone put LSD into my drink?

When he finally approached us, I looked down and saw that he had a pair of rollerblades in his hands. Whew, I was getting ready to freak the fuck out for a minute! "How are you girls doing tonight," he asked? "We're doing great," we chimed in unison. "My name is Christopher, would you like to dance? I hope you don't mind if I dance barefooted; I didn't think I would meet anyone tonight, so I didn't bring shoes to change into." "That's okay," I said, as I had another visual of a manic tribe dancing around a bond fire. I leaned over to Louise — before following Christopher to the dance floor — and whispered to her: "You tell anyone I danced to ZZ Top on this trip, and I will kick your ass!" "Of course," she just burst out laughing in my face and continued to laugh the whole night at me. This went down in the history books: Miss Thing dancing to music that she wouldn't be caught dancing to if she were back home!

I finally finished cutting a rug to ZZ Top's Greatest Hits with Christopher. He and I proceeded to exit the dance floor when I spotted Louise talking to some young guys near the bar. *Good,* I thought, *she will be busy for a while.* Christopher led me to one of the tables near the dance floor and we sat down to take a break. "You're a great dancer," he said. "Thanks," I replied, "you ought to see me when I'm on my own turf!" I then asked him if he was there on vacation and he started to laugh. "No, I actually live here. I did come here on vacation with two college buddies almost ten years ago and I never left." "That is crazy," I replied, "how did that happen?" He then went on to tell me how he had gotten there from Montana. *Hell, that's even crazier,* I thought!

They all had come down to party for spring break. The women he met on the trip were practically throwing themselves at him: buying drinks, t-shirts, and anything that he wanted. They were even offering themselves. Each one that he met kept offering to extend his stay until — before he knew it — he had been there on an extended three-week vacation, totally paid for. I could see how that story could have been perfectly true, because he was very good-looking!

He then went on to say that three weeks had turned into a year. When his buddies had already left, he decided to just get a job and take one day at a time. "You see, I'd 'Gone Bamboo,'" he said. "Of course, on the off season months, I had to work, because it was slow," he added. "Wait, wait, what the hell does 'Gone Bamboo' mean?" I asked him. I learned that "Gone Bamboo" is a term to describe day trippers, travelers and "expats" who have decided not to return to their home and lives, but to go native in the tropical locale they were in. "That is fuckin' hilarious," I exclaimed. "I've never heard, or met, anyone who has done that. You are definitely the first!"

"Every once in a while," he went on to say, "an older woman, with her friends, would show up at the restaurant, where I was employed, and offer to take me off with her. But I always turned them down; I don't know why. I guess I was already a part-time gigolo, but didn't really want to be a full time male prostitute." We instantly started cracking up. "I'm a waiter at the fine dining seafood restaurant down the strip. You and your friend should come by for lunch, or dinner." "Hey, how about it if we come by for an early dinner, tomorrow?" I asked. "That would be fantastic!" he replied. "I will put you down for 6 p.m." "Ok, sounds like a plan," I said.

Louise then stumbled over with some young dude with liberty spikes; she said she was starving, and could we please go get a burger, or something? I waited for Mr. Liberty to say something, but he just looked dazed and confused. Christopher then suggested a place that had the best hotdogs ever, so we all followed him over. *Tomorrow night, they better be playing some funky house music or something; because if they don't, I will be forced to dance to the white trash top forty mixes just to burn off all the calories I'm consuming on this vacation!* I mused.

After we finished scarfing down the pig innards wrapped in dough, I knew it was time for us to get back to the condo. I suggested to Louise to tell "Mr. Give Me Liberty or Give Me Death Rocker" that she would see him the following night at the hangout down the strip.

Later I fell into a dreamless sleep and at around 2 a.m. was awakened by a seagull screeching seemingly as loud as it possibly could. *Shit, that's fuckin' crazy; it sounded like it was right outside the window.*

I got out of bed and peered out the bedroom window. Ugghhh, yeah, there it was just sitting there: screaming with the dirtiest head I've ever seen on a bird; hmmm, it kind of resembled Gary Busey. I pulled down the windowshade and crawled back into bed.

A few hours later, I heard a knock on the door and heard Louise asking, "Hey, are you awake?" "Yeah, this loud ass bird woke me up around 2:00 this morning," I replied. She came in running and plopped down on the bed. "So hey, let's lie out and get some sun for a little while and then maybe go do some shopping," she said. "Yes, that's exactly what I want to do for a few hours: lie down on a lounger and not move for a while." So we changed clothes, then stuffed our beach bags, and headed off.

The beach was pretty active with tons of younger boys, and girls, drunk off their asses at 11 a.m. I never liked being wasted during the day. It always felt like you might as well just put yourself on the waiting list at Betty Ford; because that was where your sorry ass was headed in a few months. It was great people watching for sure, and why do girls think that it's wise to show their tits on camera? Because one day one of your Dad's associates will be talking about this video he ordered late one night when the "Little Misses" was zonked out on pills, and gin; they'll shove it in the boardroom video player and "Bah Bam!" There is Daddy's little girl with her hooters in some other chick's mouth! *Uggghhh, never give a mother-fucker that kind of ammo!*

After Louise and I both got a little more color to our already perfect skin, we went back to the condo to shower, and change, in order to go on a little shopping spree. As we walked around, we noticed there weren't really a lot of shops to choose from. We had to keep reminding ourselves that this was a small seasonal town, not the big city.

All of a sudden, a couple came barreling past us on roller blades! "Let's rent some of those for a little while, so we can get a little workout," Louise said. "I don't know about that," I replied. "If we do, the only thing you can have to drink is a non-alcoholic beverage." "Oh, all right," she snapped back. "When will you ever forget about that incident?" she asked. The incident "Little Miss Minnelli" was referring to was the one in which the whole gang decided to purchase roller blades. I don't remember who had the brilliant idea of drinking wine coolers while skating.

We would all skate around a particular area, where we could go have a drink, and do our laundry at the same time, if we wanted. Next door was a lounge bar with concrete décor; we would skate in there so Louise could flirt with one of the bartenders for free drinks. The manager of that establishment didn't really care for us too much.

One afternoon, Louise lost her momentum, and came crashing through the place, bulldozing one of the heavy metal tables over, knocking drinks and food everywhere. So the manager, with proper cause, of course, threw our asses out of there! "Okay," I said. "This will be the last time I mention it to you again, sorry."

We rollerbladed for almost two hours — which was so cool to do — especially after not being able to hit the gym. We then returned our blades, grabbed our belongings from the rental lockers, and got back to the condo around 5 p.m., just in time to get ready for our fine dining experience. I was actually a little excited to see Christopher. He was a pretty interesting dude; and, so far, probably the hottest man on the island!

Louise and I knew to really look our best that night for dinner. Christopher said it was fine dining, so we could look sexy, but "not look like were on the verge of dabbling in whorem," I suggested.

We arrived at the restaurant at 6 p.m. sharp, quickly informing the maître d that we had reservations. He started giving us the once over with his beady little eyes through his designer bi-focals. Then he grabbed two menus and said "Follow me." His fucked up hooknose was stuck so far in the air that I thought he was going to drown in his own snot any minute! *Okay girl, calm down! Don't let this ciditty prick provoke you to kick his ass and ruin the whole evening,* I thought. *Remember, we must choose our battles!*

Christopher emerged from the back of the restaurant, spotted us, and came over to the table smiling. "Hi girls," he said, "Wow, you guys look really hot tonight." "Why, thank you, Christopher," I said. Louise glanced over and looked at me funny. "What would you ladies like to start out with to drink?" he asked. "I would like a Cranberry Absolute, with a lime," I replied. "And I will have a screwdriver," Louise said. "Coming right up," he said, before trotting off.

"Man, he is looking way super cute tonight," I told Louise. "Yeah, he is kinda' fine, girl; he does have a great ass, for sure," she said. "Hey bitch, quit looking at my man's onion! Onion guar-an-teed!" We started cracking up over that!

The dimly lit restaurant was refined and elegant, with a much older crowd of patrons. I guess the spring-breakers didn't dare darken the doors of this establishment; they probably didn't even know it existed.

Christopher served us our drinks and then informed us of the specials for the evening. "I didn't hear a damn thing," Louise said. All I did was look into those dreamy eyes of his. Oh boy, I didn't realize he had stopped talking. They were both looking at me, waiting for me to respond. "Give us a minute to look over the menu, would you, hon?" "No problem, I will be back shortly," he said. "Hon!" Louise repeated, "What are 'you' guys — already involved, or something?"

I decided on shrimp cocktail and a chicken salad on a bed of lettuce. I did not want to eat a huge ass meal before we went out, because I was going to wear Thunder Pussy that night, and I had to look perfect! Louise ordered a steak. "Oh my God, girl, you're going to look like you are getting ready to deliver if you eat all that food." "I'm hungry girl, I don't give a shit. I don't know anybody here, anyway!" "All right, but when you have to suddenly take a shit while you're out on the dance floor, I won't even tell you that I told you so!"

We ordered our second drinks as I started to notice some of the customers were staring at us a little. When Christopher came over to check on us, I inquired about what was the deal with all the staring. He then started to grin. "They think that you guys are professional singers." *Well, thank God, I was beginning to get a little paranoid.*

Then a huge bearded man dressed in a three-piece suit came over to our table and introduced himself. His name was Mr. Phillips and he was the owner of the restaurant. "Anything you ladies need, just let me know!" *Now, that's what I'm talking about,* I thought. *This is service, fo sho!*

The food was truly amazing, and it seemed as if Christopher and Mr. Phillips were battling for our attention. They hovered over our table all night; no wonder the other customers thought that we were famous! After our meal, I asked Christopher about what time he would be getting off from work; and would he be able to meet us out later? To our disappointment, he said he would be working till close, and then had to stay to shut the place down. So that meant he wouldn't be done till 2 a.m. "But can we meet for breakfast tomorrow?" he asked. "Yeah, that's a great idea," I said. "So it's a date. Let's meet at that dive bar where we met the first night. They actually have a very good breakfast and brunch menu," he said. "Ok, I will meet you there at 11 a.m.," I said. "Okay," he replied, see you tomorrow."

Mr. Phillips then came over and asked, "Well, ladies, how was everything?" "It was magnificent," we replied. "Well," he said, "it's not everyday that I get to see such beautiful women in my restaurant. Your meal and drinks are on the house. Just promise me you will come back tomorrow night." Oh my God! Louise and I looked at each other, then knew we had to play it really cool, like this happened to us all of the time. "Why, thank you, Mr. Phillips," we both said. "Dan, call me Dan." "Okay…Dan. Of course we accept your invitation to come see you tomorrow evening." "Great! I'm looking for it," he announced. For a second, when I glanced at Christopher, I thought I saw a hint of whup ass was being directed toward Mr. Phillips; but then he saw me looking towards his direction, and that scowl suddenly turned into a big smile. *Man, he is good,* I thought... *He's real good...*

As Louise and I walked back to the condo to get ready to go out, we started talking about what had just happened at the restaurant. "That owner was a trip, wasn't he?" Louise asked. "Yeah, he was, and did you notice that Christopher was getting a little p.o.'d that Dan The Man kept hitting on us?" I asked. "Ugghh...I think he was mad because Dan kept talking to you and not letting him get a word in at all." "That's for sure," I said. *I felt like I was in the middle of a cave man sparring.*

By then, it was already 10:30 p.m., so I put on TP, my combat boots, and grabbed my little black box purse with my face powder, lipstick and $20. Okay, I know what you're thinking: why the hell does she need a compact on the beach? Well...because I was addicted to touching up my face; all Divas have that trait. Louise decided to wear a bustier top and short blue jean shorts with cowboy boots. Yep, we were ready for war!

When we got to the club, the sound I had longed to hear was playing: finally, House Music! They actually had a real DJ spinning, oh joy! This place was pretty much all dance floor, with restrooms inside. The bar, which was actually a banquet table, was set up with two girls selling beer and cheap vodka drinks. There were soooo many cute guys here that we couldn't believe our eyes! And that's how it used to be in the 80's and early 90's: no matter where you went, they were all fine. Now, if you see one at all, it's like playing that "Where's Waldo" game. We danced, and danced, and danced!

Just when I thought I was going to take a break, the DJ would bust out with another good one; as a sea of hot guys would surround us so that we could all dance together. I was sweating so much, and (believe you me) that was not my M.O., but I continued to powder my face until I think I started to look like a "spotted tiger quoll!"

At 3 a.m., things came to a screeching halt. I still had two drinks I hadn't finished, so I gave one to Louise and we went up some stairs to the top deck of the club. And, of course, there were more boys up there just hanging out. ♪ I want to be where the boys are, but I'm not allowed. I wait outside of the boy's bar. I wait for them to all come out♪

Chapter 23: Magically Delicious

We sat down, and a dark-haired guy who resembled the actor William Baldwin came over and started talking to us right away. His voice was very raspy and sexy. He looked at me and said, "That is the hottest outfit I've ever seen." "Thanks, babe," I said, "it's one of a kind!" He then proceeded to tell me his whole life story.

What is it about being a hairdresser? Even if you don't tell people what you do, it's like we have some kind of built-in radar device; and their built-in bitching detector picks up the signal. Then, all of a sudden, you take on the role of being their therapist!

I kind of zoned out for a few minutes and just listened to his voice; boy, this mother-fucker could talk. *He has to be on some kind of speed or something.* Then, I heard him say: "My Mom actually craved dirt when she was pregnant with me…" What the fuck? I then snapped back to reality. "Did you just say that your Mom craved dirt while pregnant?" "Yeah," he said, "and she got so good at it, that she became knowledgeable on certain types to stay away from." *Oh my God,* I thought, *ok let's go ahead and take this a step further.* "So when you say she became a dirt eating expert, what made her qualify?" "Well," he answered. "For one thing, she knew to stay away from the dirt that appeared discolored or moist in texture; that was usually the places where someone had taken a piss…" *Okay, I didn't know whether to laugh or up-chuck!* Why would a mother tell her kid that in the first place? Is that some form of abuse I'd never read about yet?

I realized it was almost 5 a.m. and Mama had to get back into her Diva cave before she burst into flames. I looked over and saw that Louise and the guy she had been talking to had fallen asleep with their heads cocked together. Awww, isn't that precious….

I was again awakened the next morning by Gary B., the dirty-headed bird. *Ughhh, I was so sore from dancing the previous night!* I looked over at my alarm clock and it read 10:35, oh shit! I was supposed to meet Christopher at 11 a.m. for breakfast.

I ran to the bathroom, brushed my teeth, and took a ho bath. I then threw on some shorts, a t-shirt and grabbed my flip-flops and sunglasses. I ran as fast as I could to the restaurant.

As I got closer to the place, I could see that Christopher was already seated. He stood up from the table when he saw me coming. "Morning, how are you?" he asked. "I'm doing well, considering we didn't go to sleep until almost a little before 6 a.m.," I said.

The waiter came and took our orders; right after he left, Christopher started pouring his heart out. "Yeah, I heard that place was rockin' last night and you were definitely the talk of the evening here at the restaurant this morning," he stated. I then took my sunglasses off and asked him, "What are you talking about?" "I got here a little earlier to talk to a friend of mine who works here; and a group of guys showed up to have breakfast. I couldn't help but overhear them talk about some hot chick with whom they danced all night long. And, they were going into detail about what you had on and what you looked like, etc…" *Hmmmm,* I thought… *I think I'm picking up on a little jealousy bear here.* "Yes, sounds like they were talking about me, but that's all that went on, dancing and talking," I replied. "Louise was falling asleep at the bar, so we went straight to the condo afterwards… totally alone." "Ohh, well, I didn't think anything happened; you know how guys like to talk," he quickly added. "Oh, I know," I replied. I had one doing that very thing from 3 to 5 a.m. this morning. *Pretty interesting,* I thought, *"Ole Christopher Robin" was a little envious that he wasn't with me last night and had to hear it from total strangers. Yeah, that would pretty much suck!* He then said, "I'm off all day today and tonight. I have to do some errands after breakfast. But would you like to meet up with me later this afternoon, and hangout, and then have dinner with me tonight?" *Wow, I like this: Mr. Man is taking charge, taking control!!* "Sure," I said, "that will be fun! I really would like to go back to bed for a couple of hours anyway." "Okay, I will come by your place around 2 p.m." he said. "Oh, I just remembered! We promised Dan that we would come back to the restaurant tonight," I added. "Oh, I already told him that we had plans," he replied. "You did?" I asked. "Yeah, it's already taken care of. I'm sure that Dan probably wasn't too happy about that," I said. "Whatever, he will get over it," Christopher replied.

I could sense that Christopher was a lot more relaxed after our little chat. He just wanted to make sure I hadn't been whoring the beachfront the previous night. I really didn't know how to take that. *Should I be flattered, or a little concerned, that he was acting like we were already an item?*

Even with all the weird psycho dreams about Gary B. (aka dirty head bird) I managed to sleep pretty well. When I came out of the bedroom, Louise was nowhere in site; something told me she was with Rocker Boy that day, which was a good thing, because that way we were both busy doing our own thing.

I showered and changed into a baby blue sundress with sandals to match. Christopher showed up at 1:58 pm and told me that he wanted me to meet one of his friends, whose name was Barry, who lived in a house near his apartment.

It was a beautiful day to go for a stroll. The next day was going to be our last full day of vacation, so I was really glad that Christopher suggested this outing. It was a fifteen-minute walk to Barry's place and Christopher made sure that he prepared me for what I was about to see before we arrived. "Barry," he went on to say, "is a little eccentric, he's sort of a collector." "Oh, you mean like art, paintings or sculptures?" "No not exactly, he collects empty cereal boxes…." I started to laugh out loud, but then toned it down to a small grin. "Okay… and what else does he collect?" I asked. "Well, that's it," he said.

I just had to tell Christopher: "That oddly reminds me of a client I had who collected salt and pepper shakers. The only problem was that he acquired his collection solely through theft. He would actually steal them from every restaurant he visited. One day, he was meeting his girlfriend's parents for lunch — for the first time ever — at a local Thai restaurant. He had arrived first. He, of course, confiscated the goods and slipped them into his jacket pocket. A few seconds later, his girlfriend and her parents arrived. Just as they approached his table, the owner of the restaurant — who just happened to be a female — came running over straight to my client, looked up at him, and screamed: 'You steal solt n peppa, you get tha fuc out!'" "Jeez! What happened after that?" Christopher asked. "Oh, they just went to another restaurant," I said.

"Oh, and Barry also dips, so he has spit buckets placed everywhere; but he never misses his target," Christopher added.

Well, I thought, *he sounds harmless enough. I actually had a baby-sitter when I was five years old, who took care of all the neighborhood kids and she collected "snuff buckets." She was probably only 60 something years of age; but since I was only five, I thought she was about 200 years old. She dipped snuff and had buckets placed strategically around her home. She never missed her aim, either. I remember very vividly watching some toddlers eating rocks and grass. I went up to her, and gently tugged on her apron, to let her know what was going on with that. She casually turned away from me and spit into one of her buckets; and then, with a smile, and a wink, replied, "That's ok, Kiddo. Let em eat it; it's good for them!"* I felt like I knew Barry already.

We walked up to a white picket fence with a broken hinge and skipped over an uneven cobble-stoned pathway, to a little blue and white one-story home. As Christopher knocked on the door, we could hear Barry huffing and puffing his way towards the entrance. "Keep your panties on!" he yelled. "I'm coming!" He swung the door open and, with one arm, flung us both into his living-room. When I first saw Barry, he looked so familiar, like I'd met him before, but I couldn't put my finger on it.

"Well, well, well, so this is the little lassie, huh? Nice to meet you!" He grabbed my hand with one of his meat hooks and it totally disappeared in his. Barry was a huge barrel of a man, looking like an old salty dog sailor. He had a full dark beard with a few gray streaks running through it. His forearms were the size of bowling pins and his head was full of salt and pepper thick wavy hair. "What are you two kids up to today?" Barry asked. "Well, first off to visit you and then take a walk around town a little and then dinner tonight," Christopher answered. "Ohh, ho ho I got cha!" Barry yelled. Barry's incredibly booming voice enabled anyone to clearly hear him blocks away. "Hey Girlie, would you like to take a gander at my collection," he asked. I looked quickly at Christopher and said "Yes, sure, I would love to see it."

We followed him out to the back part of his home through the kitchen. What looked like it had been built on as an after-thought was a huge sun-room filled from floor to ceiling with every type of cereal box that was ever created: Cream O Wheat, Frosted Flakes, Count Chocula; there were even cereal boxes from other countries. It was all kinda disturbing, yet intriguing. There were hundreds of boxes, of all shapes and sizes, stacked perfectly for display. "How long have you been collecting?" I asked. "Oh, since I was a teenager, the only thing I loved to eat growing up was cereal. Actually, I still love it. And I kept wanting to try new ones all of the time; drove my mother bat-shit, I tell ya!!" *Yeah, that would have driven me bat-shit for sure,* I thought!

"Oh, I meant to tell you that Barry and Dan are also brothers," Christopher added. "No fuckin' way, are you serious?" I replied. "Yes maam, we came from the same womb, but different sperm!" Barry barked back with a laugh. "Yeah," Barry started, "that mother-fucker thinks his shit don't stink now, ever since he opened his little 'hoity toity' restaurant!" Barry went on to say... "he makes me sit in the back, near the kitchen, so his vainglorious customers won't see me!" "Barry, you know that isn't true!" Christopher interjected. "That is Dan's special table he shares with all of his cronies!" "Well, that's not how I see it," Barry replied.

All of a sudden, I knew to change the subject, sensing a certain "feel sorry for me" tone coming up. *Ugghhh, didn't want to go there.* "Barry, how long have you lived here; and how did you and Christopher meet?" I asked. All of a sudden, Barry perked right up! *Thank God for the people skills I've acquired being a hairdresser!* I thought. "Well, I came here on vacation with my brother and mom in 1963. I was a 21-year-old and Dan was 23. I actually had the idea to move here. Of course, to this day, my dear ole brother takes all of the credit!" *Oh brother, here we go again,* I thought. "Anyway, I convinced my Mom to let me stay; and then I had to bribe Danny Boy to go back with her and for him to come back on a later date. I won't tell you what I bribed him with. It's the only thing I have on the sneaky bastard," Barry added. "Then I had her ship all of my cereal boxes to me. Over the years, many, many women have tried to get me to leave, but I knew this place was where I was meant to be." "Uh, Barry, you also left out that after they saw your box collection, and you told them that you wouldn't leave them behind, that kind of closed the chapter on those invitations, remember?" "Just a minor detail I left out sonny, very minor!" Barry said. "I met Chris the first day he arrived with his buddies. God, they were ignorant cusses! And we've been compadres ever since, right buddy boy!" "Yep, you're right, Barry. Barry definitely has schooled me in the ways of the world over the years," Christopher proudly stated.

"Hey, do you guys want to play some dominoes?" Barry asked. "Uhhh, do you want to play?" Christopher asked me. "Sure, why not, I'm not real great at playing games, but I'll give it a shot!" "Hey, let's all do a shot of whisky, huh!?!" Barry offered. "Shit, why not!" we answered. We all did a shot. *Wow, that was a nice warm fuzzy,* I thought.

Barry broke out the dominoes, walked past a bucket, and spat without losing a beat. Then he ran over to his stereo and put in… *Is that what I think it is?* An 8 track! And guess what tune came on! Barry White, that's who that mother-fucker looks like; of course, it's all coming in so clearly now!

Barry started gyrating to the soulful sounds of Mr. White. This was so hilarious. Here was this white guy who looked exactly like Barry White. Wow! We sat down to play. Of course, Barry was very good at it; that's why he wanted to challenge us in the first place.

After the third round, and his tenth shot of whisky, we knew it was probably time to head out. Our first clue was when Barry started showing us his Soul Train dance moves while sloppily using the Jim Beam bottle as his sexy dance partner. We left to the sounds of ♫Never Never Gonna Give You Up♫

Chapter 24: Prehistoric Will Destroy It

As Christopher and I approached the front entrance of his apartment, he turned to me and asked, "You didn't mind hanging out with Barry today, did you?" "Oh no, I think he might have just made this vacation all worth the while," I said. "He definitely was a real treat." Christopher unlocked his door, reached around, and turned on a light-switch to let me walk in front of him into his living-room. His apartment was small, but very tidy.

So now that you readers know my M.O., I know you have already figured out what I was going to do next, right? You fuckers are so clever! *Yes, I'm going to go check out his bathroom, yes in fuckin' deed.* Christopher directed me to his bathroom. After I promptly shut the door, my ex-ray eyes immediately started examining the room. *Hmmm…no prehistoric toothpaste fragments on the mirror, and sink, check. The toilet seat doesn't appear to have been spray painted a slight yellow tinge, check. And the shower curtain liner doesn't look like it has spent 20 thousand leagues under the sea, check. Actually, this curtain appears to be brand new! Triple check for Mr. Christopher!*

"Are you ok in there?" I heard Christopher shout outside the door. *Oh shit, I got so caught up with my inspection, that I lost all track of time.*

I quickly flushed the toilet and washed my hands. "I'm fine," I replied, as I swung the door open. "Just freshening up a little," I added.

While I was doing my cross-examining job, Christopher had changed his clothes for dinner. He looked so delicious that I could sop him up with a biscuit! "You look very nice," I told him. "Thank you," he said. "I have to look my best tonight, if I'm going to be seen with you." *Wow, how sweet was that comment,* I thought. "I'm going to take you to an Italian restaurant that one of my good friends owns. You will love it; everything is handmaid." "Cool, I'm starving. I think that whisky burned a hole in my stomach," I said.

When we arrived at the restaurant, a man who appeared to be in his early 50's ran to greet us at the door. You could tell this guy was 100% Italian. He came and kissed us on both cheeks, he was so excited to see us. "I'm Antonio. I will tell you now that this will be the best meal you will ever have in your whole life," he said to me. He seated us at a table by one of the windows of the restaurant overlooking distinctly beautiful landscaping. "This place is gorgeous," I told Christopher. "I knew you would like it," he proudly stated. "Hey, let's have some champagne," he suggested. *This guy is not holding back,* I thought. I can't wait to tell Louise that a man who asks you out, and then orders white zinfandel in a bucket of ice, is not a good starting point on a first date.

When Antonio came over, Christopher informed him that we wanted his best champagne; and you could see that Antonio was actually beaming with excitement. You could tell that this man not only loved his restaurant and his food; hell, he just loved life! When Antonio went off to go fetch the champagne, Christopher leaned over and said, "Antonio's wife Rosa and his mother Anna do all of the cooking. And from time to time you can hear them screaming at each other in the kitchen." *Now, that would be highly entertaining,* I thought. Antonio came over with another waiter who smartly brought sparkly clean champagne glasses and a long-neck bottle of grappa. "We must all do a toast together," Antonio said, as he poured us all a tiny portion of this liquid. We all "clinked" our glasses together, and then down the hatch it went. I'd had grappa before on several occasions and there was a common effect. It gave me such a huge surge of energy, that I could go non-stop all night long. It's kind of like liquid crissy, only without the bad coming down side-effects; it also made me want to party my ass off! We then ordered our meal and sat back, relaxed, enjoying the wonderful champagne. When our food arrived, I was super grateful because I was starting to feel the booze big time. I don't think I said two words to Christopher as I inhaled my meal. Before I even realized it, my plate was almost half finished. At that moment, Antonio returned to our table, looked at my plate, and then at me. He said, "I love to see a woman who enjoys her food." *Well, I guess he was practically having an orgasm then, because I took this puppy down!* I thought. After we finished eating, I was starting to get a little sleepy. *Oh no,* I thought, *I can't get tired now; the night is still young!* So I asked Christopher if I could have another grappa. It was as if Antonio had read my mind, because he came over and said to me, "I love it when a woman enjoys her grappa!" Giggling, I replied, "I love it when a grappa enjoys its woman!" Antonio threw his head back and started laughing. He then leaned down, grabbed my face in both his hands, and kissed me on both cheeks again. After the dinner, we said our goodbyes and Christopher walked me back to the condo. As we got a little closer to the condo, we both heard dance music coming from that direction. *Oh Lord, guess who's having a little party while Miss Thing is away!*

  The front door of the condo had a rock planted in front of it, so as to leave it open for anything that would dredge off the fuckin' beach! I ran ahead of Christopher while yelling for Louise, and she was nowhere in site. *Ok girl, calm down,* I thought. *Don't go to the dark side in front of Christopher. Just go to your bedroom, make sure nothing is missing and then lock the door.* Good, no one was fuckin' in my bed, and Thunder Pussy was still hanging in the closet. Tiny-figured drag queens and petite gay men have always wanted me to part with TP. I have guarded this prized article with my life! I ran back to the living-room, passing by bodies I did not know; and then I saw Christopher having a beer and talking to a security guard who was also helping himself to one. *Well, that's real cute,* I thought. "Protect and serve," huh! Oh well, everything was intact. The condo was not destroyed and it wasn't my place, anyway. If anything happened to this place, it would be on Louise's ass — not mine. All of a sudden, Louise showed up with Rocker Boy. "Hey girl, I'm glad you could make it back for our going away party!" she said. "Yeah, I'm glad I made it back too, just in time to batten down the hatches," I said. But she wasn't listening anyway. She pointed her index finger towards a cooler. Boy Blunder reached over and fished out a wine cooler for his Babyyy! *Well, I might as well enjoy the last night here too,* I thought. All we had for tunes was the local radio station, which by then wasn't so bad, since ZZ Top had broken me in! The last "Whangdoodle" finally sauntered out around 4 a.m. and Louise and her escort had already retired for the morning. Christopher was a gem and stayed to help me clean up the mess. Afterwards, I knew he wanted to stay over, and I didn't push him away from that idea. Okay, Okay, I know you guys are still waiting for me to give you all the sordid little dirty details. Well, there aren't any in this case. Christopher and I had a lovely romantic time together and that's all I'm going to disclose to you for now. There are times when there are some things you just want to keep close and sacred. I'm just fuckin' with you guys! It was hot,

hot, hot, raw, wild, monkey love! Him Tarzan, me Jane! Or was it Me Tarzan, and He Jane?

Chapter 25: Raggedy Ann and Dandy

After the Beach Blanket Bimbo Vacation, I was back in full swing at the salon. I had been going 90 to nothing almost every day for weeks. Between work and getting back in the gym, just the normal routine of life was getting pretty stressful. I still hadn't found the right balance of work and play. I knew something would have to take a back seat one day and it wasn't going to be me not working. This hectic schedule was also starting to affect my sleeping pattern.

One night, a month after Louise and I arrived back from our trip, I had the most disturbing dream. In the dream, I was a life-sized "Raggedy Ann Doll" and I was running to and fro all over the place at a very frantic pace. I didn't have real fingers. I just had those big ass white mitts for hands; so the frustrating part was I could barely grip the steering wheel of my car. My feet didn't have any feeling to them, yet they were wedged against the gas pedal. When I finally got to the grocery store, my Raggedy Ann Brain couldn't think fast enough to park in a parking space; and I crashed into the basket stall instead. I grabbed my box purse, then forcibly body-slammed the driver's side door open before high-tailing it to the front entrance of the store. Noticing the little old ladies setting up their free sample trays — as I ran by with my huge Raggedy Ann head flopping all over the place — I reached out with one of my mitts to take some snack samples; and in doing so, wiped out their neatly arranged array of food. Crackers and cheese, and meat bites, came crashing to the floor as I painstakingly tried to shove the morsels into my fake mouth! I suddenly woke up drenched in sweat with Val's flipper in my mouth! Shit; that was the most fucked up dream I've ever had!

It was already 6 a.m., so I decided to just get up and start getting ready for the day. I turned the television on to listen to a little news, and went to the kitchen to pour myself a glass of cranberry juice. I heard a commercial that was advertising pagers, which strangely perked my interest.

The salon was going through yet another change and this time it was the front desk taking on a new metamorphosis. Danny had already sold out of the salon, as he and Debra had settled down in Boulder, Colorado. They bought some ranch property with a couple of horses, took along their dog, and they discovered hog heaven at the "Ponderosa!"

When Kathy had full ownership, her attitude towards the salon really started to plummet. She was cutting back and skimping in places she shouldn't have been. In any business, we all know that whoever greets you first, and how they greet you, will determine whether the business will make it or not.

Since the salon was well-established, Kathy began to get greedy and more self-centered. Michelle, by that point, had been working with Kathy for 7 years. That's a very long time for a receptionist to stick around, but she was Kathy's right hand and very loyal to her.

As soon as Danny split, Kathy started hiring these very young, incompetent, stupid desk girls. Michelle tried her best to train the little "chippies," but they didn't want to work; they just wanted to reap all of the benefits of working in a salon. I won't even call them receptionists, because that was not the job they were doing. What most of them did during the day was fuck up our appointments; you know…having us all run behind all day while they talked on the phone with their fuck buddies. Hmmm…let's see, also getting their nails, makeup and hair done. Oh, let's not forget the waxing jobs and pedicures on company time!

One girl that was hired couldn't seem to figure out how to work the phones — like the simple task of putting people on hold — so she would hang up on them repeatedly. That was the last straw for me, so when I heard the advertisement about the pager, I repeated the number in my head, and wrote it down on the back of an envelope. *I'm going to get one of those things today,* I thought. And from then on, if my clients had any problem dealing with those "dumb bunnies," they could page me right away and the problem was solved!

I then made it a point to contact every client to give each one my pager number, pronto. It turned out to be a great investment, because nobody held back on using it, at all. One afternoon, a client named Denise, who became a really dear friend, paged me to make her next appointment. She was a police officer, so her schedule was really crazy. She would work late hours into the early mornings, usually busting drunk drivers, or Johns, who told their wives they were at a business dinner, but were really at a hotel in the downtown district with a lady of the evening. I paged her back right away and then didn't think anything of it, until almost an hour had passed; and I noticed she never responded. *That's weird,* I thought, *she always gets back to me right away.* So I paged again, actually twice the second time, adding the numbers "911" for emergency.

Later on that evening, she called me back laughing and said, "I have a very funny story to tell you when I come in for my appointment. I would tell you now, but I'm headed back to work." "Ok, girl," I said, "I can't wait!"

When Denise came in, she was laughing her ass off. "What's so funny?" I asked her. "When you paged me that last time with 911, I was in a hotel room, posing as a prostitute, and getting ready to bust this married man. We were just getting ready to talk about the money exchange when your page came through. I had to turn my head around and face the other direction, because I wanted to laugh sooo bad. The John started getting more nervous and I had to tell him it was my 'Ole Man' trying to find out where I was. So, girl, you were my pimp for the day!" She laughed her ass off. "Then, after we made the deal, my backup came in and this turd tried to jump out of the window. The whole way down to the squad car he kept screaming, 'Don't tell my wife, don't tell my wife!'" "Damn, girl. Well, I'm glad I could help you out on the job that day!" I said. "Sweet Sweetback's Baadasssss Song," Get back, you jive turkeys!

One Friday afternoon, Tammy, Louise, and I decided to go grab a bite to eat. I asked Tammy how it was going with Baby Bro. "Well…we kind of called it quits," she said. "You're kidding, when did this all take place?" I asked her. "Pretty much while you two were in Padre. He was spinning at this Latino club and the guys in that place were so hot and super sexy!" "Oh, nooo, what did you do?" we both asked her. "B.B. never minds if I dance with someone, but this time I think it really hit a nerve." "Yeah," I said… "probably the dry humping on the floor did it, huh?" "Yeah, pretty much. Next thing I knew, he had two girls behind his booth; and when I came over to escort them out of there, he escorted me out instead," Tammy replied. "Ouch!!" Louise and I both exclaimed. "Yep, he kicked my ass to the curb. So now I've got the 'Latin Fever!' Those motherfuckers can dance; and the wild sexual energy that exudes from their pelvises is ♪ Supersonic♪!" she nearly shouted. "Well, my best friend in high school dated a Hispanic guy and he was pretty good-looking, from what I can remember. He was a little older than she was and I don't think he ever graduated, either. He drove us all to the prom. My date actually was a couple years older than I was too, and my mom hated his ass, but that's a whole other story.

As we drove off, Hector casually mentioned that he brought his gun with him and it was located under the back seat. 'We have to protect our girls, you know!' And he started laughing like it was normal to carry a concealed weapon to a prom!" "Shit, that's fucked up!" Louise said. "Yeah, tell me about it," I said, adding: "Guess what else is fucked up? I'd begged my Mom to buy me this gold lame' prom dress, and she finally gave in. A year or two later, I saw that picture; and I looked like a hood ornament on a pimp car. I grabbed that ugly thing and threw it in the dumpster that very minute!" "Ewww!" they both squealed.

Suddenly, my pager started going off and I saw that it was my client Denise. "Hey, let's go ahead and wrap this up," I said. "I need to see what she wants done, because she just came in a few days ago." I called Denise as soon as I got back to the salon and asked her what was up. "I'm getting married. Dominic proposed last night!" "Congratulations!" I told her. "Thanks, the reason why I paged you is because I would love for you to do my wedding." "Great, I would love to," I responded. "This is the thing," she went on..."the wedding is going to be in San Antonio, so I will pay for your airfare and your hotel." "Right on, I'm there!" I said. "We are thinking probably June 15th. That way, it will just start getting hot. If we wait till July, the heat will be unbearable." "Ok, sounds good. I'm looking at the schedule now and I will mark that weekend off completely," I said. "Thanks, I really appreciate this," Denise responded. *Cool, my first wedding out of town and all expenses paid, yippee! If I'd only known what was in store for me.*

Chapter 26: Unarmed Forces

I arrived in San Antonio at 9 a.m. Denise's brother Marco had volunteered to pick me up at the airport. Marco was right on time, which was great, because I needed help with my luggage and my work travel bag. "Denise told me that you would be doing the hair at our Mom's house," Marco announced. "Ok, that's fine with me. I can do the girls wherever they need me to."

We drove up to an older Spanish style stucco home with lush green landscaping. Marco parked in the circular driveway in front of the house, and ran around to open the car door for me. As I was thanking him, I could hear a woman's voice wailing, and crying, coming from the front part of the house. *What in the world is that?* I thought.

As Marco opened the front door, I could tell the crying and moaning sounds were coming from a room on the left side of the front entry of the home. Denise came running up to me, helped with my bags, and started thanking me for accommodating them. "No problem, girl, I'm happy to do it," I replied.

The screaming seemed to continue to a more fevered pitch. "Who, or what, in the hell is that?" I asked her. "Oh, it's my Grandma, she's not doing so well today; and, sadly, she won't be able to come to the wedding." "What's wrong with her?" I inquired.

"You name it, she's got it. Most of the sicknesses are all conjured up in her head, I suppose," Denise said. "She may not be with us much longer, so my mom tries to make sure that she is comfortable, and has round the clock care." *She doesn't sound too comfortable to me,* I thought.

I began to unpack my supplies and decided to set up in the dining room, which was spacious enough for the girls. I only had to do three bridesmaids, her maid of honor, Mom, the flower girl, and, of course, the bride.

The family was in such great spirits, and seemed oblivious to the hair-raising shrill going on in the back of the house! How in the hell could they stand listening to that? *It's like she didn't even exist!* I thought.

It didn't take me long at all to finish the wedding party. I was like "Speedy Gonzalez" with a curling iron. I couldn't wait to get the fuck out of there! It was only the grace of God that gave me the strength to stand there and work, enduring that crazy shit for three and a half hours. Damn! What about their neighbors? Did they all keep their televisions on day and night, with plugs or cotton stuffed in their ears?

As I began to pack my things, Denise came over quickly to pay me. "You are coming to the wedding, aren't you?" she asked. I was at a loss for words. *God, I was so worn out from the screaming, I didn't think I could sit through a wedding ceremony.*

Then, Denise's mom called for her to come back to the dark cavern where Grandma resided. About ten minutes later, she came running back and sweetly suggested that I ride with the "Screaming Mimi" and her brother.

245

All of a sudden, I felt like I had been swept into a dark menacing vortex! Oh God, I couldn't turn Denise down, but I didn't want to ride with that out-of-control Banshee either. *Wait!! What's that? Has that earth cracking sound finally diminished?*

I heard Denise's mom's voice behind me speaking Spanish. I turned around and locked eyes with the woman being wheeled out into the living-room, who was supposedly on her death bed.

All of a sudden, it hit me! This woman was playing a huge fucked up game! She looked pretty damn healthy to me. Come to think of it, for someone who was supposedly plummeting closer toward death's door, ole La Abuela sure did have a set of pipes on her. Also, Grandma knew I was hip to her bullshit. The look she gave me was totally defiant. She had succeeded in directing all the attention to herself on her own granddaughter's wedding day! Wow, for the first time ever I saw the sick manipulation of a woman who had done this kind of crap her whole life. Marco took over the reins and steered grandma out to the car.

As I followed them out to the car, I could hear that death march song in my ear. Then, miraculously, Grandma got up out of her wheelchair; it's a miracle, Brutha's and Sista's!!! She confidently positioned herself into the front passage seat. All I could think of right about then was having a drink, but I knew that was going to be a long way off.

In a matter of minutes, we arrived at a colossal cathedral. This was the first Catholic Church into which I'd ever set foot. I was totally blown away with every detail of the building, from the windows to the altar. Every place I cast my eyes led me to amazing details to absorb.

I was seated on the aisle for the bride's family, and friends, as Marco and grand ma ma were ushered to the front row. I then realized that I hadn't eaten anything the whole morning. Normally, I would nibble on some crackers, and drink a lot of water, so I wouldn't get lethargic while working. But all I had was water that day and I was starting to feel a little woozy.

Finally, the ceremony started and the priest spoke a few words. Then Denise started gliding down the aisle. She looked fabulous! Then we were told by the priest to stand up, sit down, stand up, then sit down......*Oh my Lord, I couldn't do any more calisthenics, I was so worn out!* At that point, I didn't care if I offended anyone. I was going to sit the fuck down. *How long was this thing going to last, anyway?* Well, it lasted an entire hour, uggghhh!

After the groom kissed the blushing bride, and the closing of the ceremony, I ran out into the front corridor of the church and saw a little elderly lady in a room hanging up robes. "Excuse me? Is there a phone I could use to call a cab?" I asked her. "Sure, honey, there is actually one right here in this room and there is a phonebook on the table," she replied. "And here is the address to give the cab driver," she added. "Thank you so much," I told her.

I found a cab service within minutes and was told the driver would arrive in ten minutes. Then, I galloped back into the main sanctuary and spotted Marco instantly, asking him if he could come to the car with me, so I could grab my bags.

As he courteously walked me out, we opened the cathedral doors to discover that the cab was waiting right up front. Marco then told me he would run and get my bags;

and he was away and back in a blaze. I thanked him, told him to have a wonderful time, and zoomed off to the hotel. It was on like Donkey Kong!

God, I was so keyed up from when I arrived at the hotel, I was practically buzzing! As I was checking in at the front desk, I noticed there was a little gift shop that sold snacks. I went in and purchased some potato chips, and a small package of cookies, just to tie me over until I decided on what I wanted for dinner. At that point, I really wasn't hungry anymore, because my stomach had already started eating away at its own inner lining.

I walked into my room, threw my bags on the floor, grabbed the bag of chips, and dive-bombed into the bed. As I lay there on my back, eating the chips with crumbs dropping all around me, I started to subjectively go over the details of the day. That was by far one of the eeriest encounters I'd ever experienced. Was that woman really a human being, or some extra-terrestrial? Because some of those sounds that were coming from that mouth were very alien-like.

By then, in this business, I'd met manipulating females before, but that was by far one of the sickest attempts I'd ever witnessed. To go to such great lengths — as to fake that you are dying during your own granddaughter's wedding — had me in total amazement.

My 25th birthday was advancing toward me like a steamroller. Shit, pretty soon I was going to be closer to 50! What other career could I possibly consider looking into? How long should I stay in this line of work? At that point, I couldn't picture myself dealing with those crazy bitches for one more day, let alone a decade. As I deliberated over this issue, I straightaway fell into a restless sleep. The whole part of the sporadic dream state was filled with Grandma chasing me down a dark hallway in her wheelchair with a bowl of hot steaming Menudo in her lap.

A knock on the door from room service abruptly awoke me from my sweat-soaked catnap. I peered through the peephole, opened the door, and told the woman I didn't need anything. I then thanked her.

I plugged in my hot rollers, quickly took a shower, fixed my hair, and put on a new mug. I threw on some bell-bottomed jeans, a cute top, and headed down to one of the restaurants in the hotel.

It was almost 7 p.m. and people were just starting to come in for early cocktails. I knew I'd better get something in my stomach before I had any alcohol, or it wasn't going to be pretty! I told the hostess that I would just eat in the bar area, then found a table near some corner booths.

When the bartender came over, I ordered a huge plate of chicken, beef nachos, and a margarita. As I slowly sipped on my water, I noticed that several older men in army fatigues started to come towards the entrance to the bar area. At first, there were only about four of them, but then others started to pile in. Their ages seemed to be in the range of forties to early to middle fifties. One of the men — who looked like to be the youngest out of all of them, probably in his middle forties — pointed at a table that was located right across from where I was sitting.

When the bartender brought over my drink, it took only one sip before I finally started enjoying the peace and tranquility of the evening. The men were all making fun of each other, and laughing, while they ordered their beers. *Whew, this drink is strong; if I want to have another drink, I'd better switch to what I know I can handle!* I thought to myself.

The bartender took my dishes away and asked me if I would like another beverage. I then ordered an absolute cranberry, my signature "drinkie poo," and one of the guys told the bartender to put my drinks on his tab. *Whatttt?* I thought. *That's pretty cool!* The guy introduced himself as Benny and asked me, "Are you meeting someone here, little lady?" "Actually, no," I answered. I came here for work and now I'm just kicking back after a long day." "Well, would you like to join us?" "Sure, thanks," I said.

Benny got up and brought another chair over to the table for me. I sat between Benny and a guy named Steven. "What are you guys doing here in San Antonio?" I asked them. "Well," Steven said, "we're all here for an exam." "Do you think you all passed it?" I asked. "Well, I hope so, because if we didn't, this will be the only chance we'll have." Benny added, "That's why most of us decided to take it later in our career."

When someone had the great idea of ordering shots of tequila, I knew that I'd better watch my p's and q's. I could not miss my flight the next morning. On that particular night, I learned to only be a two-shot girl, and no more. No matter what people would say, or even if they called me a pussy, I never went past the #2 rule. While others continued to go past the human limit, I would just sit back and watch them become blacked out drunk.

After a while, the hotel bar was starting to shut down, so the boys decided to move it to a restaurant across the street. By this time, I was feeling no pain, so we hopped over to the next taproom. By then, it was as if I'd never experienced the siren-like blood curdling calls of that mountain lioness, which had become just a fading memory.

As we approached the bar, I noticed how the exterior resembled a log cabin with a porch with tables and chairs. As Benny held the door open for me, I noticed how the place looked just like something you would read right out of a Steven King short story. The walls were all stained wooden beams and there was a jukebox in the corner of the bar. The wildest part was that the ceiling had dollar bills hanging from it with signatures written on them in red ink. You could barely see the ceiling because of all the money hanging from it.

There were only three people in the bar: two blonde women about my age; and the biggest, most muscular man I'd ever seen in my life. His forearms were the size, and kind of the shape, of a water heater.

Benny ordered a round of drinks. The girls turned to me and started complimenting me on my outfit, and my hair. Their names were Sarah and Amy. We three separated from the guys and started talking amongst ourselves.

Sarah and Amy asked me what my profession was. After I told them, I cheerfully said, "I don't talk shop after working hours. I would rather talk about what you guys do." "We break quarter horses for a living," they replied. "Wow, that's pretty fantastic," I said.

Sarah was a very pretty girl with white blonde hair pulled back in a ponytail, while Amy wore her blonde hair down and slightly curled at the ends. The girls suggested that we get another round. I don't know how this came about, or who suggested it, but we all got it in our heads that we needed to arm wrestle each other. I did acquire a little more muscle after those long sweaty hours in the gym; so I think the girls wanted to see if they could beat this City Diva and make her eat crow all the way back home.

Amy's boyfriend was a big lumberjack of a man. She went over and told him, and the army guys, what was getting ready to transpire. Of course, you could have cut the sexual energy in the air with a razor sharp dildo! The men came charging out of the bar like water buffalo.

Sarah sat down first and Amy's boyfriend Lucas started the count. I never told the girls that I had once played softball and baseball as a teenager, so I had a lot of upper body strength. I took Sarah down faster than a ravenous fatty eating a Big Mac at McDonalds.

The crowd went wild as Sarah got up looking madder than a blue-eyed Jap! Then it was Amy's turn; and, right as she started to take her seat, I realized, *shit, this girl looks just like that actress Uma Thurman! Okay, don't get distracted. Focus, focus: you've got an audience; it's time to take the bitch down!!* I thought.

Amy was a lot stronger than Sarah, so I knew I needed some ammo. I said that magic word that makes every red-blooded American girl smile. Just when she thought she almost had me, I whispered the word "Penis…" and Pow!!! *Oooopps, did I just win?*

Amy started laughing so hard that her arm turned into a loose noodle. "I can't believe this skinny bitch just beat me!" Amy screamed. "You think I'm skinny!" I asked. *Right on,* I thought. "Oh my god, I can't believe you did that!!" she yelled. *Well, thank God she was a good sport about it.*

When we turned around to go back in the bar, I saw the guys handing each other dollar bills. *Those motherfuckers were betting on us!* I thought. Sarah ran to the jukebox and Nancy Sinatra quickly filled the air. We three girls all started dancing like the kids on

American Bandstand. ♫These boots are made for walking, and that's just what they'll do, one of these days these boots are gonna walk all over you♫

Chapter 27: It's a Comb, Not a Wand!

Oh crap, it's 1 a.m., I realized, and my flight was at 9 a.m.! Well, at least I never unpacked; so all I had to do was get ready for bed and I could wear my sweat pants and hoodie on the plane. At that point, I didn't give a flying fuck about fashion. I just wanted to be in my own bed and finally get a good night's sleep, without freaky dreams about work!

After my "winner takes all" arm wrestling victory, Steven offered to escort me back to my hotel. One thing I have to tell you is that those guys were top-notch class act gentlemen. Not one time that whole evening did they hit on me, or the girls. They were all married with children, of course; but everyone knows that doesn't ever interfere with a horn-dog on pursuit. Ten-hut!!!

We said our goodbyes and I called the front desk for a wakeup call for 7:45 a.m. Wow, I felt like I had only slept one hour. 7:45 came like a flash! I took a shower and made sure all of my toiletries were intact. I called for the bellman to come and meet me at my room to help with my luggage and he was there within minutes. I checked out and was escorted to a cab by the same nice young gentleman. I tipped him handsomely before I fell back into the back seat of the cab. "Please take me to the airport," I told the driver and off we went.

It was a very short flight, which I was grateful for; but I was so exhausted when I arrived back in town, and picked up my car from the airport, that I just knew I didn't have the strength to even make it back to my apartment. How sad was that?

I drove for about twelve minutes. By then, it was starting to get really dangerous because I could barely keep my eyes open. I saw a La Quinta Inn sign in the distance and headed towards that direction, parked, then grabbed my luggage. I walked up to the front desk and told the gentleman that I needed a room for just a few hours to get some sleep. I took the key and found the room immediately. Once again, I threw my luggage on the floor and crawled under the nice bedcovers to finally fade into the best *zzzz*'s that for so many months I had longed to achieve.

I was suddenly wide awake and had no clue where I was for a second. I was gripped with terror and thought I was still in San Antonio, having missed my flight. I leaned over to my right and felt around for a nightstand, then felt a lamp and turned it on. *Oh, thank God.* I realized I had somehow made it back to my hometown and had just taken a small pit stop on the way. I glanced at the black plastic digital clock on the nightstand and it read 5 p.m. *Damn, I slept for 5 and a half hours.*

Well, I was then extremely rested up, so there was no reason to continue to stay there at La Quinta any longer. I grabbed my bags once again. *Wow, this bag grabbing was really starting to get old!* I thought. I walked through the deserted lobby and gave my key back to the half asleep girl with earphones attached to her head.

It was then Sunday early evening and I was off from work, so I had the whole day to unpack and get ready for the next riveting week. I decided to go ahead and start doing my laundry then, as I'd already slept a whole day. I had been so busy with my trip to Padre, and the wedding, that I suddenly realized I hadn't spoken to Kevin privately in a while. We would constantly pass each other in the salon, but that was about it. I knew it was time for us to converge in a pow wow pretty soon.

Kevin answered on the second ring! "Hey Miss Thing, I was just thinking about you!" he said. "What cha been up too?" he continued. "I just got back from doing a wedding in San Antonio," I replied. "How did it go?" Kevin asked. "Oh brother, I don't have the desire to get into it right now," I said. "Oh one of 'those weddings,'" Kevin said. "Kevin, we haven't talked, or done anything, together in a while now. Would you like to meet later for dinner?" I asked him. "Yeah Girl, that's a great idea, because I have something I want to tell you, anyway, outside of the salon." *Oh great, is he tail-spinning toward the entrails of hairdresser hell again?* I thought.

I think Kevin could sense my dread over the wire. "Don't get all disturbed, girl," he quickly conveyed. "It's very exciting news and I know you will be happy for me!" Kevin said. "Will you give me just a little hint," I asked? "Nope, you will just have to hold on. Let's meet at 9 p.m.," he said. "I have to shower, shave and then make sure I put my bronzer on right. Some horrid queen asked me the other day if I was wearing Mary Kay foundation. Girl, I was outdone!" Kevin screamed. "Oh my, what did you say to him after he asked you that?" I asked. Kevin answered, "I turned to him and said: 'Bitch, I'm getting ready to do something to you the devil wouldn't do!'" "What's that?" he asked

Kevin. "Leave your ugly ass alone!" And, with that, I snapped my cute self around and strutted out of site!

Kevin and I met that night, of course, at our favorite hamburger place. I was famished because I had barely eaten anything that weekend. "Damn girl, I've never seen you finish a plate before. What happened to you, this past weekend?" Kevin asked. "I feel like I'm having dinner with a German Shepard!" he exclaimed. "Whatever, Roberta, that weekend kicked my happy ass!" I said.

I then revealed to Kevin the whole mind-numbing cluster fuck experience. "Wow, Girl. That is some fucked up shit, for sure! You will experience more of that in the years to come. Women will aspire to great heights to break a hairdresser down. Why do you think I take off, and disappear, once every 3 to 4 years? If I didn't, I would be in some 'bughouse,' braiding what little hair is left on a one-legged doll!" he exclaimed. We laughed pretty hard over that live image! "Okay, tell me this great news of yours," I said. "Well, I've thought about doing this for about two years, pretty much right after my last disappearing act," he explained. "I'm going to open my own salon; the plans are already drawn out. We are negotiating on the building right now." "Kevin, that is so cool!" I screamed. "Wait a minute, who is we?" I asked. "Lance, Roller Boy, and Rubin and I, are all partners in the salon," he answered. "That's going to be fantastic! Oh Boy, Kathy is not going to be happy to find out that some of her best chicks are leaving the nest," I added. "Well, of course not, but that's not my problem!" Kevin said. "Eventually, you have to break out on your own, remember that!" he added. "What do you think about that chick that Lance has been all lovey dovey with lately?" I asked him. "Something is not quite right with her, I can sense it," I added. "Yeah, I know what you mean," Kevin replied. "Supposedly she is a super model, but I've never seen her in any magazines or fashion shows; and have you noticed that she seems kind of masculine?" Kevin posited. "Yeah, that's it!" I shouted. "Do you think she's a tranny? It's like here mannerisms are sooo overboard. Hell, real girls don't walk and act like that! And, you know, she's going to be hanging out in the salon most of the time with her 'lover,'" I said jokingly. "Well, I will suggest that Lance takes a station towards the back of the salon; but tell him it's because that's where the "star" hairdresser should be. That way I won't have to look at that thing while I'm there," Kevin said. "Are you sure that you and 'Roller Boy' will get along?" I asked. "You know how you guys have some sort of hairdresser rivalry going, you're but pretty high strung and opinionated." "Yeah, we both have been discussing our issues with each other. She thinks that she is way more talented than I am. The bitch is in her own little LSD haze. I told her that if she doesn't go along with everything I say, I will throw her out!" Kevin said while laughing. "You didn't tell him that, did you?" "Yes, I did, and I also told her to lose the roller skates, she's way too old to be sporting that look. It was cute in the eighties but now it's just looks fuckin' crazy: her 'Dee Snider' looking ass!" Kevin said. "I'm glad that you are bringing Rubin in on this deal. I have to say he was the first person I met before you and he is one of the nicest guys," I said. "Yeah, I purposely brought him in because he is so tranquil and laid back. He doesn't get angry; he's more of the mediator type. And, to top it all off, I just found out that he is bi-sexual," Kevin added. "No way!" I replied. "Yep! He's dating a guy right now, though, who is one of those moody, dark artistic types. I will hint around a little for Rubin to tell 'pouty girl' to stay home and not visit if she can't put a smile on her face. I don't need that negative shit hovering over the salon!" Kevin complained. "But Rubin is an amazing massage therapist. His clientele is phenomenal and we need him," Kevin explained. "Right now, if everything goes as planned, the salon should be up and running in four months," Kevin explained. "That is so exciting, Kevin!" "Hey, how about you coming on board; do you think you're ready to leave the snake pit yet?" he asked. "The offer is really tempting; but, with the location, I'm pretty sure my clients wouldn't appreciate the long drive. I know them all by now and they're always telling me how they love the fact that I'm so close. But thank you for the offer. You know I'm flattered that you even would ask me to join you," I answered. "Well, I knew what your answer would be anyway. Just make sure you come out and see the process from time to time," he said, adding: "And I'm definitely going to have a huge grand opening extravaganza!" "I know you will and I won't miss it for anything," I told him.

Tuesday morning I came into work a little earlier than usual and could tell right away that Michelle was up to something; she had that look on her face again. "Okay, what did you do this time?" I asked her. "I haven't done anything yet. I wanted to run it by you first because I know if I don't, you will kill me," she said. "You bet your sweet arse I will kill you; and I happen to know from a client of mine that there are a lot of places in Oklahoma where you can hide a body. So give, what's up?" I asked her again. "Well.... There is a client who comes in quite regularly for a blow dry and style…" "Okay," I said, "that sounds reasonable." "But this one is a man," she said. "Yeah… and?" I asked. "Uhhh…he likes to have his hair curled with a curling iron after you blow dry." "Are you fuckin' kidding me?" I yelled. "No, I wish I wasn't kidding because I had to book him with you. For the time slot he wants, no one else is available," Michelle said in dismay. "There is someone else available," I answered. "Yeah, who?" she asked. "The cleaning lady Esmeralda; she can do it!" "No, she can't," Michelle answered while laughing. "Okay, Okay, I will do it!" I told her. *Shit, that is fuckin' weird. What man in his right mind wants his hair curled with an iron?* I thought to myself. "Well, actually, you're not in your right mind if you are a male and request that. Only pimps wore this sort of do, and I'm sure this oddity was not a pimp. If so, at least he would have a legitimate reason to request such a thing. What time is he coming in?" I asked Michelle. "1:30 p.m." *Damn, this was one of those days when I wished I did smoke dope!* I thought. Today I wouldn't touch a client like that with a ten foot rat-tail comb, but back in the early days I still did not know that I didn't have to take everything that dragged its sorry ass into the salon doors. The dreaded hour finally arrived and that guy was everything I imagined him to be and much, much more. This was going to be so enjoyable! *As I introduced myself to him, I extended my right hand out to shake his, and his slimy palm felt like old mushrooms, gack!! I thought I was going to heave ho right there on his light blue fake alligator loafers!*

I mumbled for him to follow me back to the shampoo area and offered for him to have a seat. I then ran like an untamed chimpanzee to my station to grab some rubber gloves; because I knew if those palms were greasy, just imagine what that scalp and hair were going to feel like. *Oh my God, I don't think I can go through with this, I didn't sign up for this over-the-top nastiness when I became a hairdresser.* I made the water a little warmer than usual hoping that he wouldn't notice, because I wanted to kill whatever might lunge at me unawares. I poured a hefty amount of shampoo on his head and scrubbed as vigorously as I could without drawing blood. After the shampoo, I escorted him to my chair. As I started to towel-dry him a little more, he began directing me on what to do with his mop. I also must add that it was extremely bleached out blonde — and super thick in texture — with a God-awful male stripper motif. I was half listening to what he was going on about; then, inexplicably, I heard him speak the word *girlfriend.* "You have a girlfriend?" I asked in disbelief. "Oh yeah, and she loves my hair this way," he said. *Wow, now I have heard it all!* I thought. I could tell he was a major boozer. How? Uhhh, maybe the blood-shot eyes and the W.C. Fields snout gave it away.

One important thing I really did notice was the fact that he didn't smell like bologna. Right now you may be thinking: "What the hell is she talking about; smelling like bologna?" Yep, that's right; let me clarify a little. When I was in junior high school, there was a boy in my social studies class that seemed a little older than the rest of us. You could tell that he had been held back a grade or two. He sat in the desk right in front of mine and on certain days of the week — usually Thursday's or Friday's — he would come in smelling like bologna. It drove me crazy, because that whole school year I could never figure out how a human being could acquire that aroma. Did he eat a whole shitload of cold cuts on the weekends, or something!?! Then, the day finally came when the mystery was solved!

Tammy had a client named Donald who was having a Saint Patrick's Day party at his house. Everyone was slamming down green beer, except for me. I stuck to my ole cranberry and vodka's. Well, Donald was really pounding the beer away and chain smoking cigarettes like a steam engine. We all got pretty toasted and decided to crash at Donald's pad. The next morning, Donald came into his living-room where the girls and I were all sprawled out on his huge leather sectional. When he passed me by to grab his remote control, I could smell that 1977 back down memory lane pong! You see, that morning it hit me! Beer+cigs+male=Bologna!!!

Now, the guy whose hair I was styling didn't smell like bologna at all but pretty much like the scent of plastic and desperation, or was it just some M.E. Moses Five and Dime cologne? He then started talking about his job...*Oh, you're a car salesman; okay, now it's all starting to register...* Then the moment of truth; the curling iron was ready and I started picking up sections of hair and wrapping it around the barrel, while everyone around me was looking and smirking. Even the clients were like: "What the hell is going on over there?" Donny was laughing his ass off! *All right...laugh it up, Donny Boy,* I thought, *I have a little surprise for you, honey bunny!* Then super-freak requested just one more little thing: "Now that's perfect. Don't comb the curls out; just leave them like they are." This was by far the ugliest thing I'd ever created. I couldn't wait to kick that bastard out! Of course, he wanted my business card. I totally bypassed that request and grabbed one of Donny's on the way up to the desk. Donny was bringing a client to his station when he suddenly saw me take his business card. He started laughing and screaming "No" at the same time. *What was he going to do?* Tackle my ass to the floor and take his card away from me? Don't think so. I then told Mozart Muppet that Donny would be better suited to accommodate him in the future; and, please, why not go ahead and make a standing appointment right then? ♫Rock Me, Rock Me Amadeus♫

Chapter 28: The Mane Attraction

I have been sensing for a long time that people who are reading this have been stomping at the gates for me to finally start tearing into the fucked up antics of hairstylists. I know you want me to elaborate on the experiences you might have had to suffer. Now, I've never said I was perfect, but I'm damn near close! 90% of hairdressers have dabbled a little in mind and body altering elixirs, and the remaining 10% were too busy traveling with the family circus. Okay, we all know the main objective when a client comes to visit you is for he, or she, to receive a service. Hairdressers: It's not for you to: a) talk about your fucked up kids, husband or wife. The majority of clients really don't give a shit; they just want you to listen to their gobbledygook! b) If you know you're going to pull an all-nighter, for God's sake, cancel your following day and deal with it later. Coming into work looking like a "Horton Plains Slender Loris," and acting like one, will cost you a few patrons for sure, you can bet on it. And finally: c) talking on the phone while a client is in your chair is a big no, no; unless you want to totally ignore one, that is a total beat down!

But the funniest thing to ever watch is an annoying hairdresser trying to deal with a client that is about as annoying as they are. I call this modern marvel "The Showdown of the Beatdowns!" That reminds me of the guy Derek I mentioned a while back; you know, the cokehead who wore the long-sleeved silk sweat-stained blouses. He actually only lasted about 30 days at the salon, but he would try to out talk his clients. So when he got one in his chair that was ready for a two hour round, it was like the battle of the vocal chords. One day, I thought he was going to have a stroke because he was talking so hard and sweating from all of that "Birdie Powder!" And, even after the visit was over, he would actually walk the client out of the salon to their car while still talking a mile a minute. Oh My God, I think those types of people are still talking even after the coffin has been nailed shut!

Kevin's grand opening of his salon was being held that upcoming weekend on a Saturday night. I was also invited to go to the circus with some gay and Lesbian hairdressers the Friday evening before. Yes, I can tell you all have a shit-eating grin on your faces! Yes, we went to the circus, grown ass men and women. Of course, with them being gay, they had to bring streamers and banners with them, too. A friend of Robert's, whose name was Bryce, worked for one of the rival salons that we always made fun of because they wore uniforms to work and never took them off after hours. They would actually wear that shit out to the clubs. Bryce told Robert that the circus was in town and that, as a child, his parents never took him; going to the circus had always been a life-long dream. Wow, that's sad, the guy was then 27 years old and this was a dream! Okay, I won't rain on a queen's parade! Hey, this could be fun! I remembered once going with my parents, but all I could remember were the clowns and hearing Bernadette Peters in my head singing, ♪Where are the clowns? Send in the clowns♪, Uggghhh, shuddersome…

So, in all, there were about twenty people going on this field trip. Robert invited Tammy, Louise and Donny; and we all carpooled together. Robert's boyfriend David didn't want to take part in the jamboree, which was fine with me. And I sensed that Robert was relieved that he wouldn't be partaking in this fun. Ohhh, was the honeymoon finally over? Had the newness of the relationship turned rusty and cankered? We arrived at the front of the venue around 5:30 p.m. The plan was to meet up with the rest of the crew there. And there they came: Lesbians and Gays and drag queens galore, with banners with inscriptions reading: "We're here, we're queer; get used to it!" And this one: "Closets are for clothes!" And the all time favorite, "Gay — It's My Designer's Genes!" *Whoa, are they going to let us in the place with this going on?* I thought. Of course, everyone was dressed like they were going to a concert; and I detected that a few of them had already started drinking, especially Bryce. He was so excited, and thrilled, that our seats were in the very front row. "We won't miss a thing," he squealed like a six-year-old girl. As we entered the venue, of course everyone was staring at us, and the banners, as the usher timidly directed us to the front row. Wow, this was bigger than life: the sounds, the smells, ugghhh…the smells! The overpowering stench of elephant dung was almost too much to bear! How can those people work around that shit all day? I then saw a man coming down the aisle selling popcorn, peanuts and, *thank God,* wine coolers! I needed something to dull the senses! I looked over at Robert, as he had his hanky draped over his nose.

  Everyone ordered more drinks and settled in with their banners, and signs, while screaming along with the crowd. The announcer finally came out under the big top and the circus began. Seating in the front row had a lot of perks, for sure, but I have never in my life witnessed so much fertilizer coming out! There was one guy who worked the whole time shoveling that stuff up; and he was quick, too. I turned to Donny and asked, "So, if that guy ever wants to change careers, what does he put on his resume, Elephant Shit Technician?" It lasted way too long for my taste and I had started to get a headache from the wine coolers with the combined smell of shit. As the circus came to an end, I thought that Bryce had thoroughly enjoyed himself because he could barely walk out of the place he was so wasted.

As we approached the parking lot, to our left was a huge sign that read "Elephant Rides." And, of course, all of the nelly queens ran over to check it out. *Hmmm, I don't know about this,* I thought. There weren't too many people in line for this. I wondered why. The carny sized up Miss Bryce and said: "You can't ride. You're too drunk, next!"

So Robert took Bryce aside to console him, while Donny came over to me and said: "Girl, let's do it, I've never ridden one of these before." "Well, I haven't either, this is a wild animal, you know," I answered. "Oh, come on, live a little!" he coaxed. "Honey, we deal with wild animals every day. I don't know if I want to pay to sit on one while it takes off down the freeway," I said. I looked over at Tammy and Louise as they were both shaking their heads with an emphatic "no." But I gave in, like I always do, and the guy handed me a waiver to sign. *Oh, this is a morale booster: ride at your own risk, you idiot!* I signed the waiver, paid the fee, and the carny man brought me over to my chariot. "This elephant is huge!" I screamed. "Oh, this one is a baby," he replied, continuing, "look at the others around you; see, they're much bigger." He was right; thank goodness I got the baby. After he threw me on top of that monstrosity, my hands brushed along the sides of its skin; and it felt like the roughest brillo pad ever! Then we were off. *Weee, it was actually pretty cool!* The baby just followed the other older elephants; and we went all around the grounds, circled the tent, and back again. Donny's elephant started taking off a little as he screamed his head off! I started laughing so hard that I almost peed myself due to all of the wine coolers I drank. It was only a twenty-minute ride, but it was worth every penny.

    Afterwards, the group wasn't ready to end the evening, but I sure as hell was. I felt like I actually worked the circus, because I could still smell the animal feces! I whispered to Robert that I was ready to go home. I asked if he could please drop me off at my house before they went out. We all piled into the car and I started falling asleep on the way. He didn't even turn the motor off; and they zipped away before I could even open my apartment door. As I walked past the couch where Val was sitting, he promptly put a flipper over his beak… "Don't even start!" I told him.

    Whoa, my butt really hurt the next morning! Was it from sitting on that hard ass chair at the circus, or the elephant ride? I think maybe a combination of the two made my sacroiliac feel like I'd been participating in a mosh pit. That night was the night for Kevin's grand opening party at his new salon; and I was pretty excited about it. I had just bought a new black evening gown for the occasion and wanted to look hotter, and more sophisticated, than usual. I knew that everyone who was anybody in the hairdressing world, and beyond, would be there that night. My first client was at 10 a.m. that morning; so I proceeded to get ready for work, when suddenly I got a phone call from Kevin. "Hey, what's up?" I asked him. "Morning, Miss Thing. I just wanted to give you the heads up on Ms. Kathy. I heard she was on the rampage because of my salon. So if she tries to corner you, and ask questions about what's going on, just ignore her wicked ass. Word just got back to me that she's trying to sabotage my clientele," Kevin added. "My clients are calling me asking me what's going on, stating that Kathy said I was sick, which means that I have Aids, or something," he explained. "Oh my God, that is horrible. I can't believe she would actually stoop that low!" I replied. "Yep, remember this day girl; because you will have to walk through the same thing I'm going through. When it comes down to you doing things to better yourself, there are very few people who will be there to back you up, and I mean that!" Kevin exclaimed.

After I got off the phone with Kevin, I grabbed Val, and sat on the couch, replaying in my head what Kevin had just shared with me. He had been with the salon for so many years, even if it was off, and on, with his mental health breaks in between. At the time, I was still so naïve to the fact that after you had given your time, energy and talent to an employer, at the end of the day you were just nail scum in their eyes.

I finished getting ready for work and arrived about fifteen minutes before the client. The whole day, Kathy kept looking in my direction to see if I was busy, or not; and when I didn't have a client, I would make myself scarce so she wouldn't approach me. I made my great escape at 5 p.m. and went home to soak in a nice hot bath before getting ready for the party. Robert and I were going together, so I knew to be ready right on time, as he was always punctual. David once again was absentee. I secretly knew that their relationship was now skidsville. But I was going to let Robert spill the beans. I wasn't going to bring up that sore subject. Robert arrived dressed in a sharp black tux; wow, he looked smashing! We looked pretty damn good together, thank God, and Greyhound, that David wasn't coming! *Now we could really have some fun like we used to before "curmudgeon" came on the scene,* I thought.

There was a valet station set up in front of the salon, with men running to and fro helping guests with their automobiles. *Kevin was really doing this right,* I thought. After Robert and I walked in, we both whispered…Wow! The salon was done in creams with little hints of gold, with beautiful flower arrangements perfectly situated. Amazing looking servers — who were, of course, all men — were dressed only in black short shorts, bow ties and combat boots. *Ooohh, lovely!* And to top it all off, house music was rocking in the background all through the salon. Kevin had really outdone himself; this place was magnificent. It was packed with photographers, magazine and newspaper people, and all of his friends and family. Even our extended drag queen family made an appearance!

I spotted Kevin near the back of the salon where a bar was set up. Of course, Kevin was flirting with the drop-dead gorgeous bartender, so you know I had to interrupt immediately. "Kevin, this place is divine. There aren't enough words to describe how amazing it is!" I added. "Thanks, Girl, I love it too," Kevin said. "Come, let me show you guys around. You're both going to shit a brick when you see what my designer has done for me!" he exclaimed. As Kevin showed Robert and me around every inch of the place, I realized that it was way more than I ever expected. The fact that it opened on time was a miracle from the start.

I was getting pretty thirsty and suddenly a blonde server appeared. I took a glass of champagne off of his tray and looked down because it was so fuckin' obvious; it looked like he had stuffed two softballs in his shorts! "Kevin, where did you find these waiters?" I asked him. "Oh, most of them are on the Gay volleyball circuit and are just helping out for the extravaganza," he replied. "From the looks of it, they are serving up more than COCK-tails!" I added. Kevin started laughing hysterically. "You got that right, girl. You know a gay man never gives up an opportunity to cruise — even during working hours!" We both laughed.

All of a sudden, the double glass doors of the salon come bursting open and a tall lean thing, dressed in drag, barreled through while sobbing, and screaming, making a huge spectacle! Four waiters, with bodies of death, went rushing to the front entrance to grab the dragzilla before it slithered too far into the main part of the salon. *Do I know that guy?* I thought to myself, *He looks so familiar!* Then Dragquilla fell on his knees to the beautifully tiled entryway while screaming Kevin's name! *Oh shit, that's fuckin' Michael. Oh my God, why was he dressed like some old Vaudeville Sea Hag!* I thought.

The mascara was pouring down his face and the bright red lipstick was all over the place. As I got closer to him, he smelled of cheap booze! And he was just screaming Kevin's name and pretty much beyond shit-faced drunk! Kevin then ran up to him with two other "Hunkies" in tow and they scooped Michael up with his feet dragging the floor. They rushed him to the back dispensary while he yelled: "I DIDN'T MEAN TO FUCK AROUND ON YOU. THE FACT WAS THAT YOU WERE STARTING TO GAIN SO MUCH WEIGHT".......OUCH! ♪Fat bottomed girls, you make the rockin' world go round♪

Chapter 29: Edwina Scissorhands

Robert and I followed the entourage as they headed towards the salon office. The "Hunkies" dropped Michael into a swivel chair as he was just balling his head off. Wow, this was awful. I hadn't seen or spoken to him since Kevin moved back. Even though Kevin gave me Michael's contact information, I never got in touch with him and I really felt bad now for not doing so. "What are you doing here; how did you find out about the grand opening tonight and what the fuck are you wearing?" Kevin issued his multi-tiered question while handing Michael copious tissues. "I moved back to town about three months ago; but I knew you wouldn't speak to me, so I had one of my friends hunt you down and fill me in on what you were up to," Michael answered before continuing through a haze of uncontrollable sobbing, "I then found out about the salon and I felt like an idiot because of what I had put you through." Kevin looked over at me while whispering, "It's been horrible because the other cheap queens won't keep him in cigarettes, booze and couture! Oh, and I'm doing amateur drag night down the street on Saturday nights now," Michael added between unruly sobs. "Well, that's exactly what you look like — an amateur — if you're going to do it, you might as well do it right. And comedy is not your deal, sweetheart; that Carol Burnett look is beastly!" Kevin yelled. "I wasn't doing Carol Burnett...." Michael went on to explain, "I was doing..." "Oh my God, that's even more disasterly!" Kevin screamed. "Don't tell me. I don't want to know whom you were impersonating!" Kevin reproached.

About that time, Roller Boy, Lance and Rubin all crowded into the office. "What the fuck is going on here?" Lance yelled. "I hope this kind of bullshit doesn't continue to happen when we open. This is a classy joint I'm running here, not a haven for wayward drag queens!" he went on to say. "Wait a minute, honey!" in piped Kevin, "I let that "Praying Mantis" you call a girlfriend hang around here during a lot of the construction with her putting her two cents in where it didn't belong. I would think this would be no big deal for you!" "You fuckin' fag; how dare you make those insulting references that my sweetums resembles an insect. I might just have to kick your ass!" Lance screamed. "Bring it on, Closet Queen. You have been looking at my ass for years. I know this is just you being jealous because my Ex came back!" Kevin nudged Lance. "Are you out of your fuckin' mind? I don't want you; you're fuckin' crazy!" Lance yelled. With all of this going on, Roller Boy was standing back taking it all in and laughing his head off, with a comment every once in a while about him not being able to wear his roller skates...*but yet this shit is tolerated?* "Because you look crazy, and old, girl!" Kevin turned and snapped at him.

Of course, poor Rubin was trying to be the referee in this madness. He eventually got everyone to tone it down to a low roar, with only a few expletives thrown out every few minutes or so. One of the drag queens spontaneously rushed the office door and whispered in a hushed tone, "Kevin, girl, you better get your ass outta here like in two snaps! Everyone is wondering what's going on, hurry!!" And he hurriedly rushed off, leaving a few scattered feathers behind. Kevin then asked one of the "Hunkies" to help get Michael cleaned up and presentable. Then we all traipsed out to meet the inevitable onslaught of grilling that was to be expected from the other guests.

The salon grand opening was a big success and went on without another hitch. With a lot of help from the "Hunkie Patrol," Michael had finally gotten his shit together and came out smoking a cigarette while standing by Kevin's side — as Kevin hammed it up for the photographers. I could tell from the way they were carrying on that the two of them were heading back to rekindling their relationship. That was probably for the best, anyway. Michael seemed like he had truly hit his rock bottom when he threw himself on the floor earlier that night. Hell: that would have gotten my attention, too, to reconsider taking back a hardship case like Michael.

I was actually beginning to feel a little tired from work and my dogs were starting to bark from the brand new pumps I was wearing. God, it was starting to feel like my feet were breaking in two, I mean four. I looked at Robert and could tell that he, too, was about ready to leave. By then I was a little hungry, because I hadn't thought about eating any of the hors d'oeuvres. "Hey, do you want to go and grab a snack somewhere and maybe talk a little?" I asked him. "Yes, that was exactly what I was thinking!" Robert replied.

We decided just to slip out and not say goodbye to anyone. I just didn't want Kevin to make me stay any longer than I had to. Anyway, that was his gig. *Now that Michael was back, he surely didn't need me around,* I thought. "I know of a place that is about 15 minutes away, with great appetizers and really nice cocktails; it's quiet and never crowded," Robert said. "Oh man, that's what I need right now after the 'High Noon Drama' affair,'" I answered him.

When we went to the restaurant, it was practically empty. "You're not kidding; this place is deserted," I said. A sign at the front entrance requested for patrons to seat themselves, so Robert steered us over to a table in the back corner of the place. *Hmmm, he is ready to spill his breadbasket over the trials and traumas that developed between he and "Ms. Nancy Know It All." Ohhhh can't wait,* I thought. The waitress appeared, looking like one of those tomato-shaped pincushions made out of cloth that your mom, or grandmother, used to stick pins in while sewing. Her hair was bright red and her face was pierced everywhere a hole could remotely be safely penetrated. This image was totally taking me back to my childhood; ♪ Looking back on when I was a little nappy headed boy♪

"What would you like to drink?" the waitress asked, as she gazed at me kind of funny. "What's wrong with you?" Robert asked me. "Nothing, nothing I just got lost in thought," I said. "Well…can the other voice in your head order the damn drink, then?" he implored. "Hold your horses, Roberta. I will have a cranberry absolute and he will have a vodka tonic in a baby bottle, please," I answered. The waitress walked off laughing. "So how's everything," I asked him. "For starters, why don't you erase that smirk off your lips," Robert said jokingly. "What smirk?" I asked, while reaching into my purse for my compact to take a look. "Oh, you mean this smirk? I'm just pulling your collar, you know that," I said. "Yeah, right. Anyway, David and I split up about two weeks ago; and frankly I'm pretty thrilled about it," Robert continued. "Really…what brought this all to a screeching halt?" I asked. "At first it was pretty intriguing hob-knobbing with the so-called elite; but, after a while, their so-called sophisticated asses were boring as hell.

"Talking with David became flavorless and mind-numbing. There was no substance at all; and to further exacerbate the situation...David couldn't dance!" Robert exclaimed, before continuing: "It was like watching someone that didn't have joints; he looked stiffer than a pirate's plank. It was sick to watch because you know how I love to dance; and I really missed our times together even more when I was held captive out on the dance floor with Pippi Longstocking!" "Hey, it's still early and it's of course Saturday night. Let's go downtown and shake our booties!?!" Robert suggested. "Right on, I'm ready! Hey what about our clothes? We look like we just came from a fundraiser." "I don't give a shit at this point. Let's just chalk it up as a costume!" he exclaimed.

So after Robert and I quickly paid the tab, the dynamic duo was then ready to tear it up somewhere. The club wasn't the same after the drug bust, so we decided to give Dane a ring; because, if anybody would know where a kick ass soiree would be, he would definitely be the first candidate! I called Dane from my mobile phone and left a message on his voice mail; within minutes, he returned the call. "Hey Girl, I was thinking about you the other day, where the fuck have you been?" Dane yelled. "I should ask where the fuck have you been? You are way overdue for a haircut!" I retorted. "Yeah, yeah, I know," he said. "Hey, there is a DJ spinning in a warehouse downtown tonight and he's from Detroit. This boy's shit is crazy good!" Dane said. "That's why we're calling your ass. Give me the directions and Robert and I are there!" I said. "Okay, I will wait for you at the front entrance," Dane said. With Robert driving like a gay superhero on a mission, we found the place in no time. Dane was waiting for us, just liked he'd promised. He whisked us through with the murmuring going on behind us. To this day, I've never stood in line for anything and never, ever will! The music was pumping and House filled the air! God, how I missed this! ♫ DANCE♫

Observing Kevin and Michael together again was kind of like watching a bad sitcom with a most highly annoying laugh track. They were both being so overly kind and affectionate that it was fuckin' weird! Kevin's salon was doing quite well, and the prices he was charging for his services had gone through the roof! He was well worth it, though. If I hadn't already been a privileged client of his, I would have had to work the streets full time just to pay for my visits!

Michael quit his night job as a waiter, and amateur performer, to take on the full responsibilities of a housewhore.... I mean, housewife. So they were just settling into the blissful life of starting over again in love. They suddenly got on a kick of watching movies at home and barely hitting the bars at all. What the hell? It was then 1993 and I was 26 years old. I cannot tell you much about my 25th year, because I spent pretty much all of it partying with Robert, and crissy, again. After Robert split up with David, we kind of went to the extreme. I was hardly ever at home again. Val was, of course, pissed and felt neglected; he even told me so! Actually, it's quite funny when Val was letting me have it. Imagine a penguin with a lisp!

So I will go ahead and skip that year, as it was pretty raunchy! When Kevin and Michael took on the Ma and Pa Kettle role, it was kind of a relief for me, because I needed to once again draw back and slow down. I knew I wouldn't be able to keep up that sort of frantic pace forever. I was seriously considering going to an AA meeting because I really didn't know if I could go out without having a drink or doing firecracker party favors…or both. I'd actually never tried AA; and, to be honest, I didn't want to, so that's why I was considering: *hmmm, maybe I have a little problem that's starting to fester?* I didn't dare tell Kevin my plan of going to one of those meetings. I just looked in the paper and found one in my area. I was a little nervous on the way there. What if they made me stand up and talk? What if they asked me what I do on the weekends or during the week? What was I going to say? "Wellll…. My friend and I party till the neon, with booze and crissy washed all over us as we're takin' it to the hardwood, or the concrete?" Uhhhh..don't think so!

I pulled into the parking lot of a white brick and plain looking one-story building. As I carefully opened the heavy tinted glass door, cigarette smoke came billowing out like it had escaped from a tee-pee. There were about twenty people — mostly men — standing around or sitting drinking cokes, or coffee, and they were all lighting up. I didn't have a problem with cigarette smoke because I was a social smoker. I didn't smoke during the day at work. I only smoked at night, and I carried my cig in a long antique rhinestone holder so I could burn people who were standing in the way as I tried to maneuver through the clubs. The majority of the people there were in their latter 40's, with a couple of people who were maybe around my age. I couldn't really figure out how old the younger ones were because they looked so beat up. Now, you AA people don't need to get all twisted off; you know that what I'm saying is true!

Anyway, I sat down in a chair next to a watercooler and about that time the person over the meeting walked in and said; "Okay, everyone, get settled. Let's go ahead and get started, shall we?" This man was probably in his 50's…maybe… *Shit, who knows?* He kind of resembled Rutger Hauer — not the super hot Rutger Hauer from back in the day. I'm talking the Rutger Hauer 100 years from now... *And these people didn't drink anymore?* Then what the fuck are they doing to cause them to look so fuckin' horrendous? I was baffled.

Then I felt someone sit right next to me; it was one of the younger guys and I looked over and gave him a half ass grin. *Okay, girl...don't look too friendly,* I told myself. He was sitting so close that his sneakers were literally touching my very cute platform sandals. "Hi, I'm Manny," he said. "Uh, Manny, it's nice to meet you; but either move those boats or sail them; you're way in my video right now!" I shot at him. "Ha, Ha, you're a funny girl!" he snorted. "Okay, Manny, save it, will you; we're getting ready to start!" Rutger retorted Manny's way. Well, anyone who has ever attended one of these knows the whole routine, so I won't bore you with it. But as I watched the people share about what was going on in their lives, I also picked up on all of their mannerisms and something was not quite kosher up in the ole' dill pickle, if you know what I mean. And if you don't, some of those people were a muy loco en la cabeza!

Afterwards, Manny started hitting on me again, asking me the single, smingle questions: "Do you have a boyfriend, blah, blah?" He was actually cute, except for the fact that it looked like his nose had been fractured numerous times. "Hey, would you like to go grab something to eat?" he asked. "Yeah, why not?" I replied. "Do you want me to follow you in your car?" I asked. "Uhh...actually, I don't have a car right now after my 3rd DWI," he casually mentioned. *Hmmm... Maybe I should bail on this character; this is beginning to sound really fucked up,* I thought to myself. But, of course, you all know me by now. Miss Thing has to push it to the limit, right? Drive it like she means it, right?

"Okay, where do you want to go," I asked him. "Oh, let's discuss it outside; people in here are pretty nosy," he replied. "I'm parked over there," I said. When we arrived at my car, he immediately said, "Hey, why don't we go grab some vodka and go back to your place and party?" "Oh, you want to party, huh?" I asked him. "Yeah girl, let's go!" he shouted. "Okay, for starters, turn around and get on your knees facing the car door so I can put my foot up your ass, then get the fuck outta here!!!" I screamed at him. He pushed the car door open. I then reached over, grabbed it myself and slammed it shut before speeding off like Daisy Duke! ♫ Just'a good ol'boys, never meaning' no harm♫

Saturday, I went in to work still reeling from the AA experience the day before. I knew I wasn't an alcoholic, because it didn't seem to control my everyday life. I wasn't drinking vodka with my fruit juice in the morning. Hell, I didn't even have breakfast. I always just started my day off with one steaming hot cup of coffee. And the coffee wasn't even spiked with Baileys.

That whole experience of seeing those people so verklempt, and dejected, just made my heart ache. All day at work, I felt like I was just going through the motions. All I heard my self say back to the clients were the words, "Uh huh? Really?" or "That's cool." Not hearing a damn thing that they were yapping about, all I could think about was Rutger and Manny, shit!! Michelle announced that I had a phone call so I quickly ran over and answered it. "Hello?" "Hey, Miss Thing, are you almost done for the day?" Kevin asked. *Wow, thank God! It's like he knew I needed to talk with him.* "Actually, I have one more man's haircut and I'm out of this bitch. So I should be heading out by 6 p.m." "Why, what's up?" I asked. "Michael and I are just going to hang out at the house and watch a movie; we would love for you to come over." "Yes, that's exactly what I would like to do tonight," I replied. "Okay, great. Oh, Rubin is coming over, too! Don't worry about bringing anything over; we're fully stocked up on beverages," Kevin added. "Okay, I will see you guys around 7:30 pm or so," I said. "Okay, see ya!" Kevin replied.

My client came in early and I suddenly became Edwina Scissorhands, cutting that bush so fast, and furious, even my client made a comment about it. I just ignored his ass and shuffled him to the front with a smile before getting the fuck out of dodge! I quickly rushed home, changed, and headed out to Kevin and Michael's place. The front door was already unlocked, so I let myself in. "Hey guys, I'm here!" I yelled. Rubin was already there sitting on the floor in the den fiddling with the VCR. "Hey, they're in the garage getting stuff out of the freezer." "Okay, how are you doing?" I asked him. "I'm doing pretty good. My clients love the salon; it's definitely a total step up," he replied. "I'm now getting more referrals because my clients are not ashamed for their friends and co-workers to experience the new place," Rubin went on to explain. Michael and Kevin then entered the room. "Hey, Miss Thing, how long have you been here?" Kevin asked. "Only about 5 minutes or so," I said. "What movie are we going to watch?" "The Color Purple," Michael answered. "Isn't that movie supposed to be really depressing?" I asked. "Oh, it has its tear jerking moments, but the ending is fabulous!" Kevin exclaimed. Kevin cocked his head a little and looked at me and then said, "Hey, come into the kitchen with me for a second." After I followed him in, he turned around with his hands on his hips and asked, "You look like you have been dragged around on a rug; what's wrong now?" "Well….. yesterday afternoon I went to a AA meeting…" "You went to a fuckin' what meeting, what the fuck for!!! I should kick your ass, girl!" Kevin screamed.

"Is everything alright in there?" Rubin asked in the other room. "Yeah girl, everything is peachy!" "Why would you do that? You're not an alcoholic!" "Well, once I went to the meeting and saw the other people, I kind of figured that out for myself real fast; but it left a really bad, and lasting, impression on me that I can't shake." "Yeah, I know, I went to one of those before years ago and a lot of those people have some real dark rooted shit built up. It's not just about the drinking and the drugs; it's what has happened to them prior to that," Kevin explained. "You're just going through that twenty-something phase — where you're trying to figure things out," he went on to say. "Don't worry about it, things are happening the way they should. You're not going back, right?" Kevin asked. "Hell no!" I replied. "Good," he said, "now grab that platter and tissue box and help me bring this stuff into the den."

Chapter 30: Hurts So Good

That following week, on a Wednesday evening, I got home after work at around 7 p.m. As soon as I opened my door, I heard the phone ring one final time and my answering machine picked up right away. I quickly threw my things down on the couch and ran to the bathroom. Oh my God, it was Frank! *Please leave your phone number!* I thought to myself, as I heard his voice coming from the speaker in the living room. I'd gotten a Christmas and birthday card from Frank and Philip since they moved to Amsterdam. We had spoken maybe twice on the phone briefly but I hadn't heard most of the details of how they coped with living in another part of the world. Just like I sensed that it would, the phone started ringing again. I leapt onto my bed, almost knocking Val to the floor, as he looked at me with a frown; and I yanked the cordless phone off its cradle.

"Hello!" I said, while out of breath. "Hey Sissy, I'm so glad I caught you! Hey Sissy, what is going on? I heard you on the machine and was praying that you would leave your number. I didn't know what time you would be home tonight or if you would ever make it home with your busy lifestyle," Frank said jokingly. "You're definitely right on about that," I told him. "Tonight was a good time to catch me because usually on Wednesdays I work till about 6 p.m., or so." "Well, I have some fantastic news for you. Philip and I are moving back in a month." "No, fuckin' way!" I yelled. "Yes, fuckin' way!" Frank replied. "I'm thinking about working at your salon for a few months, or so, just to build up my clientele again, then maybe branch out on my own, not quite sure yet," he said. "Well, that's funny that you mention branching out, because that's exactly what Kevin has done," I said. "Are you shitting me?" Frank yelled. "Yep, he has his own place with two partners; maybe you could join his team later," I replied. "Yeah, that will be definitely something I would consider." All of a sudden, I heard Frank yell, "Get down from there, Marilyn! Shit! Girl, I have to let you go. The dog is devouring a loaf of bread on the table. I will let you know when we arrive! Love you, bye!!" And he hung up.

  The next day, I was working from 1 till 9 p.m., so I made sure I got up early and finished as many chores as I could, because I knew I would do absolutely nothing once I made it back home after a long work day. I arrived about twenty minutes early and peeked over the front desk to look at my schedule. *Shit, I was going to be working my ass off that day, but that meant the day would fly by!* I thought. I did notice I was actually given a twenty-minute break. *Hmmm, to do what?* That wasn't even enough time to go take a shit, let alone get something to eat. *Well, maybe someone could grab me something when they went out for themselves.* I quickly set up my station, and then the battle began.

  By 2 p.m., I could have chewed the arm off of my cutting chair. Everyone around me had a client, so I knew they didn't have time to go anywhere for lunch. Immediately, I thought of a place that sold bagels. Actually, I loathed those things, but at that point I didn't give a shit. I just needed something to fill the void in my stomach. I didn't even let Michelle, or Penny — the other receptionist — know that I was leaving. They didn't seem to notice, anyway.

As I walked down to the bagel factory, I thought, *at least they smell better than they taste.* After I paid the girl, and started walking slowly back to the salon, I decided to go into a bookstore that I frequented from time to time. I just needed to relax and at least enjoy the little time I had to myself. I only had about thirteen more minutes to go before I had to head back into the trenches. The sales clerk behind the desk greeted me. I said hello and kind of browsed a little before heading back to an area that I knew usually carried discounted items.

As I made my way to the back of the store, I noticed a guy who was probably about 5 ft 7 inches in height with brown hair, looking up and reaching for a book that was almost at his fingertips, but not quite. That day, I was wearing my 5 and 1 half-inch "Red or Dead" platform sandals, which made me 5'11, so it was quite easy for me to reach the book for him. He turned, looked over with a smile, and said "thank you." "No problem," I answered. I then realized it was John Mellencamp, or was it John Cougar Mellencamp? He had changed his name a couple of times, so I couldn't remember which one was the current one. And, also, he was a lot shorter than I imagined him to be.

This time, I knew to keep my mouth shut and not be rude like I was to Mr. Man from Depeche Mode. "Are you looking for something for yourself?" he asked. "No, not really, I'm on a short break from work and just needed to get out and breathe for a few minutes," I said. "What do you do?" he asked. "I'm a hairdresser at a salon that's about two doors down from here." "Oh, I'm about due for a haircut," he interjected. "Well, I'm booked solid today, Honey, but I'm sure there is someone who will jump at the chance to accommodate you," I answered.

So I gave him my card and said, "Here is the main number of the salon." "Okay, I will have someone call and set it up," he said. As we both walked toward the salon, I noticed that Penny was behind the desk talking on the phone. When Johnny Boy saw her, he instantly fell in love! "Who is that?" he gushed. "Oh, that's Penny. She's not only dating someone, but she's also gay!" I answered. That didn't seem to deter him at all. He just kept starting at her, totally mesmerized. I guess I couldn't blame him, as she did resemble a pixie doll. Her hair was a bright orange pumpkin color and the short haircut perfectly framed her pixie face. She had bright blue eyes, with white porcelain skin. So it was really hard not to stare at her, to tell you the truth. "Do you think someone would come to my room and do the cut, because I have some important stuff to go over later this afternoon," he asked. "Oh sure, Michelle or Penny can totally set it up, but I have to get back to work, ciao!" I said.

Michelle came running up to me as I walked towards the back of the salon. She started walking with me. "Aren't you going to cancel your day and do his hair?" she asked, amazed. "No, I'm not going to treat my clients like that; they have been very loyal to me. I will never put a celebrity over anyone. Everyone's the same in my book," I said. "Wow, okay, I will check and see who is available," she said. "Well, you won't have to see for long, because everyone else in here will cancel their day for this guy. I guarantee it." I said.

Louise just had a no show, so Michelle summoned her to the desk and laid the bomb on her. Of course, she almost peed herself with delight. I continued to work the rest of the day, not giving much thought to the rock star status quo. *He's a man, for God's sake, shit!* No offense, JM.

Just as I was finishing up a highlight, Michelle called me to the front desk. So I sat my client under the processing lamps and quickly walked to the front. Michelle was right there in my face before I could ask her what she wanted. She leaned down and whispered to me so the clients in the waiting area couldn't hear her. "Girl, John called the front desk about twenty minutes ago and asked to speak to Penny; and invited her up to his suite after his haircut." "Fuckin' shit, are you shitting me?!" I yelled. Everyone in the reception area quickly turned to our direction after my country ass outburst.

So we both proceeded to run down the hall to the back of the salon for more privacy, with Michelle asking Donny to fill in for her at the desk for a few seconds. "You better not let Kathy see him up there by himself for too long," I told her. "Yeah, I know, so let me tell you quickly what just happened," she said. "She just left a few minutes ago, so Louise should be on her way back pretty soon," Michelle said. "Oh God, this is crazy!" I said.

You see, the whole salon knew that Penny was supposed to go on some kind of Lesbian retreat with her girlfriend Kellie. And to really break it down for all of you, Kellie was not to be fucked with! *If she found out that her girlfriend was with a Man, she would have come up there and ripped balls off; and JM would be the first one to get it!* I thought.

"They're scheduled to leave this afternoon and Kellie is supposed to pick Penny up here! I hope to God she doesn't do anything stupid and stay up there too long!" Michelle cried. "What I don't really get is why would she go anyway? She doesn't even like men. Maybe it's just that celebrity mojo that takes a hold of people," I said, before adding, "We've all seen men and women do some crazy shit when they meet a star; I just didn't have it in me." Kevin always said: "When they start shitting roses, then that's when I will bow down and say to the rose shitter, hmmm….you're different than me!"

"She better get her ass back here pronto, because Kathy will not tolerate a scene in here and Kellie will cause a scene." "Hell, I wouldn't blame her: HER GIRLFRIEND IS WITH A GUY!!" Michelle yelled. Twenty minutes before Penny's chariot was due to arrive, she came waltzing in like it was no big deal. "Oh my God, bitch, you were really cutting it close. You know how Kellie is always early! So did you do em?" Michelle asked. "We didn't do anything. He just serenaded me with his guitar," Penny answered. "Well, why do you look like you just got poked?" Michelle prodded. "Nothing happened, but it was very sweet," Penny continued, with a dreamy look on her angel face. "Girl, you better go look in the mirror and rearrange that expression on your face; or it's going to be Armageddon when Kellie arrives!" Michelle instructed her.

Michelle was the one who dealt with Kellie the most, so she was definitely not crying wolf about what would come to pass. Penny then went to the restroom to wipe the gaze off her face, and Michelle and I proceeded to walk back to the front. Kellie was already there, with a look of disapproval on her face for having to wait a minute longer. "Hey Kel," Michelle and I casually, and in unison, said. "Hey… so where is she, we gotta go," Kellie barked back at us, as she glanced down at her big man watch. Right about then, Penny slowly emerged with her flowered covered backpack. As they reached the front glass doors, Penny turned and gently placed her index finger to her lips. And, to this day, we never, ever found out the true scoop on what really happened in that hotel room….. ♪ when the walls come tumbling down♪

Chapter 31: Switch Hitter Highway

Frank and Philip arrived back in town in thirty days, just as they planned. Philip had already found them a cozy little condo near the downtown area. It would be about a twenty-five minute drive for Frank if he decided to work for Kathy, but he said it would be a small price to pay in order to get his clientele re-established. Frank had contacted Kevin the day after he had contacted me and told him their plans of moving back to town. So everyone was informed of their arrival.

Kevin invited us all to meet at the salon on a Thursday night, after hours, so Frank could check out Kevin's extravagant baby. That also gave Kevin an opportunity to show off in front of Frank and gloat. I noticed right off the bat that Frank and Kevin seemed to have some weird type of sibling rivalry between them. Frank often made cracks about Kevin's large ass and Kevin was ruthless about mocking Frank's ears. Bitches could never make fun of each other like that, but guys could do it to each other and totally get away with it — while remaining friends til the end.

After everyone arrived at the salon around 8:30 p.m., Kevin gave Frank and Philip the grand tour. "Wow, girl, I can see that things have been going real well for you since you left the barnyard, huh? Looks like you have been eating pretty good since I saw you last. Did your contractor purposely make the front doors of the salon just a little wider to accommodate that ass of yours?" Frank asked. "Ha, ha. Hell!" Kevin fired back. "Philip honey, did you notice that all of the overseas airlines have developed a prototype for a floatation device that resembles your Man's ears?" "Whatever, girl," Frank snapped. And, by that time, we were all rolling!

There was music playing in the background and, all of a sudden, I heard a voice that I didn't recognize. It was the clearest, most beautiful voice I'd ever heard. "Who is this singing?" I asked the group. "Her voice is simply captivating. God, I wish I could sing like this!" I added. "This is k.d. lang." "Wow, I would love to see her in concert," I said. "Actually, I read in the Advocate that she's coming to town in two weeks, so why don't all of us go together." Kevin suggested. At about that time, Rubin came out from the back of the salon, having just finished setting up his massage room for the following day. "What are you guys up to now?" he asked. "We've all just planned to go see k. d. lang; do you want to come along?" Kevin asked him. "Yes, that would be great, I totally adore her!" Rubin said. "Okay, good. I will purchase the tickets and then you guys can reimburse me the night of the show."

When I picked up the cd cover, I couldn't believe that voice came out of that person. I don't know what I pictured, but it wasn't that. She was very attractive; but she was so butch, with a voice of an angel, and a great haircut, by the way. It was so incredible; I was in awe of the whole package.

The following day — which was Friday — I received a call from Rubin while I was working. I was actually a little taken aback that he was calling me. "Hi, it's Rubin." "Hi Rubin, what's up?" I asked. "Would you like to come over to my place and maybe have some tea?" he asked. "Uhhh, okay, what day is good for you?" I asked him. "How about twelve noon this coming Sunday?" he asked. "Okay, that works for me," I said. And he gave me directions to his home. After I hung up, I was confused as hell. *Why is he inviting me over? And what the hell is his boyfriend going to do while I'm there; is he also joining us for tea? WEIRD...*

Rubin lived in an older established neighborhood, where the homes looked like they were built in the early 1900's. Come to think of it, it was a historical district I had heard, and read, a little about, but never had a chance to visit. Well, my chance had finally arrived; and I somehow knew it would be more than I could ever have imagined, or expected. I located the house immediately, because Rubin described it as a very large Victorian home, light pink in color, with a rounded enclosed front porch. Yep, it was definitely the only pink house on the block as far as the eye could see. I slowly pulled into a small narrow parking lot, and before I could turn off the ignition, Rubin was already coming out of the front door. "Hey Girl, I see you found my place okay. You're right on time." Rubin exclaimed. "Yes, I'm hardly ever late to anything. I think it's pretty rude to do that, especially when someone is expecting you," I added. "Well, this is definitely going to be fun," he enthused. "Are you hungry? I have finger sandwiches and herbal tea ready for us."

He opened the door and let me walk ahead of him first into the front foyer. The living room was filled with books from floor to ceiling, everywhere you looked. Books, books and more books: and they all looked to be over 100 years old. What was very odd, and eye-catching, about Rubin's décor was that the home was Victorian style, but his furnishings were from the late 50's to early 1960's. I actually really loved it, because everywhere you looked there was a little lamp, or a table, that took you right back into the Rat Pack Era. "I really like your house, Rubin," I complimented him. "Thanks, I moved here about five years ago and I couldn't imagine living anywhere else. The neighborhood is well-preserved; and, believe it or not, the neighbors actually mind their own damn business," he said. "Wow, that's a miracle. What area has neighbors that mind their own beeswax? I've never heard of such a thing, ever!" I said. I then heard someone clear his throat behind us; and a tall, thin man, with Buddy Holly glasses, stood there with a grimaced look on his face like that cartoon character Snoopy. "Aren't you going to introduce me to your little friend?" he coyly asked Rubin. "Miss Thing…this is Dexter." "Nice to meet you," I said. *Dexter didn't say nice to meet me back. Hmmm, I just arrived in a beehive and the Queen Bee doesn't like me one bit!* I thought. "Dexter is my roommate…"Rubin began to say, before being abruptly cut off by: "So now I've been reduced to being just your fuckin' roommate, huh?!" Dexter screamed. *Oh shit!* I thought. "Well hiney holes and elbows, what should I do next, get on a broom and ride on up to the attic and scrub the floors?!" "Honey, do whatever makes you comfortable…"Rubin mumbled. "Arghhhh, you are such a prick!!!!" Dexter screamed, before turning and rushing towards the front door. I noticed that he had a slight limp. *I will have to ask Rubin about that limp later,* I thought. "Never mind about that spectacle, he's just having one of his tantrums again," Rubin said. "Let's go into the sunroom, it's much nicer in there," he added.

We sat down at a little bistro table and Rubin began to pour our tea.... "Uhhh, Rubin, thanks for the tea and the sandwiches, but after I have this cup, would it be possible if I could maybe have something a little stronger, like maybe vodka?" I asked. *I knew I needed something a little stronger than herbal tea after that recent little production.* "Oh yes, I'm sure Dexter has some booze stored away in a cabinet somewhere. He claims that I'm the one who caused him to start over-indulging in the sauce; but when we first met he could suck em' down like a frosted malt," Rubin explained. I started glancing around the sunroom as Rubin poured our tea, and it was really quite lovely. Birdfeeders were strategically hung outside. I just sat back and watched while little birds came to feast and bask in the sun. The hummingbirds buzzed energetically. "How long have you and Dexter been together," I asked. Rubin explained: "Not very long, really, maybe eight months. He wanted to move in pretty fast. Against my better judgment, I gave in, and then found out later that he had bad credit and a habit of not being able to keep employment. So now he's angry because I've given him two weeks to move out." He added: "It really amazes me how people can use and abuse you, and then when you've had enough, and take charge, it's like you're the evil one." "Yes, I totally agree, I'm sure Kevin told you about his friend he sent home on a bus," I said. "Yes, he told me about that. That's why I decided to just get him out of here. It became such a crazy ass way of living. I'm not that type of person. I hate fuckin' drama!" Rubin said. "Rubin, can I ask you one more thing about Dexter?" I asked. "Sure," Rubin replied. "I noticed when Dexter was stomping out that he had a limp. Do you know what happened to him?" I asked. "Oh, why yes. He, and an asshole buddy of his, were in a convenient store stealing merchandise. There was a really bad storm. As they ran out of the store laughing, a clerk went chasing after them. His buddy made it to the car safely. Dexter was wearing a belt with a huge western belt buckle depicting the insignia of Texas. As Dexter touched a metal pole on his way towards the car, a lightning bolt came down and hit him square in the dick...." Rubin was so calm in explaining about what happened to Dexter, that all I could do was just look at him dumbfounded. And, all of a sudden, I saw a little grin spread across Rubin's lips, for just a quick second, before he took another sip from his teacup.

Rubin and I visited for five hours, and I couldn't believe how fast the time flew by. He walked me to my car. After I got in, he shut my door, leaned in my driver's side window, and asked: "Would you like to go see a foreign film with me next week...on Wednesday evening?" "Ugghhh... sure, that would be fun," I replied. "Okay, I will pick you up at your place around 8 p.m., will that work for you?" he asked. "Yes, Wednesdays are my early days," I said. "See ya soon!" he said. As I drove away, and got on the road, a world wind of thoughts started to flood in. *WHAT THE FUCK WAS I GETTING INTO NOW?!!! This guy dated MEN! HAS BEEN WITH MEN!!* I had never been in that type of situation before, EVER! This was my FIRST Bi-Rodeo! Wow, no wonder Dexter was fit to be tied. He couldn't compete with me; I was from a different order. *Okay, Okay, let's hold your horse...maam, maybe he wants to be friends, and that's all,* I thought to myself. *Yeah, that's it: just bosom buddies, someone to have tea with and go to the movies with...* Well, I can't, and won't, think about this because it will only cause me to be even more freaked out!

Monday, and Tuesday, the following week just seemed to last forever. I tried not to think about what I guess you would call "My Date" with Rubin. On Tuesday night around 10:30, Kevin called me. I knew he would call because surely Rubin had told him we were going out. "Hey Girl, ♪ I know somebody who wants your Cooter Cakes♪!" "Oh cut it out, he does not want my cakes, at all." "Whatever Girl, I know you're not that naïve!" he coyly added. "But if you decide to go down the 'Switch Hitter Highway' — and get down and dirty — make sure you use a condom!!" Kevin said. "We're not going to get down with anything!" I yelled back. "Ha, Ha! Okay, Okay, I'm just making sure, you know how Yo Mama can get over-protective," he said. "I know, and I really appreciate your concerns. But to tell you the truth, I don't think I'm attracted to him in that way," I clarified. "Well, you may not be now, but Rubin is a charmer and has very mesmerizing qualities. Before you know it, Ba Bam! His shit can sneak up on you without any warning!" Kevin spoke ominously. "Okay, well, I will make sure I wear my chastity belt whenever I'm with Don Juan," I emphasized.

  So then the blessed Wednesday had finally arrived and my last client canceled at the last minute, so I had a couple of hours to figure out my date outfit. I was thinking that I probably should go a little Rockabilly rhinestone cowgirl, so I wouldn't look too far off from Rubin's attire. Rubin rang the doorbell at 7:45. *Damn, he's ready to roll!* I thought. I opened the door and... *yep, I was spot on, he was dressed the same way he always did: white t-shirt, black jeans rolled up at the bottom 50's style, with black combat boots; and his shaved head appeared extra shiny tonight.* "Are you all set to go?" Rubin asked. "Yep, I'm ready," I responded. I followed Rubin out to the apartment parking lot and he led me towards a bright red car with a white top. *Wow! Such an absolutely stunning car!* "Rubin, your car is gorgeous, what is it?" I asked. "It's a 1957 Bel-Air Sports Coupe," he answered. "It was my Grandmother's car. She was actually a mechanic and she gave it to me before she died," he said. "Grandma must have been amazing," I added. "Yes, she really was. Actually, I think she was a lesbian, but could never, ever come out in those days. She always wore pants and men's work shirts; and she smoked a cigar," he explained. *Hmmm, that explains a few things about ole Rube,* I thought.

As Rubin opened the car door for me, I started looking inside at the interior. The car was in perfect condition inside and out. It looked like it just came off the showroom floor. *Uh oh, all of a sudden, I heard Kevin's voice,* "Rubin is a charmer and has very mesmerizing qualities...."

As we started to head out, I began to tell Rubin about what I thought of him when I first saw him on the bus, how he scared the living shit out of me. He started to laugh out loud and replied, "That's pretty funny. I guess I do appear to some people to be pretty menacing, but I couldn't even hurt a fly. I used to frequently take the city transit because I didn't feel that my car would be safe in those parking garages at the old place. Now, with the new salon set up, I don't have any worries about that anymore," he explained. "What movie are we going to see?" I asked. "The name of it is called 'KiKa.' It's a drama/ comedy. A cosmetologist is called on by a guy to provide makeup for the 'corpse' of his stepson, but I can't tell you the rest, because I will give it all away." "Please don't tell me the rest, because what you just told me sounds utterly dreadful, and this is supposed to be a comedy?" I asked him. "Yes, but you know how some foreign films can be; they are always a little quirky," he replied.

We arrived at the theatre and noticed that quite a few people were already there. There was a lounge that was adjacent to it and we were early, so Rubin asked if I wanted to get a drink beforehand. "Yes, that's a great idea," I said. *I knew I needed something before the show, because it didn't sound like it was going to be your average Hollywood fluff at all,* I thought. Tammy and I were actually kicked out of this lounge bar too, no, not the one that Louise and I skated through. This was a different one. The female manager hated us.

One night, we got a little tipsy, *okay, maybe a lot tipsy,* and she told us to leave and never come back. Well, that was a few years back, so I hoped the old bitch was gone by then. *Thank God! There was a new manager there, whew! I would hate to embarrass Rubin at a movie theatre lounge! How would that look?* When we finished our drinks, and walked to the other side of the building, Rubin took out his wallet to pay for our tickets. The female attendant behind the booth had all the personality of a backdoor. I suddenly remembered back in the early days, when I was trying to get a job, and not one person would give me a shot. *How in the hell did this girl get this position with the attitude she was sporting?* I was baffled.

Well, to pretty much sum it up, the movie was weird and disturbing; but the cranberry vodka I had earlier had numbed me up pretty good, so I could glaze my way through it. I just sat there and thought about being with this guy. Do you know the feelings you get ever so often when you have particular recollections of your childhood? *And you can actually remember the smell of the air that particular day or have a glimpse of the curtains waving in the breeze of an open window in your bedroom?* That's how I felt being with Rubin, like I was experiencing things for the very first time, only on a slight acid trip level. Finally, the flick was over and, as we walked out of the theatre, Rubin asked me what I thought. "Rubin, that was some crazy shit, but who knows; maybe it will be some good material I can use one day if I ever decide to write a book!" I replied.

♫Well, you don't know what we can find, why don't you come with me little girl, on a magic carpet ride♫.

Chapter 32: Constantly Craving Surprises

Rubin invited me over to his home again the next evening, which was Thursday night. I hadn't been out with a guy that many times during a week, ever! It was like he couldn't get enough; and we hadn't even held hands, or kissed. I think we were both a little nervous about starting some type of intimacy thing. *I sure as fuck was, I can tell ya!* But I kept being drawn back, like a junkie to his smack.

I arrived at his place a little later than usual, because Thursday nights were my late nights at the salon. I couldn't help wondering if the Killer Bee was going to be lurking around the hive this evening. As I pulled into the parking lot, I could see lights on downstairs, inside the house, and there was one lonely light on in a room on the second floor. *That must be the room where Dexter resided while making his killer bittersweet honey,* I thought.

Rubin opened the door as soon as I was about to ring the doorbell. "Come in; you're right on time, as usual," he said. I followed him into the den area and, instead of offering me tea, Rubin handed me a cranberry vodka. *Whoa, this is a surprise!* I thought.

"I have a treat for us this evening. I have some poetry I would like to read to you that I personally wrote a few years ago," he said. *Oh boy, what a treat,* I thought. *Is he fuckin' serious?* The only time I ever read any type of poetry was in high school, because they forced me to. I just didn't want to sit back and reflect on what the author was trying to say. Who gave a shit, anyway! But I was nice and gracious, like always, and said: "Sure, that would be nice."

We took a seat on the couch; and as soon as Rubin started to read, Dexter materialized out of nowhere like a "phantom housekeeper" and started dusting around us with a feather duster. But Rubin just ignored him, and continued reciting his works, as I started to gulp my cocktail. Rubin finally interjected just about the time when Dexter started dusting the couch that we sat on. "What the fuck do you think you're doing?" Rubin yelled at him. "Just a little dusting, you know how this old place can get," Dexter replied. "You had all day to dust and you start now?" Rubin asked. "Oh, I've been meaning to ask you something," Dexter went on speaking, like what he was doing was all perfectly normal. "A friend of mine is having a birthday party on Saturday for his 'Lover' and he said I could bring a guest. So do you want to be my guest?" Dexter asked Rubin. "No…sorry, Miss Thing and I have plans to go see k.d. lang in concert," Rubin said. "Oh, so you already have plans, huh? Well that's fine, suit yourself I will just have to look through my Rolodex, because there are plenty of men who are just waiting to be in my presence…" Dexter drawled. "I'm sure most of the homeless bums that you normally trick out with are just waiting for you to ride up on your bicycle and take them to the nearest park," Rubin snapped. "You are such an asshole!" Dexter screamed while limping off again upstairs toward his lair. Through this whole scenario, all I could do was just sit there with my mouth wide open. Rubin then looked over at me and asked, "Another one?"

Saturday at work was fuckin' crazy. I was slinging hair all over the damn place. There is nothing more satisfying than cutting a bunch a hair off and slamming it into the wall! Okay, I have to tell you the truth. I had the privilege of doing a Mohawk on a chick that day, and it was fun! And yes, for some reason, people still want that type of do!

Afterwards, I met the guys at Kevin's salon because we were all going to carpool together; but, of course, Kevin had something else in mind. I parked my car in the rear parking lot and made my way through the back entrance. I could hear Dead or Alive turned way up ♪ I want surprises! I want surprises! ♪

As I walked to the middle of the salon, everybody was dancing and screaming along to the song. "Well, you girls are in full swing, I see. You all have definitely worn the fuck out of this tune!" I yelled. *Hell, even Rubin was cutting a rug. Wow he cannot dance... Strike 1, 2, and 3, strike, strike, strike!* I thought. About that time a man dressed in a tuxedo walked in and said: "The limo is ready, sir." *No fuckin' way, we're going in a limo?* I then tried to control myself so I wouldn't get all country on everyone. Yes, girl, I decided that we had to do this right. "No queen goes to a concert with her friends piled in a station wagon honey!" Kevin replied.

The concert was starting at 8 p.m., so we all decided to go to a little lounge bar near the venue. Kevin then told the limo driver where we wanted to go and he answered back, "Very good, Sir." Kevin then leaned my way and whispered to me: "Girl, he's (the driver) kinda cute, don't you think?" "Yes, he's kinda cute," I said, "but I'm not in the mood right now Kevin," I said. "Girl, you are so strange. When do you ever get in the mood?" he asked. "Well, if you must know, it's when you're not around!" I retorted. Kevin threw his head back and laughed. We arrived shortly at our destination. When we walked into the bar, it looked like a dyke fest was taking place. *Hmmm…these women are obviously going where we're going,* I thought. Is it just my imagination or are 80% of the people in here trying to clone k.d. lang? Even some of the men, *or I think that's a guy over there by the bar…* Shit, I can't tell who is, or who isn't, in this place! The place was very crowded; but Michael knew one of the bartenders who managed to get in our drink order pretty quick, which pissed off at least a few of the patrons. My drink was small and pretty watered down by the generic "Donald Duck" cranberry juice and mixed with the "skull and cross bones vodka," but of course I managed to get it down without a hitch in my "get a long."

We then soon all piled back into the limo and arrived at the concert venue fifteen minutes before show time. Our seats were located on the left hand side and the sixth row from the stage. "These are amazing seats!" I exclaimed to Kevin, with him smiling and nodding back to me. A few minutes later, k.d. entered on stage and the crowd went berserk! "We love you, KATY! We love you, KATY!" a woman kept screaming towards the stage over, and over, after every break in a song.

Finally, k.d. got sick of that stupid bitch pronouncing her name wrong, and promptly corrected the drunk, moronic audience member. "MY NAME IS k.d. NOT KATY!" k.d. bellowed back. Of course, that didn't stop that dingo at all, as she seemed to go up to an even more feverish pitch… "KATY, KATY, KATY!!!" *Oh my God, I could never be a performer and put up with that shit night after night!* I thought. I would totally be arrested for coming down with two cases of whup ass on one of those individuals. Almost halfway through, I heard a commotion to my left. I was sitting between Kevin and Rubin; and Frank and Phillip were on Kevin's left. There was an empty seat next to Rubin, and guess who showed up to make a spectacle? "I DO HAVE MY TICKET STUB!" Dexter sputtered. An attendant tried in vain to escort Dexter to his seat, but the dumb ass was so stinking drunk he didn't realize it. Rubin started to lower his head into his hand, he was so embarrassed and probably pissed. "I finally made it. You had no idea I was coming…Well, surprise, surprise, motherfucker!!!" Dexter ranted. *Ohhh shit and shinola, this is going to get real good!* I thought.

    A real butch mamasita with wild, untamed curly red hair turned around towards Dexter and said in a surly voice: "You need to calm down. We're all trying to enjoy the concert." "Shut your face, Raggedy Andy, and turn your ass around in your seat before I shut it for you!" Dexter screamed. Oh God, that did it! Raggedy Andy's black girlfriend stood up and then we all stood up. Kevin, Frank and Michael all took a hold of Dexter and lifted him out of his seat. His shoes went flying off his feet down the stairs, while Dexter yelled: "Security! Security!"

    Rubin quickly got up and followed them out of the auditorium. As Phillip and I sat back down, he turned to me and said: "I was wracking my brain trying to figure out where I'd seen that character; and when his shoes came off, it finally dawned on me." "What?" I implored. "On Friday afternoons, I like to go to this particular park near our condo, and sit on one of the benches, so that I can read the paper and have my coffee. One day, I saw that guy riding a bicycle barefoot with a homeless guy hanging on to the back of it…"

It was then 1995. God, I was 28 years old! Believe it, or not, my clientele had gone through the roof; and I was happy about that, but I needed something more. Robert and I tried to do the club scene off and on; but, after a while, we just felt old and stupid being out. Everyone was much younger…you know, the age we used to be when we started out. Hell yeah, we could still out-dance most of those fuckers, but that didn't matter at all because the dancing styles were starting to change, too. The time of the costumes was coming to a close because everybody was wearing those baggy ass clothes! What the fuck was that, anyway? And the sad day finally arrived when I knew I had to get rid of Thunder Pussy. Of course, I could still wear it because I didn't get all fat and nasty, if that's what you're thinking. But I knew that unless I was going to start working in a strip club, I had definitely outgrown it. A couple of my gays had their eyes on TP forever, but that was my baby and no hairy ass bitch was going to squeeze into disco history, baby! Hip-Hop had been around for years, but it was starting to take over the world. Now don't get me wrong, those artists were, and are, very talented, but it was never my love. Because you know what is, let's say it all together now, HOUSE MUSIC! So I knew that my party life was going in for a dramatic change forever. Tammy, Louise and I decided to go to a Mexican restaurant for some margaritas, and we noticed a woman who was probably in her early 40's raising up her blouse and showing her girlfriends her belly-button ring. Oh hell, nawww, now the old girls are getting pierced. Check that as #2 on my list: remove belly ring soon!

Two weeks later, my friend Trenton came in and invited me over to his place for a little get-together. Trenton and his boyfriend Brandon were a blast to be around. The one thing that I noticed about them was the fact that they had no close gay friends. All of their friends were straight people. And Brandon took on the job of trying find me a boyfriend. "Girl, I have a friend who is Gorrrrrgeous! He owns his own business and he works out. Body of Death, Girl. Pecs as rock-hard as Ellie Mae's biscuits!" Brandon would say. "How tall is he, Brandon?" I would ask. "Why do you have to be so judgmental!?!" he would yell back. It was great hanging out with them, but I knew I needed to get away by myself for a few days and sit on a beach somewhere so I could think through some decisions I needed to make about my career.

One Monday evening, I came home from doing errands and went to the closet. I grabbed TP, put her in a sack, and — as I was headed toward the front door towards the dumpster outside — noticed Val was smiling and clapping his flippers with glee! *Oh, so you thought it was about time I got rid of it too, huh?* He nodded in total agreement. The next morning, I went to the gym and the site of my belly ring was making me nauseous. After my workout, I went to a hardware store and the proprietor greeted me as I walked in. "How can I help you, young lady?" "I've had this belly ring in for about 7 years, and I can't take it out myself. I tried using pliers to snap it in two, but I'm not strong enough," I said. "Well, I'm sure I can help you with that, let me see now," he said.

He walked around to the other side of counter, reached down and brought up the biggest set of pliers I'd ever seen. "This should get the job done," he proclaimed. He pinched the two sides together with this monstrous instrument and the ring shot like a rocket into the air and flew across the store. "How much do I owe you?" I promptly asked him. "Little Lady, this pretty much just made my day, it's on the house!" he replied.

I then drove to a Chinese restaurant near my place to grab something to go and there was a television sitting on a table near the back. And my good ole' friend Robin

Leach was on again, full of enthusiasm and excitement over a new resort that just opened its doors in Costa Rica. Lush rolling hills, oversize quaint bungalows, ya da, ya da…*That's the place I must go for my sabbatical!* I thought. I paid for the food. Shit, I wasn't even hungry then, anyway. I headed straight to the travel agency where the Miami trip was booked. When I walked in, the older woman that helped Donny and me before wasn't available, but a nice young guy told me he would be glad to accommodate me.

I told him about the resort I'd just seen on television and he immediately looked it up and said, "This place just opened about three weeks ago. Right now, they're offering phenomenal deals," he gleefully explained. "Great, would you please print out the information for me; and I will get back with you tomorrow afternoon right after I check my work schedule," I told him. The next day at work, I ran in and told Michelle my plans and we booked off for a full week. On my first break that day, I went back and booked the trip. I told the gang at work where I was planning on going and they didn't ask to come along; so, I knew it was the right thing for me to do. Three weeks later, on the night before the trip, I packed my bags *and, yes, Val was going to accompany me on this venture.*

My flight was scheduled for early in the morning, so I took a cab to the airport. I was to fly into San Jose first and stay overnight at the Marriott. So when I arrived, I took a cab straight there. As we drove towards it, I was totally blown away. The lobby was very busy but the front desk clerks were fast and prompt. The bellman escorted me to my suite and it was breathtaking. After I tipped him, I walked over to the window of the room which looked over the magnificent grounds and landscaping.

I decided to order room service for dinner, because I had arranged for a tour guide to pick me up early the next morning. Right after dinner, I went down to the hotel bar and had a kick ass martini! After that, I went back to my room and fell into a soundless sleep.

I was awakened by the sounds of men outside, who were yelling in Spanish, and the loud buzzing of lawn equipment. I glanced over at the clock and saw that I had 45 minutes to get ready before my guide would arrive. When the front desk buzzed my room, they informed me right away of his arrival. I was greeted not by one guide, but two. Hector and Percy were their names, and they had to be around my age. And, boy, were they a barrel of laughs. After showing me to a resort company van, we were off. I was a little worried that there would be a language barrier; but soon I realized by talking to these two that practically everyone in Costa Rica pretty much spoke English. Also, there were a lot of Americans that came to vacation there and decided to set up businesses and never left. The cost of living in Costa Rica was very inexpensive, so you could do minimal work and still live like a king or a queen.

The resort was only thirty minutes away from the Marriott hotel; it was so unbelievably magical. The television show could not capture all of the beauty of the place. My guides grabbed my bags as we entered the lobby. I was quickly checked in and given instructions on where my bungalow was located. As we all walked down the cemented path, it almost felt a little like Gilligan's Island, because it seemed as if we were in the middle of nowhere. There were not many people out and about at this resort; in fact, I felt like I was pretty much the only one here. After finding my bungalow, Percy and Hector waited while I threw my bags down. I then turned to them and asked, "Where can a girl get a drink around here? I'm thirsty!"

We got back into the van and began to drive through a lush tropical forest and then on to a well-known national park. There were a lot of little out of the way shops and make-shift local restaurants that were hidden and out of the way. Most of the shops sold t-shirts and souvenirs for the many tourists that frequented the area. The restaurant owners were usually all locals that were born and raised in Costa Rica.

Percy began to drive down a dirt road and we finally arrived at a little shack of a place, with chickens everywhere. They were also inside of the restaurant — walking around perfectly content, like they owned the place — and you were definitely an intruder. It was definitely a first come, and first serve, establishment.

We decided to sit at a scratched up, lime green formica table. A waitress approached us and in Spanish asked us what we wanted to drink. Percy immediately told me that I had to try a drink called guaro, which is one of the traditional alcoholic drinks of Costa Rica. He went on to explain that it is a form of rum and that the taste and quality vary in different parts of Latin America. Some locals insist that guaro was invented by the Guaro Indians, but they were such a tiny tribe that no one has been able to find them to confirm this. I found out a little later, while reading an article about this drink, that a lot of people find it a powerful, even crude spirit. But some tourists go home overjoyed about the stuff. If you want to experience it safely, the most important thing to know is to not drink it straight like tequila; a couple of shots could numb various parts of your body that you might have planned to use later in the day. Guaro-based mixed drinks usually consist of pouring a shot or two in a glass of Fresca and ice. That's how most Costa Ricans prefer it except, of course, those sleeping on the gritty streets of downtown San Jose. Guaro also mixes well with other tangy soft drinks, Coke (but not "coke!") and fruit juices. Wow, this shit was good! And before I knew it, I'd had three of them and my tongue started to feel like a sausage in my mouth. Hmmm… I'd better stop slamming these things down before I black out and they find me a week later in some cave in one of the rainforests.

As Percy and Hector continued to indulge in that sweet nectar, I began to wonder, *if they continued to drink like this, who was going to drive me back to the resort?* I then decided that we needed to rap it up. I paid our tab and we all stumbled into the van.

As Hector took over the wheel, Percy and I noticed that he couldn't place the key into the ignition. Percy immediately spoke something sharply to him in Spanish and they switched seats. *Thank God, all I could picture was the three of us plummeting off a cliff and dive-bombing into the Rio Tabacon!*

After they promptly got me back safely to the resort, I tipped them handsomely and walked the very short distance to my villa. I practically kicked the door open and pole-vaulted into my lovely posh king-sized bed! The next two days, all I did was workout at the resort's incredible facility and sit out by the pool with Val, who was sitting in a lounge to my right. While being served bad-assed cocktails, I was able to contemplate the most important decisions I was going to embark on in my life. By the time I had my second cocktail, on my last day at the resort, it finally became crystal clear that it was time for me to step out on my own. I knew that I didn't want to open a huge salon with partners like the set up Kevin had. *I didn't want to be THAT involved in it.* So I made up my mind that I would be my own boss. When I arrived home, I would start my search and see where I ended up. But I had no idea that it would take me almost a year to get the fuck out of that place!!

Chapter 33: Final Chapter: The New Frontier But Not the Final One

The year was already half over and my 30th birthday was coming up over the horizon in 9 months. The salon had finally taken several turns for the worse. It started out as a commission-based salon, which meant that the hairdresser would take home a certain percentage of his, or her, weekly gross. And that percentage increased as the years progressed; but it also meant that the employer's percentage was elevated, as well.

After eleven years, my clientele was well beyond established. I also had to tackle a waiting list. Concerns began to surface; because the more money I made meant that more was taken out. Also, the way the salon was being run was ludicrous and downright embarrassing. The receptionists that were continuing to be brought in had become an even bigger joke. One day, I walked in and peeked over the front desk to find — much to my amazement — a guy performing oral sex on one of the desk girls while she was on the phone! *What if I'd been a customer? Wow, how low and unprofessional can we go?*

For the past few months, I knew it was time to move on, to finally take the plunge and become self-employed. I already knew the ins, and outs, of running a business, because I watched and observed what not to do when you have one. Every week, it was one thing after another. Stuff was happening that should, and could, have been prevented. But Kathy seemed to be on a destructive mission to destroy everything around her — including the relationships she had built up with her employees over the years.

She didn't give a flip about her employees, or the clients: only the money. That was the beginning of some sad, frustrating, and very dark days. Product cost had increased, which was understandable, because the year was then 1996. I couldn't expect to be paying the same we had 10 years prior to that time. The "sticky wicked" was that we purchased the products from the salon inventory stock, so I was sure she was making a little extra off of us from that, too. All of the hairdressers who had been there for several years were starting to be disgruntled about the way that things were being handled. No matter how much we complained, or made suggestions to Kathy, she would not budge; and she would continue to rape and pillage the town folk. It was pretty much like working for a politician. Whatever they promised you along that golden brick road was forgotten in the end. The only ones that will get that pot of jewels is the T.H.A.I.C, which stands for The Head Asshole In Charge!

About once a week, I would call Kevin and rant, and rave, so much about what was going on, that even Val was sick of hearing my shit! Kevin would always come back with the same answer: "Miss Thing, you've got to get the fuck out of there!" Five months later — on a Friday afternoon, while walking with Donny to go pick up something for lunch — it's like a lightning bolt hit me in my Chi Chi's! As we were talking, I knew that day was the day to start looking for another place to work. All of sudden, it became so crystal clear to me that things in that place were never going to change and it would eventually implode on itself. I had to get out of there before the avalanche took place. Right away, I knew if I was going to act, that I had to do it right then before I thought myself out of it. I then told Donny that I just remembered I had an errand to do; and I ran to my car and went to one of the distributors to inquire about what was going on in the booth rental world.

As I drove about 15 minutes down the road, I knew if I asked any questions about going to another salon, I would have to say I was gathering the information for a friend. You see, just like every other profession, everybody knows everybody in the hairdressing galaxy; and some disgruntled Klingon would squeal on you just for the hell of it. A lot of hairstylists have never mastered the art of keeping their traps shut! Then I started to wonder if I could trust any of my friends at the salon. I would definitely have to ask Kevin about that, because this had to be the smoothest move in history. Employers don't take kindly to you leaving — with a kick ass rock solid client base — and 90 percent of them will sabotage you for sure; so I knew I then needed Kevin more than ever. I already had profile listings of every single client, so I knew I was prepared in that category.

As I pulled into the parking space in front of the store, I thanked God that there was no one inside. Behind the counter was a man who was about 6'2, very thin, with dark chocolate brown hair that was swept back with hairspray. "Can I help you?" he asked. "Yes, I was wondering if you knew of a place where a friend of mine could work who wants to be self-employed?" I asked. "Oh sure, I know of a place that opened a little over a year ago. It's about 10 minutes from here," he said. I didn't even write the directions down or get the man's name. I just thanked him and leapt out the door. *Do you know that's the first and only time I ever saw that man, even though I went to that particular store at least once a week? I always wanted to thank him for telling me about my New Frontier. I believe now that he was an angel sent from God to guide me away from the hell in which I was then residing!*

I recognized the area right away because I used to frequent an old gas station that was right around the corner from this place. When I found the building, I pulled in front of the place practically sideways — like the Formula One racing driver Michael Schumacher. As I got out of my car, I instantly knew I was supposed to be there; that was it. I slowly walked in and the place was breathtaking! Chandeliers were in the entryway, suspended over a round mahogany table with a gorgeous centerpiece. Right behind that was an office with a sliding glass partition. There was a young woman sitting there. I went up to her and asked if they had anything available at the moment. She asked me to come into the office and have a seat.

She introduced herself, saying her name was Casey, and she politely told me that there was nothing open at the moment. She urged me to leave my contact information and she would put me on a waiting list. I have to admit that I was a little disappointed, but at least she gave me the time of day. I would not give up hope. At least I had found a place that was right; so I made a mental note to call and check the status of the waiting list. If you're persistent enough, they have to eventually acknowledge you one day, right?

When I got back to my car, I immediately called Kevin on my cell phone and told him the news. "That's what I'm talking about, Girl!" he yelled. "I wanted you to get off your ass and quit bitching about that place and do something about it! Where are you now?" he asked. "I'm still here in the parking lot but I'm done for the day at work."

"Good!" Kevin exclaimed. "Meet me at my place in thirty minutes. We have a lot of things to cover," he said.

When I arrived, Kevin pulled me into the house and told me to sit down. "You better listen to me and listen good!" "Number one: Don't tell anyone that you're planning to leave, because as sure as I'm standing here they will all throw you under the bus, honey! Even your little bosom buddy party friends, girl, believe me…I've been through it all and they will turn on you like rabid drag queens! So keep your big mouth shut!" "Okay, Okay, I got it. I will not say a fuckin' word to anyone!" I said. He went on, "Number two: We have to write and send out a letter to all of your clients; so as soon as you hear from the manager at the new place, let me know, and I will get the girls on it! And it has to be top-notch, nothing ghetto. I have the perfect person to help with that, my cousin Emilio. She thinks she knows it all and I have to bring her ass down to the common denominator that she is sometimes; but she knows her stuff about writing. "Okay, as soon as I hear from Casey, I will let you know," I said. "Good, because we have to do everything quick and precise; so when you let the boom down on Ms. Kathy, she can't come back and bite you in the ass," Kevin replied.

Approximately one week passed and I got a phone call from Casey the manager on a Thursday mid-morning. She told me to start getting ready to transition over because they had someone moving out of one of the suites in a week or two. Wow, my heart started beating like crazy! "Okay, I will definitely be ready to go!" I told her. I then called Kevin and told him the news! "Yes, Girl, here we go!" he yelled. "I will contact Ms. Emilio right now and tell her to come over after she gets off from work today." "She will do that?" I asked. "Oh yeah, If she knows I need help with a writing assignment, she will be all over that so she can throw her weight around and be moo moo bossy cow! I only call her when I 'really' need her because she gets on my fuckin' nerves. But believe me, we need her!" *I had met Emilio only once and he was this chubby Mexican queen who was a major one upper, "Ms. Been There, Done That," but if Kevin said we needed his help with the letter, so be it!* Then Kevin called four of his volleyball playmates and invited them over so he could put them in charge of stuffing the envelopes. He also ordered them to bring liquor. *I could smell a party brewing up,* I thought. *Yeah!!!* Emilio showed up wearing a grey suit with a pink tie. *Whoa, you could surely spot this queen from the back row!* I thought. "Okay, Girl... he said to Kevin... "What do you want me to do for you guys?" "Miss Thing needs a very precise, professional — but humorous — letter written to send to her clients about her new, and exciting, adventure she's getting ready to embark upon!" Kevin responded. "Okay, that sounds easy enough. How about if we start it out this way?" Emilio asked him. "No, no, no...don't start it out that way. She's a hairstylist — not a mortician!" Kevin yelled. "Whatever, bitch. I know this is the way it needs to start out in the beginning to really grab them!" Emilio barked back. Then the cat-fight proceeded between the two of them.

  Suddenly, I became distracted by the sound of someone ringing the doorbell and laughing outside. I ran over to open it and it was Steve with three other guys I hadn't met yet. And they were all holding bags filled with booze. "Hey Miss Thing, congratulations on moving on up to the east side!" he cackled. "Thanks, Steve," I responded. "Kevin and Emilio are in the living-room fighting over the way the letter should be written." "Oh hell," he said, "I guess I better get in there and referee!" "Girls, put these bottles on the bar and whip me and Ms. Kevin up a gin and tonic, will ya?" So the girls pranced over to the bar area while Steve and I tried to break apart Kevin and Emilio. Finally, after an hour of name calling and gay bar insults, the product was finished. Kevin ran next door to his neighbor's house and ran off copies of the letter.

I immediately put the girls to work in an assembly line type fashion on the couch to get the ball rolling much faster. Steve went over and slipped in a Cher cd, then started lip-syncing to ♪ If I could turn back time♪…Kevin chimed in, "and if you could, hopefully you would change that tired hairstyle of yours and the way you dress, girl!" We all pissed our panties over that one!

It took over two and a half hours to get all of those letters stuffed, and stamped, but we accomplished it. That was so exciting and couldn't have happened at a better time; because a week and a half prior to that, the hot water heater in the salon finally needed to be replaced. And Kathy had someone put in a smaller unit instead of the original size….Why, you ask? Because she was being fuckin' stupid and cheap, not taking in consideration that there wouldn't be any hot water left after an hour, or so, on a busy Saturday! By twelve noon, when the waters were icy cold, guess what brilliant solution Ms. Kathy brewed up? Can you fathom the horrors that took place? I bet you can't! Water was boiled in a microwave and then poured onto the client's heads. If you could have seen the looks on the clients' faces. I guess the word I could use is flabbergasted! I didn't do that fucked up shit, but a lot of hairstylists did because they went into terminal shock. My shock treatment was handled a little differently. I actually walked a couple of color clients to neighboring salons with foil, or tint, on their heads in broad daylight, in front of other people!!! Uhgggg! More confirmation to get the fuck out of "Dodge City" before I lost everything I'd worked so hard to achieve.

Kevin then told me to mail the letters as soon as possible so the clients would receive them before receiving my three-day notice. Kevin and the guys were all hyped up to go out on the strip, but I graciously declined. I was in stealth mode then, driving to a post office near my apartment and dropping them all in. On Tuesday, I knew I had to tell Michelle first. We had a bond, and a mutual respect for each other, that had grown over the years. When I walked in, I called out to her, "Michelle, I have something I need to talk to you about." She cocked her head and looked at me, replying, "Okay, give me a few minutes. I have to call Kathy about something." "Okay," I responded.

She came back and we walked down the hall to the very back of the salon away from everyone. She looked at me and asked, "You're quitting, right?" "Yeah, I am," I said, "my last day will be this Saturday." "Well, I won't tell Kathy today because she's late with the payroll," she said. I then responded by saying: "Yeah, imagine that musical merry-go-round payroll where you just never know these days when you're going get paid. Even though you work like a fuckin' mule days before…you see, Michelle, that's one of the many reasons I have to go! This is all fuckin' insane!" I said. "Yeah, I know, I know, you have all the reasons to leave," she said. "Well, Girl, wherever you go, I only want the best for you and I know you will do well," she continued to say. Michelle was the only person in that whole dungeon that ever said any kind, encouraging words to me those last few days. Kevin was spot on about the treatment that I received. My co-workers literally turned their backs to my face as I approached them in the hallways, as if I had the "scarlet letter" B attached to my couture! Robert seemed indifferent about it though I could detect a hint of jealousy. Tammy and Louise wouldn't even look my way or talk to me the rest of the week. Kathy also played out the cold shoulder routine, which was a little hurtful at first. Their actions proved to me right then that most of them were not for me at all, but totally against me doing something to better myself. Donny, on the other hand, took it well and told me he would come and visit me after I got settled. I then told him about the set up and he said something shocking to me that rang in my ears for years to come: "Girl, I couldn't be locked up in a suite with 'them'!" "What are you talking about?" I asked him. He then began to say, "Well…I couldn't be that close to them, is all…" I never got what he meant, until eight years later. My last day at the salon finally arrived and it was a long one. My last client Bob helped me with my things and walked me to the back door of the salon. There were a few people left but the only one I said goodbye to was Donny. He blew me a goodbye kiss as he was styling out his client and the metal clad door of "Shawshank" slammed abruptly behind us.

That was a little over two years ago, and I had successfully made it as a self-employed stylist. Ninety-eight percent of my clients followed me and were genuinely happy for me. Plus, they loved the new surroundings and the privacy that this place had to offer, so it was a great move for everyone. The last time I spoke with Kevin was a month after I left the other place; and, of course, he called me to drop another bomb on me. "Girl, Michael and I are moving away again; this business is wearing me the fuck out!" he shouted. "Where are you two headed off to now?" I asked. "Not sure yet," he replied, "maybe San Francisco…still trying to decide. But I will keep in touch and fill you in for sure," he said.

Kevin never contacted me and no one seemed to know of the place to which he disappeared. Some of the bitter queens that we mutually knew kept telling me that Kevin was dead. I knew that shit wasn't true; they were all just hateful bitches! But one summer day — when I went down to the gayborhood to meet Trenton and Brandon for cocktails — I glanced up for a moment, as I was locking my car door, and saw a man that looked exactly like Kevin walking down the sidewalk! *Oh My God, he's back!?!* Where had he been for two years? I cupped my hands around my mouth and yelled, "KEVIN!" He turned around, looked in my direction, and started smiling.

I looked both ways quickly before I ran across the street and gave him a big hug. "What are you doing back in town?" I asked him. "Oh, I just arrived about two weeks ago," he answered. "Well, why didn't you ever get in touch with me?" I frantically asked him. "Miss Thing, you know how I am when I'm ready to go. I just go, and when I'm ready to make an appearance…." "Yeah, I know," I replied. "So how is everything going with you? I know you're still at that same place you moved to, right?" he asked. "Oh, everything is good. Everyone followed me over," I answered. "Well, I never doubted that," Kevin said.

Then Kevin started to instruct me on certain things with the business that I had already mastered years prior to that day: little things like booking my clients correctly, and what not to do with my money, and so on. He kept on — and on, and on — until I started to get really pissed! Finally, I yelled at him, "Who do you think you're talking to? I'm not some dumb ass bitch that just fell off the Massas's wagon! I know what the fuck I'm doing now, as I've had some experience by now, you know. I am fuckin' 32 years old!"

Kevin then just looked at me with a twinkle in his eyes and said: "You don't need me anymore, my work here is finished…" He walked away, with me just standing there stupefied! "Hey, bring your faggot ass back here, I'm not done!!" I screamed. "Kevin, come back here!!!" He just kept walking farther away — with his right hand doing the Miss America wave behind his head. And I never saw him again…

CPSIA information can be obtained at www.ICGtesting.com
Printed in the USA
LVOW01s0329210415

435421LV00029B/624/P